WHITE LIKE YOU

by

SPENCER J. QUINN

Counter-Currents Publishing Ltd.
San Francisco
2017

Published in the United States by
COUNTER-CURRENTS PUBLISHING LTD.
P.O. Box 22638
San Francisco, CA 94122
USA
http://www.counter-currents.com/

ISBNs
Hardcover: 978-1-940933-73-3
Paperback: 978-1-940933-74-0
Electronic: 978-1-940933-75-7

Library of Congress Cataloging-in-Publication Data

Names: Quinn, Spencer, 1976- author.
Title: White like you / by Spencer J. Quinn.
Description: San Francisco : Counter-Currents Publishing Ltd., 2017.
Identifiers: LCCN 2017023824 (print) | LCCN 2017032729 (ebook) | ISBN
   9781940933757 (electronic) | ISBN 9781940933733 (hardcover : alk. paper) |
   ISBN 9781940933740 (pbk. : alk. paper)
Subjects: LCSH: White nationalism--Fiction. | White supremacy
   movements--United States--Fiction. | Whites--United States--Politics and
   government--Fiction. | United States--Race relations--Fiction. | Adventure
   stories
Classification: LCC PS3617.U5845 (ebook) | LCC PS3617.U5845 W55 2017
(print)
   | DDC 813/.6--dc23
LC record available at https://lccn.loc.gov/2017023824

CONTENTS

PART 5: NATHAN'S FORD

PART 6: MUNCIE

PART 7: TEHRAN

Part 1: Little Rock

Chapter 1

What is a test? Ben Cameron never had to ask because he always knew.

"I see you have D as the answer," Phil said, "but A, 'go extinct,' could also be right, or at least not wrong. If the bird's already on the verge of extinction, that is." Portly and short, Phil slid his pudgy arms on the table and shifted his weight in his seat. Eyebrows over alert sunken eyes pushed up into his bald head like furry crescent moons.

"But you're making it seem like mass suicide," Ben said. "Can a species really react to a new population by going extinct? It seems that extinction is something that happens *to* a species over time, not something a species can actively achieve."

Ben rapped his fingers on his company's tiny device. Thirteen hundred fifth-grade science test questions, known simply as items, waited on its memory drive. Four months of work producing them for the Arkansas Board of Education. One week in committee with a dozen Arkansas educators to see which ones survive.

"I agree," Phil said. "But our curriculum does not require students to interpret extinction like that."

"So, it's possible a kid could know his science and still get the item wrong?" Franklin suggested. "Because he views going extinct as being active rather than passive?" Franklin was a tall, middle-aged man in short sleeves despite the frigid air conditioning. Crossing his long legs alongside the table, pale skin peeked out from where his pant leg ended and his sock began.

Ben laughed. "You'd have to hack through some hairy logic to come to that conclusion. Arkansas must have some pretty scary fifth graders."

Laughter rippled through the hotel conference room leading to weary wisecracking from some of the teachers: "You'd be surprised!" "That's not all they hack through!" "Scary in other ways!"

"I'm not saying it's a bad item, Ben," Phil said, pointing to the projected document. "It's just that A will distract kids a little too well."

Ben squinted at the item with one eye. "Fair enough. Let's change A from 'go extinct' to 'interbreed with thin-beaked birds'. The wide beaks certainly can't do that. Then we'll change it to B because of its length."

Janet nodded. "That will work," she said. Janet was the committee chair, a serious, middle-aged woman in a navy-blue business suit with shoulder pads. Girlish eyes flashed beneath straight dark eyebrows and wavy gray hair. The rest of the committee murmured its assent.

"So we should accept this one?" Ben asked. He looked over his committee. Some had PhDs. Some were administrators. Others were ordinary teachers who had driven to the Holiday Inn in Little Rock from points across Arkansas, exhausted from travel and clocking their miles. All to pare Ben's work down to the 700 items they needed for their end-of-year fifth-grade science exam.

As the teachers studied the projected item, Ben observed with a thin, confident smile. He recited the item from memory:

"Thin-beaked birds move into a habitat containing a different species of wide-beaked birds. The birds occupy the same level on the food web, but the thin-beaked birds can better compete for food and shelter. What is a possible response from the wide-beaked birds?

    A. prey upon thin-beaked birds.
    B. interbreed with thin-beaked birds.
    C. occupy a lower level on the food web.
    D. migrate to a more hospitable habitat."

Silence never sounded so good, Ben thought. This was how he liked his committees, searching for faults in his work and finding none. "Not too shabby," one of them said.

"I say go with it," Franklin said, cracking his knuckles and leaning back.

"Me too," said a few others.

Janet folded her hands beneath her chin. "Another winner. Got the edit, Ben?"

"Got it," Ben said, now correcting the item on his device. In seconds the new item manifested before the educators. He then walked around the table, making sure the correction uploaded to their personal devices. Ben was a tall, slender twenty-nine-year-old with thin sideburns and brown hair tousled with a touch of mousse. In his custom suit and designer silk tie, he made a curious waiter for the drably-dressed educators. Their smiles radiated mutual warmth.

"What does that bring us to, Ben?" Janet asked.

"I think we're hovering around ninety percent," Ben said, sliding back into his chair. He performed some calculations on his device. "90.21 percent accepted. We've read 235 items today and got 212 through. At this rate we'll be done by Thursday. You'll all go home a day early."

A committee member clapped twice and startled everyone. Laughter rumbled and then rolled away as the teachers grabbed their jackets and purses. "Good. Let's wrap up for today," Janet said, redundant amid the hubbub.

"Did you write all these items yourself, Ben?" Phil asked.

"About 900 of them," Ben admitted. "Couple item writers took care of the rest."

"By item writers you mean independent contractors who write for Benchmark Testing?"

"Yeah."

"Well, good work so far," Phil said, smiling. The committee members then stopped what they were doing to further congratulate Ben. Their day was over, and they had no obligation to stay, yet they shared with him their frustrations and fears regarding standardized tests. A bad test can do so much damage, they said. Not just to the children but to their schools and communities as well. Teachers also find it frustrating to teach to a test they're not confident in. They were especially grateful to have someone competent and conscientious like Ben developing it for them.

Ben cleared his throat, touched by the spontaneity of it all. He had met these people for the first time that morning. He thanked them as graciously as he could and worried he wasn't being gracious enough. Janet, the ranking educator in the lower school science committee and sitting member of the Arkansas Board of Education, looked askance at him. The stakes were high, and she wanted to see if Ben understood that.

After a moment, Ben smiled back at her playfully as if to say, "Who? Me?"

Janet smiled and put her hand to her mouth to stifle a short laugh.

It was almost four-thirty by the time Ben strolled out of the committee room with his Benchmark Testing Company device in his pocket. The meetings were supposed to last until five, and it was a pretty bold statement to quit early, especially on a Monday. He was hoping his project manager Nigel Polite would see him sauntering the halls. Perhaps this would help persuade the BTC brass to give their star content specialist his much-deserved promotion.

He noticed that the door to the high school science committee room was open. That was odd. He was expecting Benchmark Testing's new science content specialist Sono Kofi Mensah to still be working with his committee. Born and raised in Ghana but schooled mostly in England and America, Son, as he preferred to be called, had been with BTC only three months. Ben wondered if Son could have finished before him. He didn't want to be upstaged by anyone, especially a new hire. Still, Son only needed to get 300 items past the committee that week. Ben guessed it was possible.

He slowed his pace as he approached the room. He could tell it was nearly empty, yet two voices were projecting from it: Nigel's and a woman's he'd never heard before. He couldn't make out what they were saying, but he could tell that she was interrupting him, bullying him, menacing him almost. Only a high-ranking member of the Arkansas Board of Education could talk to Nigel that way. So much for being upstaged by Son, Ben thought. Something horrible must have happened in the high school committee that day. The scene was made even more cringe-worthy by Nigel's sycophantic appeals rendered almost eloquent by his Mancunian English accent. Suddenly, looking good next to Son Mensah lost much of its charm for Ben. Thinking of how this might affect Benchmark Testing, small and fi-

nancially beleaguered company that it was, made him sweat
with worry.

Not wanting to eavesdrop anymore, Ben picked up the pace
and whizzed past the door. The only tidbit of information he
could catch was that the high school committee had broken for
the day at two. Early. If the committee wasn't passing Son's
items, Ben thought, why would they quit *early*? Wouldn't they
want to review as many items as possible?

Still pondering this, Ben passed the doorway of the middle
school committee room. It too was open, and at once he noticed
the arresting figure of Ariya Mohammadi, BTC's middle school
science content specialist, standing in front of it. A tall woman,
she was conversing eye-to-eye with her committee chair, a
paunchy, grey-haired man of sixty. Splotchy skin marked his
face, and his pants must have been a size too small given how
his belly spilled out over them. He seemed keen on extending
his conversation with such a majestic woman for as long as he
could, even as other committee members were filing past.

Ariya clearly had a passion for fashion. Her suit, shoes,
makeup, and hair all worked in tandem to revamp the attainably
attractive woman that she was into something unattainably seductive. In the office Ben snuck looks at her hazel almond eyes
and delicate pinup-girl chin whenever he could. Although she
was from Iran, her golden fair skin recalled the Mediterranean
and made her seem more Greek or Italian. She could have lost
fifteen pounds, but Ben was grateful she hadn't since the extra
weight, especially in her breasts and naturally toned arms,
seemed to bolster her self-confidence and made her a sweetly
fearsome presence at BTC. Meanwhile, a modest tummy roll
suggested that an innocent girl lurked somewhere within the
alluring curves of her body.

It was well known in the office that Ariya spent at least half
an hour on her appearance each morning with an array of
topflight cosmetics and perfumes always present in her tote bag
of a purse. Yet she was married and supposedly a devout Muslim. Early birds at BTC would often see her scurrying across the
parking lot in her traditional cloak and headscarf only to appear
from the ladies' room a radiant new woman.

Despite these efforts, Ariya never *acted* sexy. Never once had Ben seen her flirt or even socialize with colleagues. Rarely did she smile, and she never spoke about herself. She spent most of her time either writing items or barking orders in Farsi to her gaggle of writers back home in Iran. Until Ben's arrival five years prior, Ariya had been BTC's most successful content specialist. She was also the costliest since her friends and family were making their fortunes in thirty dollar increments every time she accepted an item. This was BTC's typical pay per item, about ten dollars less than the industry standard. Rumor had it she wasn't above accepting inferior items just to keep the money flowing from BTC to Tehran and other points scattered across the former Persian Empire.

Ben slowed down and noticed something new in her womanly arsenal: orange highlights in her long, lustrous black hair. He paused to take them in until her eyes met his. She had a way of looking at you as if picking through fruit at a grocer's bazaar. He didn't want to be the one to pull his eyes away first. She had to, since she was still in conversation. When she looked at him again, he was still looking at her.

***

It was eight-thirty in the evening. Ben had just reclined onto his hotel bed and was paging through a novel about the battle of Thermopylae when startled by sharp knocks on the door. Through the peephole he saw Nigel leaning heavily against the doorframe.

Ben opened the door. "Nigel, what's up?"

"It's Son," Nigel said. "He needs your help." Nigel's brown hair fell down almost to the bridge of his pelican beak nose, and his laughably fat neck made him seem a month or two away from having to buy a new shirt. His cheeks were a rose-tinted pink.

Ben had always had a shaky opinion of Son as content specialist. Son often arrived to work late, and his attitude could charitably be referred to as lackadaisical. Ben also could never get a good conversation going with him about science. Rumblings from colleagues who had worked with him only strengthened his suspicions. But Ben was sensitive enough to the racial taboo which followed Son around like a long black shadow not to rumble along with them. He knew such discussions would be distasteful and would stir up unsettling memories about race which he had kept comfortably un-remembered for many years. Despite sensing an impending disaster, Ben was still prepared to give Son the benefit of many, many doubts.

"Really?" Ben said as he let Nigel in.

"Unfortunately. His items are crap."

"All of them?"

"Enough of them. We just went over them in his room."

Ben rubbed the stubble on his jaw and closed the door, watching his boss pace frantically around the room.

"Ben, I need you to…" Nigel began, pointing his finger. He then checked himself, softening his appeal. "Please. If you would be so kind, help Son meet his quota. He needs new items."

"New items? You mean, like, from scratch?"

"Yes."

"Can't he just fix the ones he already wrote?"

Nigel's tiny jowls jiggled as he shook his head. "No, he can't."

"Okay. How many items are we talking?"

"Around 280."

"He needs to write 280 items, or he needs to get 280 accepted?"

Nigel clamped his mouth shut before answering. "He needs to get 280 items accepted this week. The Arkansas Education Commissioner chewed me out over this. It wasn't pleasant."

"Was that the lady who had you begging like a cocker spaniel in Son's committee room this afternoon?" Ben asked, smirking.

The left half of Nigel's face lifted in shock. "You were spying?"

"No. There was a bunch of us in the hall watching the show. I was just selling tickets."

Nigel laughed. "That's not funny. They're worried about this. If we don't meet our quota this week, Arkansas won't have enough for their eleventh-grade exam."

Ben folded his arms. "And then we lose our contract."

"Yes. But not before we fulfill our obligations to them at a loss. And take a big hit reputation-wise."

"We can't afford that, can we?"

"No," Nigel sighed. "So, can you do this?"

Ben threw up his hands. "I have a vacation in San Diego planned for this weekend with friends. I bought plane tickets."

"But how would that impact your week here?"

Ben's only answer was a chagrined smile.

"When does your flight leave?" Nigel asked.

"Thursday evening. I was gonna tell you."

Nigel recoiled, utterly scandalized. "What? We're here all week!"

"I know."

"You were that confident you'd finish a day early?"

"Well, yeah. It's only 700 items, and we're already a third of the way there almost. We even quit early today. You didn't notice, but—"

"You've never even seen this committee before! How did you know you'd finish a day early?"

Ben hesitated just a little. "I have good items."

Nigel blinked and raised his hands like he wanted to shake Ben. "Can't you transfer your ticket for Friday?"

"It's non-transferrable. Anyway, it'll take me well past Friday to get 280 items through. You're basically killing my vacation here."

Nigel let his hands flop to his sides. "What can I say? We're desperate. Can't you reschedule?"

Ben squinted as he considered. "I don't know. We've been planning this for months."

Nigel waited for Ben to reconsider. It didn't take long. Ben stamped his foot and swore under his breath. Nigel held up his hands as if to pray. "Oh, tell me you'll do it. Tell me you'll do it!"

"Will BTC cover my unused tickets?"

Nigel nodded eagerly. "You can comp it. I'll sign."

"What about all the overtime?"

"I will give you a month's paid vacation. In January, when it's slow."

Ben scowled at his boss. "It's a good thing for you I like writing items."

Nigel clasped his hands together and rushed over to Ben for a thank you bear hug. Ben patted him twice on the shoulder. "I'm a sucker," he said.

Nigel released him. "No, you're a star."

Ben laughed. "Well, star or no, I don't know if I can fill the hole Son dug for us by Friday."

"Sure you can," Nigel said. "I've been in testing since before the ban. I've never seen anyone write as fast as you."

"Nigel, I can max at about forty a day, and that's going from eight to five with a working lunch. I'd have to double that to make 280 by Friday. I'm assuming I'll be working nights since I'll be in committee all day, right?"

"You can work in the day too."

"What about the fifth-grade committee?"

"I can sit in."

"You're not a content specialist. You don't know anything about science."

"Do I have to? Your items sell themselves. You've said so yourself."

Ben shook his head. He *liked* his committee and enjoyed working with them. "280 is still a lot."

"Ariya will help," Nigel offered.

"Have you asked her?"

"No. But she's always very nice to Son. I'm sure she will."

Ben grimaced at Nigel's naiveté. Ben suspected that what Ariya said, in English at least, and what Ariya thought were not always the same thing. He was liking this less and less. Nigel put his hand on Ben's shoulder, his eyebrows steepling in worry. "I need you to ask her for me."

"Me? Why can't you do it?"

"Because I have to explain all this to St. Clair right away."

Peter St. Clair was the president of Benchmark Testing and a difficult person to talk to even when bearing good news. Stern and quiet, he had a way of singling out project managers he didn't like and burdening them with tedious work until they resigned. The stubborn ones he managed to eventually fire. Nigel was clearly dreading their conversation.

Ben looked longingly at his novel lying on the bedspread. "You know me, Nigel. I can't say no."

Nigel clapped his hands once. "Capital. Ariya is in room 210. I cannot thank you enough for this, Ben," he said, heading to the door.

"Oh, I'm sure you could, now that you'll be talking with St. Clair," Ben said, lifting an eyebrow.

Nigel got his meaning and pointed at him. "You will be rewarded. I promise." He shut the door without looking back. A thought came to Ben a moment later, and he opened it.

"Nigel!" he called.

Nigel had been jogging down the hall and stopped. "Yes?"

"If the committee was rejecting Son's items, why did they quit early?"

Nigel did not hesitate before answering. "His items were that bad."

***

The stark, almost violent, pockmarks riddling Ariya's cheeks and forehead rendered her nearly unrecognizable. It was the first time Ben had seen her without makeup. Their sudden, unexpected proximity also imbued him with a new feel for her age, which he pegged at around thirty.

"I will not help him! No!" she snapped through the half-opened door. Barefoot and in a bathrobe, she was clearly not prepared to receive visitors. A braided towel gripped her hair like a foot-tall vice.

"Think of it as helping the company," Ben reasoned. "Think about the Arkansas contract—"

"I said no! They should never have hired him! Okay?"

Ben held out his hands. "Ariya, please. Without you I have to write all the items myself."

Ben knew this was a dicey gamble. He and Ariya had always been friendly, but not that friendly. Ariya took a deep breath and folded her arms. "That's stupid! You're too smart for this, Ben. What's wrong with you?"

"Nigel came to my room and asked me to—"

"Do you know what that man did to me?"

"Who? Nigel?"

"No. Come inside!" she commanded without opening the door further. Ben snuck in, banging his forearm painfully against the door handle. He shut the door behind him. Still with her arms folded, Ariya stood before him like a prison guard. She was nearly as tall as he was and held her chin high as if to make up the difference.

"So, what did Son—" Ben began.

"Shush!" she barked, pointing at Ben. "You cannot tell anyone!"

Ben turned his head, beginning to resent the woman's abusive tone. "Tell anyone what?"

"Son almost ruined my New Mexico project!"

"New Mexico? I thought that went well."

"And he was no help. He gave me seventy-five items, Ben. They were all rejected. All of them! He is stupid and lazy. My six-year-old nephew can write better items!"

At this, Ben realized that Ariya had not inspected Son's items before submitting them to committee. This was a cardinal sin at BTC and probably why she had just sworn Ben to secrecy. He decided not to mention it. "So what did you do?"

"I called my cousins in Iran. They were sleeping. They stayed up all night writing. A hundred items they gave to me on this!"

Ben looked away, realizing that the more time he spent arguing with Ariya the less time he had to clean up Son's mess. He was also tired of getting yelled at. In his professional experience it was considered unseemly for whites, especially white men, to raise their voices at anyone, especially non-whites, even though Ariya seemed more white than non-white. It made one vulnerable to complaints, all of which were taken seriously and could lead to summary termination. On the other hand, complaints from whites of discrimination, harassment, and abuse—like what Ariya was heaping on Ben—were acted upon much less often. "I'm sorry that happened, Ariya," he said. "But I need to know if you'll help."

"Of course not. Son should be fired."

"Okay, but does BTC deserve to go out of business? Because

that's what will happen if we lose this contract."

Ariya blew through her nose like a bull. "That's not my problem, Ben. It is BTC's problem for hiring so many of the blacks!"

"What?"

Ariya remained silent, refusing to take back what she had just
said.

"You're saying BTC should discriminate *against* black people?" he asked.

Ariya slapped her thick, round thighs. "What did I say? Do
you not listen, Ben?"

"But affirmative action hiring policies are now —"

"It is stupid! Everything these people touch they ruin. Look at
them!"

Ben noticed the puffiness around her eyes, the unflowed
tears. Ariya refused to wipe them. Ben had always admired immigrants for their fearless honesty, but he had never seen it this
brazen before.

"I'm sorry, but you have to leave now," she said.

"So I guess I'm a team player without a team," he said.
"Thanks, Ariya." He slammed the door behind him and didn't
care. With his life now infused with meaning, Ben Cameron was
excited and fearful at the same time. Benchmark Testing was his
to save.

Chapter 2

French naturalist Jean-Baptiste Lamarck was one of the first
men to develop a scientific theory of evolution. Later scientists
disproved his theory by discovering that individuals cannot
inherit which of the following?

A. DNA
B. RNA
C. genetic traits
D. acquired traits (correct)

Son's hotel bed was littered with paper, and the man sat on it
like a bald Buddha in white pajamas, putting a visible dent in
the mess.

"Hello, Ben!" Son hailed with a thick hand in the air. Papers rustled in a perimeter around him as he shifted his weight. His dark face smiled brightly. "Welcome to the eleventh grade!"

"Thank you! Nigel says you need some help," Ben said, removing his BTC device from his pocket. He just realized that he had never been in a room alone with Son before.

Ben was almost six feet tall and athletic. He had played basketball and tennis in high school and, as a point guard, had even been first off the bench for a season at the University of California, Santa Cruz. But Son was a real heavyweight of a man, two inches shorter but outweighing Ben by at least sixty pounds, most of it in his chest and shoulders. His tugboat thighs suggested he was in the 99th percentile for the powerlifting squat. Ben was prepared to ooze politeness before such a gargantuan presence.

"Yes, that is right, Ben," Son said. "This committee is not reasonable, I'm sorry to say. Nigel agrees."

"Does he now?" Ben said, flipping through some of the items piled at the foot of Son's bed. They *were* bad, he noticed. Dingdong dumb and unswervingly so: 'Which of the following is an example of this?' 'Which of the following is an example of that?' Rote memorization items, all of them. Even rookie item writers knew that state boards eschewed rote memorization for items that tested analytical thinking. If rote memorization were all they wanted, the boards could write the items themselves. So why did Son produce so many rote memorization items? Ben marveled at the shamelessness of it all.

"Nigel says this is the worst committee," Son added.

"I see that," Ben said, putting the items back on the bed in a neat pile. He wondered why, in a post-electronic age, Son insisted on reproducing all of his items on *paper*. He noticed the letters 'DNU' in big capital letters on almost all of them. DNU stood for 'Do Not Use.'

"These are good items," Son asserted, waving a partially crumpled one in the air. "I have a master's degree and doctorate. I am qualified. Nigel agrees." The authority with which he made this pronouncement would brook no contradiction, and Ben was not about to offer any.

"Okey-doke," he said, grinning tactfully. "Let's get started."

Son raised a finger. "But you first must consider, Ben. This is not the fifth grade. This is high school. That is much more harder than the items you write. Moreover, I was hoping that Ariya would come since she also has the academic background in education."

Ben blinked twice and understood he was being condescended to. He glanced to the door and felt the Spartans at Thermopylae beckoning from across the hotel.

"I have seen your items, Ben," Son went on. "They are pretty good. This is not criticizing you. Understand? I just want to warn to you that this will be a new experience if you are prepared for it."

Ben took a deep breath as if to suck up all the hatred which was now ravaging his insides. Ben *wished* he could write high school items for Arkansas. Son was apparently too ignorant to realize that lower school items were 'more harder' to write than high school items. Lower school standards tended to be basic and vague, and teachers everywhere lived in fear of challenging their precious little darlings. With the range between too-easy and too-hard being only a hair's width, getting lower school items through a committee was often like threading a needle with oven mitts. Ben bristled at the man's gall.

Son had at least six years of graduate education under his belt and claimed to have taught for an additional ten. Yet he had little understanding of the item writing process and less inclination to learn. It was as if he felt his degrees and seniority could do this for him.

Ben, on the other hand, dropped out of UCSC as a junior and drew only upon his talents and industry to get where he was. He knew he had accomplished more at twenty-nine than Son, already in middle age, could have hoped for in a lifetime. Ben could do one thing well, and that was write standardized test items. Once he discovered this, he wanted to do nothing else. Holding back the desire to fire nasty sarcastic barbs at Son, Ben felt an uncomfortable pressure in his forehead. He understood the racial politics of the situation. He knew Son was not worth the trouble he could cause. Ben wanted to keep his job. "Thank you, Son," he said, and then hated himself for saying it.

The evening proved to be tedious and frustrating for both men. They started by writing independently to different standards and then reviewing each other's work. Ben's attempts to infuse critical thinking into Son's items met with stubborn resistance. Son appeared to take it personally every time Ben questioned him. Then, seemingly in retaliation, Son began to challenge the content of Ben's items, repeatedly accusing him of bad science. This led to several fruitless arguments in which Ben had to *prove* to Son certain science facts that all Arkansas eleventh graders are supposed to know: Yes, the organelle called the mitochondrion contains DNA. Yes, the density of ice is less than the density of water. No, the mid-Atlantic ridge is not where tectonic plates descend into the Earth's crust. Son was wrong every time yet never stopped trying. He seemed pathologically immune to embarrassment. Ben couldn't understand it. Only he could, but didn't want to.

Ben sat at the tiny desk in Son's hotel room with his BTC device. Son still lounged on the bed with his. It was past two in the morning. Dizzy with fatigue, Ben took a close look at his colleague who had just nodded off. The freakishly wide shoulders, the prominent jaw, the conspicuous bulge in the back of his neck, the calloused hands, the positively elephantine bare feet. Son's massive belly rose and fell with every snore.

That Son was stupid Ben was certain. That he was lazy, he was also certain. But the question was why? *Why* was Son like this? Ben had been taught since high school that blacks tend to 'underperform' due to the 'psychological slavery' inflicted upon them throughout hundreds of years of oppression. You oppress people long enough, the theory goes, and you enter a vicious cycle of poverty, violence, and low standardized test scores. This seemed to make sense, although the mechanism which connects oppression to these dismal outcomes was never made clear.

Throughout his life Ben had known few if any truly intelligent blacks and many, many stupid ones, ones that made even Son seem brilliant in comparison. Of course, there were those he liked, especially at work. But the idea of socializing with them outside the office was never something he took seriously. He always chalked it up to not having enough in common with them. But was that really the reason?

With his eyelids growing heavier, he looked again at Son. The resentment he had been feeling over the course of the evening began to morph into something ugly. He now despised Son, not just for his incompetence, but also for drawing a healthy salary by masquerading as a content specialist. Son was worth nothing to the company, less than nothing, actually, since BTC began throwing away good money after bad the moment they took him on.

A queasy sense of race guilt would normally begin fermenting at this point and remind Ben that it was time to start hedging. How could he judge a whole race of people? Was he a geneticist? Did he want to lose his job? Ben had witnessed up close the ugliness of racial strife back in San Diego years ago and left town wanting absolutely no part of it ever again.

But for some reason guilt did not seep into his mind that evening. Nothing did, except the gentle lull of the air conditioner and the distant rumble of traffic filtering through the window. Five hours was all it took. Five hours of working as an equal alongside a black person for the first time in his professional life. Five hours of un-forgetting things that he, now an established and highly successful content specialist, was no longer too afraid to know.

His device alarm jarred him awake. His body longed to sleep, but sleeping in a chair all night had given him a sore neck and a real gem of a backache. He banged his shin against the desk as he tried to open the curtains. The early morning sunlight hit him like a sledgehammer. It was Tuesday. He had four more days and nights of writing items with Son.

It was 7:15 am. Conferences began at eight. He still had to shower, shave, get dressed, and get his own committee started for Nigel. Son remained unconscious on the bed in the same position he was in the night before. Occasionally, he waved his hand in front of his face as if swatting flies.

The plan was for Son to meet with his committee while Ben formatted the items they had written. Ben had produced twenty-three. Son, eight, but only two that Ben had deemed acceptable.

Looking about the chaos of Son's room—towels, clothing, and papers scattered everywhere—a truly evil idea occurred to Ben. What if, he thought, he were to leave Son here still sleeping? The idea had consequences he liked. Son would be late for his committee, the client would be even angrier, and BTC would have another reason to fire him. Ben could see himself delivering passionate testimony in St. Clair's office about Son's ineptitude, his laziness, his...

Ben tapped Son on the leg until he woke. He said he'd meet him in the committee room in forty-five minutes. Son grunted and rolled over without saying thank you.

The week settled into a grueling routine for Ben. Holed up in his hotel room, he sent items to Nigel in batches. During breaks from the fifth-grade committee, Nigel would edit them for spelling and grammar, and then send them to Son in the high school committee. Ben was facing a peculiar challenge since he was unfamiliar with the high school standards and the tastes and biases of the committee members. This left him taking chances on items more often than not, which he hated to do. By five pm on Tuesday, Ben had written sixty-nine items, sixty of which had been accepted. Several times on Tuesday and Wednesday Son volunteered to contribute items, and Ben graciously accepted each time. In private with Nigel however he would emphatically refuse, explaining that Son would only clog the process with unacceptable items. Nothing can sour a committee worse than that. He left it to his boss to figure out how to delicately put this to Son. He also noticed how Ariya avoided the team entirely during this trial. She would take breakfasts and lunches in her room and retreat there as soon as the meetings concluded for the day.

On Wednesday they met with setbacks; disagreements by the committee members over the meaning of certain standards revealed that Ben had interpreted them incorrectly. Eleven items that had been accepted on Tuesday were unceremoniously DNU'ed. Further, Son wasn't adept at selling items. If a committee was waffling on an item, it was the content specialist's job to demonstrate how the item met its standard or offer ways to revise it so that it would. This required finesse and a large amount of trust on the part of the committee. By two in the afternoon, Ben had produced another eighty-three items, including the ones from the night before, but was hovering around a sixty-three percent acceptance rate, which for him was appallingly low. They still needed 168 items with little more than two days remaining.

To keep from panicking, Nigel installed himself in Son's committee by three o'clock and put Son in the lower school committee where Ben's items were passing at a healthy eighty-five percent clip. He hoped he could get some of Ben's items through on charm alone.

This helped. Ben managed another thirty items by close of business Wednesday. The committee accepted seventeen outright, and Nigel finagled an additional six with last minute re-writes. They were still not even halfway there. The bias committee, which operated concurrently and without oversight from BTC, rejected only two items up till that point, both Ariya's.

That evening, Nigel called an emergency meeting in Ben's room, but was embarrassed when Ariya refused to attend, claiming a headache. Son again offered to write items and expressed frustration that his offers kept getting spurned. Nigel did his best to placate him, but Son got the hint. After several minutes, he threw up his hands and left.

Finally alone with Ben, Nigel loosened his tie. "Son tells me you're only down to eighty percent in the fifth-grade committee," he said. "So that's good."

Ben chuckled fleetingly. "With him in there I'm surprised we're doing that well." He hadn't shaved or showered since Tuesday morning and was still wearing the shorts and T-shirt he had slept in the night before.

"He says they only have 125 items to go," Nigel said. "They should wrap tomorrow with items to spare just like you said they would. Nice work."

"Thanks."

"Have you heard back from your writers?"

"No. One's on vacation, and I can't get a hold of the other. I told them both they'd have off this week, so I'm not surprised they're unavailable."

"That's too bad."

"Did St. Clair say we could use any of Ariya's writers?" Ben asked.

Nigel shook his head. "They're busy putting out a fire in New Mexico."

"Another one?"

"Yes. Anyway, we'd have to pay them to train on the fifth-grade specs as per our contract as well as write items. Their acceptance rate isn't high enough. We'd go over budget. And you know how St. Clair feels about that."

Ben looked away and bit his lip. "How does he feel about his employees working eighteen-hour shifts?"

Nigel patted Ben on the knee and stood. "I spoke to him, Ben. I insisted that he promote you to BTC's lead content specialist. I told him what you're doing here and that you deserve it. He said he was inclined to agree."

"Inclined to agree," Ben repeated.

"Yes."

"That I deserve the promotion or that he'd give it to me?"

Nigel made a show of shrugging and smiled.

"I get the feeling that clearing the hurdles here in Arkansas may help him make up his mind," Ben mused. "Am I right?"

"Possibly," Nigel said.

"Thanks," Ben said, falling flat between heartfelt and sarcastic.

After Nigel left, Ben started some coffee and set his alarm for midnight to guarantee a full day on Thursday in the most literal sense. He then shaved and took his much-needed shower. He transposed it into a luxurious bath and began feeling sorry for himself over his cancelled vacation. At eight, he ordered dinner via room service but made the mistake of lying in bed soon after. Sleep ensnared him almost immediately. Room service left his dinner in the hall after knocking for a minute without an answer.

Chapter 3

After assassinating President Abraham Lincoln, John Wilkes Booth was fatally wounded by Union soldiers. As he was dy-

ing, he asked a soldier to raise his paralyzed hands to his face
and said which of the following last words?

A. "Sic semper tyrannis!"
B. "I have done it. The South is avenged!"
C. "Tell my mother I died for my country."
D. "Useless, useless." (correct)

Except in math, testing companies had for the past decade
largely given up using artificial intelligence to write test items.
Pirated versions of item writing software were too easily obtain-
able and allowed students to sync correct answers to their personal or implanted devices. After several years of widespread
cheating and the ensuing scandals, the testing industry returned
to relying on human ingenuity for its content as it had before the
temporary ban on standardized testing twenty years prior. It
was the more expensive option in the short term but worth it
considering the averted legal and IT expenditures.

Although Ben didn't understand it as completely as Nigel
did, he was almost as cost effective as AI. This made him an extremely rare and valuable commodity for Benchmark Testing.
He generated his items himself and relied on very few item
writers. For him, it was *easy*. The trick was to write clearly and
succinctly, to test one idea per item, and to dream up appropriate scenarios in which to apply these ideas. Right answers must
always be right, and wrong ones always wrong. He never understood the charge that standardized tests were culturally biased. Having written them for almost seven years, he knew that
they were biased only against students who weren't very bright
or didn't work very hard — or both.

Ben didn't hear the alarm until a few minutes after midnight.
He then brute forced his way out of bed one foot at a time,
poured himself some coffee, and got to work. Thursday was
make or break day for BTC. And if things broke, he imagined
he'd next wake up in a hospital.

At this point, Ben had internalized the canon of forty or so
Arkansas science standards and was scouring the internet for
unique situations into which he could fit them. Dew on a leaf to
teach the water cycle. The edges of the universe to teach the

Doppler Effect. Some precocious kid's science project to teach photosynthesis. A news report on the Kibaale virus to teach the immune system.

Fingers shaking from a combination of nervous energy and caffeine, he produced forty-three items before sunrise. Nigel got up around six to edit them. The eleventh-grade committee was gathering in the room when Ben appeared with megabytes of fresh items. This was the first the committee had seen of him. They had expected a gaunt, bearded recluse with vampire skin and bad breath. That Ben had donned his suit and was his usual chipper self was a pleasant surprise. With a cocky flourish he scrolled through his items with Nigel and rattled off possible rewrite ideas for some of the riskier ones. Nigel sat there red-faced and grinning as Ben shook hands with the committee members and made introductory chit-chat. He feigned modesty about his work, but his swagger and confidence told a different story. He was carrying his company on his shoulders. He was someone *important*. Despite the fatigue and the pressure, it felt tantalizingly good.

Ben then made a quick stop in the fifth-grade committee room. Within seconds he was fielding hugs and handshakes and was presented with a gift of chocolate inside a large coffee mug. Son arrived a few minutes late, and Ben had the vindictive desire to sit down with him and discuss the progress of the fifth-grade items. This was entirely unnecessary since Nigel had been keeping Ben apprised all week, and Son knew it. But Ben couldn't resist the temptation to act like Son's boss despite technically being the junior content specialist. He spoke to Son as if to an errant child. Son responded with a series of grunts and murmurs and wouldn't even look at Ben, clearly chafing under the kid brother treatment from his skinny white colleague. Being surrounded by committee members, there was little else he could do.

After going over the last item, Ben asked, "Are we clear on that, Son?"

Son cleared his throat and made a show of putting his papers in order.

"Son. Are we clear?" Ben repeated, moving his face into Son's field of vision.

Son glared at him. "Yes."

Ben smiled and patted him on the back twice. "Good. And let me know as soon as you finish up today, okay?" As Ben slipped through the door he took one last resentful look at Son's powerful shoulders, muscular arms, and rough-hewn hands, so grossly overqualified for the delicate task before them.

By ten-thirty that morning, Ben brought in twenty more items. By the time the committee returned from lunch, there were an additional twelve waiting for them. By the three-thirty break, the committee was close to caught up. Of the forty-three items submitted at start of business, thirty-six were initially taken. The bias committee wouldn't even look at the Kibaale item since they were afraid that a deadly virus originating in Africa would stigmatize African Americans. It was DNU'ed so unconditionally that Ben had no interest in salvaging it. Only thirteen of the batch of twenty initially passed, but Nigel saved an additional four through clever wordsmithing. Not counting the twelve items submitted during lunch, ninety-three items remained to be accepted. Ben was relieved to hear that the fifth-grade committee had successfully concluded, and that Son would soon be on a plane back to Muncie, Indiana where the BTC headquarters were located.

After dinner in his room, Ben set to work right away, but was crippled with fatigue. He watched three sitcoms in a row while lounging on his bed. The episodes were pretty good, so he had that going for him. He gazed at his neglected novel opened face down on the nightstand, too tired to read. The Persians had just discovered the mountain pass leading around the Hot Gates. The Spartans were doomed. Ben took another cup of coffee and brought his device to the bed with him. If he had to work, at least he would be comfortable about it. But his sluggish mind could not grasp ideas quickly enough. After an hour and a half all he could produce was a cluster of six geology items about the former Aral Sea and a couple cheap items on mitosis which he was pretty sure would get rejected.

By nine-thirty his pathetic rally was about to fizzle. He was mentally preparing for a near miss with the committee. If he could get all but twenty or thirty items through, would they give him the weekend to meet quota? Or even just Saturday?

A gentle knock woke him. It was Ariya, dressed casually in a polo shirt and jeans with a satchel strapped over her shoulder. Her hair enjoyed a post-shower shine and fell behind her in an unostentatious ponytail. Foundation makeup expertly disguised the flaws on her cheeks and forehead. "Do you need help, Ben?" she asked, business-like but not unfriendly.

Still a little piqued over her rebuff on Monday, Ben made her wait for an answer. "Oh, if you insist," he said.

Ariya bit her lip and darted her eyes up and down along Ben's long, slender body. Ben remembered that he had nothing on but a pair of boxers. "Ah! One moment," he laughed. He slipped back into his room, threw on a T-shirt and a pair of shorts, and then let Ariya in. This unexpected intimacy, innocent as it was, killed whatever tension still lurking between them. Each revealed their embarrassment through a row of teeth.

"How's it going?" she asked.

Ben rubbed his face. "Slow. I don't think I can make it."

"Nigel told me the committee finally caught up with you. First time all week."

"That's true. Did he tell you to come here?"

Ariya offered him a tight, secretive smile. "Maybe. Did you really write 250 items since Monday?"

"Something like that. Still got eighty-six to go."

"You did it all by yourself?"

Ben nodded rather than answer such a flattering question.

"Wow," she whispered, scanning the room as if looking for item writers hiding behind the furniture. "I knew you were fast, but...wow."

"Yeah, but I'm losing it. I only wrote twelve items this afternoon. They accepted seven. I think I'm done."

Given Ariya's change of attitude, he was expecting a soft exclamation of surprise or pity. Instead, she clapped her hands. "Come! Let's see what we can do!"

Despite her religion and marital status, Ben felt the urge to kiss her on the cheek. His face morphed into a smile, and he looked away. He cleared away the remnants of his dinner, and

they placed their devices on the desk. He then walked her
through the eleventh-grade standards, which fortunately resembled the eighth-grade standards. They discussed the committee
members, their tastes and biases. He showed her his accepted
items so she wouldn't duplicate them. Then they set to work.

While Ben went back to scraping the bottom of his brain for
new science scenarios, Ariya took a close look at his rejected
items. By 2:30 that morning, she had rewritten twenty-six of
them. Ben recognized that the woman had an uncanny talent for
editing.

"I have nine item writers working for me!" she snapped, pretending to get defensive. "What do I do to them but edit?"

Ben laughed. He had produced a meager eight moon phase
items, but they were so listless that Ariya herself rejected half of
them.

"Go to sleep," she commanded. "I will handle this. In morning, you will write more."

Ben stretched out on the bed, muttering his thanks.

"You are welcome," Ariya said, working rapidly on her device.

"Ariya."

"Yes."

"How did your eighth-grade items do?"

"We may not make it."

"What?"

"We need seventy more to get accepted. We only have one
hundred left."

"But why come here if your committee isn't done?"

"Stupid question," she said. "So stupid."

Ben turned over and yielded to the clouds of sleep now
numbing his mind. Lamplight glared onto his sleeping face until
Ariya got up and turned it off. She rolled the bedspread over
him and returned to her device. Its blue glow cast a thin and
sickly haze across the room.

Ben woke up at six-thirty, refreshed and remembering what
strength and vigor felt like. Sleep was all he needed. A burning
hunger in his gut matched his sudden desire to get the job done
once and for all. Sitting up, his heart stopped as he noticed Ariya

waking up alongside him. The blinds were open, and sunlight silhouetted her as his eyes adjusted. They looked at each other without embarrassment for nearly ten seconds. Ariya opened her mouth, but not to speak, her eyes laden with intent. Only Ben's girlfriends had ever looked at him that way. He felt a tremor of desire, but it vanished when he looked past her flaking foundation and noticed again the deep pockmarks populating her forehead.

She turned away the moment his expression changed. "Good morning," she said, sitting up. She hunted for her sandals on the floor with her bare feet.

"Hey," he said, smiling self-consciously. "How late did you stay up?"

"I don't know," she yawned. "I edited thirty-nine items. Sent them to you. They should pass now."

Ben did the math in his head. Thirty-nine plus the Aral Sea, mitosis, and the Moon phases equaled fifty-one. Eighty-six minus fifty-one was thirty-five. Thirty-five items in one day was possible, he knew. "I can't thank you enough for this, Ariya," he said.

She chuckled as she packed up her device. "Maybe you write for me one day. I could use you. Pay is pretty good."

Ben laughed.

"I have to get ready for my committee," she said. "Oh! I don't have enough time!"

"You still have an hour and a half."

Ariya slung her satchel over her shoulder and hurried for the door, sandals clapping against her heels. "Yes! Not enough time. Must prepare!" Ben surmised that 'prepare' for Ariya meant selecting her wardrobe, hairstyle, and makeup like a soldier gearing up for battle.

She opened the door and waved to him. "Bye!" she said in a high, girlish voice. He had never heard such birdsong sweetness from Ariya before and fell back onto his pillow thinking only of her.

After sending Nigel the fifty-one items for editing, he sat down for a working breakfast. Within an hour he gathered that he had pretty much exhausted his resources there at the hotel.

His electronic textbooks and magazines were becoming all too familiar, and the internet, vast as it was, had limits when it came to Arkansas eleventh-grade science standards. After inadvertently plagiarizing himself a few times, Ben decided to make the three-mile trek to the nearest bookstore and sit himself down with an ice coffee and a stack of books to finish the job.

By one o'clock, he had forty-seven items and gambled that that would be enough. He was ready to lead the committee by the nose to accept each and every one of them. He was *not* going to falter on the finish line. He stepped into the committee room with the same determination. Thanks to a message from Nigel, he knew that forty-nine of the fifty-one items developed the night before had passed. Only his mitosis ones didn't make it.

He sat down next to Nigel and watched as the committee members discussed his items. One by one, they passed. It was all too easy. The committee seemed to appreciate the herculean effort Ben had put in and did whatever it could to save or rewrite items. That the items were of high quality to begin with made it easier. By the thirtieth item, Ben had fallen asleep in his chair, and the meeting continued in whispers since no one had the heart to wake him. When it was over, they had made it with two items to spare. A teacher nudged Ben on the shoulder to congratulate him. As he woke, the committee broke out into gentle, heartfelt applause. Nigel joined them and then shook his hand for all to see. Ben sat there and soaked it all in, all the while resisting the urge to yawn and rub his eyes. The accomplishment felt good, and he appreciated the attention, but all he wanted to do at that moment was go back to sleep. He knew the elation would come later, after everything had a chance to sink in.

Chapter 4

The Regents of the University of California v. Bakke (1978) was the first Supreme Court case to allow which rationale for racial discrimination?

A. affirmative action
B. separate but equal
C. redress of past wrongs

D. attainment of diversity (correct)

"Don't continue," Nigel said, pretending to ward Ben off with his hand. "I just might let you go after all."

Ben laughed. He looked pleased with himself—if still a bit frazzled—with scruff dulling the edges of his sideburns. Eyebrows curved over his half-closed eyes like handlebars. Beneath it all, his tie remained impeccably snug around his neck.

"I got two rooms full of Arkansas school teachers who'll vouch for me in writing," Ben said, thumb poking the air behind him. "After my performance this week I can go to any testing company I want and name my price." Sitting in the hotel restaurant, Ben's sense of direction must have gotten confused. The committee rooms were in front of him, not behind him.

"I know half the people at those companies, Ben," Nigel said, slicing cleanly through his beef cutlet. "As soon as they receive a resume bearing the letters 'BTC', they will call me before they will call you." Nigel seemed even more pleased with himself, if that were at all possible.

Ben swirled his half-filled glass of beer as if it were wine. His mind swirled along with it. "Then I'll apply with the other half."

Nigel waved his fork at Ben like a scepter, dripping gravy on the tablecloth. "All I have to do is tell them you're a Right-winger, and you'll be banned from the industry."

Ben drained his glass. Alcohol on an empty stomach after his week-long ordeal was brutalizing his equilibrium. He couldn't wait to sleep on the plane. "I am not a Right-winger," he said pedantically. "I am a libertarian. That means I'm a liberal, but with a capital 'L'."

"Come on, Ben. What's the difference?"

Ben's dinner arrived. Massive cheeseburger and steak fries. Hunger hit him like a flash flood, and he forgot all about his napkin. He smiled his thanks to the waitress. "You know full well what the difference is, you Leftist twit," he said, cheek bulging with food. "It's more likely that wherever I go, I'll win over hearts and minds to my point of view than the other way around."

"All the more reason to let you go!" Nigel concluded through a fat grin. "You can muddy the waters someplace else and not at BTC."

Ben reached over and clasped a slice of Nigel's dinner between his thumb and forefinger. He drew it to his mouth. "Well, if I remember correctly, you were wanting our waters muddied up pretty good Monday night."

Nigel handed Ben his own napkin still lying next to his plate. "Ben," he announced, "please accept this napkin as a token of our esteem here at Benchmark Testing. The valiant work you performed this week was above and beyond the call of duty."

"Yeah. You say that now," Ben said, snatching the napkin and using it. "But you'll throw me to the curb when you're done with me like you do with all your writers. Why don't you just drop a hundred bucks on the dresser and be done with it?"

"Can't we make it fifty?"

"Uh-uh. Man's gotta keep his self-respect."

"We'll take it out of your forthcoming raise then," Nigel said, sliding his elbows on the table and resting his chin in his hands.

Ben looked up, startled. "Seriously?"

"Yes. St. Clair told me this morning. It will be a sizable raise and a promotion going into effect the next pay period. I just hope you'll invite me to the party."

Ben brightened into a jubilant half-smile, and his eyes positively glowed. Nigel folded his arms. "You deserve it, Ben," he said. "I only wish there was something more we could do."

A small frown spoiled Ben's expression. "There is one thing."

"What?"

"I think this might be inappropriate for me to ask, under normal circumstances, that is."

"Ask what?"

"But I think I've earned the right."

"Okay. Ask me what?"

Ben sighed, appearing to gather his nerve. "Why did you hire Son Mensah, and when are you going to fire him?"

Nigel's response was to engage Ben in a staring contest, but Ben was not about to blink first. Nigel soon gave up and sipped his beer. "You're right. That is inappropriate," he said. "Can we change the subject please?"

Ben said nothing, still aiming his tired eyes at his boss.

Nigel held up a hand as if to thwart them. "Okay, okay. You have to promise not to tell anyone."

"I promise."

Nigel started with a high-pitched sigh. "Well, you know *why* we had to hire him, don't you?"

"Diversity requirement."

"Yes. Tammy in language arts wasn't enough. The department needed at least—" Nigel glanced both ways and reduced his voice to a whisper. "—at least two African American content specialists, and HR was putting tremendous pressure on us to find suitable candidates."

"Why were they doing that?"

"What do you mean 'why'?" Nigel said, still whispering. "We get tax breaks and avoid audits and lawsuits if we do. And it is everyone's obligation to even the playing field for disadvantaged minorities. We're in the testing industry, Ben. The slightest whiff of anything racist and we're done for."

"But by law every state board of education has a bias committee checking our items for racial or cultural bias," Ben reasoned. "And these committees consist largely of black and Latino women!"

"Keep it down," Nigel ordered. They looked around. Fortunately, the only other diners were white. Their Mexican waitress was on the other side of the dining room. "Bias committees don't matter," Nigel went on. "If people can find a reason to blame the tests, they will. You know that. Why do you think there was a ban on testing in this country for ten years?"

Ben held up a hand. "Okay, fine. That explains why you had to hire Son. Now are you going to fire him? Or next time will *you* be the one cleaning up his mess? Because it won't be me."

Nigel puffed up his cheeks and exhaled. "We're not going to fire him. At least not right away," he said, leaning in close. "Believe me, we've wanted to ever since New Mexico. But we currently have two under-performing African Americans in the department—"

"You mean, the *only* two African Americans in the department."

Nigel rolled his eyes with an impatient sigh. "Regardless, HR will not let us fire both at the same time."

"Why not?"

"Because it would look bad. It would invite a civil rights audit from the government. It would make us vulnerable to lawsuits. It's not worth it."

Ben leaned in close as well. Their foreheads were inches apart. "Can't you fire one and then fire the other?" he asked.

"Yes, we are in the process of doing that. We started with Tammy. But we have to amass evidence. We have to follow our operating procedures to the letter. We have to consult our attorneys. It's expensive and time consuming. We have to present a watertight case, and her case is less cut and dry than Son's. This can take months. It also didn't help that Shawnia in HR resigned last week."

Ben nodded down, but not up. "You mean you need black people to fire black people?"

Even though Ben said this in a whisper, Nigel once again checked if the coast was clear across the dining room. He fidgeted in his seat before responding. "Ehhhh, not necessarily. A Muslim, Hispanic...some kind of minority. A Native American would be fab. The problem is that it's hard to find qualified ones, and when we do it's hard to keep them since they are in such demand. And the firing really should at least come from the VP or director level. It just looks better that way."

"But Sushma and Shangbin are directors. Why can't they —"

"They are the wrong kind of minority, Ben. You know that."

"That's insane."

Nigel finished his beer. "It's the mid-twenty-first century. You and I are not in the majority anymore." Nigel held up a finger to correct himself and stopped whispering. "Well, I should say that *you* are not in the majority anymore. I will always be part of a minority, fortunately."

"Because you're gay."

Nigel grinned instantly. "Yes."

Ben gave him an empty smirk. "That's great, Nigel."

"It *is* great, Ben. It means we are making progress."

"But what about people like me?"

Nigel sighed and ran his tongue across his lips. "Unfortunately, you are the bottom of the barrel."

Ben blinked. "Come again?"

"According to HR, that is. We could fire you in a heartbeat. All the precautions we're taking for Tammy and Son wouldn't apply to you because you are a SWM."

"Straight White Male."

"Yes."

Ben studied the fancy floral wallpaper behind Nigel as he took this in. The waitress came and refreshed their water glasses. Nigel asked for the check. Ben hardly noticed. "Bottom of the barrel, huh?" he said.

Nigel shook him by the wrist. "Oh, don't let it bother you, Ben! You're our best content specialist. We're privileged to have you."

Ben pursed his lips, mostly to hide his growing anger. "But I'm the bottom of the barrel."

Nigel let him go. "I didn't mean it like that. You know that I have the greatest respect for you. I wouldn't be confiding in you like this if I didn't. This is just the way the HR is *forced* to feel about you. There are political reasons for this Ben, reasons that have been building for a long time. This is a great world we live in now. You can't deny that, can you?"

Ben looked down, blinking in fatigue, mouth open and saying nothing.

"Can you?" Nigel asked.

Part 2: Muncie

Chapter 5

Despite being a radical Leftist early in his career, American author John Dos Passos began a political shift to the Right in the late 1930s which culminated in his campaigning for conservative candidates in the 1960s. What initially caused Dos Passos to change his political beliefs?

A. the Japanese sneak attack at Pearl Harbor
B. the Bolshevik victory in the October Revolution

C. the Arab invasion of Israel during the Arab-Israeli
   War
D. the murder of his friend and translator during the
   Spanish Civil War by Soviet NKVD officers and the
   nonchalance with which many of his left-wing
   friends, including Ernest Hemingway, either accepted
   or approved of the murder (correct)

Ben couldn't sleep on the plane and set his car to auto-drive
on the way home since he had real concern he might doze at the
wheel. The trip from the Indianapolis airport to Muncie was
pretty much a straight shot northeast along I-69 and usually took
an hour and fifteen minutes. Ben always found the Indiana terrain exceedingly boring along 69, mostly just farmlands and
wide horizons bristling with forests and corn. Of all the people
he'd met in Indiana, only the indigenous white Hoosiers ever
referred to the Indiana landscape as beautiful.

Ben had grown up in San Diego close to the beach. As a kid
he used to cruise the Pacific Coast Highway and surf at La Jolla
Shores. He moved to Indiana for the work and liked the people.
But the flat Indiana topography held as much interest for him as
the hair follicles on his right arm. With twenty miles still to go
and the radio blasting, his car's fatigue sensors caught him nodding off and woke him with a shrill alarm which kept his ears
ringing for the remainder of the trip.

Ben lived in one of the middle units of a three-story townhome on North Wheeling Avenue in Muncie. It was 11:30 at
night, and under the street lights he could see a few teenagers
listening to music and a woman walking her dog. As he turned
into his lot, a lone figure jumped down the front stairs of one of
the units. He wasn't sure if it was his.

Ben parked in his garage, but instead of taking the elevator to
his unit, he set out for the mail station, which was about fifty
yards away. The figure, a slender man in khaki shorts and blue
jacket, turned the corner just as Ben was pulling envelopes from
his box. He was young and carried a large duffel bag over his
shoulder. Flipping through his mail, Ben heard him approach
and spun around for a brisk walk back to his garage. His neighborhood was safe enough, but with strangers, you never know.

Ben was relieved to see that this person was white and only five-and-a-half feet tall. His windbreaker fluttered in the breeze revealing a tight-fitting polo shirt. They nodded as they passed each other, and the stranger gave Ben a short wave.

"What's the matter, Ben? Don't recognize your own brother?"

Ben whirled around. "Isaac?"

Isaac smiled, holding out his hands and standing on his heels. In the street light Ben could barely make out the brownish sheen of his crew cut.

"What the heck happened to you?" Ben asked. Spit flew from his mouth without his realizing it. "Where have you been? What have you...?" Ben stepped close to make sure it really was his wayward younger brother and started to smile. "Look at you! Last time I saw you, you had a ponytail!"

"All gone now," Isaac said as the brothers shook hands and bumped chests. "They say it made me look too much like a girl. How are you?"

Ben got a close look at Isaac and liked what he saw. The short hair, the preppy pretentions, the bulging muscles in his arms and chest. Isaac had always been pale and less than healthy, and this was as vigorous as Ben had ever seen him. His teeth had been fixed too. Only his hardened bare feet and slightly glazed eyes which always seemed to wobble around whatever he was looking at served as artifacts of what he once was. Isaac had been a hippie ever since he was old enough to shave and had never taken much stock in clothes, money, or hygiene. He had never bothered with college either and lived in their aunt's basement until he was twenty, spending most of his time on music, marijuana, and catching up on his sleep. After that he disappeared and would pop in and out of Ben's life only when he felt like it, usually whenever he needed money. He had no personal device, no implants, no permanent address. Just 'friends' with whom he would stay and move around. He never provided specifics of his life to anyone. He was two years younger than Ben.

Ben had last seen Isaac at their father's wake five years ago, shortly before he moved to Muncie. It had been a small affair, held back in San Diego, and attended mostly by distant cousins.

No one from their mother's side came, of course. How Isaac had found out about it Ben never knew. Isaac just showed up in cut-off corduroys and sandals. At least he wore a clean shirt, half-way-buttoned and untucked as it was. His girlfriend was his exact same height and wore a pair of faded men's jeans and a tank top. She was not pretty and, aside from the conspicuous hair under her arms, had a body unnervingly similar to that of a pre-pubescent boy. They had the same brown hair, same ponytail. From behind, kneeling at the casket, they were almost indistin-guishable. Given Isaac's well-known history with his father, no one felt that their pleasant, easy-going airs were inappropriate. They stayed no longer than forty minutes and left with barely a word.

Considering that their father Stillwell had brutalized Isaac as a boy and ultimately gone to prison for it, Ben was surprised his brother showed up at all. In the final incident, Stillwell had twisted Isaac's right arm until it broke and then knocked him unconscious with a punch. Isaac was twelve. He had always been such a gentle boy. Their father had never broken him of that despite depriving his son of the ability to lift his right arm over his shoulder due to the repeated beatings.

"I'm fine, Isaac. I'm fine," Ben said, still clasping his brother by the shoulders. For the first time in his adult life Isaac Camer-on seemed normal. Ben sang a high note considering the possi-bilities. "It's good to see you. Have you decided to rejoin civili-zation?"

"Or take it by storm," Isaac said with his typically insipid smile.

"What are you doing here?"

"Visiting friends. Thought I'd pop by and say hey. One of your neighbors said you'd be back late tonight. So here I am."

Ben noticed something that made him catch his breath. Isaac's right arm. It was white, pale, and empty. Previously it had been covered in tattoos.

***

Chinese food extended almost the length of Ben's small kitchen table. Chopsticks in hand, Isaac gorged himself on noodles and sweet and sour pork straight from the box. Ben handed him a napkin for his nose. "Tell me more. Tell me more," Isaac urged with his mouth full of noodles.

"Not much more to tell," Ben said, feeling his words begin to slur. He was corresponding with clients and colleagues on his BTC device while taking intermittent bites from his eggroll. He reclined with his stocking feet on the table. Wooden shutters, fancy pre-fab furniture, and stylish prints coordinated nicely with the wallpaper. Ben's townhome hinted of a domesticity which clashed with his bachelor attitude. "Did I tell you my boss Nigel 'fired' me again this morning?"

"Didn't he just give you a promotion?"

"Yeah. It's a running joke between us. He always threatens to 'fire' me for being a Right-winger even though he won't fire me, and I'm not really a Right-winger."

"I would agree that you're not on the Right."

"He thinks it's funny, and I guess it kinda is."

"I think it's obnoxious," Isaac said, opening a new box. He dumped noodles into a bowl of greasy moo goo gai pan and began stirring.

"Yeah, but I know he doesn't mean it. It's just how he is. I mean, this morning, he said I was the bottom of the barrel because I'm a straight white male."

Isaac stopped stirring and glared. "He said that?"

"Yeah," Ben said, startled by this punch of intensity from his brother. "He said that BTC doesn't need to take the same legal precautions to fire or reprimand me as they would for so-called 'minorities'."

Isaac's mouth tightened. "Ben, you need to find yourself a good civil rights attorney and sue. You need to win a sizeable settlement for pain and suffering caused by harassment and intimidation in the workplace. What your company is doing is racist and unconstitutional. Your boss should be selling pencils on street corners for what he said to you." Isaac went back to his food and didn't notice Ben's mouth snake into a grin. He looked up when his brother started to laugh. "I'm sorry. I don't remember telling a joke," he said.

"I've just never heard you speak like this before," Ben said.

"There's a lot I do now that I've never done before."

"Well, it's not what you think," Ben explained. "I like Nigel. We're almost like friends. He lobbied to get me that promotion. I can't go to war against Benchmark Testing. They hired me when I didn't even have a college degree."

"They also didn't have to call you the bottom of the barrel, Ben. This is why we should stand up for ourselves. No one else is gonna do it for us."

Ben squinted his eyes into slits. "What's this 'we' stuff? This doesn't sound like you, Isaac. Last time I checked you were some hippie moonbat liberal who kept *The Autobiography of Malcolm X* and *The Chomsky Reader* under his pillow. Now you're acting like some Wahoo Yahoo."

Isaac nodded six or seven times. His eyes no longer seemed glazed. "You seem tired," he said.

"Well, yeah. I am. But enough of this!" Ben demanded, dropping a fist on the table. "You're talking to me like we last hung out a month ago. I haven't seen or heard from you since the funeral. You're the only family I have! What the hell have you been doing all this time?"

Isaac groaned and put down his chopsticks. "Thanks for the food. All I need is a place to crash. I'll be out of your hair in the morning."

"Oh, no you don't."

"What?"

"The nearest homeless shelter is two miles that way," Ben said, pointing to the window. "You will be hoofing every inch of it if you don't tell me where you live and what you do."

Isaac slid his chair from the table and got up, heaving a little bit from his full belly. "I understand. It was good seeing you again, Ben. Glad you're doing well. Hope you hold on to that job. I'll look you up next time I'm in Indiana."

Ben waited until his brother picked up his duffel bag before abandoning his bluff. He bounded to his feet and grabbed Isaac by the arm. "Hey! Wait—"

Ben had been knocked back two feet by a well-executed, open-handed strike to his chest. He hadn't seen it coming, and now faced Isaac, who was assuming a fleet-footed martial arts stance from across the kitchen. The blow hadn't hurt, but Ben felt the strength and power behind it. He knew he would have been on the floor gasping for air had it been aimed two inches lower at his solar plexus.

Isaac held up his hand, part peace offering, part wave good-bye, and turned to leave. He was crossing the parking lot when Ben burst from his door. "Isaac! Wait! You can stay!"

Isaac turned, and the men faced each other under the street lamp. The teenagers had gone inside, and at one in the morning, the place was as still as death. Even the dry midsummer night air didn't seem to move. "I'm sorry I hit you," Isaac said.

"It's okay. You can come back inside."

"You sure?"

"Yeah. I just want to know one thing, though."

"What?"

"What happened to your arm?" Isaac looked down at his right arm and made a half-hearted effort to hide it behind his back. "You used to have seven or eight tattoos there," Ben said, pointing. "Mystic symbols, Buddha, whatever."

Isaac held out his bare arm under the lamplight. "That was sloppy of me," he said, more to himself than to Ben. "I guess it was too hot today for long sleeves."

"What happened?"

Isaac sighed. The glazed look was back. "Let's just say that the friends I'm with now don't care very much for tattoos."

Ben leaned in closer. "Who are these friends?"

Isaac smiled. "You know, if I told you, Ben, I'd have to kill you."

Ben gaped at his brother for nearly five seconds before a wink informed him it was okay to laugh. Isaac kept smiling but wouldn't join in. Ben put his arm around him and led him back to his door. "Have it your way. I'll take you to the bus stop tomorrow and give you all the cash you need."

"Did I ask you for cash?"

"Okay. Just thought I'd offer."

"I should give you money. You're letting me stay with you."

"Don't worry about it. Just don't hit me again, okay?"

Isaac yawned. "Okay. No hitting."

"Where did you learn to fight like that? Your new 'friends' teach you?"

"No. I just joined a gym. Started taking taekwondo classes."

Ben opened the door for him, and Isaac ducked under his arm to enter. Once inside, he said, "Look, I'm sorry I haven't been in touch. I'll try calling more, I promise."

"You know, public libraries have free internet. And if you can access the internet you can send an old-fashioned email. It's like you're living in the 1980s, Isaac."

"The 1980s were a good time."

"So I've heard."

The brothers smiled awkwardly at each other. Suddenly, Isaac remembered something. "Listen, speaking of internet, do you mind if I stay up and surf a bit on your device? I'd like to catch up on some news."

"Sure," Ben said as he headed into the hall. "Sheets and pillow are in the linen closet. Couch opens up. And don't use my toothbrush, you filthy animal."

"Good night, Ben," Isaac said, settling down at the table with Ben's device at his lap.

Ben looked back and noticed how much Isaac resembled their father. The straight mouth and thin lips. The high cheekbones and small, deeply set eyes. Not until that moment did he ever see his father's face in Isaac's; the two were so different in so many ways. The light from the device took away Isaac's human pallor and replaced it with a dry, bluish glow which for the first time that evening made him seem as if he belonged in the modern age.

"Good night, Isaac," Ben said, and turned down the hall to get that full night of sleep he'd been needing for the past five days.

Chapter 6

As of January 1, 2016, 108 athletes scored official times of less than 10.00 seconds in the 100-yard dash. How many of these athletes were NOT of African descent?

A. 19
B. 18
C. 17
D. 2 (correct)

The new Muncie Indiana Transit System terminal was located on High Street, between Jackson and Main, and was probably the most presentable face one could put on an area which seemed to grow sketchier by the month. Traditionally, Jackson, which ran east and west, was the dividing line between what was sketchy and what wasn't in Muncie. Most robberies and shootings and gang activity took place in South Muncie. This was also where people were hardest hit when a number of manufacturing businesses closed down around the turn of the century. Ben learned shortly after starting at BTC that South Muncie was where most of the town's eighteen thousand blacks made their homes. He made the connection, of course, but like most white people in the office said nothing about it.

The terminal cost $60 million and epitomized the current trends of post-contextual architecture, which, with all its smooth, aerodynamic curves, seemed little more than a return to the postmodernist style of the previous century. It was basically a concrete and glass arc opening up to High Street. After constructing it, the state government also demolished an abandoned office building across the street to make room for a three-story parking garage and a small city park with basketball courts. They gambled that with new factories opening and the sudden influx of over four thousand new workers and their families, efficient public transportation would be vital for the town's economic resurgence.

It had almost no effect. Instead, the facility was understaffed, poorly managed, and burdened by high rates of crime almost from the start.

'You don't come to South Muncie. South Muncie comes to you.' This was the joke floating around town a couple years before Ben arrived. It referred to how the town's worst sector was burgeoning north with new inhabitants who were nearly as shiftless and violent as the old ones. The bus terminal, the courthouse, the library, and many government buildings were caught in the literal crossfire. Only a heavy police presence kept the peace. Still, gunshots rang out weekly. Incidents of violence and robbery on the bus lines further soured the public to public transportation. Despite still being in operation, it stood as an embarrassment for city and state officials who years later continued to scratch their heads about how such a fiasco could have happened.

Dread thudded in Ben's chest as he followed the instructions of his car's GPS. He noticed not a single face in the vicinity that wasn't black or Mexican. There were many, and most were under thirty. People glittered in tasteless jewelry and revealed themselves in vulgar displays. The ones who didn't kept their heads down and kept moving. Ben had lived in Muncie five years and never once took a bus anywhere. This was his first time in this part of town, and his stomach kept tightening the longer he was there. He didn't savor the idea of leaving Isaac in a place like this.

Their conversation for most of the ride had been pleasant enough and only grew tense when it became clear that Ben was not simply dropping Isaac off and saying goodbye. Ben parked in the parking garage and stepped out of the car with him, insisting on accompanying him to the terminal.

"So that's what this is about," Isaac said as he slung his duffel bag over his shoulder. "You want to see where I'm going, don't you?"

"Can you blame me?"

Isaac closed his eyes and kept them shut. "For the millionth time. I stay with friends. We live in an itinerant farming community. We've worked the land. We've done cattle ranching. We've contracted with the government. We've—"

"I know. I know."

"We don't have a permanent address, and we don't have personal devices."

"But where are they now? You must have an idea since you're about to buy a bus ticket."

Isaac turned away and then turned back again, letting his hand fall on his thigh. "I just don't want to share that part of my life with you, Ben. Try to understand that."

Ben shook his head. "Okay."

"Okay."

"So, that's it, then?"

"No, it isn't. But just let me go, okay? I need to go."

"All right."

"All right."

They stood on either side of a chasm of silence before Isaac initiated an uncomfortable hug.

"One thing," Ben said when they let go. "What are your long-term plans? Do you think you'll be doing this for the rest of your life, or do you have something else in mind?"

Isaac smiled. "Yeah."

"Yeah, what?"

"I think one day I'd like to be a songwriter."

"Songwriter?"

"Yeah."

"Yeah?"

"Yeah."

"What kind of music?" Ben asked. "No, let me guess. Folksy, rootsy music, right? That's all you listened to at Aunt Jean's."

"Naah."

"What? Not hip hop."

Isaac smiled and shook his head. "Satire."

"What?"

"Satirical music. I wanna be a satirical songwriter. Real sharp. Real political, you know?"

Ben opened his mouth to speak but couldn't think of something suitable to say.

"I've taught myself the piano," Isaac continued, pretending to tickle the ivories. "I'm pretty good with words, too. One day, you're gonna hear a real sharp, real political song, and you're gonna say, 'Yeah, that's my brother. My brother wrote that!'" Isaac pointed in the air and did a half-strut to the music in his head.

Ben smiled. "It's good to see you again, Isaac," he said. "Take care."

Isaac waved and then headed for the terminal without looking back.

***

The fuel levels in Ben's dashboard display hovered just below empty. He stared at them at a red light, relying on the car's auto-drive function to remind him when it turned green. He regretted leaving his brother, and it ate at him the further he drove away. At the next red light, he noticed a superstore across the street and had an idea. He hung a dangerous U-turn and skidded into its parking lot, emerging from the store twenty minutes later in a new T-shirt and with a bag of snack food and a gallon of iced tea. After filling his tank, he tempted law enforcement to clock him for speeding on his way back to the terminal.

The bus stops in front of the terminal were simple two-sided structures of steel and plastic. Buses followed the concave curve of the terminal's arc on either side of the stops to pick up or drop off. The route facing the terminal was for local transit. The route facing the parking garage across High Street, where Ben planned to post himself, was for out-of-town travel.

Ben parked on the roof, immediately realizing that he wasn't the only person up there. It occurred to him that regarding bus travel through his personal device from a parking garage roof might seem suspicious. He was also pretty sure there were cameras rolling when he entered the building. Convinced that spying on his brother from such a perch was a bad idea, he decided he needed another tack.

Ben stepped out of his car and walked to the wall facing the terminal anyway. He saw Isaac sitting cross-legged on one of the benches with his duffel bag at his feet, leafing backwards through a book and jotting notes with a pencil he kept behind his ear. He wore a tweed cap that Ben hadn't seen on him before. Ben waited till no one else was around and peered through his binoculars app. The book was old and leather bound. He couldn't make out the text on the spine, but he knew it wasn't anything close to English.

The park, which was adjacent to the parking garage, was well within Isaac's line of sight. On the south side of the terminal, a strip mall hung back behind its wide-open parking lot. There were people about but not enough among whom to hide. On the north side, across Main, was the Delaware County Building, but Ben couldn't get a good look at Isaac from there thanks to tree cover. There was just no place from which he could spy on his brother and not raise suspicion.

Ben took the elevator down to the first floor and stepped out facing Main Street. Where he stood, a brown brick wall next to the sidewalk obscured him from the bus stops. But the wall stretched only another twenty feet. To reach the terminal he would have to turn right and cross High Street in the open, in plain view of the people on the benches and right under his brother's nose.

He didn't think he could make it.

Leaning against the wall and listening to the wind and the traffic and the thump thump thump of men playing basketball, he had an idea. He put on his sunglasses and jogged around the west end of the garage, away from the terminal, hoping his backside would be less distinctive than his front if his brother was looking. He planned to take the long way around and keep an eye on Isaac while on the basketball court either as an observer or a player. He was careful not to run. Seeing a white man hightailing it anywhere in a minority neighborhood might convince the denizens that he was running away from *them*. Like he was racist or something. They would not take kindly to that. Not that they took all that kindly to white men *walking* in their neighborhoods either, but Ben knew he had a much better chance of making it around the block if he didn't hurry.

So Ben ambled and kept his nose in front of him most of the time. He nodded at a few people who nodded back, friendly enough. The west side of the parking garage served up a view of a few flat-roofed, dilapidated houses which adhered to a tan brick building like infected spider bites. Patches of grass sprouting up amid concrete compromised their lots. Ben couldn't be sure, but he thought he saw people *living* in those structures.

The park emerged on the left as he passed an African themed hair salon. The courts were surrounded by a chain link fence. The baskets had only the remnants of nets, and kids had somehow managed to spray graffiti on the backboards. Ben figured that if Isaac saw him there, he had the perfect alibi. He wanted to play some hoops.

Three half-court games were in progress, and Ben selected the one farthest from the terminal where he would least likely be noticed.

"You wanna play or wha?"

Ben took a look at the guys he was about to play with. Five dudes. They needed a sixth. Three of them were big, hard looking black men in their mid- to late-thirties with scraggly yet creative facial hair: sideburns, goatees, soul patches. Not a mustache in sight. All were six-two, six-three, big-framed dudes. The other two were the shorter, speedier type with smooth milk-chocolatey skin and well-kept afros. One of them could have been Puerto-Rican. They wore a hodgepodge of faded athletic apparel — navy blue, grungy white, blasted orange, gym class gray — all promoting various sports teams and colleges. A cooler filled with Gatorade and water on the sideline indicated that these guys were serious about their Saturday morning basketball.

Ben glanced up once more at Isaac and then joined them.

At five feet, eleven inches, Ben had been one of the more imposing players in his high school district. He had played point guard his junior and senior years, quarterbacking his team to the state semi-finals as a senior. He had reasonable speed and ball-handling abilities, but his strongest assets were a solid understanding of the game and an unerring awareness of all the crucial goings on around him: the intricacies of the plays, the clock, the timeouts remaining, who was in foul trouble, the strengths and weaknesses of everyone on the court. He also had an excellent jump shot. Of course, none but the last part mattered in pickup games like this one where defense is always man-on-man, and 'plays' rarely go beyond pass to the shooter, muscle your way to the hoop, or take the open shot.

Ben's charge was one of the big men who had him by at least thirty pounds and was as strong as an ox. Ben hadn't played any kind hoops in almost half a year, and the play was much more physical than he was accustomed to. For the first ten minutes or so, his defense was nearly ineffectual. The man would literally shrug him off and then spin into the lane for a smooth hook shot or layup. He hit his mark most of the time. Wanting to keep his jaw in one piece, Ben didn't even think about contesting rebounds.

Offense was another matter. Ben had a knack for finding the open court, and his fadeaway jumper was reliable provided his teammates could feed him the right passes. A few disastrous drives to the basket convinced him to stay on the perimeter where he would do the most good. Over time, his defense improved. Basically, he was remembering his bag of tricks, like timing his man's spin, going easy on his weak side, and blocking his line of vision whenever he took a shot. If anything, he proved irritating and was forcing his man to work harder for every point.

Ben was careful to keep checking on Isaac between scores, but the game was growing intense. They were playing twenty-one with the winners needing an edge of at least two points. The score was twenty-five to twenty-four with Ben's team up. Neither team had scored in a while, and both were getting winded. Ben's defense was proving especially stubborn this late in the game, and after his man's third drive to the basket, he swung violently to his left when Ben wasn't expecting it. The point of his elbow cracked Ben in the nose.

Ben took the impact coming in. He saw a white flash and felt its stabbing aftereffects in his forehead. His knees buckled. He felt himself dropping, no longer in control, not even able to lift his hand to brake his fall. He crashed to the asphalt, knees first, shoulder second, wondering if his nose would ever stop bleeding.

Personal fouls like charging and blocking are typically overlooked in pickup games of this nature, but this foul was so egregious that all play stopped. Ben's team was immediately awarded the ball.

"I gotcha! I'm sorry!" the man said, full of good nature and holding out his hand. Ben knew the foul had not been intentional. The game had been rough and physical throughout. Although he preferred to stay down, Ben took the man's hand and let him hoist him to his feet. Athlete to athlete, he wanted to earn the man's respect.

Ben's teammates checked on him and thoughtfully handed him some ice from the cooler wrapped in a towel. Ben flashed a blood red smile and handed out high fives. Experienced with nosebleeds, Ben held his face high and stanched the bleeding. The guys offered to let him sit out the rest of the game, pointing to a couple of new players who were waiting to be rotated in, but Ben shook his head. In a few minutes he was ready to resume play.

He insisted on playing point for the first time, the position he played so well in high school. Up till then the point had been played by Rashawn, the Puerto-Rican dude, who was electric quick and far more suitable for the job. Ben had always known that there were things blacks could do on the basketball court that whites simply could not, the running, the jumping, the explosive movements. By the way he was strutting and talking smack, Ben was acting as if his injury had inspired him to change all that.

It was a bad idea, and the other team knew it. "Aww, look out! Here he comes!" they crowed, clearly not taking him seriously. Rashawn looked doubtful as well until Ben shot him a wink and pointed with his eyes to the left side of the court.

Ben wiped his nose, checked the ball, and started play. Acting the speedster, he faked right and bolted left, drizzling blood as he went. He was trying to dribble around his opponent to gain space for a layup. It was hopeless. Just as he jumped, two dudes were about to close in on him for the block. While in the air however Ben fooled them both. He executed a last-minute no-look backwards pass to Rashawn who was still on the left perimeter. Rashawn drilled the open shot and won the game.

With blood spilling from his nose, Ben didn't stop to look. He walked off the court while the ball was still in play and grabbed hold of the chain link fence with his right hand. With his left he tried to soak up the blood with his sweat-drenched T-shirt. He looked up, tasting blood between his teeth. Isaac was still there. Ben suddenly realized that Isaac was not leafing backwards through his book. He was reading right to left.

***

Ben played approximately every third game that morning and outlasted the five dudes he had started with. By noon, he was playing with a whole new set of guys and having about the same measure of success. His swollen nose, a livid knot below his right eye and a scrape on his chin made him seem as if he'd been brawling rather than playing basketball. Twice he witnessed fights at the other end of the court. The first was a one-on-one slugfest which started as a shoving match over a presumed foul. Neither guy landed a significant punch, and the fight was broken up after about a minute. But the blows had been thrown with murderous intent. The second fight directly involved five guys—three blacks against two Mexicans—and indirectly at least a dozen spectators, mostly teenagers of both sexes, who egged the combatants on and joined the melee for brief seconds whenever it was safe. They reminded Ben of a gang of shrieking hyenas.

Ben sat down in the far corner of the park and rested his chin on his forearms, trying to be as inconspicuous as possible. He didn't want to see the fracas, of course, but he couldn't leave since he figured Isaac was watching as well. Shock melted into cold, jaded disgust as he watched on.

The brawl ended when one of the Mexicans whipped out a homemade weapon from the pocket of his thick, denim shorts. It was a slender, metallic chain which took the shape of a curved blade when shaken. In one swift motion, he slashed the thigh of the largest black, who crumpled gracelessly onto the asphalt as blood began to spurt. The other two blacks were no match for the Mexicans in any event, let alone with one of them wielding a jerry-rigged scimitar, and promptly fled along with a handful of supporters, leaving their erstwhile associate to the tender mercies of their enemies. Police arrived minutes later as the Mexicans were stomping and pummeling their helpless quarry to the roaring cheers of the crowd.

After another couple hours of basketball, a bus pulled up near where Isaac was sitting. Isaac got up, slung his duffel bag over his shoulder, and boarded. Finally. Ben saw the bus from its side, so he couldn't make out its number or destination, which he presumed was posted only on its front. He had to hurry, since the bus wasn't hanging around. High fives and hugs all around, he took off from the court making the dudes wonder who the hell that halfway decent white kid was and why he was hanging out so long in their neighborhood. He did have a pretty sweet shot, though. Ben never did get any of their names.

In order to get a clear look at the front of the bus, Ben had to exit the park the way he had come in and once again brave the parking garage's west side. He caught a few nasty looks as he hustled past and fortunately little else. He turned right onto Main and knew that if he reached the intersection after the bus had left the terminal, he'd be sunk. Despite his exhaustion, however, he made it, catching the bus number and destination just as it pulled out of the terminal: Bus 1297, headed for Richmond, Virginia.

What was Isaac doing in Richmond, Virginia?

Ben guessed it would take ten to twelve hours for the bus to get there. He peeled off his shirt and wrung a half pint of sweat from it. He put it back on as he hurried back to his car. He booted up his car's computer and booked the next flight to Richmond out of Indianapolis. It departed in two hours and fifteen minutes. Barely enough time. Once again, Ben found himself tempting law enforcement as he sped through town. He really picked up speed once he hit I-69 West. After spending a grueling morning amid the decay and neglect of the inner city, the flat, wide expanse of Indiana farmlands was looking beautiful indeed.

Chapter 7

Which conquistador declared himself the 'Wrath of God', sailed the Amazon to find the legendary El Dorado, crowned himself king of Chile and Peru, and murdered his own daughter when surrounded by Spanish soldiers bent on his destruction because he did not want someone he loved "to be bedded by uncouth people?"

A. Hernán Cortés
B. Hernando de Soto

C. Juan Ponce de León
D. Lope de Aguirre (correct)

Ben had imagined that his return to BTC after his triumph in Arkansas would be something like a homecoming. His biggest concern was how to tell his colleagues *two* stories: how he almost singlehandedly saved BTC from bankruptcy and how he came to resemble a polychromatic victim of a protracted mugging. On the drive to work that Monday he considered contriving a droll narrative which intertwined the two.

A considerably more worrisome predicament presented itself after he reached his desk, which was in an open cube in plain sight to almost everyone in the spacious first floor office. His BTC device wouldn't boot. Irritated, Ben had only five weeks to prepare for his Kansas language arts meeting and was anxious to see the new standards. He had already been forced to tell his stories to a half-a dozen colleagues on the way to his desk. Not wanting to waste any more time, he snuck down the back stairs and took the long way to the IT department in the building's basement.

"Bendo!"

"Ben! Whassup, yo!"

"The hell happened to you? You get that shiner eating your girl's pussy or what?"

Ben liked the IT guys. They were a healthy relief from the distaff-dominated Research and Development department. Their cramped office might as well have been a tool shed with all the reconstructed computer machinery lining its walls and tech minutia scattered everywhere. The guys treated it as if it were a locker room. Ben relished any opportunity to go down there and disappear for a while.

"I'd say it was *your* girl's pussy, but you don't like girls very much, do ya Joe?" Ben snarked. He and Joe clasped hands and pumped chests.

"Learned that from you, baby," Joe said. "What's up?" In his early-thirties and about six-and-a-half feet tall, Joe managed to stay good-looking despite a small mouth, receding chin, and sunken eyes. God had given him a serious face which he used to hide a wicked sense of humor.

"Nuthin'. What's up with your ugly ass?" Ben said.

"It's that time of the month for old Jo-Jo here," Nate said, leaning back in his chair. "I wouldn't want him diddling around my device right about now." Unlike Joe, Nate *was* ugly. He had an asymmetrical face, thinning blonde hair, and rosacea crust corroding his left cheek. Photographs of his pretty wife and three kids all over his cube were not going to change this. His little American flag also made him one of the few conservative holdouts at the company. Ben always enjoyed discussing politics with Nate, especially when they were alone.

Ben fell into an empty chair with his back to the door. "Then maybe you can help, Nate. Device froze up on me. Turned it off and on again three times. It still won't boot."

Nate rolled over to Ben. "First, let me look at that eye," he said in his Piedmont drawl. He was the only transplant Southerner in the office. "Lordy, how'd ya get that?"

"Playing basketball at the bus station."

"Jackson Street?" Nate asked, incredulous. "What were you doing over there?"

Joe whistled. "Got off easy if you ask me."

"Boy, you're lucky you're not dead," Nate said through a grim laugh.

"I know," Ben said, seeing his chance to release some pent-up anger. "It's a different world over there. Like violence is no big deal. In the few hours I was there I saw two fights. One almost turned into a riot. Three dudes were whaling on these two guys. People just rooted them on or they would join in for a kick or two, all screaming like savages."

Ben realized it too late, but Joe and Nate blanched and were trying to tug themselves away from the conversation. They were no longer alone. Ben turned and noticed August Little, the new African American IT specialist standing by the door which Ben had left open. Ben didn't know how much August had heard, but Joe and Nate's timid retreat to their desks wasn't encouraging.

"Hey, Ben," August said. "What are you doing here?"

"Hey, Aug," Ben said, keeping cool. "Device's on the fritz."

He hadn't once mentioned race in his little diatribe. He could have been talking about anyone. He knew the ramifications were dire for white men accused of racism, but he didn't think August had heard enough to go beyond a reasonable doubt.

Ben stood and looked August in the eye. August was about five-nine and solidly built. *Café au lait* skin. He spent a good deal on his wardrobe and today he wore black slacks and a silk, platinum gray shirt. A gold chain glittered around his neck. Ben remembered that August had a pretty stolid personality to begin with. Today he seemed particularly humorless. August stared right back at Ben and held out his hand. "Well, let me take a look," he said.

Ben hesitated. He was expecting Joe or Nate to inspect his device, not August, someone he barely knew and didn't particularly like. He felt uneasy about handing his device over to this person, and not having time to plumb the depths of his apprehension only made it worse. He also knew that he couldn't look back at Joe and Nate because that would indicate a lack of faith in August, which, by extension, could be interpreted as a lack of faith in August *because he was black*. Of course, that would raise suspicions of racism, and Ben had been extensively trained when he started at BTC not to let that happen. He was trapped. He handed over the device.

After hanging out with Joe and Nate a little longer, Ben climbed back up the stairs, trying to think clearly about his situation. He hadn't said anything explicitly racist. If August wanted to make trouble, his claim would be pretty tenuous. Ben had the feeling that Joe and Nate would act on his behalf rather than August's if called upon, given the number of times he had heard them grumble about the man's questionable abilities as an IT specialist. Ben had that going for him at least. That, and his overall chumminess with Nigel. Still, it was close. Disquiet was gnawing at his gut.

A sign that the day was growing even more surreal appeared as Ben was heading for the common-use device. He was almost there when he heard the murmuring.

"...terrorist attack..."

"...foiled..."

"…bomb scare…"

"…Muncie mosque…"

All work had stopped in the office as people were viewing live streaming newscasts. A man who claimed to be one of the imams at the Muncie Islamic Center on McGalliard Street was ranting for the cameras. He had been there early in the morning with his young nephew and happened to discover something strange behind one of the toilets in the Men's bathroom. It was an apocalypto bomb, fully operational and capable of razing a third of the free-standing, 22,000 square foot building. Experts were not sure why the bomb had not detonated but were much more concerned about this being the third attack on an American mosque that year. A brand new one in Akron, Ohio had been blown to bits in January. Another exploded in Tulsa, Oklahoma in April. Both incidents had occurred at night with only two casualties overall. The worldwide Islamic population had been livid all year over these outrages and was now ready to boil over.

The imam was a puffy-faced, middle-aged man with dark armpit stains and a long, black beard. He had no mustache. He also seemed perfectly oblivious to his jiggling man-boobs as he explained to a reporter with ringing righteousness what had occurred. He had a fuzzy recollection of detail, however. One version of his story put him in the bathroom to clean it, but another had him following up on his nephew who had been charged with the task. His voice was deep and hoarse, but his control of English was smooth and complete. He must have been born here despite his fourteenth century haircut, Ben thought.

The imam then took to his bullhorn and segued into a lengthy condemnation of the United States as a terrorist nation which harbors Zionism and Islamophobia. Standing outside his mosque he rallied a sizeable crowd with strident calls for justice. Others were doing the same with bullhorns as well. Things were beginning to get ugly as the crowd churned with hatred and hurled insults and threats at any reporter attempting to interview them. Only a line of police in riot gear protected the news crews and anyone else nearby from the impassioned violence of the mob.

People in the office, especially the women, were verbalizing their shock.

"Is this happening right now?"

"That's only six blocks from here!"

"I pass that mosque on my way to work!"

"Who would do such a thing?"

Someone opened a window, and sure enough, the distorted fury of the bullhorns came through and seemed closer than they really were.

For their parts, the mayor had declared a state of emergency, and the police had sealed off the entire block. The police chief, an older white gentleman with a thick neck and mustache, was assuring reporters that the Muncie Police Department was taking this matter very seriously and that it would do everything in its power to find the terrorists. Already the FBI had been called in. Chopper footage of the mosque dominated the internet even though the bomb had been removed and disabled hours before. Numerous white supremacy organizations were being proposed as possible culprits. Names and locations of likely suspects were splashed on virtually every mainstream internet site.

Ben winced. He had actually *voted* for one of these people six years ago, back when he was still a viable GOP politician. He even had one of his bumper stickers on his car for a brief time.

Congressman William Stark.

Two weeks after Stark had been elected to the U.S. House of Representatives representing California's fifty-second congressional district, a Left-wing watchdog group captured video of Stark speaking at a function held by the editors of Patriot Press. Patriot Press was a white nationalist and race realist publication which was freely branded a white supremacist hate group by its plethora of enemies. Stark was the first elected member of Congress to associate with such a group in over a hundred years. This sparked a worldwide outrage over which the media in every major nation obsessed for weeks. In the face of civil unrest and rioting crowds consisting largely of unemployed blacks, Arabs, and Latinos—egged on from a comfortable distance by an unshakable cadre of Marxist college professors, super-rich media personalities, and overweight third world dictators—the

House Minority Leader had Stark impeached. He was almost unanimously voted out of Congress. Stark went into hiding rather than risk increased danger for himself and his family. He famously took his case to the Supreme Court where he argued that what he had done was protected under the First Amendment, and despite what he had said he had every right to serve his constituents. There were only four whites remaining on the Supreme Court at that time. His case was heard and summarily rejected. Two of the white judges defended him but neither dared even author a dissenting opinion.

After this, he became an attorney dedicated to the civil rights of native-born American whites. These were his only clients. Several lawsuits, an IRS audit, and a brief prison sentence later, he disappeared, much to the consternation of the U.S. government.

William Stark was commonly acknowledged as the guiding light and inspiration behind the burgeoning American White Nationalist Movement, which fifteen years prior had gained traction in many parts of the Midwest and in the former Confederacy. While he was still at large and number one on the FBI's Most Wanted list, the authorities had been unable to track him. They were reduced to collecting conflicting information from his supposed associates and downloading pirated copies of his writings and recordings like everybody else. This was due as much to the White Nationals' innovative use of computer and communication technology as it was to the FBI now being almost seventy-five percent black, Latino, or Muslim. They simply could not recruit enough willing and reliable whites to infiltrate the communities that would harbor Stark and his associates.

Some believed Stark had perished in the recent explosions around Wichita, Kansas. At the time, the government denied responsibility for the attack and decried it as the culmination of an internecine power struggle within what was known as the 'Redneck Mafia.' Five homes in a six-mile radius were blasted clean with Hellfire Junior missiles in the middle of the night. They were launched from what must have been stealth choppers. Twenty-seven people were killed including eight children. The massacre lasted all of two minutes. There were no survivors, no witnesses, and the killers didn't leave any obvious clues. Remains of several cocaine and methamphetamine labs were uncovered in the debris. This had happened two years ago.

The Ear Muffs, as they were called, recruited heavily among the White Nationals, especially when they were in prison or on the lam. Ear Muff kingpins Ralph 'Bonzo' Johnson and Silvio Norton were ultimately convicted and sentenced to life in prison in upstate New York. Within six months, Norton hanged himself. Johnson ultimately converted to Christianity and for a brief time starred in his own internet reality program entitled *The Sinners of Cell Block 10*. After that came his popular *Born-Again Humor Hour* on Prison Web Radio. He never claimed he knew which of those Wichita homes Stark was in at the time, but under oath he claimed that according to the scuttlebutt there was a good chance he was in one of them.

Others believed that Stark had met his self-imposed end *à la* Adolf Hitler in the bunkers of the Wahoo compound three years before Wichita. It was possible. Hundreds of bodies had been charred beyond identification, and not all were women and children. The defeat at Wahoo was widely considered to be the death of the American White Nationalist Movement.

Perhaps the most farfetched theory explaining Stark's whereabouts involved the fledgling African nation calling itself South Zion. One year before the Wahoo disaster and after a few Wahoo-like setbacks for white nationalist organizations in Europe, nearly two hundred white, European millionaires made a move that no one had expected. Led by Noah Herzog Bollinger, a former Swiss rugby star and descendent of the twentieth-century German filmmaker Werner Herzog, they, along with a couple dozen wealthy South African Jews, purchased thousands of acres in the Sofala Province along the coast of Mozambique and bribed members of the corrupt Mozambican government to look the other way as they surreptitiously imported arms, food, and materiel in preparation for a hostile takeover. These millionaires, disgusted with the rise of Islam in their own countries and disheartened by the inevitable Nazi backlash, decided to start over with a homeland for all white Caucasians, Jews included. They founded their nation approximately 3600 miles due south of Jerusalem along the thirty-fifth meridian, placed the Star of David alongside the Christian cross on their flag, and pronounced South Zion the new Great Protector of the so-called Judeo-Christian tradition.

The strategically selected location on Africa's southeastern coast allowed nearly a quarter million disaffected white South Africans, white Zimbabweans, and Afrikaners to flood the country and join Mozambique's legacy Portuguese population and approximately 15,000 expat Europeans for the upcoming war. After declaring themselves an independent state and inviting whites the world over to join them in their righteous struggle, they were invaded by South African and Mozambican forces from the south and Zimbabwean and Zambian forces from the north and northwest. Tanzania seemed content with just absorbing the northern half of Mozambique, which they acquired almost without resistance.

Of course, white Africans who hadn't escaped to South Zion within two days of independence were hunted down and slaughtered. The bloodbath began in Centurion, a subdivision of the South African city Tshwane—formerly known as Pretoria—and quickly metastasized throughout South Africa and Zimbabwe. It resulted in the violent deaths of 1.5 million whites and mulattos and effectively ended the near-600-year presence of white Europeans in the southernmost regions of Africa. The white Africans referred to this catastrophe as the *Uitwissing*, which means 'annihilation' in Afrikaans. The black Africans referred to it as the Week of Atonement.

At first, the South Zionese, with their superior technology and organization, were able to fend off the much more numerous invaders. They converted every privately-owned boat, airplane, and land vehicle at their disposal into implements of war. Nearly five thousand former officers from the great armies of Europe came to lead the fight. Women and children as young as ten fought alongside men. The allure of taking part in a righteous race war was too strong for many whites, even as far away as the United States and Canada, to resist. Thousands flooded the shores of South Zion in those heady early days of independence.

Things soured for the South Zionese however after they took the city of Beira and killed nearly 100,000 of its citizens in reprisals for the Week of Atonement. Included among the dead were over 9,000 Indians and 7,000 Chinese. This ended any hope of support the South Zionese were likely to receive from the international community, including Israel, which distanced itself from its sister nation soon after. The double standard of supporting barbarous African states while opposing a much less barbarous white one did not seem to impact the decision-making of many of the great powers. Within a month, the United Nations pulled its recognition of South Zion and declared it a rogue state. UN forces scuttled its navy and placed strict sanctions on the young nation, essentially laying siege to it along the Mozambique Channel. Currently, its population of 300,000 was being starved into submission by an international alliance which was also covertly supplying its African enemies. South Zion's future was never more in doubt and its people never more desperate.

Could Stark have escaped to South Zion? A plausible theory, Ben thought. Then again, all the theories were plausible.

Ben had once met William Stark and recalled when he last saw him, standing on the stage at that Patriot Press event, beckoning to him across the wreckage to join the cause. Ben had been there. He had witnessed everything, perhaps more than anyone else in attendance. Unwelcome emotions rattled in his head as blood seemed to explode in his face. That night had been the single most consequential night of his life. It had convinced him to flee California and take his chances in faraway Indiana. Years later he was still trying to live it down. Ben forced himself from his bitter reverie. So much had happened since then, he thought. While following the streaming news stories he remembered writing a series of eighth-grade social studies items about the historic changes America had undergone in his lifetime:

In the twenty-first century, the DREAM Acts granted full citizenship to millions of undocumented Americans. How many DREAM Acts have been passed so far in the twenty-first century?

A. 1
B. 2
C. 3
D. 4 (Correct)

How many undocumented Americans were granted full citizenship as a result of the DREAM 4 Act?

A. 5 million
B. 10 million
C. 15 million
D. 25 million (Correct)

What right did DREAM 4 give these Americans that they did not already have in the United States?

A. The right to vote (Correct)
B. The right to health care
C. The right to public education
D. The right to government welfare

What Ben couldn't include in his items was the fact that most of these twenty-five million new Americans were either Hispanic, Muslim, or black. Also prohibited was mentioning that these blacks and Hispanics were converting in increasing numbers to Islam.

Chapter 8

The hairstyle in which a man has a beard hanging below the jawline and no mustache is known as a

A. Van Dyke.
B. toothbrush.
C. muttonchop.
D. chin curtain. (correct)

"Is this what you wanted?" someone shouted. "Hey, Cameron! Is this what you wanted?"

Ben turned and noticed the young man's fat, pimply nose inserting itself into his life. All he knew about this person was that his name was Jamal, he was an Arab, and he worked in the editing department. He also smelled.

"Answer me, redneck. Is this what you wanted?" Jamal taunted, gesturing to the streaming newscasts. His voice was hoarse and loud, his natural way of speaking.

Almost amused that this lanky, twenty-two-year-old cream-puff could fashion himself a bully, Ben crowded Jamal back in his ill-proportioned beak. "No, I am not glad it happened," he said. "I had nothing to do with it. And call me a redneck again. Go ahead! Say it again!" Ben had recently taken hard shots in the face from real men and knew there was nothing Jamal could do to stop him from popping all the pustulous zits on his nose with his fists. Ben figured that sending his resume to ETS in Princeton would be a small price to pay for disabusing this punk of his tough guy pretensions.

Practically everyone in the office was on their feet watching. They were mostly women, so Ben knew they would be of little use in an altercation. Nigel and the other managers were in a meeting with St. Clair, so at that moment there was no leadership. Ben also knew that the two other white men in the office, Tim and Alex, would be too timid to get his back. Thin, flabby, and almost pathologically shy, these two wouldn't be much help regardless. Ben suddenly understood that there were reasons why nerds got bullied on the playground. Meanwhile, Carlos, a short, tubby Mexican with an eyebrow as thick as his mustache, and Osama, a slender, serious item writer from Pakistan, posted themselves nearby. They folded their arms and narrowed their eyes at Ben.

Jamal didn't know this, however, and retreated as Ben stepped forwards. "Well, how do we know you weren't involved?" he shrieked.

Ben took another step, forcing Jamal into a last stand by the supply cabinet. "Who is 'we'?" Ben countered. "And what makes you think you have the right to interrogate me, you racist punk?"

"You're the racist!" Jamal accused, pointing his finger. Ben smacked it aside when it touched him in the chest. Jamal began to sweat and jerked his eyes around the room. "Come on!" he said to the crowd. "You know how the whites get!"

"I'm white too," a woman warned.

"Yeah. Me too," said another.

The two black women in the group cooed in embarrassment and went back to their desks to follow the news reports, muttering sarcastically to each other. Carlos simply left the room, shaking his head. Jamal noticed Osama for the first time, but that didn't seem to bolster his confidence.

"You know, Jamal, we have two choices," Ben said. "We can go outside and handle this one-on-one like men. Or we can stay inside. In which case as soon as management is out of its meeting, I am going to file a formal complaint about you for racial harassment."

Jamal snorted out a laugh that wasn't entirely faked. "You can say what you want. It won't matter," he said, waving his hand.

"Will it matter if I complain too?"

Everyone turned to see Ariya. She wore a gray knee-length skirt and a sleeveless red blouse. Her eyes glistened beneath dark eyebrows. "I gave you seventy-three South Carolina items to edit, Jamal. Have you started them?" she asked.

Jamal turned from Ariya to the dwindling crowd and back again. "Uh, no...I..."

"It's after ten, Jamal! How could you not start? I have a plane to South Carolina in one week! And many more items to come!"

Jamal gestured to one of the newscasts. "There was an attack on—"

Ariya walked up to him and faced him brazenly. "I see. You'd rather talk about an attack that didn't happen and accuse innocent people than do your job. I have more to complain about now!"

Red-faced and speechless, Jamal tried to disguise his shock with anger. But his flushed cheeks and dangling lips only made him seem like an insolent child being scolded by his mother.

"This is an office, Jamal!" Ariya went on. "Go back to your desk and edit for me. Or I will complain. And not for first time!"

Jamal must have finally realized that standing there slack-

jawed made him look idiotic. He stormed out of the room, presumably to the building's exit, rather than to his desk. One cool
look to Osama from Ben made him disappear as well.

Alone at last, Ben and Ariya shared a smile. "It's good to see
you, Ariya," he said.

"What happened to your face?" she asked.

Ben smiled and touched her shoulder. "Nothing. It was basketball. Hey, I'm really sorry about what happened at the
mosque."

"Yes. Me too. Come to my desk. Come!" Ariya ordered, tug-
ging on his arm.

Ben turned towards his desk just as Ariya was pulling him
away. "But I haven't even started my —"

"Shush! Come!"

Ariya's cube was a cramped space backed up to a window. It
resembled a right triangle with an inward arc for a hypotenuse.
Aside from e-documents and textbooks everywhere, only a calendar of Monet nudes, a library eBook bodice-ripper, and a
pendant hanging from a chain personalized her space. Ben
looked carefully at the pendant. It was circular, with an upside-
down triangle inside. The triangle contained a thin, red oval
which opened just so at the bottom point.

Ariya sat in her chair and spun around to face him. "You
know, I know him," she said. "That man making all that noise
this morning."

"You mean the one with the bullhorn?"

"Yes." Ariya turned to her personal device and started
streaming the newscast of the botched bombing. Since nothing
much was going on in Muncie anymore, the newscasts either
consisted of chopper footage of the dwindling protest or of pun-
dits discussing the event. Ariya replayed the segment in which
the bearded imam with the puffy face and no mustache was de-
nouncing the United States as a terrorist entity.

She bit her lip and shook her head. "Ben, how many people
were killed in the mosque bombings in Ohio and Oklahoma?"

Ben held up two fingers. "And the revenge attacks on
churches were ten times as deadly," he said. "It's been happening so often they almost don't even report it anymore. Not in the

mainstream media at least."

"And how many were killed in Nebraska?"

"You mean the Wahoo, Nebraska compound?" Ben clarified. "Ehh, that's not quite the same. That was an organized secessionist movement. Technically, what was going on there was war."

"Against women and children? Against the elderly?" Ariya challenged. "You write social studies items, Ben. Did the United States not sign the Geneva Convention?"

Ben rubbed his forehead and nodded reluctantly. "About 700 people were killed. Not including thirty-four federal agents."

"Yet this man gets angry over a bomb that does not explode. So stupid."

Ben peeked around the corner of Ariya's cube to make sure they were alone. "You know, Ariya," he said, leaning closer to her. "I agree with you. But I wouldn't expect you to say these things. It's almost as if you have no sympathy for him."

Given the chance to deny it, Ariya glumly watched the news report and said nothing.

A smile crept along Ben's face. "But I think your imam does have one legitimate reason to be mad."

"He does not."

"I think he does."

She turned to face him. "What is it?"

"He can't find his mustache," Ben said, running his finger under his nose. "I'd be pretty broken up too if someone stole my mustache." He then puffed up his cheeks and began imitating the imam, gesture for gesture, issuing a fatwa against whomever absconded with his facial hair.

Ariya laughed, and its joyful, ringing sound caused Ben's heart to surge. She tugged his wrist as if that would help her regain her composure. When she realized what she had done, she pulled her hand back, gradually. It was almost a caress. Ben took a deep breath, checking his desire. They looked at each other until they became aware of their own smells, their own oppressive carnal attraction. Despite his excitement, Ben was relieved when Ariya broke away and looked back at the streaming footage. The imam was still with the bullhorn, agitating the world.

"You said you know him?" he asked.

Ariya nodded ponderously.

"How?"

"I know him."

Ben's mouth fell open as he wondered what she meant by that. His personal device vibrated before he could find out. "It's Nigel," he said. "He wants to see me in his office."

She patted his knee. "Go to him. This is when you get your promotion. You deserve it."

Ben stood. "Thanks. We'll talk more about this later. Okay?"

Ariya flashed him a proud, vulnerable smile. "Yes," she said.

Chapter 9

Witch: "All hail, Macbeth, that shalt be King hereafter!"
—Macbeth, Act 1, Scene iii

The above quote is an example of

A. satire.
B. metaphor.
C. hyperbole.
D. irony. (correct)

A few strands of hair fell into Nigel's face as he watched Ben enter his office. Behind him, postcards from Europe and photos of Westminster Abby decorated the wall along with a framed snapshot of Nigel vacationing with his boyfriend, a short, muscular redhead. A single piece of paper lay face down on his desk between a pen and a teddy bear waving a mini flag of England. Nigel brushed the hair from his face and stood. "Have a seat, Ben," he said, all humor drained from his face. "And close the door."

Ben had a feeling that his promotion was going to have to wait. Did Nigel somehow *hear* his confrontation with Jamal? Could Jamal have contacted Nigel? Ben tried to remember if he had said anything offensive while Jamal was accusing him of being a terrorist. His mind flushed with dreadful possibilities as he took his seat. "Nigel, you know what happened, don't you?"

he said.

Nigel said nothing and didn't take his eyes off Ben.

"A bomb was found at the Muncie Islamic Center."

"I know about that, yes."

Ben shrugged defensively and held out his hands as if holding a melon. "Well, what was I gonna do? We were in front of everyone!"

"What are you talking about?"

"Jamal."

"What about Jamal?" Nigel asked the question but didn't seem too interested in the answer.

"What abou—" Ben froze and carefully regarded his boss. This had nothing to do with Jamal, he realized.

Nigel folded his arms. "Ben, there are some things I must tell you."

The idea flashed across Ben's mind that this was all a joke. Nigel often wore gravitas like clown makeup—although in this circumstance it would have been in extremely poor taste. Nigel was also no stranger to poor taste, so Ben couldn't be sure. "This wouldn't have anything to do with my promotion, would it?" Ben asked through a delicate grin.

Nigel's slow blink indicated that it did not. He groped his way through a few introductory sentences and then dropped his hand on his desk as if to interrupt himself. "What websites did you visit on your work device Friday night?" he asked.

"Friday?"

"Yes. In the evening."

Ben took a moment to remember. "None. I got home from the airport, checked my mail, and went to bed."

"Well, you gave your device to August Little this morning, yes? According to him the reason it wouldn't boot was because whoever used it on Friday visited a brood site which deposited a cookie onto it. A couple months ago all BTC devices had been programmed not to boot if they find cookies like this."

Remembering his brother's visit, Ben looked relieved. "Yeah. I can explain everything. On Friday night, I ran into my—"

"Ben, you don't understand," Nigel interrupted. "This was a *brood* site."

Ben shook his head. "I give up. What's a brood site?"

"We sent a memo about it last month," Nigel said. "I didn't remember either until August reminded me. Basically, it's stolen space on a sap-serv. A hacker will release some kind of..." Nigel waved his hand. "...bot, worm, scorpion, some autonomous program onto a server. It replaces content with its own instructions and creates a brood site."

"I've heard about those. And when the webmaster finds them, they take them down."

"Yes, but depending on the skill of the hacker, it could be days before the webmaster even knows they're there. If the hacker has the webmaster's IP addresses, he or she could even publish the correct version of the website to the webmaster and the hacked version to everyone else."

Ben began to relax as the two fell back into their usual chummy rhythm. "I saw a piece about that once," he said. "You can select, like, the first five characters of the URL. And if they're blinking real fast that means the site is constantly refreshing itself to maintain the illusion. That's when you know you're looking at false material."

"Yes. It's basically a temporary website set up by people who don't have access to a sap-serv."

"Nigel, I'm sorry this happened. I hope no damage was done to the device."

Nigel blinked again, more reluctantly this time. "This is much more serious than that, Ben. Whilst it is not illegal to view a brood site, it is illegal to make one."

"I know."

"Do you know *why* it's illegal?"

"Yeah. It's cybersitism. Stealing sap-serv space that other people are paying for."

Nigel shook his head. "No. Well, yes. That's technically true. But that's not the real reason. Do you know what the *real* reason is?"

Ben gestured in exasperation. "Nigel, why are you playing games? Just tell me!"

"Because I am giving you every opportunity to get yourself off the hook, Ben!" Nigel said through his teeth.

"What hook?"

Nigel squinted at Ben. "You really don't know, do you?"

"Don't know what?"

"That according to the FBI, brood sites are the primary source of communication for underground white supremacist groups."

"What?"

"I said that according to the FBI—"

"I heard you. I just can't believe what you're accusing me of."

"Why's that?"

"You're saying I used my device to view white supremacist brood sites!"

"No."

"Then what are we talking about?"

"The fact that the FBI reports that over ninety percent of the brood sites out there are run by white supremacists."

Ben shook his head. "I am not a white supremacist nor have I ever viewed white supremacist brood sites on any device, let alone BTC's."

Nigel leaned back and thought for a moment. "You also visited a site called Jihad-Jihad, which the FBI calls an anti-Muslim hate site."

"Waitaminute," Ben said. "So what?"

"You're serious? You're asking me so what? Seriously?"

"Yes. Jihad-Jihad is a valid site. Nothing wrong with it. Is it against the law now to go on Jihad-Jihad?"

"Of course not."

"You know, as a gay man, you should check it out too. Just last week, four Saudi men were accused of sodomy and were stoned—"

"Ben! That doesn't matter! At the end of the day, *you* used a company device to visit a brood site and a hate site. That twice violates standard operating procedure 112!"

"I see people in the office all the time viewing sites that bash white people," Ben reasoned in a wave of spite, "and Christians."

Nigel sighed through his nose. "Come on. You know that's not the same thing."

"It is."

"It isn't."

"Why not?" Ben inadvertently smacked his hand against Nigel's desk.

"Because given the events of the past few years," Nigel explained, "especially in Ohio and Oklahoma, and what happened this morning, we, that is, all of us, must be, by law, sensitive to these kinds of things. White supremacists, by definition, are not sensitive."

"But I don't support white supremacy."

"I know, but the fact that you had one of those cookies on your device, and the fact that you visited an FBI hate site, and the fact that you're a Right-winger does not look good!"

Ben felt blood erupt in his face as he finally grasped where this was heading. Nigel had been mentioning the FBI a lot, which made Ben think that if he gave up his brother's name to save his job, Nigel would be obligated to report Isaac to his favorite law enforcement agency. It was an open question whether he would do the same to Ben. "But Jihad-Jihad is not a hate site!" Ben argued, suddenly wanting to throttle Isaac. "A lot of former Muslims write for it. As for the cookies, anyone can put up a brood site, not just white supremacists. And as I told you before, I'm not a goddamned Right-winger. I'm a libertarian!"

Nigel put his hand on the piece of paper on his desk and slid it towards him. "I don't want to argue about this anymore," he said.

"The hell is this?"

"We want you to succeed, Ben. You are our best content specialist. The last thing we want to do is fire you."

Ben's breathing cut short as he looked from Nigel to the paper. He turned it over. It was a long, groveling letter of apology with his name at the bottom and a place for him to sign. Ben was too sickened to read beyond three sentences.

"So," Nigel went on, "we can say that during our heartfelt discussion, you admitted that you inadvertently violated SOP 112 by visiting a hate site on a company device. That you were only doing what's known as opposition research for your own personal edification and that you staunchly oppose the positions held on that site. You also confirmed that you're not a white supremacist, nor do you support their activity. As such, you don't know how that cookie appeared on your device, but you are deeply sorry for any offense you've caused. And finally, you've consented to undergo and pay for an extensive two-week-long racial and religious sensitivity training program both with BTC and the city of Muncie to ensure this never happens again."

Ben didn't move or change his expression except to slit his one good eye at his boss. "It's all in the letter, Ben," Nigel went on, handing him the pen. "You should sign."

Staring at the cheap utensil his boss was handing him, everything seemed to crystallize for Ben. He had never seen so clearly the contempt others had for him. They *all* mistrusted him, not just malformed children like Jamal. They saw in him something that needed to be brought down and dragged under. They viewed Ben as an artifact of centuries past when men like him were establishing overseas trade routes and authoring treatises on physics and assigning scientific names to microorganisms and fine-tuning their ancestors' machines and rocketing themselves to the Moon when most everyone else in the world considered themselves lucky to have the proverbial pot to piss in. And this difference, this crushing expanse, persisted, or, if anything, grew larger the closer these people got to Ben. And being able to write test items better and faster than they could with nothing more than a high school diploma made his presence even more galling. Of course, this would have been forgivable when people like Ben made up the majority of the political class and wielded most of the power. By the mid-twenty-first century however this was decidedly no longer the case.

Ben saw this now. He saw all of it. He had absolutely no intention of signing that offensive, humiliating document. Instead, he wanted to complain about the preferential treatment non-whites received at BTC. He wanted to complain about the racial harassment he endured that very morning and demand that Jamal be dragged into his manager's office to sign such a ridiculous confession. But he knew that would never happen.

Nigel pushed the paper closer. "August is a recent convert to Islam. Were you aware of that? He's quite upset."

Ben gave him no answer.

Nigel put down the pen. "Ben, try to understand," he pleaded. "We are a *testing company*. Any taint of racism and our business is ruined. We will be audited. We will be boycotted by every state board in the country as well as face lawsuits from the government and from the NAACP, CAIR, and other civil rights organizations. It will be the end for all of us."

Ben slid the paper back to Nigel and stood. With his sympathy for Benchmark Testing evaporating, he wasn't even looking at Nigel anymore. The disgust writhing in his belly wouldn't let him. He figured if BTC wanted to fire him and retain clueless fools like Son Mensah and Jamal, then they deserve what they get.

As Ben turned to leave, Nigel acted as if he were still seated before him. "August said he overheard you saying racist things about African Americans this morning. Is that true?"

Ben stopped and said the last thing he ever intended to say to Nigel Polite. "Yes."

Ben heard Nigel get up and follow him to the door. "I was hoping it wouldn't come to this," Nigel said, putting his hand on the door as Ben opened it. "Because of your violation of SOP 112 and your refusal to cooperate with sensitivity training, we are forced to terminate your employment, effective immediately," he whispered through his teeth.

Ben forced a chuckle and then stepped into the hall where Antonio Jones, BTC's assistant facilities manager, had been leaning against a cubicle wall. Pens, paperclips, and other items rattled as he pushed his linebacker frame off of it. His mouth twitched as he came forward, gingerly favoring his left side. A hip injury which ended his college football career years ago had recently been operated on. Antonio was clearly still recovering.

Ben caught the secret nod from Nigel and understood that whatever Antonio's normal responsibilities were at BTC, he was now their ad hoc security guard and, if necessary, bouncer. Nigel obviously had this all planned. If Ben signed, all was well, and Antonio could go back to surfing the net and eating candy bars or whatever it was he did all day. But if Ben didn't sign, then guess who would be escorting him out the back door.

"I'm going to have to disable your clearance, Ben," Nigel

said, hair falling back down past his eyebrows. He was not bothering to brush it back in place anymore. Ben held his personal device below Nigel's BTC device and waited for them to finish transacting.

"Thank you," Nigel said. "You are to leave the premises immediately. We will box up your belongings and ship them to you today."

"This way, sir," Antonio said with neither regret nor enthusiasm. Antonio was nice and well-liked in the office for his easy humor and respectable knowledge of Indiana sports teams. Ben always got along with him fine. But when Antonio put his hand on his back like a police officer guiding a convict, Ben recoiled. Arching away from Antonio, he spun around and glared into the man's Paleolithic African features. There was much that was stereotypical about Antonio. He was big and athletic, not too bright, and not too industrious. He went to church on Sundays, loved R&B and hip hop, and always talked sweet to white women. Probably ate fried chicken and watermelon every Saturday at the barbecue, Ben thought. None of this he ever held against him. Now, however, it was different.

"You don't have the right to touch me!" Ben barked. "You can lead me out of here, but you don't have the right to touch me!"

"This way, sir," Antonio said, stupidly nonplussed.

Ben turned and started walking but as soon as he felt Antonio's hand again, he whirled back at him, full of venom. "I said don't touch me!"

Antonio was about to shove Ben into the wall when Nigel intervened. "It's okay, Antonio," he said, trying to smile reassuringly. "Just let him go."

Ben led the sullen march to the back door along the uncarpeted hallway and away from the cluster of offices in the center of the building. They had to descend the same flight of stairs he had taken that morning to visit Joe and Nate. Several yards before reaching it, however, Ben fixed upon the idea of going up instead of down. There was something he wanted to do. As if reading his mind, Antonio sped up in order head him off, but Ben bolted before he could. He slipped through the door and bounded up the stairs three steps at a time.

Antonio and Nigel followed him amid a welter of alarm and profanity. On the second floor, which BTC shared with a local real estate company, Ben could only turn right since he was at the edge of the building. He knew that if he tore down the hall the two of them would have a hard time keeping up, with Antonio not being able to run well and Nigel being blocked by an aging bruiser with a thirty-nine-inch waist and a bad hip.

The BTC offices were in a T-shaped three-story building, and Ben had dashed almost to its center by the time the door opened behind him. Antonio and Nigel burst into the hall, still shouting. As he overtook Antonio in a lumbering sprint, Nigel looked almost comical as his chin bounced upon his neck like a jiggling poached egg. He was pleading with Ben to let himself be escorted from the building. Ben passed the elevators and darted into the building's central stairwell. Clutching the banister and taking five steps down at a time, he knew he'd reach the first floor before either of his pursuers could get to the door above him. But as he jumped onto the landing, his right heel caught the edge of the bottom step, and his ankle turned hard. Upon hearing a distinct 'click', Ben knew he had sprained it. His shoulder slammed into the wall as he fell. He righted himself and exited the stairwell the moment Antonio and Nigel entered from above. A split second later, and they wouldn't have known which way he had gone. This would have given Ben perhaps a minute or two to do what he needed to do. Now he had seconds.

The hall was empty, to Ben's relief. He darted to his right, ignoring the shards of pain in his ankle and then slipped into the first doorway on his left. He was back in the R&D department. The office contained about forty people with room to spare thanks to impromptu window cubes like Ariya's. His plan had been to creep along these cubes out of plain sight. But his sprained ankle squashed that idea. Instead, he loped painfully down the center aisle.

Ariya was editing an item while listening to her romance novel when he snuck up behind her. He fell to one knee and tapped her on the shoulder. Startled, she gasped and then smiled. "You're back!" she said.

"Ariya, I forgot to ask you something," he said, red-faced and huffing. "Your items on Friday. How did they do?"

"What?"

"I know you put your own project in jeopardy to help mine. Did you get all your items through committee?"

Ariya smiled. "We barely made it. Five items to spare!"

"I'm glad," Ben said. From the sound of it, Nigel and Antonio had just entered the room along with a few others, all looking for Ben. There was a commotion. Ariya tried to stand to look, but Ben guided her gently back to her seat.

"Is something wrong?" she asked.

"Yeah," he said, wishing he had more time to admire her hieroglyph eyes. In the five seconds they shared before the sky fell and changed Ben Cameron's life forever, he leaned forward and gave her a shameless, sensual kiss on the mouth. Eyes wide in shock, Ariya lifted her hands to stop him but then rested them on either side of his face. She held him gently as if he were a delicate thing.

Ben pulled away as soon as she closed her eyes. The moment she opened them, three men set upon him in blurring action. His head, neck and arms became engulfed in the violent, churning pile. Ariya screamed as they dragged him away.

***

The perfect end to the perfect day. Bruised, battered, and disheveled, Ben was sweating a riot through his cotton clothes as he limped across BTC's parking lot. He stopped when he noticed the sunken frame of his silver Honda. All four tires had been slashed. Jamal, that little prick, he thought. That's why he disappeared and never came back. Ben imagined Jamal explaining to the police that anguish over today's non-attacks had caused him to commit such a crime, and therefore he should be let go. Ben forced a chuckle realizing that such a tack would probably succeed.

Anger, disgust, and frustration flashed across Ben's mind like razors. He couldn't even kick his car like he wanted to. Eventually, he leaned against the driver side door and laughed at himself as if he were some comic book villain getting his much-deserved comeuppance. It was the only way not to be consumed by hatred. And he guessed such a turn of events would be funny if you shared cultural sympathies with someone like Nigel Polite. He tried to imagine what that would be like.

"Ben!" someone called. "Good morning!" Ben looked up and saw Son ambling towards him. He was in sandals, brown slacks, and some ivory-colored, muumuu-like garment which swayed in the breeze. He was late, even by his standards. It was going on eleven.

"Hi, Son," Ben said, now looking at the root of all his troubles in his bald, brown, bespectacled face. If Son Mensah had possessed even a shred of competence, Ben could have flown out of Arkansas on Thursday like he had originally planned. He would have met up with his friends in San Diego, dodged that knucklehead Isaac, and gotten his hero's welcome as soon as he set foot in the office.

But it was not meant to be.

Son did not seem to notice the state of Ben's tires, nor did he wonder why Ben was loitering in the parking lot in the middle of the day. He also failed to notice Ben's disheveled state, his pained expression, his squashed nose, and that prune of a shiner below his right eye. Instead, he walked right up to him and shook his hand.

"I want to thank you for saving my project last week," he said. "It was quite an accomplishment, and you should be proud of yourself."

Ben smothered a sarcastic laugh in its birth throes and said nothing.

"And perhaps I was not fair," Son went on. "I underestimated you. I did not think you could do it, but you did. And that is something that deserves respect."

It took Ben a moment to realize that Son was actually being nice to him. Ben was too surprised and too touched to respond coherently. He couldn't even manage a smile. Son put his hand on his shoulder and stopped him from trying. "And I want to tell you that in all my experience I have never seen anyone do what you did so quickly and so well," he proclaimed. "You, my friend, have a bright future in the field of educational testing!"

Chapter 10

In 1969, psychologist Arthur Jensen proposed that genetic factors play a major role in IQ differences across races. As a result, Jensen was

A. largely ignored.
B. awarded the Nobel prize in psychology.
C. paid in secret for his propaganda services by the John
   Birch Society.
D. roundly denounced and excoriated by his colleagues,
   picketed and harassed by his students, given death
   threats against himself and his family, assigned bodyguards by police, and labeled 'The world's most
   loathsome scientist' by a famous newspaper. (correct)

Ben finished his Thermopylae novel feeling like a complete
wimp. While his foot was iced and elevated on the armrest of his
couch, the heroic Spartan warriors were holding back the Persian hordes to the last man. Sprained ankles hurt, and, being his
first on that ankle, his had swollen to the size of a grapefruit. Ben
was no Spartan, but he had a feeling he would have to be one for
a while if he wanted to survive.

It dawned on him after several weeks of unemployment that
Nigel's threat, although made in jest, had been genuine. Nigel
did have the power to ban him from the industry. This realization came to Ben while he was re-watching footage of two dozen
young Muslims swinging sledgehammers into the St. Mary of
the Angels bell tower in Chicago as a reprisal for the Muncie
non-bomb. He had sent out résumés to every single educational
testing company in North America and had been invited to six
interviews from California to Massachusetts to Florida. He had
hoped that Nigel's reach wasn't as long as he had vaunted it to
be. He had also hoped that his experience and outstanding accomplishments would overcome his lack of a college degree. He
had been so comfortable for so long under the peaceful aegis of
BTC that he was now regretting never preparing for war when
he should have. Of the six interviews, he felt that five went exceedingly well and the other only tolerably well. Still, no job of-

fer materialized. Over half of the people he met with were Hispanic, Muslim, or black.

He didn't want to say it, not even to himself, but he pretty much knew after a month. He gave it another couple weeks to be sure. He was being blackballed. A self-serving conclusion, but accurate, given that he couldn't even scare up *contract* work with some of these companies. He knew eight science content specialists across the country and nearly a dozen in language arts and social studies. Only two responded to his inquiries and both claimed they didn't have any work for him. They were always pretty anxious to get off the phone whenever he called.

Ben surmised that on the day he left BTC, Nigel contacted every testing company in the country and ruined his reputation, likely broadcasting that he was a racist and a troublemaker. But why? These companies were BTC's competitors. Wouldn't it be *good* for BTC if one of its competitors got embroiled in an ugly racial scandal? Wouldn't that offer BTC a greater portion of the testing market? Being fired from BTC he could understand, but being banished outright from the testing industry he could not, especially not by Nigel, someone with whom he had always gotten along so well.

Loneliness is difficult to contemplate when one is not truly alone. But with his career now swept out from under him, Ben began to fathom how much he had been his work and how empty his life was without it. In the many blank afternoons he spent in his townhome, trying to read, trying to work, trying to do something, he consumed hours considering what his life was like before he came to BTC.

Back in San Diego, after he quit college, what did he do? He surfed. He smoked pot. He played bass in a few forgettable beach bands. He worked on his tan and got laid whenever he could, which was often. A friend introduced him to a small testing company looking for part-time question editors. Bell Ridge Measurement. Standardized testing had recently been brought back on the federal level after a ten-year hiatus due to the reduced standing of American universities on the international stage. As such, there was a sudden demand for workers, and qualifications ran second to availability in many cases. Ben needed the scratch, so why not? It wasn't long before Bell Ridge saw his potential and recruited him to write items. Soon he was printing his own money.

It was as if a powerful light had switched on in his head. Within a month, he knew, he just *knew* that he was the most capable item writer in the company. Didn't matter the subject matter. Didn't matter if you had advanced degrees in psychometrics or education. It didn't matter if you had taught for decades. If the tall, skinny hippie kid in the cutoff shorts and flip flops said it was a bad item, then it was a bad item. And if this selfsame kid vouched for an item, there was a 92.4% chance that it would pass through a committee. Preston Brooks Smith, the president of Bell Ridge, had done the math. He had also taken a liking to Ben and started grooming him for greatness. He coached him on statistics and other scholarly fine points. He shared with him all the literature available on educational testing. He brought him to clothing stores, insisted he take night classes, and even took him under his wing socially. Most importantly, he introduced him to classic texts of economics by writers such as Adam Smith and Friedrich Hayek.

The man, known as PBS by friends and enemies alike, hailed from South Carolina, and brandished his out-of-fashion Southern accent like an officer's shiny blade. His features were straight and handsome, but deeply lined. He was almost completely bald except for a stubborn tuft of gray in the center of his forehead. He was old, already established in testing prior to the great boom around the turn of the century when the No Child Left Behind Act funneled billions into the industry. He was old enough to remember the 1980 presidential election and in his office prominently displayed a photograph of him as a young boy with dark, tousled hair brandishing a campaign button which read, 'Let's make America great again.'

Ben remembered the books that PBS kept in his office, books written by psychometricians, philosophers, and eugenicists. Some were close to 150 years old. None were newer than fifty. These were infamous books by infamous writers: Charles Spearman, Arthur Jensen, Charles Murray, and many others. The field of educational measurement was once a field exclusive to white men, the very class of people who first devised ways to measure and codify racial differences. Now the field was over-run with people who weren't white and who weren't men who were trying to eradicate these differences, to pretend they never existed. They were also demonizing their white male predecessors. To them the past was evil. Something to be 'progressed' away from. But PBS was the past. He embodied it. He'd look you straight in the face and tell you so.

Ben flourished under PBS, but left the company in little over a year and a half. To hear him describe it, he was an arrogant youth who looked past what in hindsight was the best thing that had ever happened to him. He was a rising star who started distributing résumés because he presumed he was worth significantly more than what Bell Ridge could pay him. It wasn't the truth, but at the time Ben didn't care. Upon hearing from BTC, he put in his two weeks and loaded up his car for Indiana.

Ben worked hard at BTC and would frequently put in the twelve-hour days and weekends to be the only content specialist in the country not bolstered by a cadre of item writers. His life became his work, and with greater dedication came greater re-sponsibility, and more work. He socialized from time to time with colleagues. He dated four girls during his five years at BTC, two from the office and two from nearby Ball State. Nothing that would threaten his freedom or his career, of course. Perhaps if St. Clair ever dubbed him vice president in charge of Research and Development he'd consider getting married. Maybe when he was in his mid-thirties. He dreamt about it, but wondered if it would ever happen. Not one single relationship he had ever had even threatened to last. He wasn't sure why, but in his moments of self-pity would ask himself that very question and others like it, and then enter the dark, fearful corners of his mind seeking an answer. He could always rely upon a deadline at BTC to pull him out empty-handed.

About a year after Ben moved to Muncie, Preston Brooks Smith collapsed in his kitchen from a massive stroke. He was paralyzed and bedridden in a San Diego hospital for two months before another stroke did him in. Ben was saddened to hear of this but was too busy leading four projects and going on

consecutive week-long trips across the country to attend the funeral. Ben learned of his old boss' death while watching a baseball game in his hotel room in Florida. He turned off the game,
closed his eyes, and remembered how hard these things are to
take. It's like a cruel pressure on your mind that you just can't
wriggle out from under. It forces you to either get stronger or
give in. Ben *liked* the old man and would have loved him like a
father had he only stayed in San Diego.

Sitting on his back porch in Muncie, nursing a beer and trying
not to feel sorry for himself, Ben remembered the last time he
saw him. The old man had walked him to the front door and
waved goodbye with his cane as Ben drove out of the Bell Ridge
parking lot. Ben waved back. A line of palm trees along the
boulevard cut him out of Ben's life forever.

For the past weeks, Ben had been building a pyramid of empty beer cans on the uneven patio table in his back porch, manag-
ing at least two cans each night. He had gotten it as tall as three
feet when he inadvertently toppled some of the less soundly
placed cans on one side. The back of his hand brought the remainder of the structure down with a crash. Ben stared for a
long time at the mess.

Would Preston Smith have fired him? If he had been in Nigel's shoes that morning, would he have fired him? PBS hated
the expansion of government and the excessive borrowing and
the constant spending and the punitive taxation. He hated how
government insisted upon regulating the affairs of private industry. On the other hand, he never had to withstand a diversity
audit or a civil rights lawsuit. Ben thought that if he had he
probably would have fought it in court on constitutional
grounds. The man came from an old and extremely wealthy
South Carolina family, so he would have had the resources to
make a go of it. He died shortly before the last two DREAM Acts
and never lived to see the aftermath of Ohio and Oklahoma.
Would he have been like Nigel Polite, dangling like a puppet in
the hurricane winds of the modern age? Or would he have stood
firm and suffered a fatal fracture in the gale?

Or would he have been like Representative William Stark?

Preston had introduced Ben to Stark at a party he hosted in

Stark's honor one evening. Stark had just been elected representative of California's 52nd Congressional district, and Preston was one of his biggest boosters. Actually, it was Preston's slim and stylish Viennese wife Lena who first introduced them when she and Ben were both waiting for the bathroom. Stark had just stepped out. Firmest handshake Ben could remember and still somewhat wet from the sink. Stark barely looked at Ben as he walked past, saying hello to Lena. Ben watched his round jaw and longish gray-black hair as he stepped back out to the veranda where most of the party was. He smelled thickly of scotch.

Later that evening Ben received a formal introduction. After a flash rainfall had ushered the partygoers into the Smith's sepia-themed Victorian living room, Ben was still shaking water out of his hair when his boss approached with the new congressman from California. After a few crude witticisms regarding their first encounter, Stark began grilling Ben about his career prior to Bell Ridge. His attention dulled when he discovered that Ben hadn't had one and had dropped out of college after three years. He showed no reaction whatsoever to Ben's listless history of beaches, babes, and bands. Stark was at least four inches taller than Ben. His face was unremarkable except for a cleft chin and a deep dimple on his left cheek. The dimple darkened as he apologized to Ben for interrupting him and announced that he needed to discuss something urgent with a colleague who was preparing to leave. They parted with another firm handshake, dry this time, and that was the last time Ben had ever spoken with William Stark.

Ben had a nice time socializing that evening, but the fifteen-to-forty-year age difference between him and the majority of the crowd made the tedium difficult to stave off. The only other people under thirty were the bored and somewhat cliquish relatives of Preston and Lena. As he pretended to listen to political gossip, Ben counted minutes in his head as he waited for his beer buzz to wear off. He made sure to give Preston a warm goodbye before he left.

As he was about to close the front door behind him, Lena approached and discretely slipped an envelope in his jacket pocket. "Preston hopes you will be able to attend, dear," she said as she kissed him by the ear. The perfume the woman had on earlier had given way to the smell of clean but heavy perspiration. Mrs. Preston Brooks Smith had a flat, pleasant face with dyed blonde hair and a proud Roman nose. Slim from the gym, she handled herself with confidence and grace. From a distance, she seemed forty, but Ben discovered beneath her porch light that she was much older than that.

"Attend what?" he asked.

"It's best we not talk about it," she said, her Austrian accent appearing for the first time that evening, transposing the 'w' in 'we' with a 'v'. The woman seemed looking forward to falling asleep after the party. "But Preston wants you to know he is keenly interested in your development. He has high hopes for you."

Ben smiled. "Thank you. He says I need more experience before he can promote me to lead content specialist at Bell Ridge."

Lena held him by the shoulders and said nothing. For a moment Ben noticed a deep, almost clinical, scrutiny in her eyes. It evaporated so quickly that he couldn't be sure it had even been there.

"You will always be welcome in our home, Ben, if you ever need us," she said. "Drive home safely, dear."

Ben waved goodbye to his host, wondering what she could have possibly meant by that. Why would he ever need Preston Smith other than for a job? The man's professional guidance and tutelage was welcome, of course. But Ben knew that theirs was essentially a business relationship, not something he wanted to threaten with too much personal contact.

Ben couldn't wait and opened the envelope as soon as he entered his car. Unfolding the document, he saw it was an invitation to the nineteenth Patriot Press Conference to be held in two weeks at the Poway High School gymnasium, thirty-five miles north of San Diego. Poway was Ben's old high school, and that gymnasium was where he had played basketball for the Titans.

'This is a private and secret event,' the invitation read. 'For safety purposes, discretion is required.' The topic was the crisis of white nationalism and the 'browning' of America. Bios of a dozen speakers cluttered the page. At bottom, beneath a description of a talk entitled 'Colonialism: It's a White Thing' it read, 'Speaker to be revealed at event.'

Ben hollered in alarm and cracked the steering wheel with his knee as the paper disintegrated in his hands. Combustible spy paper. Only the FBI and CIA have this stuff, he thought. How did PBS get his hands on combustible spy paper? Ben had to open the door to release a cloud of thick, gray ash which made him gag as if inhaling sawdust. He practically fell out of the car. It was another ten minutes before the air inside was breathable again. Finally driving off for home, he thought he'd never get the stench out of his car.

Chapter 11

'Property is theft' and 'Propaganda through deeds' were slogans of an internationalist movement which committed acts of terror against world leaders. These include the assassinations of French president Sadi Carnot in 1894 and U.S. president McKinley in 1901. What best describes this movement?

A. Nazism
B. Fascism
C. Communism
D. Anarchism (correct)

The two guards gave the inside of Ben's car a cursory look and then let their scanning devices do the rest. The Sun hadn't yet sunk below the trees and the air was imbued with the orange hue of dusk. It was still light enough to see, and the guards quickly dismissed any suspicion that Ben was a security threat. After frisking and scanning him, they let him go. Wearing his black windbreaker, navy blue Polo shirt, jeans and hiking boots, Ben stepped into his high school gymnasium for the first time in six years.

The gym was decked in green and white as he remembered it but now boasted a few more championship banners. As visitors entered, they were confronted with the image of the pugnacious Poway Titan himself, Ol' Greenskirts, as he was known, painted on the wall. He assumed a nineteenth-century boxing stance and wore the helmet of a Teutonic knight, the kilt of a Scotsman, and an Irishman's green jacket. Ben let go an edgy snicker. Patriot Press could not have selected a more perfect mascot for their clandestine rendezvous.

Around 700 folding chairs were neatly arranged on the court before a portable stage which didn't elevate more than six inches. On the stage were twenty more folding chairs, a podium with microphone, and three folding tables dressed in a black pleated table skirt. Ben estimated that nearly 300 people were already seated and another hundred or so were still milling about. The ratio was five-to-one in favor of men.

Why they didn't make use of the bleachers on either side of the gym, he couldn't fully understand. When in use, they could seat two thousand. When not, they folded nicely into twenty-foot layered fortifications against the walls. One had been pulled out over a third of the way, freeing up the top five rows, inaccessible as they were. It seemed however that the Pat-Press people had hit a snag with the bleachers—which were notoriously cranky, Ben remembered—and opted for a more traditional approach midway through the preparations.

Ben heaved a delirious sigh once he confirmed that he recognized no one, and that, more importantly, no one recognized him. He tramped once again on his home turf, collecting memories, and then took a seat near the back, right next to the semi-opened bleachers. He smiled as he remembered how many girls he had invited to join him back there throughout high school. Very few turned him down.

At this point, Ben noticed serious-looking men armed with various computer-assisted weaponry guarding the place—four by each exit. He took a deep breath and looked longingly at the gym's entrance, which was now growing more jammed with traffic. More people, he thought. Then why do I feel so alone?

Ben judged that the man who plopped down next to him was a few years older than he was and perhaps three or four inches taller. He had straight brown hair, a clean-shaven face, and an abnormally square jaw. Both shabby and formal, his dress shoes and herringbone tweed sports jacket might have been presentable ten years earlier. His bleach white shirt needed ironing with its collar jutting out over the jacket lapel. He didn't look at Ben but instead leaned forward with his elbows on his knees and kept his eyes glued to the stage even though only a handful of presenters had appeared. Every couple minutes or so, he would glance at his personal device.

The event began at seven pm with two minutes of silence in tribute to Pat-Press's recently-deceased octogenarian founder. Ben found most of the talks surprisingly enlightening, sober, and well-reasoned. Topics ranged from straight economics to anthropology to constitutional law, focusing mostly on the second and tenth amendments. Several themes kept cropping up, however. Most prominent was that genetics matters. There is a racial intelligence and behavioral hierarchy hard-wired into the human genome, and civilizations ignore it at their peril. It was so central to all the talks that speakers and audience members alike seemed almost bored with the idea.

If there was a competing theme, it was that whites had all but lost America to the blacks, Mexicans, and Muslims, and now regrettably faced the sharp and swiftly approaching Morton's fork of either fleeing to the far corners of the anglosphere such as Australia or South Zion—which was then enduring its birth pangs in a three-front war—or taking a stand in the United States, which could only mean seriously considering a second Civil War.

A particularly tense moment occurred when a speaker, a bearded, middle-aged man with a thick South African accent, held court on anti-Semitism. Dressed like a biker, he seemed almost inhumanly stocky. Ben had trouble following his rapid, Dutch-like pronunciation. But the gist, he got. Jews have historically been the enemy of European civilizations. But they are extraordinarily gifted. For what they can give humanity, they must be allowed to maintain the state of Israel. This garnered intense jeers from certain corners of the crowd, but the majority reacted warmly, even vocally. While speaking directly to the anti-Semites before him, whom he addressed as brothers, the South African rattled off all the grievances that white Europeans have against modern, secular Jews, a class of people he clearly detested. He avowed that the characterizations of Jews as scheming, dishonest, bloodsucking parasites were dead-on accurate considering how they had been deliberately weakening the racial resolve of whites since their emancipation in the 1870s. After intense applause from about three dozen men died down, the speaker then pointed to the holographic image behind him and began scrolling through the names and faces of hundreds of Jews who made noteworthy contributions in science, math, medicine, and economics in the last 200 years. With this, he told his anti-Semitic friends in language colored with archaic profanity to, in essence, sit down, shut up, and take a whiff of their own farts for a change. He concluded by saying that Israel must be preserved at all costs because only by nurturing something as precious as a state, as gentiles have always done, would the Jews ever realize what skelmy turds they'd been acting like throughout history.

For a speech which inspired nearly as much rancor as it did rapture, the reaction in the end was downright tepid. The crowd took a moment to recognize that the man had concluded and then responded with applause that could almost be described as polite. Ben didn't clap. Neither did the nervous man sitting next to him who was now shaking his leg like a machine.

It was nearly nine in the evening when the last scheduled speech had concluded. The new editor of Patriot Press, a bearded, ordinary-looking man in his fifties led the crowd in sustained applause for the speakers, whose recordings, books, pamphlets, music, and other media were available for download on the hologram behind the stage. He then thanked everyone for their support and asked five interns to pass out banking devices for secure contributions from the crowd. A guitarist-violinist duo played acoustic heavy metal while the crowd members made their contributions. The entire operation took thirty minutes. Ben gave fifty dollars.

Ben half-expected his jumpy neighbor to rise and walk to the stage by the time they were about to invite the mystery speaker to the podium. Instead, for the final talk of the night, the Patriot Press editor asked the crowd to welcome newly-elected Congressman William Stark.

For a U.S. Congressmen to appear at such an event was extraordinary. At this point in the twenty-first century, Patriot Press and about ten other nonviolent white nationalist or race-realist organizations had achieved real samizdat status in the United States. The men who edited or contributed to these organizations were not outlaws, per se. But they were tracked carefully by the government. They were aggressively audited. Their websites and sap-servs were routinely shut down, their web activity monitored, their inboxes overladen with hate mail, their reputations shredded in all public media. Their faces and addresses became permanent fixtures on the internet where they were branded as hate criminals. Their public appearances were met with gangs of violent protestors. They were often rejected service in restaurants and hotels. Even more disturbingly, other forms of intimidation began to occur with near-impunity, such as bricks thrown through windows, muggings, petty thefts, death threats, and, in the case of the teenage daughter of a prominent writer, mysterious disappearances. Forced racial integration of law enforcement in almost every state caused the police to be less than enthusiastic about pursuing leads. The Justice Department and FBI largely ignored such cases, focusing more on 'domestic terrorism', a euphemism for neo-Nazis and other violent white groups. They would also look the other way whenever churches were looted or burned or whenever Hispanic-black gang warfare threatened to approach sub-Saharan levels of violence and depravity.

Anyone who wished to maintain a respectable career stayed away from the Patriot Press crowd and its ilk. Of course, collaborating with the government invariably made careers more respectable. So the remaining true-believers, the 'race patriots', if you will, had no choice but to resort to brood sites and combustible spy paper and coded messages and Cold-War-vogue sobriquets in order to keep striving for relevance.

But why would William Stark appear at such an event with so little to gain and so much to lose? A stunned Ben asked himself this as the man he had shaken hands with two weeks prior now stood behind the podium.

Stark raised a finger, and the hall fell silent. "I am not here," he began, "for me!" He pounded his chest twice and then pointed with both hands at the crowd. "You are not here…for you! There's too much at stake for selfish aspirations." He waved his hand dismissively. "We are here…" he said and then stopped as if he had forgotten the remainder of his speech. He turned his head left, but his eyes snuck devilishly rightward, putting the lie to this impression. "…to remember and prepare." He licked his lips, smiled, and continued.

"It is barely within living memory — barely, mind you — and it is now only a matter of months, perhaps weeks, until we may finally forget a time when we could speak the truth without fear. A society declines the moment good men can no longer speak the truth without fear. Once, the states of modern Europe were truly masters of the world. They seized colonies with impunity, ruled them as a matter of course, took from them what they needed, what they felt was theirs, and treated the indigenous cultures with contempt at best. This was all predicated on the manifest superiority of white over brown and black."

It took him almost ten seconds to say these last five words. He was met with dead silence.

"This is the truth. God's truth. We knew it. They knew it. No one doubted it. But what happened? What happened was we began to apply white men's laws and white men's ideas to the black and the brown…as if they were white. Thus, the black and the brown were elevated to the level of the white where they didn't belong. This very act improved their lives more than their blighted minds could ever have imagined. But it also had one curious, and I'm sure unexpected, consequence…"

Stark placed his hand to the side of his mouth and whispered, "It made it impolite to tell the truth."

He smiled disarmingly. "White people, I'm sure, must have a politeness gene somewhere. Many of us can't ever speak the truth because we cannot imagine ourselves being so impolite in front of a black or a brown. We might hurt their feelings, you see. From there, truth inevitably became rude, then offensive, then taboo. Now," he said, once again whispering, "speaking the truth is all but forbidden.

"As for relations with people from our former colonies? Well, that has gone to the opposite extreme, hasn't it? We extol their virtues while denigrating our own. We take pride in debasing ourselves while turning a blind eye to their abject barbarism. We insist—insist!—that they are our equals yet ignore scientific and psychometric evidence to the contrary. We listen like guilty schoolchildren when they talk of the debt, *what we owe them!* We are their greatest benefactors, and they complain that we—owe—them! I assure you there is no end to this debt. They will not be satisfied until they swallow us up and take everything we have!"

Ben had not heard as much as a cough during Stark's impassioned oration. A few bodies adjusted in their seats. Clothing rustled. Feet slid centimeters on the hardwood floor. Ben struggled to remind himself that this was the same person he had been joking with two weeks ago.

Something wasn't right. Ben turned to his left and saw that the man who had been shaking throughout the entire event now sat stone still. He was a hell of a specimen, Ben noticed. Thick veins popped out of his neck and hands. His blazer would have fit him better if not for the well-formed muscles in his arms and shoulders. He stared out to the stage with determination, purpose even. Ben surmised that the man was inspired by Stark but he soon reconsidered. The man's eyes were too fierce, too focused. Something definitely was not right.

The man whipped around to face him, arresting Ben's attention with riveting contempt. The hardening eyes, the clenched teeth, the primal sneer, it was all there in the man's all too scrutable expression. Ben's heart slammed into his sternum in a fear best described as Pleistocene. He had to grip the seat in front of him to keep from falling backwards.

"So what do we take from all this?" Stark asked the crowd. Both men turned. "What's the lessoned learned?"

"We should've picked the damn cotton ourselves!" someone shouted.

Stark waited for the laughter and applause and further commentary to die away before continuing. "Well, yes, but it goes deeper than that. I think the biggest lesson we can take away from all this is that...our ancestors got it right the first time. We are superior to those people. They deserve our contempt for what they do. Anything less would be tantamount to our complete submission to them. They are more virile than we are, more robust physically, and they cannot control their passions. If we treat them as equals, it's only a matter of time before they overrun us and wipe us out."

It took a moment or two for this to sink in for the crowd. Stark's tone was more defeatist-sounding than they were accustomed to hearing—but no less irrefutable. Murmurs of half-hearted approval rumbled in the gym below sharp sounds of exasperation.

"So," he continued. "We've gone full circle. Now that we are second class citizens in a land that we built through our own sweat and our own genius, what is left for us to do except peer out at the wreckage of this once great nation and say, 'Dear Lord in Heaven, what do we do now?'"

Stark surveyed the crowd from end to end. "Well, I'll tell you," he said, and then looked up as if for inspiration from the heavens beyond the fluorescent lights and ceiling fans and championship banners hanging from the Poway High School gymnasium ceiling.

Ben's neighbor bolted upright, jerking Ben's attention away from the stage. He thrust his hands out with a curious flick of both wrists, and something rippled beneath the sleeves of his blazer. As his formerly muscular arms thinned out, a silver powder streamed into his hands and scattered in clouds all around him. Sitting so close afforded Ben a clear look at what this powder was: photo-crystal. Light sensitive computer chips the size of sand grains in thin phototactic casings. When thrown in the air at a light source, these ultra-light pellets turn to 'look' at objects opposite the light source and then trap their images much like film emulsion. A bio-replicated computer program then emits digital versions of these images, millions per second, via wireless to a remote sap-serv, which uses sophisticated software to reassemble them into a coherent whole, ready for worldwide download in minutes.

In a flash, so to speak, those who wanted to know who was attending the nineteenth Patriot Press convention thirty-five miles north of San Diego now knew, or were about to know. The man, whom Ben now understood to be some kind of mole, stooped low before hurling his two handfuls of photo-crystal into the rafters.

"Racism must perish!" he proclaimed in a thespian's stentorian voice. "Even if we must all perish with it!"

Ben knew what was coming next. He was also feverishly aware of what was at stake if he, talented young item writer that he was, were ever caught attending such a convention. He hesitated for the longest second of his life, and then tucked his chin into his chest and covered his face with his hands. Looking frantically for a place to hide, he saw the partially-opened bleachers, remembered what he used to do in them, and knew what he had to do now.

The crowd shifted into conflicting gears of alarm. Seconds after Ben knew, everyone knew. Their anonymity blown, their livelihoods ruined, their futures in doubt, the crowd members grew frantic with action. Some panicked and tried to flee or hide; some called for calm and order. Others, screaming in orgasmic rage, threw themselves upon the man and his confederates like swarming linebackers.

Ben's neighbor had not been alone. He had been joined by two others who also threw photo-crystal in the air and recited the same righteous mantra. One was tall, bald, and rakishly slender in tattoos and fashionable denim; the other, a bearded weight-lifter of medium height in short sleeves and khakis. As he watched the chaos ensue from beneath the bleachers, Ben saw that it was no accident these three men were physically exceptional. They were trained in various martial arts, and at first had no trouble keeping the Patriot Press crowd off of them. Kicks to the ribcage, knees to the belly, punches and elbows thrown from unexpected angles. Grown men were lifted off their feet and tossed over shoulder and hip. Ben witnessed a punch from his former neighbor crash so hard into someone's jaw that a tooth shot out and bounced off the bleacher above him.

Soon, however, as the bodies of dogged crowd members began to pile on the beleaguered saboteurs, clinging to a leg here, an arm there, the three exceptional men began to resemble exceptional water buffalo being pulled down by a pride of lions.

The tall one went down first after someone managed to catch one of his whip-like kicks and tackle him to the floor. The weight-lifter was knocked out cold from a punch he didn't see coming.

Ben's former neighbor however would not go down. He threw off man after man as he backed into the thin alley between bleachers. This afforded Ben an excellent view of the melee. He noticed that the man had a funny mannerism of biting his lower lip and expelling breath through his nose like a horse. This made it seem like he was smiling at his adversaries. He hit so hard that, even though he was faced by four men, not one of them was terribly anxious to dive in for more. Soon, however, they were pushed from behind by others and had no choice. Within seconds, he was pinned against the wall, and two men were about to rip his left arm out of its socket when the lights to the entire building abruptly went off.

Booted footsteps clamored through the chaos.

"There has been a security breach!" announced the Pat-Press editor, still on the podium. His voice had become an enervated rasp. "It is being handled! We have a professional security team on it now! Please remain calm and return to your seats!"

The closer the boots came, the less people acted and the more they waited. Ben remained crouched in the bleachers, gripping the metal girders like prison bars. By the time three security guards turned into the little alley between the bleachers and into Ben's full line of sight, the fighting had all but stopped. The lights were back on. Men backed out of the alley. They didn't want to get in the way of what was about to happen. Ben's neighbor spat in pugnacious defiance and performed an odd little two-step before charging the guards head-on like a soldier in the final, tactics-free stages of battle in which all fighting is hand-to-hand.

Supersonic air vibrations imbued with a strong magnetic pulse coming from the guards' stun guns caused the man's heart and brain to shut down before he could travel two feet. He collapsed cinematically with his left leg folding beneath him and his head striking the floor with a concussive thud. Even in deep unconsciousness, his arms jerked this way and that as if he were still throwing punches, destroying racism one patriot at a time.

The entire altercation had lasted less than forty-five seconds. Ben's memories of the incident, vivid almost to the point of pain, seemed to dilate and throb. He couldn't believe what he had just witnessed. It was as if his limited imagination had just been cranked open with a crowbar. His mouth was dry from lack of breath.

As the scene cleared, he tripped over one of the bleachers' iron girders despite having climbed over them many times before. Dead remnants of photo-crystal crunched loudly underfoot. Wading into the aftermath, it was all he could do to keep from falling as scores of people were scuttling past him to the exit. He could have looked into their faces, but didn't more out of embarrassment than anything else. Ambulance and police sirens wailed faintly in the distance.

"Why are you leaving?" the editor asked. He was on the verge of losing his voice and apparently unaware of the pathetic figure he was striking. His arms were outstretched in candid supplication. "Don't leave! Please! Do not leave! We cannot be ashamed of who we are! Our heritage! Our race! Our ancestors! We are a great people! We are a great people!" He stamped his foot on the stage, attempting to revive his diminishing authority. Dull, uncanny dread felt like a brick in Ben's stomach as he realized the man resembled a petulant child not getting his way.

"If we can't admit this even to ourselves, then we are lost!" the editor proclaimed. "We are lost…"

He trailed off as he watched nearly half his audience streaming out of the gymnasium. Ben noticed that there were many more people than when he had entered. Perhaps several hundred more. Over half the crowd remained standing before the podium, either exhorting people not to leave or watching on helplessly. Fistfights broke out between the faithful and the faint of heart. Many of the women who chose to stay were in tears, clinging to their husbands or boyfriends. A chant arose, "We're white! We're right! We know it!" but failed to sustain itself. Chants of "Remember Centurion!" did little better. "Embrace your Race!," one of the many rallying cries of the American White Nationalist Movement, fared best, but trickled out shortly after half a minute.

The editor ceded the podium to the South African who wasted no time imprecating the scampering throng. He was a natural orator and fluent in profanity. He managed to stanch the exodus to a minute degree. Five young men in mid-retreat decided to stay. But it was too late. Those who wanted to leave, by and large, had already left, hoping to abscond with their anonymity and their reputations still intact. The sirens were growing louder. The time for outspoken candor was rapidly coming to a close.

Ben stood stunned amid the wreckage. Overturned chairs, spilled drinks, various trash items, and inert grains of photocrystal littered the floor. Several of the wounded still writhed on their backs, waiting for medical help. The three saboteurs remained unconscious and were watched carefully by the armed guards.

The South African interrupted his tirade to address Ben directly. He pointed his finger so there could be no mistake. "Howzit, yooit. Hey!" he taunted. "In a dwaal, bra? Check the skaapie dere! You stay or go, ne? Ya fokking kont! I should klap ya in the fokking head. Don't understand, hey? Retard! Retard!"

Unaccustomed to being addressed like this and still in shock for having to process a whole generation of bloody strife in a span of minutes, Ben stood there like an imbecile until the South African speaker gave up on him and zeroed in on some other poor soul waffling uselessly in the gym. Ben then noticed William Stark who was clearly noticing him. Stark stood a few feet to the right of the podium. He was oddly serene and comfortable with what was happening all around him. He held out his hand to Ben, face tensing into a small smile. For Ben's sake at least, he didn't seem to mind waiting for a response.

He got it when police cars and ambulances could be heard skidding to a halt in the gymnasium parking lot. Ben turned and joined the final three dozen stragglers as he fled as fast as he could into the tumultuous night outside.

Chapter 12

Excessive heat, usually above 43°C, stimulates a protein called

TRPV1 which signals the sensation of burning to the brain. Chemicals that stimulate TRPV1 in a similar way can be found in

A. milk.
B. honey.
C. bananas.
D. Trinidad Moruga Scorpion chili peppers. (correct)

Ben recognized the man immediately. With his puffy face and missing mustache he could be none other than the Bulbous Bullhorn Bleater who pervaded the airwaves the moment the Muncie Mosque bomb did not explode. The day of the dud, as it were. Ben blinked and stammered as the man served him chicken curry with rice and stewed green beans cafeteria-style on a plate. The restaurant, two miles east of the Islamic Center off of McGalliard Road, was called Spice and Kabob, or S&K for short. It, along with a jewelry store, occupied the first floor of a two-story brick building and was surrounded on all sides by a parking lot. In front was a row of young birch trees which were too small to provide shade. Ben had seen the restaurant a bunch of times but never had a desire to eat there. By the way the man was speaking to his co-workers, it was clear he was the owner. He smiled nicely at Ben and reminded him in facile diction where he could find napkins, utensils, straws, and the drink machine. Ben smiled back and went looking for Ariya in the crowded dining room.

She was wearing her hijab along with her stylish work clothes, which was why Ben hadn't noticed her at first. She was also where he least expected her, at a table with six other people in the middle of the room. Four of them were middle-aged women, also in hijabs, and two were peach-fuzzed adolescent boys. Ariya sat at the head of the table, gesturing forcefully and speaking rapid-fire Farsi into her BTC device. She barely looked up when Ben sat down. He noticed that she hadn't ordered lunch and didn't look like she was going to.

He took the only seat available, which was to the right of the chair opposite Ariya. He had to lean forward past the others to get a good look at her. He sat between one of the boys and the oldest woman whose flabby jowls shimmied as she struggled with her legacy smartphone. While Ariya continued to chat, the other women waved and made tedious conversation with him in broken English. Every couple minutes or so, the boys would stare at him in rapt wonder before going back to their meals.

The curry was the spiciest Ben had ever had and forced him to use up his napkins wiping sweat from his forehead. He had to take a few more with which to blow his nose. He was grateful when, five minutes later, Ariya ended the conversation on her device and acted as if she wanted to strangle someone with her purse strap. "Oh! These people! They never listen!" she exclaimed, and then followed with a tirade in Farsi which caused the other women to sigh, nod sagely, and throw up their hands. Ariya donned a syrupy smile and looked to Ben. "Ben! Nice it is to see you. How are you?"

"I'm fine," he chuckled. "I was a little surprised when you invited—"

"Good!" Ariya said, slapping the table with both hands. "There is something I must share with you. I don't have much time."

Ben looked askance at her. "Okay…"

She breathed deeply through her nose, still with her hands on the table. "Meet Mohammad," she said, looking at the boy sitting to Ben's right.

Mohammad smiled self-consciously and waved at Ben. Ben did the same, muttering a stiff but sincere "Hello."

"Mohammad will be your writer in Iran," Ariya announced. "He is my cousin. He is here to visit family."

"Excuse me?" Ben said, looking from Ariya to Mohammad and back again.

"You write items for me, Ben," she explained. "You send them to Mohammad. Mohammad sends to me. BTC sends Mohammad money. Mohammad sends most back to you. Understand?"

Between the generosity, suddenness, and shadiness of the offer, Ben at first didn't know what to say. That everyone was staring at him like a star witness made things even more awkward. "Thank you for that, Ariya," he said, nodding at her in formal acknowledgement. "But I don't understand. I thought you said you had nine writers at your beck and call."

"The two best have started medical school. They don't have time. And one just got married. She cannot write anymore."

"Why not?" Ben asked. This elicited some amusement from the women. Ben blushed and looked down at his food.

"Because husband does not want her to, okay?" Ariya snapped.

"Okay. I was just asking."

"So you take my offer?"

Again, all eyes landed on Ben. "Well, this isn't exactly legal. Is it?"

Ariya sighed forcefully and muttered something to one of the women. "Ben! Why do you say such things? Embarrassing me like this!"

From her tone, she seemed to expect a sheepish apology or something like it. Instead, Ben looked straight back at her and said, "I'm only being as blunt as you are, Ariya. Putting me on the spot like this in front of people I don't know? Come on."

Clearly, Ariya was not accustomed to people saying no to her. Everyone at the table turned to her to see how she would respond to such impertinence. "Are you saying no, Ben? Do you really think Nigel would let you work for any other company after what has happened?"

"I'm saying I'll think about it. It's a generous offer, and I appreciate it. But I will need to think about it."

Ariya took a deep breath and then stood. "Good! You think. Then you call. I need you for New Mexico. We start next week!" She slung her purse over her shoulder and said her goodbyes in Farsi to everyone else at the table. "I must return to work. Bye!" With that, she walked briskly to the door, high staccato heels clicking against the tile floor.

Flabbergasted, Ben didn't even watch her leave. He would have left as well, right then and there, but he didn't want to bump into her in the parking lot. When she had invited him to lunch, he assumed it was a date, an idea that excited and intrigued him more than what had actually transpired. Ariya's proposal contained too many unknowns for him to be comfortable. How illegal was it to fraudulently earn tax-free money through an intermediary in another country? What percentage of his earnings would 'most' amount to anyway? He also entertained the frightful and not altogether unlikely possibility that Nigel had informed the FBI on him. He had no idea if they were monitoring his bank accounts. They could even be observing him right now in a van across the street or twenty feet away over a plate of lamb masala.

Suddenly despondent, Ben was worried about something a little more real. He didn't have any other cards to play. He had no professional contacts, no family to fall back on. What friends he did have were still getting high and surfing uselessly in San Diego. *I'll think about it,* he mused scornfully. Think about what? What *was* there to think about? How nice it is to pretend that you have other options? Ben laughed and figured there was an item in all of this somewhere.

> A stupid and tactless item writer gets fired from a testing company and becomes persona non-grata in the industry. Aside from a decent 401K and a modest IRA, he has little over fifty grand in savings. What should he do?
>
> A. keep fruitlessly applying for jobs in testing despite being blackballed by his former boss
> B. accrue enormous debt to finish college and then embark upon a new career fraught with uncertainty
> C. return to his beach bum life in San Diego where his biggest concerns were his tan, scoring quality weed, and comparison shopping for brands of condom
> D. accept Ariya's offer so he can make a living doing the only thing he was ever good at as well as entertain the tantalizing possibility of one day sleeping with her. (correct)

His curry wasn't looking so good by the time Mohammad nudged him in the shoulder with an envelope. Ben looked at it and then at Mohammad. The kid's face was not unfriendly. The envelope was thin and couldn't have contained more than a slip of paper. Ben opened it and found a handwritten note. What it said raised the hairs on the back of his neck and caused blood to rush almost painfully into his cheeks. 'Go upstairs behind the bathroom. Pass code QUBAD1# Close door behind and lock. Meet me on last room to right. Show this to NOONE!!' Ben looked at Mohammad who was still staring back at him with unquenched curiosity. None of the others were paying attention.

Ben took two more fiery bites of his curry and polished off his green beans. He then drained his iced tea and stood. After saying his goodbyes with a few ungainly waves, he dumped his plastic plates in the garbage, deposited his tray, and went looking for the bathrooms in the back of the restaurant. Although the building itself may have been twenty years old, the door to the stairs was a recent install. Above the knob was a state of the art code reader called a portcullis which synced to a person's device. If the person entered the appropriate code for that device, it would unlock. Ben made it on the second try, realizing that 'QUBAD' should have been written in proper- rather than upper-case in Ariya's note.

Even though the door shut heavily behind him, Ben snuck like a thief up the stairs and winced every time the wood squeaked beneath his feet. As his footsteps echoed through the well-kept, hardwood hallway, he realized the futility of tiptoeing. Door open or shut, anyone on this floor would know he was coming. This must be unrented office space, he thought. The bare walls and cobwebs made sense. But why no carpets?

He noticed the last door on the right. Ajar, it allowed a splash of daylight to kiss the dusty hallway floor. The door didn't make a sound as it swung on shiny new hinges into a thin room with a long-shuttered window. There Ariya sat on a full-sized mattress, dressed as before but barefoot and smoking a cigarette. The mattress had only an old box spring between it and a deep maroon, floral patterned area rug. Ben noticed her shoes and purse between a mini-fridge and a four-foot-tall rotating fan. Next to them were her pantyhose crumpled into a ball. There was no sign of her hijab. Ben smelled dog food and spotted a bowl of it in the corner. Chew toys and colorful plastic items littered the floor. A slender Pomeranian puppy with smooth auburn hair slept on a well-worn quilt at the foot of the mattress. The creature had a mane like a lion. The quilt beneath it featured five side-by-side pillars with words in Arabic beneath each one.

Neither said a word. Kitchen sounds—clanking plates, running water, whirring appliances, orders barked in some central Asian argot—leaked through the floor, a muffled, cacophonous soundtrack for what they were about to do. Ariya ground out her cigarette in an ashtray on the floor and stood. Ben could tell she was trying to look sexy, standing before him in her tight blouse and skirt as if to fill his eyes with her statuesque body. She gazed up at him, fearless and expectant, but her fluttering jaw caught Ben's attention the most. He cupped it in his hands and pulled her to him.

They stood there for a while, listening to their breathing escalate. As he opened his mouth to kiss her, she pulled back and began undoing the clasp of her skirt which she let fall to the floor. She looked to the door. "There is a lock," she said.

Chapter 13

Many butterfly species of the genus *Polygonia* hibernate by hanging from tree branches. Their dark, marbled colorings and unevenly angled wings resemble dead leaves and provide excellent camouflage during winter. One such species takes its name from a conspicuous mark on its underwing which resembles a

A. semi colon.
B. dollar sign.
C. forward slash.
D. question mark. (correct)

Ariya lay beside him on the bed wearing nothing but Ben's undershirt to protect against the air conditioning. With the lunch rush over, the kitchen clatter had lost its urgency, but a pot clanging rhythmically against the spinning dishwasher blade almost made up for it. Men could be heard from time to time stomping back and forth and shouting.

Ben had his arm around her, and between them her little show dog nuzzled against her owner. Her name was Sura.

"We will take you away from this place, Sura," Ariya said, clapping the dog's paws. "We'll live in a real home one day!"

"You keep the dog here?" Ben asked. "Above the restaurant?"

"Shh!" she snapped. "You hurt her feelings." She then held Sura's paws as if teaching her how to play patty-cake. "You've been here a long time. Haven't you? Haven't you?"

Sura sat up and yelped on cue causing Ariya to laugh. "Um, Ariya, shouldn't we keep it down?" Ben asked. "This place isn't exactly private, is it?"

"You're right. It isn't," she said, playfully biting him in the chest.

Ben saw that her makeup had been artfully applied to refine her chubby cheeks just so. It hid her acne scars well, but not so much the ones on her forehead. "So does Abraham Lincoln know we're getting all friendly up here in the middle of the day?" he asked.

"Who is that? Are you talking about someone named after the American president?"

"You've seen five dollar bills, haven't you? I'm talking about the imam with the bullhorn a month ago who couldn't find his mustache. He's been shouting at people downstairs all afternoon."

Ariya's expression changed, and not for the better. She pulled back from Ben. "He is *not* an imam. His cousin is."

"But the news reports—"

"Yes. I know," Ariya said, waving her hand. "Reporters believe whatever we tell them. If he had said he was grand mufti of Jerusalem, that's what American reporters would have said."

Ben leaned on his elbow. "So is he affiliated at all with the Muncie mosque?"

Ariya gave him an enigmatic smile. "He worships regularly I would imagine. He is very wealthy. He owns four businesses in Muncie including the new Fantastic Pizza near the University. He is well known in the community. But that's it."

"So what was he doing there that morning? And so early?"

It was a topic that Ariya seemed to have mixed feelings for. She snatched Ben's pillow and turned away from him. Ben took this as a challenge and tickled her ribs until she was begging him in urgent whispers to stop. She turned to him, still clutching his pillow. "Remember, he was not alone."

Ben shook his head, trying to recall the details of the day when the Muncie mosque did not explode. "I don't remem— Wait! They said he was with his young nephew." Ariya lifted an eyebrow, prompting him to delve a little deeper. "That wasn't his nephew?" he asked.

Ariya shook him by the chin. "You innocent boy. Yes, that was not his nephew. Very good. You get correct answer on test. Next question. Do you know who that was?"

"How could I possibly —"

"That was the son of Osama Rizvi, a man from the same village in Pakistan as our friend Lincoln," she said, squeezing his face not-so playfully. Ben noticed that at some point Ariya had started whispering. "Mr. Rizvi sent his boy to Hassan Moammar Khan, our Lincoln friend downstairs, to learn the restaurant business and to get an American education. His friend, in return, violates the boy any way he chooses. That's why he took him into the mosque that morning. Their hiding place where he wouldn't be caught."

Something vile squirmed on Ben's tongue as he took this all in. "That's sick."

"Yes. But it is not sick where he comes from in Pakistan. Over there, it is normal."

"How do you even know him?"

"There are six thousand Muslims in Delaware County, Ben. It's hard for us not to know each other, especially prominent ones like Abraham Lincoln."

"Yeah, but what are we even doing here?" Ben asked, darting his eyes around the room. "Why not go to the police?"

Ariya looked away, gently shaking her head until a smile emerged.

"Oh, I'm sorry," he said. "I didn't realize I was being funny. Since when is it funny that a grown man abuses young boys?"

She shook him lovingly by the ears. "You think like a white man! How is it that white men can be so smart and so stupid at same time?"

"I'm stupid because I oppose sexually assaulting children."

"No, because you assume everybody thinks like a white person. And they don't. Unfortunately, they don't."

Ben's mouth hung open in a confounded gape. Ariya cupped his shoulder in her hand. "I am sorry to offend."

"It's okay."

Ariya sighed. "But the truth is that both parties see this arrangement as symbiotic and good. The father places his boy with a wealthy, influential Muslim and countryman in America so he can send money back to Pakistan. And Abraham Lincoln gets another lover. They say he likes them under twelve."

"But what about the boy?"

Ariya rolled to her side of the bed and took a moment to get comfortable. "Yes. The boy. What about the foolish boy who comes to America with head full of Koran and dreaming of jihad? He hates you, Ben. He doesn't know you, but he hates you and would kill you if he could. So if he wants to be slave of Abraham Lincoln, and if Abraham Lincoln wants rape from him, why should I stop them? Maybe they give each other disease."

Something worldly in Ariya's expression seemed to age her by about ten years. She had stopped looking at him for some time.

He touched her cheek. "You don't really mean that, do you?" he asked.

In response, Ariya grabbed his pillow and whacked him with it.

Ben retaliated with the other pillow, and the two had at it until they felt they were making too much noise. "Abraham Lincoln must have heard us," he said. "You think he knows we're here?"

"He may."

"Really?"

"Seriously. He may."

Ben disguised his increasing concern in a facetious laugh.

"Does that disturb you, Ben?"

"Only because he owns the building, and he might tell your husband."

Ariya reached for a cigarette in her purse. "He won't."

"How can you be so sure?"

"Because I know his secret," she said, giving herself a light. "And he knows I know because I show him photographs and video of what he does with children. But I say nothing. And in return for my silence, he gives me this room where I keep Sura. Husband is allergic to dogs."

"So you *do* keep Sura here."

"Yes," she said, leaning against the wall. She spread her legs beneath the sheets and took a long drag from her cigarette. "This is also where I meet my men."

Ben gagged out a laugh once he realized she was serious. He sat up and put one foot on the floor.

Ariya clutched at air, reaching for him. "Come back. Please. All white men behave same way as this. But they always come back."

"White men? You mean as opposed to black men? What are you, keeping track?"

"How can I?" she asked in a haze of smoke. "I sleep only with white men."

Ben shook his head and for a moment would rather look at the cobwebs in the window or the paint chipping on the walls than at Ariya.

"Don't be so surprised," she said. "I say these things because I am white too."

He looked back at her. "You're—"

"Yes. White, like you." Ariya took Ben's stunned silence as a cue to continue. She put her hand on her breast. "We are the Aryans. We. The Iranians. Iran means birthplace of the Aryans or land of the noble people. That is where you get the word, 'Aryan.' The people from the steppes. The Caucasus. The Alani. They originate in Iran. Some had blonde hair. These were the masters of the country for thousands of years, and many still live in Iran today. We had great wealth, few slaves. Our cities, our art and science were the best. We didn't repress women like they do today. We had women leaders and warriors and professionals and scholars. We were really enlightened back then, not like the current power in Iran. I show you pictures of my mother with her blue eyes!"

After some time, Ben asked, "Ariya, you're not really a Muslim, are you?"

She finished her cigarette, crushed it in the ashtray and then glared at him through a billow of smoke. "I *hate* Islam," she said.

"Really?"

Ariya lifted her hands as if to push Ben away. "When I was nineteen..." she began and then halted. She got up to tend to Sura whom she tickled behind the ears. "My father's family was from a suburb of Tehran. We lived there like good citizens. But my mother's family...eh...from the south, to the east. Near Yazd. We visit them. One time, okay? One time!" She lifted a finger while Sura rolled on her back, whining for more attention. "Me, my mother, and sisters go for big winter festival like your Christmas and Halloween and Fourth of July all wrapped together. Father would not go. We go. An ancient village. We had the fireworks and bonfires and feasting and music and singing and stories and laughing and children running. The whole village. Many of us.

"My grandmother introduced us to her cousin. A man, not too old. His family was still of the old religion which Islam has no place for today. He used to be an athlete, a gymnast, I think. No one could leap higher over the fires. He spoke of history and long-ago women rulers and warriors. Things I know now, not then. He showed us the dances. The Dance of Fire!"

Ariya bit her lip as she gathered her nerve. She released a still-whining Sura and assumed a dancer's pose with her hands on her hips. Standing on her toes, she began kicking and spinning and raising her arms in a stately yet sensual dance while humming some traditional Asian melody. She quit after nearly a minute and blushed fiercely through a smile. Ben had a look of dreamy wonder throughout and duly applauded when she took her bows. Even Sura was transfixed.

"If I had a rose, I'd throw it at you," he said.

She clapped twice. "And he taught us a trick! He took my sisters and me and many of us youngsters to hills nearby. We bicycled there. There was frost on the ground. Somehow he knew the path. I remember it was still light. We could see, but the Sun was going down fast. He took us into a forest, to trees with the strangest leaves! Do you know what those leaves really were, Ben?"

Ben smiled and shook his head.

"Butterflies!" Ariya whispered. "In winter. In hibernation."

"Really."

"Yes! Thousands of them. From distance they looked like leaves. They were above us. All around us. A butterfly forest!"

"Did you catch any?"

"They were asleep! Qubad forbade us even to touch them. But then I found one fluttering on the ground. He was so cold. There was frost on his wings. He would surely die. I showed Qubad. He let me climb onto his shoulders so I could put it back on the other butterflies in the trees. He said that's how they keep each other warm."

"Wow," Ben said.

"We wore hats," she continued, taking a deep swallow. "Thick hats made of wool. Like I said, it was cold. But it was warmer under the trees, and less wind, so we took them off. But when I found that butterfly on the ground, we all wanted to find more butterflies. So we dropped our hats and went searching. And when it was time to go back, it was dark, and I had lost my hat!"

Tears began to pop out of Ariya's eyes. She blinked, and they began streaming down her face. Ben stood. "Ariya, what's wrong?"

Ariya backed up and stepped on one of Sura's toys, making it squeak. She laughed and rubbed her eyes with the back of her wrist. "My hijab was in that hat," she said.

"What?"

"It came loose from the bicycle ride. And I didn't have a cap. It just came off. And when it was time to leave I couldn't find it!"

Ben reached out to hold her shoulders, but she pulled away. She scooped up Sura and crawled back on the bed. Ben joined her as she stroked Sura behind his ears.

"You have done social studies, Ben" she said. "Are you aware of historical act by the Iranian government almost ten years ago, after the war?"

Ben thought and answered. "Yeah. Something about changing the Constitution to not recognize religious minorities?"

"And their traditions and their festivals. All illegal now."

"You were arrested?"

"The government people came in vans and broke up our festival," she said. "They put out our fires. Stopped all the music.
Man and woman are not allowed to dance together. You know
that, don't you? This was one day *before* they change the Constitution, okay? One day! We didn't know anything! They knew
we were going to have our festival. And said nothing. Not on
internet, television, nothing! They came anyway and said they
did not want to arrest anyone. But when we returned, and they
saw me without my hijab…"

"Oh, no."

"Thirty days I spent in their jail. No trial. Hundred kilometers
away."

"Ariya—"

"I lived near Tehran, Ben!" she said as if reminding him of
something he should already know. "Already we came 500 kilometers. For this to happen to a nineteen-year-old girl…"

Ben curled his lips and shook his head and said nothing.

"You know what happens to men in prison, don't you?" she
went on. "With women, it is double, okay? Thirty days I was
there. Thirty days…" Her voice trailed off into a near squeak
and ended with a deep sniff and a cough. She used Ben's shirt to
wipe her eyes.

"Ariya," Ben began, "I can't—"

"Shush!" Ariya said, lifting her finger. She spoke between
sharp, little rasping gasps. "Do you think it ends? Do you think
it ever ends? When I got out, and in front of my mother, my sisters, my father, they pinned some dirty old hijab onto my head! I
got infections. I know you know. I saw you looking at my scars."

Ben had heard enough. He took a weeping Ariya into his
arms and kept her there despite her efforts to break free. Sura
whined as the pair struggled in the sheets. She dug her nails into
his arms and shoulders and tried to push herself free. It took almost all he had to keep her and not cry out in pain. She finally
gave up in a welter of tears, leaning her head on his chest and

hanging her wrists around his neck.

Many moments passed. Her face was dry but Ben's undershirt was still damp. With a sweeping gesture, she invited him to lie back down on the pillows together. The bed squeaked as they got comfortable.

"Say something to me please," she said.

"I'd like to. I'm trying to think of something that no one else has said to you. Or something you haven't thought of before. And I got nothin'."

Ariya laughed. "You mean I am the first girl to make a fool of herself before you on our first date?"

"Sweetie, I'm afraid this might have to be our last date," he said as he pinched her on the chin. She sat up, seeing that he meant it. Ben guided her back down. "No, Ariya. I don't *want* this to be our last date. But after that bloodcurdling story, I'm afraid to put you at any more risk."

"But that was a story from my childhood. It was long ago."

"What about Mr. Mohammadi, your husband?"

Ariya interrupted him with a snort and chuckle. She turned onto the pillow and looked back up to face him. "That is nice of you to have concern, Ben. But it wouldn't be my husband to punish me. He is a small man. And quite fat. My parents married me to earliest available suitor the moment I left jail. We are like your Boris and Natasha."

"Our who?"

She looked to the window. Sunlight seemed on the verge of bursting though the shutters. "It is nothing," she said. "But you are right. It is a risk. My father's surname is Kayani. His family converted to Islam only for two generations. My mother's family never converted, okay? My husband's family knows this. His brother would want to beat me for what I do and put me in hospital. And his father. And cousins. No shaming them, of course."

"But you're not there, Ariya," he reasoned. "You are here. You have rights."

"But Sharia law is becoming American law now. My husband's family could keep me in house and refuse to let me leave. They could capture me, drug me, put me on airline to Iran, and kill me there, where it would be legal. Or they kill me here and escape home as 'religious refugees'. Punishing someone who attacks people in Allah's name violates religious freedom. And that violates your Constitution. So because of your Abraham Lincoln I am slave to my Abraham Lincoln. In language arts, I believe they call that irony."

"Muslim men game the system so they get away with peder-asty and wife battery, and the best we can do is talk about the irony. Isn't that wonderful. Oh, and that's not irony, Ariya. That's sarcasm."

"I did not notice," she deadpanned. Ben turned sharply to her and smiled wearily. He rolled over to the edge of the bed and got up.

"I'm sorry, but I have to leave soon," he said as he searched for his pants. He found them on two of Sura's plastic toys. "Not to sound selfish, but if your husband's family would kill you, imagine what they'd do to me."

"I said what they could do, not would do. Don't worry, Ben. My husband's entire family lives in Tehran, and they are not in-terested in pursuing my infidelities. They were grateful enough to me for marrying that little jelly donut Pooya, whom we all suspect is homosexual."

"No shit," Ben said.

"Shit," Ariya said back, and they both laughed for a moment. "Pooya left for Singapore this morning, Ben. As long as you leave discreetly through the back door whenever you come here you are safe."

He finished putting on his pants and then walked over to the bed, towering over her. He looked around and wondered what this thin room with the one long window was originally meant for. He held out his hand. "I need my T-shirt back."

Ariya said nothing as she raised her hands above her head in seductive surrender. It took her almost ten seconds. The T-shirt was dry now, but it was tight enough on her body to reveal en-gorged nipples bulging through the cotton. They were the size of silver dollars. He put a knee on the bed, his hands on either side of her, and slid his T-shirt up and off of her.

She then wrapped her forearms around his neck, and pulled him close for a hot, open-mouthed lover's kiss. She stopped be-

cause he wasn't responding. "Am I so distasteful to you that you
refuse to see me again?" she asked.

"I want nothing more than to see you again. I just need you to
first find an attorney and divorce your husband."

"I am distasteful to you."

"No. I just don't want to slink around like a thief just to be
with you."

"It's too dangerous, Ben."

Ben put on his shirt. "I'll protect you. And if I have to I'll take
you somewhere where you'll be safe."

She chuckled at the gesture.

"Don't underestimate me, Ariya," he said. "I will do this for
you. That's a promise." He had no idea where this confidence
was coming from, but he knew it felt good.

"You are a sweet boy," she said, both condescending and not.

"I have to go now," he said. "Flight leaves in almost three
hours. When I get back, we will talk more about this." After
finding his shoes, he leaned over to give her the kind of kiss she
wanted. They relished it, and then he pulled away.

"Only one week?" she asked. "Do you promise?"

"Yes. One week at the most."

"I hope you find your brother."

"Me too."

"Virginia, is it?

"Yes. A town called Nathan's Ford."

Still topless, she reached into her purse for another cigarette
and lit up in bed. "Well, bring a device. I need seventy New
Mexico eighth-grade earth science questions by next Friday. Fifty multiple-choice. Twenty essay."

"Template?"

"I worry about that."

"Rubric?"

"My problem."

"Sample answers?"

"If you want. Not necessary. I am easy. Check your inbox
with information. You get all the money minus tax and five percent for Mohammad's time. No cent less. I promise."

"Thank you, Ariya." He stepped back to her and waited for

her to finish her drag on her cigarette before kissing her goodbye. She slapped him twice on the thigh. "Go. Go!" she said in a
throaty croak.

Just before he left the room, Ben turned her around and
looked into her reddened eyes. "Ariya?"

"Yes?"

"Why did Nigel blackball me?"

"Why did he what?"

"Why did he tell all the other testing companies not to hire
me?"

Her quick response startled him. "He called you radioactive."

"Radioactive?"

"August was going to call government lawyers. They were
going to go public and ruin your reputation."

"So Nigel did it all for my sake?" Ben asked, flabbergasted.

"Yes, but it was more. August's lawyers would have sued
any company that hired you."

"What does Nigel care if they sue ETS or Pearson or any of
the other companies? Doesn't BTC compete with them?"

"Because everyone has become afraid of tests in the home of
the brave, Ben," she said. "Our industry could not survive such
scandal. He did it to save testing."

Part 3: Nathan's Ford

Chapter 14

East Carolina barbecue Sauce differs from most other American barbecue sauces because it lacks which of the following
ingredients?

A. pepper and tomato
B. vinegar and pepper
C. brown sugar and vinegar
D. tomato and brown sugar (correct)

Nathan's Ford.

Ben concluded that Isaac must be in Nathan's Ford, Virginia.
That Saturday afternoon, Ben's flight had beaten Isaac to

Richmond by several hours. After arriving in the airport, he wasted no time in buying new clothes and renting a car. He pulled up to the Richmond bus station less than an hour later, still chomping on his fast food dinner. Obscured by a jacket, cap, and new pair of sunglasses, he discreetly tucked himself behind a public device display in the far corner of the station and dug in for a long wait.

This time there was no mystery. The Muncie bus arrived around the time the arrival screen said it would. Isaac got off and twenty-five minutes later boarded another bus, this one headed for Nathan's Ford. Ben tossed off his cap and shades and whooped in relief.

Sixty-six miles south of Richmond, twelve miles north of the North Carolina border, Nathan's Ford's very existence seemed dependent on its proximity to I-95, which runs up and down the eastern seaboard. Aside from a few modern service stations and a recently refurbished hospital, the place could only boast of its thriving agriculture and spacious courthouse where people caught speeding were forced to go if they wished to argue their case before a judge. The Nathan's Ford downtown contained all of twelve traffic lights, Ben learned. There wasn't much else there. What was Isaac becoming now? A tobacco farmer?

Ben resolved to visit Nathan's Ford one morning during the fourth week of his unemployment. He wanted to see his brother, yes, and crack the mystery that was Isaac's life. He was also lonely. But there was something about Nathan's Ford that disconcerted him. After nearly five hours of research at the Ball State library, he sat down at a sushi restaurant but left before the waitress arrived. He browsed for over an hour in his favorite bookstore, but read nothing and bought nothing. His fire alarm went off that evening after he forgot about an egg he had boiling on the stove. At around one in the morning, it came to him. In the hundreds of news reports he had read going back twenty-five years, there wasn't anything that wasn't mundane or local. A school sporting event here, a farmers' convention there. Occasionally there would be a fire or a crime or a concert or a controversial vote by the town council. Nathan's Ford had a relatively large East-Asian population for a town so rural and Southern. It also seemed to have slightly more than its share of winos. Other than that, nothing. Why would Isaac be so secretive about a town which had nothing remarkable about it whatsoever?

And no mention of itinerant communities, Ben realized before finally drifting off to sleep.

***

Ben touched down in Richmond and stepped into the airport with only his carryon bag and device. He picked up his guitar at baggage claim and then plopped down at a café to order a large coffee. While eating the banana and muffin he brought with him on the airplane, he polished off five multiple-choice items on the nitrogen cycle. He placed them along with ten others in a compressed file and uploaded it to a secure, password protected sapserv located in Iran.

He checked Ariya's communication portal. Only the tall plant silhouetted by the shuttered window behind it appeared. She had apparently stepped away from her desk. He began a message to her but deleted it halfway through.

There was hardly anyone on I-95 South that evening. It had been a beautiful June day, and the Sun was just beginning to descend upon the tree tops on Ben's right. With his window rolled down and his arm lolling comfortably outside, he could taste the invigorating wind. He felt tempted to push his late model Japanese rental car beyond the speed limit, but didn't, and instead allowed the machine to drive itself. After his afternoon with Ariya and what he hoped to have waiting for him in Nathan's Ford, risk-taking lost a lot of its edge. He wondered what his brother could be doing so far away from home.

Seventy uneventful minutes later, Ben reached his destination and came to the melancholy conclusion that Nathan's Ford is nothing more than a sieve. A place for people to pass through on their way to Washington, DC or Myrtle Beach. A place for people to spend the night if they're traveling from New York to Florida. There was little that was remarkable beyond what you could see from the highway. Bennett Street, one of the main roads, boasted six of the town's twelve traffic lights. It also featured two of the town's most elongated buildings. One was a two-story brick structure with large garage doors which must have served as a fire station around the time the internet went public. The storefront read, 'FARM EQUIPMENT.' Next to it was a rickety prefab structure with olive drab aluminum siding. A massive blue roof loomed over its porch like a bad haircut. White letters spelled out the words 'FRED'S DESKTOP PUBLISHING' in italicized courier font. The first letter of each word stood out, being several sizes larger than the others, in a crude, almost guileless attempt at logo design. Between the buildings was a thin, nearly leafless dogwood which had sprouted through the sidewalk years ago but now leaned so far to the right it looked in danger of needing a cane. Ben wondered if the same shabby panorama welcomed GIs returning home from Iraq or Afghanistan.

Ben had considered various less-than-honest schemes to get the citizens of Nathan's Ford thinking about Isaac. Instead, however, he decided to hurl himself straight as an arrow at the problem with a smile and a handshake. At nine sharp the next morning, he walked right up to 100 Bennett Street, the one-story gray concrete building that was the Nathan's Ford police department, intending to fill out a missing persons report. He planned to later distribute copies of Isaac's 'Have you seen me?' flyer while playing his guitar on the street for chump change. He tripped on the steps while contemplating this plan, however, and cracked his knee on the concrete. He then suffered the embarrassment of being yanked back to his feet by a woman coming out of the station. She was a stocky, light-skinned black police officer. Homely, but beaming with health and energy, her front left incisor was chipped and crooked. It made her smile seem both devilish and sweet.

"Better look where yer goin' there, sport!" she warned, wiping her hands as if Ben were covered in dust. He fought the urge to rub his knee as he showed her a photo of Isaac and asked her if she had seen him.

The woman studied the image with a squint and a frown. She pursed her lips from left to right and back again. "I haven't seen 'im!" she announced. "But that don't mean he ain't here!" She smiled big at him again and pointed to the police station. "You go through them doors. You talk to officer Penny Gass. Y'hear?"

"Penny who?" Ben asked, shaking his head. "What's her name?"

The woman snorted. "Uh-uh. Her's a he! Pendergast. The officer y'all wanna talk to is Charles Pendergast. He'll he'p ya find yer boy!" She clapped him hard on the shoulder and walked off.

"Thank you!" Ben called as he went inside, regretting that his shoulder was now another part of his body he needed to rub.

Cream-painted concrete bricks lined either side of the lobby, and at the far end waited a square window and a door, each reinforced with bulletproof glass. Only the muted sparkle of photo-crystal in the ceiling indicated that this was the twenty-first century.

An overweight, slow-moving black officer got up from his post on the other side of the window and lumbered five-and-a-half feet to the door. Ben noticed that he was protected around the neck by a thick tube of fat. An erect nipple of a wart bulged from his cheek. He cracked the door open and leaned the left side of his body into view. After Ben told him what he wanted, the man shuffled back to his seat and started thwacking his old-fashioned keyboard with fingers as thick as quarter rolls. He leaned towards his screen with a myopic squint.

A whirring sound above the ceiling caused Ben to look up. He was being scanned. Sure enough, his personal device logged off and shut down. The door buzzed and cracked open and then started closing again. The officer in the window said nothing and did nothing except stare at his embedded screen and slide his finger back and forth on his desk mouse. Recognizing his fleeting opportunity, Ben jumped for the door handle.

The police station was done up in catty-corner glass cubicles with diagonal halls which made one feel like a bishop on a chessboard. The low, brown-stained ceilings were clearly from the previous century, and the thin carpet seemed almost as old. Two officers, one uniformed, the other not, one black, the other white, were watching a sports talk show projected from the ceiling while discussing the prospects of UVA baseball.

Without being told where to go or to whom to speak, Ben resolved to get the attention of the white officer.

"Hold it a second, dear."

It was a female voice, coming from an older lady, and it stopped him before he completed his first step. Right away he knew this woman was a Yankee transplant. Boston, he thought. Somewhere in New England, definitely. He turned and noticed a plump, middle-aged lady behind a long wooden desk built before the days of personal computing. Archaic reading glasses on a chain clung to the tip of her nose. She was playing 3D solitaire on her device.

"I'm here to see to Officer Pendergast about a missing person?" Ben said. He blinked three times, kicking himself for ending a statement as if it were a question. It made him seem weak and indecisive, and always at the worst possible times. He handed her one of his flyers.

The woman took it and then pointed her long, well-manicured forefinger to Ben's left. He looked and saw a six-and-a-half-foot tall borderline obese man in a white shirt, tan slacks, and yellow tie leaning against a pillar in the back of the hall. He was watching the same sports program as the other two officers. Such a big man. Ben was surprised he hadn't noticed him before.

Officer Pendergast didn't notice Ben until he introduced himself and offered him his hand. Pendergast barely shook it, all the while regarding the replays of last evening's games. He bit his lower lip and squinted when a play didn't go his way. He then shook his head, smiled, and turned to Ben.

"Hey there, Benny, how ya doin'?" he said as if he'd known Ben his whole life. His chin sunk into his well-shaven neck like a spoon in pudding. Ben guessed he was on the underside of thirty.

"Fine, thanks," Ben said. "I'm here to talk about a missing person. Perhaps." This last word he added after a moment's hesitation and regretted it immediately.

The right side of Pendergast's face lit up. "You mean perhaps he's missing, or perhaps you're here to talk about it?" Officer Pendergast spoke in the kind of slow southern drawl common to that part of Virginia. He seemed to slow it down even more, as if deriving pleasure from trying the patience of the uptight Yankee he was talking to.

Not wanting to embarrass himself further, Ben said nothing. It was a smart move, because Pendergast nodded in lazy laughter and rapped his knuckles lightly against the wall. "I get it. You wouldn't even be here if you didn't want to talk about it. All right. Come this way."

Without looking back, Pendergast led Ben past the cubes to his office. Ben didn't dare walk beside him in the thin hallway because he wasn't sure there'd be enough room. Unlike what he had seen before, Pendergast's office was a real room with ceiling-to-floor walls and a window made of thick, bullet-proof glass. His desk was empty except for one personal device, one binder and a pen. A bookshelf contained only a photo of Pendergast and his middle-aged parents leaning against the railings of a boat. He was bigger than both of them combined. Pendergast fell into his plus-sized swivel chair and took several moments to get comfortable while the chair squeaked and rolled backwards under its owner's prodigious weight. He clasped his hands behind his neck and treated Ben to armpit stains the size of tortillas.

"So the way we deal with missing persons is—" he began.

Still rolling backwards, his leg collided against the desk, disturbing his device and causing its most recently run application to run again. A hologram of a stereotypical redneck in overalls, mullet, and cowboy hat appeared and began hopping and dancing to loud banjo music. Rather than turning it off to spare Ben the inevitable embarrassment, Pendergast simply smirked and waited for the show. Soon the thing was mangling the chorus of 'Dixie' by shrieking the following lyrics over and over:

Oh, the South is gonna rise again!
South is gonna rise again!
Look away! Look away! Look away!
South gon' rise again…

During the first verse a bulge in the thing's crotch became noticeable. After the second, a torpedo-like erection burst through its overalls. What had started as some poor-boy shuffle was ending as full-on pelvic thrusts to "Look away!" as the thing grabbed its inhuman phallus with one hand, waved its hat with the other, and concluded the performance with the perfunctory "Yee haw!"

Pendergast cleared his throat and turned it off just after it began its encore. "I am so sorry you had to witness that," he said, affecting to be more annoyed than he really was. "I shoulda turned that off. Typically, we use HVRS to get information from people like yourself. You know, to avoid the paperwork."

"HVRS?"

"Holographic Voice Recognition Software. It takes a non-threatening human form, like a cute little Japanese lady, and asks questions. You give answers which are piped into the state's database lickety-split."

Ben shook his head. "But that wasn't a Japanese—"

"No, it wasn't. Was it?" Pendergast said, pounding his desk and cackling. "Ha! Didn't look like a Japanee-HA! That was somethin', wasn't it? Hee-hee! The IT guys gave me that last Christmas. Bless their twisted little hearts."

Ben was amused despite himself but said nothing to keep Officer Pendergast on task. Pendergast coughed and scratched his eyebrow which was covered partially in red crust. "All right. I apologize for making you wait," he said, placing his device before him on the desk. "Please tell us about your missing person. And I assure you, the Nathan's Ford Police Department will do everything in its power to aid you in your time of need."

Pendergast spun his device to face Ben as the holographic image of a Japanese woman appeared. She was slender and pretty and wearing a stylish suit. She looked directly at Ben and smiled.

"Good morning," she said in a crisp American newscaster accent. "Welcome to Nathan's Ford, Virginia. I am the HVRS animated receptionist for the local authorities. I am here to assist you. Please state your name, address, government ID, and business."

Of course, the programmers remembered to make her smile, adjust her hair, and breathe while she waited for Ben to respond. "Tried to get one with bigger tits, but..." Pendergast said. He laughed again and didn't seem to care that Ben wasn't laughing along.

"Do I really have to talk to this thing?" Ben asked.

Pendergast pursed his lips and turned the HVRS system off. "All right," he said. "We'll do this the old way." He gathered his device onto his lap, leaned back further in his massive swivel chair, and, one by one, placed his size-fourteen feet on the desk. His well-worn boat-like shoes each struck the wood with an abrupt 'thunk'. Ben noticed something brown and messy clinging to the bottom of his right shoe between heel and sole. It was the squashed remains of a large insect.

"According to Barbara up front, your name is Benjamin Cameron," Pendergast began, consulting his device. "You're from Muncie, Indiana. Had a school teacher from Muncie or thereabouts. Biology, I believe it was. You're looking for your brother Isaac. He's gone missing. For some reason you think he's here. Why?"

"The last time I saw him he was boarding a bus to Nathan's Ford," Ben said, handing Pendergast one of his flyers.

Pendergast took it and tilted his head as he scrutinized it. Then he gave it a keen double take. "When was this?" he asked.

"May sixth."

"Over a month ago."

Ben made three halting little nods. "Yeah."

"That's it?"

"He doesn't keep a personal device. He has no known address. No permanent job. He won't tell me—"

"Whoa, Benny. Whoa. Whoa!" Pendergast interrupted, waving the flyer. "This ain't a missing person. Isaac's over eighteen, right? Maybe he just don't wanna be found? Least not by you, if you'll pardon my sayin'. Did you two have a falling out, or—"

"No. He just came by my condo to visit. Then he left. Wouldn't tell me where he was going."

"Yet you tracked him to Nathan's Ford."

Ben nodded.

Pendergast put his finger in the air. "Now, I'm kinda flattered, but I didn't think that buses went all the way from Muncie, Indiana to this little redneck village we got goin' on here."

"He got on a bus to Richmond. I followed him there in an airplane. I waited for him at the bus station and saw him board a bus to Nathan's Ford."

Without taking his eyes off of Ben, Pendergast slid his meaty arm onto his armrest and rested his chin in his hand. "You wanna find him that bad, huh?"

Ben couldn't meet him in the eye. Instead, he looked about the room. Again, there wasn't much to look at. No diplomas, no staplers, no coffee mugs. Nothing. After three seconds he did notice an Extra Strength Rolaids wrapper in the trashcan. "He's my brother," he said.

"Well, shoot, there ain't nothing we can do for ya," Pendergast said through a wide, protracted yawn. "I'd like to help, but I cannot justify officer hours on a task such as this. My hunch? Your brother's fine, wherever he is. But you're welcome to search the county, talk to people, put up your flyers. I know the manager at the Red Lodge Inn. I'll tell him to take care of ya gratis for a couple nights while you do what you gotta do. How's that sound? Barbara out front will give you the details. You'll know her 'cos she's the only one here who talks funny."

Pendergast sucked down some snot and held out a fat hand for Ben to shake. He was practically lying on his back in his big chair and had no intention of getting up.

Ben stood to shake it, but was forced to come uncomfortably close to Pendergast's voluminous shoes. That insect was a spider, he noted, and its legs were still dangling. "Thank you, officer," he said. "One more thing if you don't mind. Isaac mentioned that he worked in an itinerant farming community."

Pendergast smiled almost in wonder. "A *what*?"

"Groups of people who, you know, move from town to town doing whatever needs to be done in exchange for food and a place where they can camp for the night. That kind of thing."

"Haven't heard that one before," Pendergast said, shaking his head. "Tell it to Barbara. Maybe she can help."

"All right, I will. Thank you."

Ben was halfway through the door when Pendergast stopped him. "Oh, when you get hungry? Don't eat at the Red Lodge. Continental breakfast is okay, but their dinners are pretty off the wall. Had a Cajun dish there once. Jambalaya, I think it was. Bland. Can you imagine! Ha! They have the gajones to serve a Cajun dish and they still found a way to make it bland. I had to ask the waitress for some Worcestershire sauce, oregano, garlic powder, cayenne pepper. She didn't even know what half that stuff was. Ha! Only in Nathan's Ford."

"That's pretty funny," Ben said.

"So if you want a good place to eat, we got Conrad's Q on Vernon. Best ribs you're gonna find in the state. They use vinegar-based sauce. Just the right touch of mustard. Not that molasses and ketchup crap they serve everywhere else in the Piedmont."

"I'll have to check it out," Ben said, inching his way out the door. He figured if Officer Pendergast knew anything, it was food.

"Good luck finding your brother," Pendergast called. "And remember, down here in Virginia, it ain't ribs. It's ri-i-i-i-i-i-ibs!"

***

By seven o'clock that evening, Ben had driven on every road, every street, and every avenue, paved or not, in Nathan's Ford. He took County Highway 473 twelve miles west out to the municipal airport. It had been closed down for years and was overrun with tall grass and weeds. He took the same road ten miles east. Nothing out there but trailer parks, superstores, services stations, and strip malls. He found the same with Highway 12, headed southeast just past the North Carolina state line. He took Route 611 southwest to the county line. He discovered nothing but churches, forests, some residential areas, and billboards advertising strip clubs, gun shows, and chain restaurants.

The only farmland he found was heading northeast on 611. He canvassed this area carefully, looking for any signs of itinerant farming communities. He handed out flyers and queried locals in drugstores and service stations, supermarkets and hardware stores. Black, white, Hispanic, or Asian, they all met Ben with the same befuddled gape. More often than not, Ben had to explain what an itinerant farming community was before he could get any kind of answer. As expected, no one had ever heard of such an outlandish thing. They assured him with a kind of rustic condescension that nothing of that nature had ever existed in Nathan's Ford. About one in four handed him bible literature and told him to have a blessed day.

The thick orange dusk began to feel like fog when Ben was ready to give up. He was confident he had been everywhere. The only other way out of Nathan's Ford was by the interstate, north and south. He looked with speechless admiration at his fuel gauge. He had driven the car sixty-six miles from Richmond to Nathan's Ford and then let the thing drive itself for *seven hours* on one tank, and it still had a wee bit to spare.

He parked at the hotel and found Conrad's Q on foot. It was part of a tiny strip mall set back thirty yards or so from Vernon, which ran parallel to Bennett. To the right of the Q was a Methodist church. To the left was a UPS store. A single, half-dead tree towered over the structure with branches reaching over either side of it like a protective mother. It had few leaves, but enough to partially cover the Q's logo on the roof: A pink, happy pig jumping through a flaming letter Q like a circus horse.

The place reminded him of the old diners his parents would take him to when he and Isaac were kids. The term 'time capsule' popped into his head a few times as he noticed the vinyl booths, the ceiling fans, the cheap tablecloths, the help-yourself fixings station, the soda and ice dispenser, and the glass counters displaying garish cakes and homemade cookies. The heavy smell of pork tickled the bottom of his empty belly, and suddenly he was ravenous.

Ben ordered a rack of pork ribs with a side of collard greens and mashed potatoes. He ignored the complimentary salad and was on his second beer by the time the main course arrived. Forgetting the steaming napkin and packets of wipes which came with the meal, he dove in, blind with hunger, and set upon enjoying at least one thing about Nathan's Ford before getting on an airplane the next day and returning to his life in Muncie.

He had just finished his ribs when he noticed a disturbance. A tall, broad-shouldered drunk was stumbling in the dining room where the wait staff was telling him he was not allowed. He wore cutoff jeans and muddy boots. Bright red with alcohol corruption, the man's face bore an expression of perverse determination. Judging from the long lines on his forehead and his receding hairline, he seemed to be in his early sixties. A basketball-sized pot-belly expanded his untucked bowling shirt and offered unwelcome glimpses of the impossibly white cellulite underneath. He seemed intent on talking to one of the waitresses, who, upon his appearance, refused to leave the kitchen. Ben remembered the reports of all the winos in Nathan's Ford and waited for the police to arrive. The drunk, however, became unmanageable after a few minutes. "Lucinda!" he bawled, with a waiter on either arm attempting to drag him to the door. Either the man was especially powerful or the waiters especially weak since neither could prevent him from reeling an erratic path through the dining room. It was almost comic as the man swayed and staggered and nearly crashed into diners at their tables. For a moment, Ben felt the man looked directly at him, but couldn't be sure.

The manager arrived. Young and stocky, and with an unfortunate case of asymmetrical gynecomastia bulging through his shirt, he put his hands on the drunk's shoulders in an attempt to calm him. "Jerome, you have to leave now," he cautioned. "Jerome! Leave now before the police get here. Please, you're embarrassing all these people."

"I want...t'talk...t'Lucinda!" Jerome babbled.

The manager winced in the miasma of Jerome's breath as he tried to shepherd the big man to the exit. "Lucinda isn't here. We sent her home as soon as you showed up. Come on."

"Let me go, Gene!" Jerome hollered. "Lemme GO!"

The tussle grew more violent as the four men grappled in the dining room. Jerome engulfed Gene in a bear hug as the waiters clung to his waist, trying to drag him down. Women screamed, and a few diners bolted from their seats. Jerome's knees then buckled in a fit of nausea. He fell backwards and tripped over one of the waiters. Upon regaining his feet, he pitched toward Ben. With his chin in the air, a streak of chunky yellow vomit spewed from his mouth and onto Ben's dinner before all two-hundred and seventy-five pounds of him belly-flopped onto the table. Tainted slaw, Brunswick stew, and vinegar-based barbecue sauce saturated Ben's face, hair, and clothing before he clambered out of the booth and fell into the adjacent one, displacing a family of four in the process. The loud thud of Jerome's unconscious body striking the floor indicated that the regrettable incident at Conrad's Q had at last concluded.

Gene placed his hands on his hips during the confused silence which followed and shook his head. "Now, Jerome," he scolded, "why'd ya have to go and do that again?"

Chapter 15

'Desktop publishing' refers to self-publishing using computing tools that offer many layout and typographic options. All of the following were crucial to the beginning of desktop publishing in the 1980s EXCEPT FOR the

A. HP LaserJet printer.
B. Apple Macintosh computer.
C. Aldus PageMaker software.
D. Windows XP operating system. (correct)

The cardboard sign in the door of the only laundromat in Nathan's Ford read 'Out OF SERVSE.' It was scrawled in pen and barely readable. Staring through the window at the crude 2D graphics of an antique arcade game, Ben reconciled himself with the idea that he had tramped three blocks in vomit-speckled clothing for nothing. Spaceship armadas sparred in a suspenseless blaze of fireworks and destruction as the machine waited patiently for quarters.

Back at the hotel, which also lacked a functioning washing machine, Ben was reduced to scrubbing his clothes in the bathtub with shampoo, and even that couldn't fully remove the smell. He spent over an hour drying them with a hair dryer.

Ben resolved to enjoy his drive back to Richmond as soon as he fueled up and hit the empty highway the next morning. The GPS display presented an accurate digitized image of his rental car as it drove itself along, complete with trees, road signs, and other automobiles. It even captured his hand when he stretched it out the window and waved. He zoomed the GPS out, past the city, county, and region until the highway was a thin gray line, a capillary in the vast green piedmont of Southern Virginia. He imagined viewing himself from the perspective of one of the thousands of all-seeing satellites floating in the stratosphere and keeping robotic watch over the lives of millions. 'Baby Sitter Skies' is what the government once called them as part of an effort to root out domestic terror and deter criminals. 'Baby Sitter Guys' was more like it, ran the inevitable internet blowback. Ben liked the idea when it originated. He wasn't so sure anymore.

There was little traffic on I-95 North that morning, but an abrupt slow-down put his eyes intently on the road. He was still a few miles south of the Sussex County line and had been driving for almost twenty minutes. For several miles, he'd been trailing a dusty 6-wheel box truck, the kind not often seen anymore: smaller than a semi, larger than a pickup. The left rear flap was missing, and the right had so much mud caked on it that its design had become unintelligible. Printed on the sliding backdoor were the words 'FRED'S DESKTOP PUBLISHING'. Bold, italicized courier font. First letters of each word larger than the others.

It dawned on him. This was the same Fred's Desktop Publishing logo he had seen the day before. It *had* to be. Could this company still be in business? Unlikely, he thought, given the ramshackle headquarters back in Nathan's Ford. According to the internet history class he took in high school, desktop publishing died out as a viable business model years before he was born. And why would anyone use such an amateurish logo, anyway? Ben voice-searched the internet and found nothing. Billions of records meticulously searched by his car's computer, and not one could find a site containing both 'Fred's Desktop Publishing' and 'Nathan's Ford.' Broadening his search to simply 'Fred's Desktop Publishing' netted Ben one prize, an anodyne article scanned from the pages of a local newspaper about the store's opening in a different Virginia town. It was from 1994. He selected the first five characters of the site's URL. They did not blink.

The truck was turning off at Exit 27 onto County Route 421 which stretched on a bridge over I-95. Ben watched the truck go, billowing dust and dirt as it clanked along the thin, bumpy exit ramp. For several seconds, it ran parallel to Ben. He got a good look at the driver. He was East Asian. He was looking directly at Ben and then quickly looked away.

Burning with curiosity, Ben pulled over immediately. He looked to his GPS and knew he couldn't let the car drive itself anymore. Hugging his arm right arm around the passenger seat and gripping the wheel tight enough to make his knuckles ache, he overrode the car's auto-drive function and sped backwards under the bridge along the shoulder.

"You are breaking the law!" his GPS squawked in a husky female voice. "Please be advised. You are moving south along I-95 North. Please pull over and wait for assistance. You are breaking—"

Ben smacked the GPS to shut it up. He was almost there. Northbound traffic was edging away from him even though he remained well within the shoulder. The gravel kicking up into traffic earned him venomous looks and several stiff-armed honks from annoyed motorists, but that didn't slow him down. His quarry was at the top of the ramp, waiting at a red light.

As he finally turned off the highway and sped up the ramp, he noticed the light turning green and the truck turning left. There were three or four cars between them, and Ben made the turn two seconds after the light had turned red again. Cars executing their right of way bore down on their skidding front tires to let him pass. More looks. More horns. Ben saw the truck disappearing beyond a turn on 421 just past the bridge.

Hitting the turn, he hoped to find the truck but met instead with a stretch of open road. He slowed down, careful not to miss any byways obscured by the copious foliage. Two miles later he found one, Hammond Drive, to the left. He took it, figuring that this was as good a shot as any.

The road ran downhill, past a couple residential neighborhoods and what looked like an abandoned state park. The road then turned abruptly left. Ben felt a violent bump and crunch as his tires transitioned to older pavement. Drops of sunlight scattered by leaves kissed his windshield as he sped south amid the road's tall, deciduous envelope. Ben was headed back towards

Nathan's Ford. There were no adjoining roads, only an abandoned service station, an old church set far back from the road, and a handful of residences pocketed in the trees. Thin mailboxes leaning haphazardly over man-made gullies gave them away.

"So why didn't you pick this up yesterday?" Ben asked the now-dormant GPS. He knew exactly what would happen if he turned it back on: it would tell him the police and his auto insurance company have been notified of his illegal activity back on I-95, and his bank account has been dinged around $300 for the infraction. He preferred that to finding himself back in Nathan's Ford watching Officer Pendergast's chin waggle during another tedious conversation about spices and food. Ben did not want the South to rise again. He also did not know where he was going. Three or four wide turns in the fully shaded woods voided him of all sense of direction. The roads that eventually did appear on either side were paved with gravel, if they were paved at all, and offered little temptation to change course. So preoccupied he was with divining his whereabouts that the sudden appearance of the Desktop Publishing truck up ahead startled him. It was slowing down. It was turning right.

Ben sped down the hill in front of him to keep up. To his left was more impenetrable forest. To his right was an empty field of tall grass which could have been a farm years ago. A wire fence linked by weathered, wooden beams separated it from the road except in places where the beams lay supine as if overrun by a stampede of large animals.

Two bare lines of dirt, eroded through years of traffic, stretched down the gravel road where the truck had gone. With deep drops into gullies on either side, it looked dangerously thin. Ben came to a complete halt. Never had he felt more like an intruder. The dark green depth and the unreasonably steep decline that lay before him told him not to follow. He suddenly did not feel obligated to discover where this secluded thoroughfare led.

He sat there for thirty seconds.

Isaac is a big boy, he thought. I did my thing. It was an honest effort. 650 miles worth of honest effort. What more can a brother do? Ben turned onto the road and then listened to gravel scrape the underside of his car as he backed out. With dust billowing all around him, he struck a neat, noisy K-turn and headed for home.

Nearly half a mile down the road, Ben noticed a black, early century Ford Explorer up ahead. It was sluggishly hogging the middle of the road, trying his patience as it stuck scrupulously to the speed limit. Ben found it odd. Where did it come from? No one had passed from the opposite direction before he turned around. Could it have appeared from one of the unpaved side roads?

Following the truck through the twists and turns, Ben noticed a recurring disturbance in his rearview mirror. Flashing here. Flickering there. It was a car or a bus or another truck. A gang of bikers. Whatever it was, it kept getting lost in the turns. Until it didn't. Ben looked again and saw it clearly. His body reacted before he could tell it to. He gasped and shuddered. His heart rattled. His elbows pulled inward as he squeezed the wheel. It was a white box truck. *The* white box truck. But *why*? Why would it go all this way into nowhere just to turn back around again? As he reached a shady patch of road, he sought to invent a few plausible multiple-choice answers to this question when the Explorer in front of him finally decided to pick up speed. Its engine hummed through the quiet of the early morning.

This time Ben didn't ask any questions. He looked to overtake the it as soon as the road straightened out, which would be any second now. He gunned it, only to lean hard on the brake seconds later. The Explorer had executed a stunt driver swerve and stopped perpendicular to the road. Ben was lifted almost entirely out of his seat as he came to a pristine halt thanks to the friction generated by his car's airless tires. He missed the truck's driver side door by a good two feet.

Instantly he knew. It was a trap.

Athletes in motion don't think. They never have time. On the tennis court, on the basketball court, any move Ben made had been made before, countless times, when he had the time, when he had nothing but time. Athletes don't think so much as they remember. Their practiced habits embody these memories, and whoever has the more artful or diligent habits has the best chance of harnessing the whims of luck during competition and snatching the prize. But Ben was not a professional driver. In the second or two in which he had to act, he had no memories from which to draw, no practiced habits he could instinctively summon. Instead, a wide, swift hammer of anguish slammed into him. He had to bully this emotion back into its hole before he could think clearly again.

By the time he had concocted a plan, it was already too late.

There were steep gullies on either side of the road, and he backed into one, intending a sharp U-turn. The underside of his car scraped dirt, and his rear wheels could not get the traction they needed at first. As soon as they did, however, the entire electrical system of Ben's car seemed to shudder and die a silent death. Stamping desperately on the gas pedal, Ben could only feel his incapacitated vehicle inch back towards the gully under its own momentum and then halt. His wrists ached trying to turn the locked steering wheel. His personal device was dead too.

Fred's Desktop Publishing then executed the same stunt driver stop behind Ben, extinguishing all hopes of escape on foot. No billowing dust this time. No gravel crunching under wheel. Just synthetic rubber kissing asphalt. In the now quiet morning Ben could hear birds chirping and leaves rustling. Up close, he noticed the outline of an ancient personal computer beneath the Fred's Desktop Publishing logo. He hadn't noticed it before. There was no one in the front seat. From his perspective he could not see the driver.

The sight of a man in bulky black coveralls and black mask pierced his mind. The man was about seven yards away and closing fast. To get away, Ben tried to crab-walk to the passenger seat, forgetting that he was still strapped in. By the time he released the buckle and lurched backwards, the black apparition reached its gloved hand under the door handle and tried to yank it off.

Ben screamed, but two hard pulls by the apparition indicated that the door was locked, a mechanical override to whatever electromagnetic force had paralyzed his machine. More men in black crowded Ben's periphery. Ben spun around and saw one staring him squarely in the face through the passenger side window. His nose was almost touching the glass.

Only there was no nose. Ben could not make out the fabric, but the mask resembled shiny burlap and fit over his shoulders like a box. There were no holes for eyes. He banged his palms against the window, screaming, swearing, reasoning, pleading. He saw an additional apparition approaching the driver side door. This one carried a shiny cylindrical object. As soon as he pointed it at Ben's door, Ben knew what it would do. It would unlock it, forcing checkmate.

Ben stopped screaming. Searching about briefly, he put his feet in the one place he could use them, on the passenger seat. Then he squatted and leaned forward like a lineman in a three-point stance. As soon as they forced open the door, he was going to charge through it and punch and bite and claw at anything that stood in his way until they fried his nerves as well. Or blasted his skull with a bullet. He tasted his tears on his teeth and realized that he had been crying all along.

The first apparition stopped and turned away. He was much shorter and sturdier than the others. There must have been some kind of signal since the others stopped as well. The one about to break through Ben's door gestured impatiently. The men seemed to be talking to one another although Ben couldn't hear them. One stamped his foot. One shook his head in dismay. The one at Ben's door kept gesturing. Without the least warning, the apparitions darted to the front of Ben's car. They all squatted by the front bumper, and, in a synchronized clean and jerk, hoisted the vehicle's front end over their heads. They were going to push the car into the gully on the side of the road. Ben was completely powerless to stop them, and for a moment enjoyed a degenerate sense of wonder as if viewing this incredible scene from a distance. His stomach rolled as his car sank into the gully.

Ben's front wheels hung two feet in the air as his car tilted at a thirty-degree angle from its new pocket on the side of the road. He tried to stay calm as he listened to the apparitions hustle back to their vehicles, slam their doors, and speed off down the road.

Swearing and kvetching, Ben waited a minute or two before manually unlocking his doors and trying to extricate himself from his inclined automobile. To the left was a wide cotton-wood, so Ben didn't entertain any realistic hopes of opening his driver side door into anything other than a wall of brown bark. A rock or root or something gave Ben's passenger side door a crunching rebuke when he tried to open it as well. There was barely enough room to fit his leg through. Unlike his doors, his windows wouldn't open in the car's current anelectric state. He couldn't imagine how he would explain this to the rental car agency back in Richmond.

Ben was about to smash open the passenger side door with his feet when he heard a car pull up on the road. Then another. Bad luck dictated that the curve in the road and the dense foliage all around gave Ben little idea of who was approaching. Peering through the windshield over his elevated hood could only tell him so much. The cars sounded big, but not too big, like bulky American-made sedans. Ben decided that these new arrivals would either signify his salvation or his doom and resolved to sit back in the passenger seat and find out.

The stocky, black policewoman from the day before appeared from the edge of the road. Ben couldn't believe it. This time she had two beefy blonde cops behind her. "Hiya, Sport!" she called through her inscrutable, chipped-tooth grin. "Whatcha doin' out here?"

Almost as annoyed as he was relieved, Ben couldn't decide if the woman's casual exuberance was a sham. He also started re-cursing through his mind for a story that was both plausible and accurate. How could he possibly explain this to someone who hadn't seen it happen? She scrunched up her face waiting for a response and then gave up. After taking a moment to judge the terrain, she slid into the gully. "Would ya mind lowerin' your window, please?" she asked as she stepped up to Ben's car.

"I can't!" Ben explained. "Car's broken down. These guys in a truck, they—"

"Didya try to make a U-turn or somethin'?" she interrupted.

"What?"

"I said, didya try to make a U-turn or somethin'?"

Ben shook his head. "Look, I'm stuck! Can you get me out of here, please?" he asked. It was a demand born out of irritation for having to make such an obvious request in the first place.

"We sure can!" the woman announced. She leaned closer, still with the chipped-tooth smile which was growing more devilish than sweet by the second. "But whatcha doin' out here?"

Ben looked askance at the woman and began to wonder if she could ever let go of that rictus of a grin. He then felt the passenger side door give way behind him. He'd been leaning on it. One of the other officers must have forced it open it behind his back. Ben whirled towards the driver side to keep from falling backwards into the unknown. This propelled him closer to the policewoman on the driver side, and when he turned to face her, she was a lot closer than before. She wasn't smiling. Her chubby cheeks made her look like a fat fourteen-year-old boy discovering the joys of bullying.

"Third time I'll ask ya now," she said. "Whatcha doin' out here." This time it wasn't a question. A hint of a growl in her voice made her seem almost masculine.

"I'm looking for my brother," Ben said. "Pendergast knows about it."

The woman waved her hand towards the highway. "That why you drove backwards on I-95, is it?"

"I was on the shoulder."

"Still against the law. And for almost a quarter mile, too."

"It wasn't that far."

"Is that also why you ran a red light off the exit and disrupted traffic? And what about the complaints that you been followin' people? You been followin' people?"

Wholly unprepared to answer such probing questions, Ben could only stutter something about being preoccupied with a flaky GPS when the woman stopped looking at him altogether. She was looking past him to one of the policemen standing in the gully on the other side of the car.

"Would you mind stepping out of the car, sir?" he asked through the open passenger side door. "And keep your hands where we can see them." The officer's gun wasn't drawn, but the one belonging to the officer still standing on the road was. He was pointing it at the pavement but was an easy hip pivot away from drawing a bead on Ben.

Ben studied the gun for a moment and tried to imagine it was made out of paper or chocolate or anything that would render it innocuous. He swallowed hard and then stepped out of his car, completely misjudging the distance to the bottom of the gully. He turned his right ankle as soon as he set foot on the uneven ground. The joint clicked again, and he fell straight to his back, cursing to what little heavens he could see between the thick, verdant treetops.

After being cuffed and Mirandized he was led up to the road and into one of the police cars. One of the male officers kept his hand on the center of Ben's sweaty back until the moment Ben fell into the backseat. Ben had to rub his back against the hard plastic seat a few times to make the feeling go away.

Chapter 16

In the brain, the olfactory bulb is part of the limbic system. Some scientists believe this could explain why there is a strong connection between

A. sight and fear.
B. taste and pleasure.
C. hearing and balance.
D. smell and memory. (correct)

Three walls of canary yellow concrete welcomed Ben to the holding cell which would be his home for the next twenty-four hours. Because the route to the jail had consisted of back roads, he had no idea where he was. Given the meager size of Nathan's Ford, he presumed it was the same police station he had visited before. The two blonde officers who deposited him there didn't say. All they said was that he would appear before a judge the next morning and would probably be fined and sentenced to a few hours of community service before being allowed to leave. The town of Nathan's Ford would also charge him for towing his rental car and assume no responsibility for damages. After removing his handcuffs, they locked the bars and walked back towards the interior of the building.

Ben peered after them as best he could with cold metal digging into his face, but couldn't see past the narrow hall. The blue concrete floors faithfully reported sharp clacks with every step the officers took in their hard shoes. Ben could even detect a hint of an echo. As they turned left and escaped from view, he wondered if the architect had acoustics in mind when he designed the place. They could be heard opening a door to what sounded like a busy office. Phones, chatter, internet. Amid the hubbub came the sounds of Dixie Dick warbling "Look away! Look Away!" and someone cackling in a high-pitched, "HA!"

Pendergast.

Ben turned away from the bars taking nominal comfort in being able to place himself in the universe once again. He couldn't stop blinking at his new surroundings even though nothing was irritating his eyes. The cell was somewhat larger than a boxing ring and featured a long bench on one side. It smelled of laundry, vomit, and urine. He had to check for puddles before setting foot anywhere. The floor was suspiciously sticky. In the far corner, and well within view of the hall, was a large, stainless steel toilet. It had no seat or lid and was almost two-and-a-half feet off the floor, presumably to force all but the tallest of inmates to dangle their legs like children when using it.

Ben laughed imperceptibly when he noticed Jerome's rotund body snoring face down beneath it. His bowling shirt was filthy with vomit, and gravity seemed to pull it down across the better part of his back where he lay like a bloated tick extracting its meals from the floor. He was otherwise naked. Pants, underwear, and shoes were strewn against the wall behind him. He had on only one sock.

Still blinking, Ben hobbled to the bench and sat down. He wanted to see Ariya again. Such longing made him feel less warlike, less cold, and made him wish every ten seconds or so that he could fall down on a mattress with her, wrap her up in his arms, and sleep.

The bars slid open. Two tall East Asian men entered and didn't bother to close the bars behind them. The man in front was bald and wore a black, long-sleeved, buttoned shirt without a collar. His jeans appeared brand new. He was looking right at Ben. Ben stood. It seemed like the thing to do. They were swiftly closing in.

At four yards, Ben knew the men were hostile and intent on something unpleasant. At three, Ben took a step back, noticing that the man leading the charge was a broad-shouldered athlete who had him by three or four inches. At two, Ben backed away further, holding up his hands, and asking why they were bearing down on him. At one, Ben realized an altercation was inevitable and began to take fast evasive action. His right heel however sank into a patch of floor where some of the concrete had crumbled away. His sneaker then caught against a part of it that hadn't crumbled. Ben pulled it free, but not after jolting his damaged ankle and sending jabs of pain up his leg. He winced, and the attention he needed for his assailants had to be spent finding a solid space of floor on which to squarely place his foot.

He needn't have bothered. A straight right from the first man connected with Ben's jaw. It was an expert punch and it landed with full effect. Ben felt the skin on the other side of his face tremble under the force of the blow. His neck stretched and pulled as his chin snapped one way and then the other. He was in a cold, dark place. He felt his body collapse. His right foot remained planted on the ground as he toppled, bending his knee in an unnatural direction beneath his suddenly freefalling weight. Fortunately, his foot shot out from underneath, easing the strain on the knee. But it couldn't save the rest of him. Hip and shoulder struck the floor first. Then came his head. The last thing he saw before succumbing to the cold and the dark, was the Asian man standing over him with his fists clenched. It was something Ben would never remember.

***

Fire in his nose woke him and caused him to gag. Trying to escape the unbelievable stink of ammonia, he smacked the back of his head against what felt like a massive wall. Opening his eyes through a prism of tears he discovered that he didn't have hands with which to wipe them. His mouth wasn't available for screaming either. Something large was wedged inside of it, propping his mandibles apart like some uncrackable nut. Drool dripped past whatever it was onto his chin. Despite his throbbing head, Ben blinked and shook the tears from his eyes so he could at least see. Staring at him was the same bald Asian man who had knocked him out moments ago. He seemed in his mid-thirties. Handsome. Prominent chin, wide jaw. Chinese, Korean, Ben couldn't quite tell. He had heavy, heavy eyes.

"Hello," he said casually. "We have your brother. Do you understand? Just nod yes or no." His accent was American. Very American. Ben was fully awake now and aware that his hands were tied behind him. Some cruel and intricate knot pitted the backs of his hands against each other and bound both pinkies together down to the last knuckle. He sat on a small, foldable chair designed for a child. With his ankles bound to the chair's front legs, his knees pointed up like legs on a grasshopper. He was in a traffic jam of discomfort. Ten feet to his right, Jerome still snoozed on the floor.

Rather than answer, Ben made the natural decision to struggle and scream. Wrenching his shoulders, arching his back, kicking, twisting, writhing, none of it worked. The man watched patiently for a moment and then pulled on two thin cords which Ben hadn't realized were in his hands. Something closed around Ben's throat and pulled him back towards the wall. Immediately Ben knew that the arteries in his neck were being constricted. Struggling only made it worse. He couldn't shout or move. He couldn't even stamp his feet or tap his hands to signal surrender. He could breathe, he could panic, he could sleep, he could dream...

"No, no. Can't have any of that, can we, Ben?"

Ben opened his eyes. Fighting his way through a thicket of oblivion, he noticed the second Asian man leaning against the wall behind the first. Slender. Khakis. Olive drab jacket over a red T-shirt. He seemed less-than-concerned about what was going on. Whatever was constricting Ben's throat was still there but with just enough slack to keep him awake.

The first man held up two thin, waxy cords and smiled. "Peppermint dental floss," he said and then dropped the smile. "Through tiny holes in the wall behind you. Any struggle, any noise—" He pulled. Ben squirmed. He stopped pulling. Ben stopped squirming. "—and you go down. Are we clear on that? Just nod to tell me that, yes, indeed, you are clear on that."

Aware of the rivers of drool now dribbling down his shirt, Ben looked at him and didn't nod.

"Do it again till he gets it," said the other without looking. The throbbing monster in Ben's forehead seemed to resent being disturbed as Ben thrashed back and forth in protest. The dental floss stopped his thrashing, not the throbbing. Ben was getting tired of the ordeal. He was getting tired in general. Too tired to even close his eyes.

Ben saw the gray concrete floor beneath him. He looked up. There was that Asian man again, still with those calm, heavy eyes. "I'm going to ask you again, Ben," he said. "Are we clear on our relationship here?"

Ben looked at him and nodded. Once.

"Shoot, he broke easy," said the other one. "Usually they go to sleep three or four times before they give in."

The first man smiled almost playfully. Ignoring Olive Drab was what he and Ben now had in common, a new starting point for their absurdly unbalanced relationship. "Are you going to struggle again, Ben?" he asked.

Ben shook his head.

"Good. Now, listen carefully," the man went on, gesturing deliberately with the dental floss and adjusting the circumference of Ben's neck with each gesture. "Firstly, you will say *nothing* to anyone about our conversation. This never happened. Secondly, when you appear before Judge Baker tomorrow morning and he sets you free, when he proclaims you innocent of all charges because the police should not have incarcerated you for a couple of minor traffic violations, when you *walk*, Ben, you will enter an old, black Ford Explorer which will be waiting for you on Bennett Street outside the courthouse."

The man paused, seemingly to gauge Ben's lack of a reaction.

"Hey, can you hurry up?" called the other.

The first man bared a picket fence of straight white teeth. He leaned in closer. "If you don't do any of this, Ben, your brother Isaac will lose his life, and you will lose yours. Do I make myself clear?"

Ben tried to speak, to beg, to ask questions when the man put his fingers to his lips. "Shhh! Ben, please. You are wearing a ball gag. It's a gag shaped like a ball. It's designed to prevent speech. So stop trying to speak."

Ben twisted and squirmed and shook his head out of frustration, and then settled down. He had forgotten that his monster headache fed off of motion of any kind.

"So will you do as we say, Ben?" the man asked.

Ben hissed at him like an animal through a well of tears and attempted a desperate lunge. The back of his skull cracking against the wall stunned him. The floss around his neck soon made it impossible for him to think. The last thing he heard before he fuzzed out was, "I sincerely hope that you do."

***

Ben awoke feeling the cold cell floor on his back and waist. He was untied. Jerome was bending over him, somehow not toppling from the weight of his bulbous torso. Jerome had been concentrating, caught in the suspense of whether Ben would wake up at all.

The first thing Ben noticed were Jerome's eyes. Otherworldly. Reptilian. Upside down. Ben spun around and began crab-walking away until he remembered where he was and who was looking at him. He stopped screaming.

"Well, dag!" Jerome exclaimed. "Didn't think I was that ugly. You all right, boy?"

Ben darted his eyes this way and that, remembering, plotting. "How long was I out?" he asked.

Jerome stood to his full height. "Well, I 'on know. Jus' got up m'self."

"You just got up yourself? How long have you been up?"

Jerome shrugged and let his hands fall on his thighs. "Two, three minutes, I guess. Maybe five. My watch is broke." He waved his wrist revealing an old self-winding watch on a brown leather strap. He put it to his ear to make sure it was still dead.

Despite his questionable balance Ben attempted to stand. "Did you see or hear anybody come in here?"

Jerome pointed to the bars. "You mean the po-lice?"

"No," Ben said, blinking through his ruthless headache. He grimaced when his ankle reminded him of its delicate condition.

"Asian dudes. You didn't see anyone like that come in here, did you?"

"You mean they arrested a buncha them Chinese fellers now?"

"No," he said, hobbling over to the wall. "Wait. I think I can find out."

Jerome put his hands on his hips. "Find out what?"

"Holes. There's gotta be holes here, right? Or was I just dreaming?" Ben dropped to his knees and started groping the concrete. "Couldn't have been dreaming. Where are those freaking holes!"

"Boy, what's gotten inta you?" Jerome said, a frown darkening his right eye a little more than his left.

"Holes. Holes!" Ben said, gesturing vigorously. "They used holes in the walls to...you know...pull the...you know...to pull!" Ben stopped talking and gesturing when he noticed a small string of dental floss tied around the pinky on his left hand. He smelled it. Peppermint. He started to laugh and then stopped. He pushed himself upright one foot at a time. He leaned against the wall wiping his hands on his shirt.

"Feelin' better now?" Jerome asked.

Ben bit his lip and looked to the ceiling as if praying to it. He closed his eyes and squinted a few times. Jerome took a step towards his meditating cellmate. The quiet lasted ten seconds. Ben lunged for the bars in a tenderfoot sprint and started screaming about halfway there. With his good foot he jumped onto the lowest rung and grabbed two vertical bars to keep from falling. "HEY!" Ben shouted, shaking the bars like an orangutan. "Hey, Guard! Guard!" His appeals descended into obscenity as his voice deadened with effort. He stopped when he finally heard footsteps. Crisp, echoing footsteps. He looked to his right, to the door through which the two blonde guards had earlier exited. Nothing.

He looked to his left. There was another door. This was the door through which he had entered. The footsteps were coming from the other side of that door. They were getting nearer. The door opened. A lone police officer stepped through. He was East Asian, same as the other two. Ben almost gagged when he saw. Badge, gun, decals, sergeant's rank on the sleeve. He had a thick neck, and pale, pockmarked skin. His mouth seemed in a permanent scowl.

"What do you want?" he asked, barely moving his lips. It was one word, four syllables. The subtleties of language were apparently not anything he needed to be worked up over. Ben stepped off the bars, taking much more care than necessary. He walked back two paces. He shook his head a couple times like a nervous tic and then retreated another step. The officer took the bars one hand at a time, the same two bars Ben had clung. "What do you want?" he repeated. This time he made sure to enunciate each word.

Realizing his defeat, Ben trudged back to the bench and sat down. "I want nothing," he said.

Chapter 17

Private Voice Networks, or PVNs, allow users within a certain area to speak without being heard by others. PVNs do this by generating sound waves that

A. have shorter wavelengths than spoken words.
B. exhibit higher frequencies than spoken words.
C. carry enough amplitude to overcome spoken words.
D. destructively interfere with spoken words. (correct)

The bag over his head scratched like burlap and smelled like raw onions straight off the farm. Ben dreaded thinking about all the insects and bacteria currently calling it home. At least his hands were tied humanely behind his back and his feet were free. They had even strapped him in his seatbelt in the backseat as soon as they got moving on Bennett. This was before they applied the bag execution style. The two men who led him to the car were the same Asian men he had met in the holding cell the day before. He never got a good look at the driver.

They drove for less than fifteen minutes on what must have been a pre-industrial rocky trail. Ben heard the windshield being slapped and scraped numerous times by overgrown foliage. He mourned for the car's paint job. Turns were sharp. Hills were sudden, steep, and jarring. He could feel every tree root and stone the car jolted over. The road smoothed out for a minute or two before they entered a garage and parked. The electric door and a vague shift in light gave it away. He could smell the oil and grease saturating the walls.

He didn't ask any questions as he was led, almost respectfully, up a small flight of stairs and into what seemed like a kitchen. A dishwasher was running. So was a nearby dryer. His guide, probably the broad-shouldered bully with the peppermint dental floss, led him with nudges to his back and elbow, through a hall, up a flight of carpeted stairs, into a room, and onto a chair. He told him not to make a sound or else he would be shot.

Three or four men followed them inside and shut the door. They communicated wordlessly. They must have been debating something. Even with a sack over his head, Ben could feel their gestures and their movements. After a moment, he realized the men were ensconced in a private voice network which kept them from being heard by anyone but themselves. He had written a few science items on the physics behind PVNs. These guys might have technical savvy, he thought, but they seemed fairly clueless about what to do with compliant hostages.

At first Ben wondered when he would get his hands back and be allowed to see the world again. He wondered about Isaac and all this cloak and dagger business. He even allowed himself the hope of one day getting his life back and seeing Ariya again. He nearly laughed at the irony of stumbling into captivity in Hick Central, USA, while Ariya waved her expensive skirts at Islam like a red cape and remained free.

After a few minutes his primary concerns sank into his lower brain. When would he eat again? When would he be able to stretch his arms or scratch his back or rub his ankle or wipe his leaking nose? How long could he hold out away from a bathroom? He tried to get up a few times, but each time was guided back onto his chair with increasing firmness. Only when Ben began squirming did his captors get the message.

They led him down a brief hallway and into some child's bathroom where he tripped on a plastic stool and bumped into a window. Aluminum shutters crashed like thin symbols. His captors didn't untie him. They just pulled down his shorts and

forced him onto the toilet like a three-year-old and kept him
there until his business was concluded. No need to wash hands.
Back in the hall, Ben tried arching his back and squirming until
his shorts fell to a more comfortable place around his waist.
They took this for insubordination and practically carried him
back into the room. Men pressed him in his chair until they were
convinced he had no intention of getting up.

Half hours feel like days when you're hungry. Ben estimated
that he had been there for three hours, but he knew it couldn't
have been that long. Sitting there with his head down, he was
trying not to think. The men had long given up arguing. Some
had entered. Some had left. He really wasn't sure how many of
them were still there. He tried counting them by their breathing,
but the clues were too scattered and fleeting. The dryer cycle
ended, but not the dishwasher's.

Something happened. It was hard to pinpoint what between
the clinking of glasses and the air conditioning and his own muffled breathing inside that putrid sack. A door slam? Footsteps?
Shouts from outside? He held his breath and restricted all volun-
tary movement. He surmised that the men in the room with him
were doing the exact same thing.

Gurgling coughs of an infant in the adjacent room unexpect-
edly clouded the afternoon's swirl of tensions. Things somehow
got worse and better at the same time. Captors and captive first
attempted to wait it out, hoping their little witness would fall
back asleep. More gurgling and more coughing dashed that
hope irreparably. Ben wondered if the child's mother or nanny
were nearby. The men must have been wondering the same
thing since gesticulations resumed with renewed vigor. At least
three of them left the room at one time. The door to the child's
bedroom opened, and one of the men entered. Immediately, the
infant fell silent, most likely enveloped in the man's PVN.
Rhythmic squeaks from the floor revealed that he was rocking
the child in his arms.

More men entered Ben's room. More men exited. Some activity. Footsteps, gestures. Nothing unusual, Ben thought, until
someone pushed his head down and sawed through the rope
that bound his wrists together. His hands parted to his immense

relief. His elbows flapped like listless wings. There was something of a scuffle. A couple men exited in a huff slamming the door behind them.

Ben raised his arms like a reluctant surrender and then slowly lifted the hood from his head. Fully expecting to be facing the diameter of a gun barrel or a baseball bat, Ben dropped the sack and protected his head with his forearms. He squinted to get used to the light and then looked about.

There were two men in the room. East Asian, as expected. One he recognized. Bald, good-looking. Super hero chin. It was his captor from the holding cell. He was seated near the door with his arms folded upon the back of a chair. The other, Ben had never seen before. He was Asian too and younger. His white polo shirt extended past his tan shorts. He wasn't puffed up and muscular like his friend, but with lean arms like cables, Ben could tell he was no stranger to the weight room. Prominent epicanthic folds obscured his eyes and gave him a kind of glazed expression which made it seem as if he were looking around Ben instead of at him. He handed Ben a tiny earpiece. It was an invitation to their private voice network. "Hi, Ben," the man said with a sneaky grin.

Ben nearly tripped over the corner of the bed trying to get away. He recovered like a ballet dancer on one foot but then banged his elbow hard against a heavy, wooden desk and knocked over a tall floor lamp. He saved it at the last moment with his fingertips after a compulsive lunge. Righting the lamp behind him, he stood there, every muscle in his upper body flexing in panic as his eyes and ears reported irreconcilable things. It was Isaac. But it didn't *look* like Isaac. The two men smiled at Ben's clumsy athleticism.

"It's me, Ben," Isaac said, rubbing his face. "This is just a disguise."

"What?"

"We call it Fickleskin. It's a paper-thin body mask that gets absorbed by your body. It's an organic computer program."

Ben babbled incomprehensibly as he took a few steps towards his brother. "Isaac?"

"Yeah. It's me."

"Oh, my God! That looks so real!"

"It's what happens when you have computer chips the size of molecules," said the other captor. "It takes a reading of your face as its starting point and then stretches and folds and moves your skin and cartilage according to predetermined triangulation points ascertained from a selected racial template. A little remote device is all it needs."

Ben wouldn't even look at him, chafing under the familiarity of a person who so recently threatened to execute him.

"Our tech guys developed it, Ben," Isaac said. "Real cutting-edge stuff." Ben leaned closer and pored over every detail of Isaac's protean face, trying to make sure that he really was who he said he was.

"Yeah, you can look old, young, dark, light," the other captor went on. "It damages your skin's DNA like UV waves and makes it produce melanin. We have standard templates for vari-ous Asian features: Arab, Uzbek, Iranian, Chinese. We use that one a lot."

"It works fast," Isaac added. "Give it an hour and it can even make you look black."

"Actually, you could even do that in ten minutes if you don't mind a 104-degree fever and blistering pain all over your body," the other captor said. "But the UV damage the Negro templates cause is so great that your body can't entirely repair it. So, once you go black, you never go back." He enjoyed mild, guttural convulsions as a result of his little quip, which, considering the circumstances, Ben found utterly tasteless.

"Isaac, but what am I doing here?" he asked. "What is this?"

The men looked at each other and then to the floor. Isaac sighed and bit his lip. The other captor decided to respond for him. "Listen, Ben, we had no choice but to take you here."

"I wasn't talking to *you*," Ben said, not even looking at him.

The man stared at Ben, leaning towards him as if coiling for a strike. Isaac raised his hand, "I got this, Michael. It's okay."

Michael's right leg started shaking. "Really? Your brother needs to learn not to insult the people who just saved his life."

"I really wish you hadn't come, Ben," Isaac said.

"Yeah, me too," Ben said.

"I told you not to. Many times. You didn't listen."

Ben contorted a spasmodic shrug as he motioned around him. "What—what is this? What are you doing here? What are you up to?"

Isaac bit his lip again. "If I tell you, Ben..."

"I know. You'd have to kill me. Right?"

"No," Michael answered, leg still shaking. "But if you try to escape, someone will."

Isaac aimed his hand at Ben like a halfhearted karate chop. "Why did you come here?"

"I wanted to find you."

"Why?"

"Well, for one, I don't have a career anymore. Thanks to you, I was fired. Blackballed."

"What are you talking about?"

"You used my work device. That night. You visited a white supremacist brood site, didn't you?"

Michael's leg stopped shaking. He looked to Isaac. Isaac looked back and then to Ben. "They caught that?" he asked.

"Yeah. That following Monday my device wouldn't boot."

Isaac blinked three times and looked to Michael.

"Where did you go?" Michael asked Isaac. Isaac hesitated, trying to remember. Michael looked to Ben.

"Don't look at me," Ben said. "They were too busy hauling me out of the building to tell me anything."

Michael turned back to Isaac. "Was it Pelion? Vardusia?" He looked to Ben. "You're from Muncie, right?" He looked back to Isaac. "Ossa? It was Ossa, wasn't it? You visited Ossa on an external device, didn't you? Why did you go to Ossa, Isaac?"

Isaac's hands flopped to his sides as blood flooded his ruddy, artificial face. "Ossa's secure," he whispered. "Isn't it?"

"Sonofagun," Michael said as he lifted his leg over the back of the chair and then shoved it into the wall behind him. Ben was afraid he'd rip the door off its hinges as he bolted from the room.

"Everything okay?" Ben asked.

Isaac bit his lower lip. "Yeah. We'll fix it. I'm sorry, Ben."

"Forget it."

"How? I got you fired. I'm really sorry about that. I wish I could make it up to you."

"Well, you can start by telling me what you're doing here."

Isaac closed the door softly. "Why did you come here, Ben?"

"Answer my question."

"You came here for a reason, Ben. What is it?"

"Answer my question, Isaac."

Isaac smiled. "You came here to join us, didn't you?"

Ben made like he was about to lunge at Isaac and shouted, "I came here to *find* you, Isaac! Now answer my goddamn question!"

The second story hallway floor creaked and groaned under rapidly approaching storm trooper boots and tipped the brothers off that the bedroom was about to endure a paramilitary raid. Isaac had to jump to his left to not be struck by a suddenly weaponized bedroom door. Three heavily armed men crashed into the bedroom muzzles first. They seemed to know exactly where Ben was without having to sort out the scene in front of them, but they didn't seem to know what to do with him once they got him. Screaming contradictory instructions such as "Hands in the air!", "Freeze!", and "Get down!" to the hysterical squalls of the baby in the next room, they practically impaled Ben with their gun barrels and forced him onto the floor. Isaac patted the men on the back, and they lowered their weapons. As soon as Isaac ushered them out, Ben let the back of his head collide with the floor. He looked up again when he realized that Isaac was leaving with them.

"I can't spend any more time up here," Isaac said. "We're having lunch in the mess hall in about 20 minutes. Chicken. Rice. Veggies. Nothing special." He was about to close the door but then thought better of it. "I'm also gonna talk to them about never pointing a gun at you again. This is your new home, Ben. Okay?"

Ben sat up. "You didn't answer my question, Isaac," he said.

"All you need to know," Isaac said, "is that I've embraced my race."

Chapter 18

Which nineteenth-century white supremacist vigilante organization labeled itself the 'Invisible Empire' because of its
clandestine meetings and use of elaborate disguises?

A. The Red Shirts
B. The White League
C. The Knights of the White Camelia
D. The Ku Klux Klan (correct)

The first thing Ben discovered when he donned his black
helmet was that he could barely hear himself breathe. The thing
latches around both ears with suction cups. After that it's like
taking off in an airplane. No need for eye slits. The helmet ap-
proximates the density of a wedding veil. On bright days it's as
if it's not there. At night, vision descends into an exquisite black
and white. A panoramic scope gives the wearer 320 degrees of
view. The contraption also forces you to bite down on a soft sili-
cone mouthpiece in order to speak into a PVN. Lightweight and
flexible, the suit couldn't stop a bullet, but with its wide neck
and shoulders, hard blows to the head shouldn't be too much of
a problem. Blades would depend on the blade wielder and the
blade.

The same tough, bendable material composed the remainder
of the costume. Walking in it was easy; running less than graceful. Photo-crystal technology captured composite live images of
what was beneath the wearer. Wide shoulders and a flat, Frank-
enstein head broadcast these images upwards, making the
wearer invisible to aerial surveillance, even in daylight, as long
as he remained upright. Spherical invisibility could also be ob-
tained but at the cost of a rapidly drained battery. That technology however never made it out of its beta stage and remained
buggy. Wearers were warned against using it except in emer-
gencies. Pressure plastic gel on soles of boots changed from solid
to liquid and back again with every step, ensuring silent footfalls
and barely visible foot prints, even in mud and snow. The apparition emitted no heat and almost no sound, even if the wearer
should scream. Nathan's Ford had only twenty-four of these

suits, nine of which were nearly useless as daytime stealth gear due to weak batteries.

Isaac rushed Ben through these details after dinner that night. Sitting in the basement of the house in which Ben was held captive, Isaac taught his brother how to don the armor and how to use it. They practiced stealth movement, invisibility, and using the PVN.

As Isaac packed the suits back in their nondescript cases, Ben sat on one of the bunk beds and took in his new home. It was a long basement, much longer than the house above it would suggest. No air conditioning or heating vents that he could see. Rugs of all designs and shapes covered the floor, and maroon carpeting lined the walls. There were no windows, and three eighteen-inch fluorescent bulbs in the ceiling provided adequate lighting for the thirty military grade bunks directly beneath them. Ben poked his finger into the pita thin mattress above him and lifted it with ease.

"So, we basically do two things," Isaac told him. "Most people here are what we call earners. They earn money to fund the movement."

"How?" Ben asked.

"Protein modeling, mostly. We use quantum computing. Real probabilistic stuff. Devices called QTMs"

"Quantum Turing Machines?" Ben said. "I've heard about those."

"Yeah. They basically generate three-dimensional images of proteins, which we manipulate. Since we don't have neural chips, we're stuck with Manin gloves, which are still the industry standard, but don't offer the speed we would like. Imagine massaging Gordian knots as if it were a game of go. Essentially, we run algorithms to see if our modelling conforms to known behaviors of proteins, and if they do, our AI interfaces produce megabytes of hairy, inhuman code, which we provide to our clients."

Ben smiled. "This is all over my head, Isaac."

"I thought you were a big science guy."

"Yeah. High school science. Ask me about the Doppler Effect or the Mohs Hardness Scale, and I'm there."

Isaac widened his eyes over a lethargic smile. "Well, this is no different what many other tech companies do these days. It's very lucrative. We run temp agencies and farm out gamers in a variety of industries."

"Gamers? Why do you call them gamers?"

"Because it's a lot like playing video games. You need excellent spatial sense and hand-eye coordination. You also need a cold-blooded lust for logic. It's a lot of work. Guys can easily put in fifteen-hour days. That's what you'll be doing, I'm sure."

Ben found such single-minded attention from his brother exhausting. "I've never done this sort of thing before," he said.

Isaac waved his hand dismissively. "It's okay. That's how I started too. You'll learn on the job. We'll train you."

"And all the money I earn goes to your organization?"

"*Our* organization. Most of it, yes. No getting rich for you. We have tens of thousands of soldiers overseas who need weapons and materiel and food. It's the best way."

"What do you call...our organization?"

Isaac smiled wistfully and looked at nothing in particular, seeming to revert to his previous half-baked self. "Nothing. We don't have a name. The people at Wahoo had a name. We don't."

"Then how do you...what words do you use?"

Isaac shrugged. "We don't. We just don't."

"Really?"

"We're a secret organization plotting the overthrow of the United States government," Isaac said. "How better to keep it secret than not give it a name?"

"Okay. What's the second thing you guys do here?"

Isaac sealed the case and sat on the bunk opposite his brother. "Agitation raids," he said.

"What?" Ben asked, tucking in his chin.

"Agitation raids. We're agent provocateurs. We commit clandestine acts of terror against targeted segments of the enemy population. This agitates them and encourages reprisals, which further radicalizes whites and makes them easier to recruit. That's been my main focus for the past year."

"You kill people?"

"Uh-huh. But we can't be too obvious about it. That's one reason why we use apparition suits. We don't want to tip off the feds, you know? We haven't done many agitation raids, but soon they will be the primary focus of Nathan's Ford."

"Nathan's Ford? You mean the town of Nathan's Ford?"

Isaac shook his head. "We're based in Nathan's Ford. But we are not Nathan's Ford."

"That's good. Last time I checked the mayor and half the town council is black. Does anyone in town even know you exist?"

"Some do. In government. In the police. They work with us. We work with them. It's symbiotic. So I'm told. Very hush-hush. Only Michael and Eli know those things. They run the show here. They're the ones in contact with the others."

"Others?" Ben asked.

"People not directly involved in the rebellion but who help us anyway."

Ben noticed how in the fluorescent light Isaac's Asian façade resembled a cheap mask. It was too flat. The eyes were too deep. His hair was all too Caucasian, to say nothing of his teeth. Ben wondered why he never noticed this before. People must see what they expect to see when they're not looking carefully, he thought. "What do you do?" he asked.

"Me? Well, to the town of Nathan's Ford, I am Shenglin Wu, born in Shantou in the Guangdong province of mainland China. My American name is Perry. Until a couple years ago I worked for a Chinese shipping company. I now work as a quantum gamer for Bayliss Recruiting, a company which we secretly run. But I'm on vacation right now." Isaac continued with his sham autobiography, but in fluent Mandarin. The nasal intonations, inaccessible cadences, and alien vocabulary brought Ben's comprehension to a rude halt.

Ben placed his hand on the side of his face. "You guys use neural language chips too?"

Isaac smiled and demurred. "If only. We don't have the budget."

"You learn the old-fashioned way, huh?"

"Yep. Simulation software. Drill and study. An hour every

night, minimum. Can't read or write it so well, though. And they say our accent is straight out of Beijing and not the hick part of the country where Shenglin Wu is from. Fortunately, there are very few native-born Chinese here. They'd catch on to us almost immediately."

"Aren't you worried about that?"

"Eh," Isaac said, shrugging a shoulder. "There are probably less than thirty mainland Chinese in the entire county, and we know where they are. Nobody else in Nathan's Ford can tell the difference. We don't go above ground much anyway." Isaac showed Ben his digitized driver's license. Looking directly at the camera with his epicanthic eyes and empty expression, Isaac resembled a corpse.

"So how often do you wear that fickle stuff?" Ben asked.

"Most of the time. You need to disable it for a few days every couple weeks or risk permanent damage. Michael is the only one who doesn't do this."

"He wears it all the time?"

"Yeah. It's the perfect disguise. Our modern day white hood. East Asians are practically invisible in this country anyway. Keep your head down and mind your own business, and no one suspects a thing. We've had a five-to-one male-to-female ratio in this town for years, and, so far, no one's noticed."

"Is there a real Perry Wu?"

Isaac picked up the cases and took them to Ben's side of the basement. "Probably."

"Probably?"

Isaac kneeled by one of the smaller rugs and manipulated its circular designs with his index finger like a combination lock. "Well, you know the Chinese control a lot of the drug trade in Central America, right? Real mafia stuff. We work it out with them somehow."

"And Isaac Cameron? Where's he?"

The floor beneath the rug rose a couple of inches. Isaac spun it to the left and then placed the suitcases in a dry crawl space underneath. "You're looking at him," he said. "No reason why I can't be two people at once. I still make authorized calls to Aunt Jean from time to time."

"Why not me?"

"Because I was afraid you'd try to guilt me into answering all your questions and then follow me down to Nathan's Ford after I explicitly told you not to." Isaac closed the crawl space door and secured the lock. He looked at Ben. "Imagine my surprise."

"You could have tried telling me the truth."

"I didn't because I couldn't trust you to have racial consciousness. We have to be careful with libertarians like yourself. They make sense on economic policy, sure. It's good they oppose socialism. But by never addressing race, they think people are fungible. And they're not."

"Fungible? What—"

"I didn't know what the word meant either," Isaac explained as he returned to the bunk. "Basically, a dollar bill is fungible because one is as good as another. Human beings are definitely not fungible."

"I know that now," Ben whispered.

"You do?"

"Yeah. After working closely with black people and knowing how hard it is to find really competent ones, I have to say that the racists are right. Or at least they are *more* right than non-racists."

"I'm glad to hear you say that."

"You know, I was more or less fired because I was white," Ben said. "Blacks or Muslims can go to worse sites than the ones you visited and nothing happens to them." Ben laughed. "You should meet this African guy, Son. Oh, my God. I mean, he's nice. But he's stupid and he's lazy. And BTC refuses to fire him! A guy like that—"

"I don't need to meet him," Isaac interrupted. He held out is hands as if about to throttle someone. "It takes all the discipline I have not to want to kill people like that in large numbers. Sometimes I think that if I didn't study yoga and meditation, I'd be a mass murderer living in the woods."

Ben waited for Isaac to look at him but he never did. "Isaac, I see you, but I don't recognize you. And I hear you, and I still don't recognize you. Is that really you in there?"

"Oh, it's me. See?" Isaac lifted his right arm to shoulder

height and grunted trying to lift it higher. "Legacy of Dad."

"You just seem so focused now. You used to have this glazed look all the time like you were on drugs or —"

"That's just how I was in front of you and Aunt Jean," Isaac said. "It kept you from asking questions. But when I was editing Leftist websites and giving black power salutes with the Campus Panthers ten years ago, I was a different person."

Ben shook his head a half-dozen little no's. "Why did you change?"

The glazed expression seemed to return as Isaac waited a long time to respond. Ben decided to give him all time he needed. "Have you ever heard the 'Scept'red Isle' speech from Shakespeare?" Isaac asked.

Ben shook his head. "Sounds like something from one of his histories."

"*Richard the Second*," Isaac told him, clearing his throat. "It was spoken by a dying duke, mourning how a corrupt and fickle king was dooming his beloved England.

This royal throne of kings, this scept'red isle,
This earth of majesty, this seat of Mars,
This other Eden, demi-paradise,
This fortress built by Nature for herself
Against infection and the hand of war,
This happy breed of men, this little world,
This precious stone set in the silver sea,
Which serves it in the office of a wall,
Or as a moat defensive to a house,
Against the envy of less happier lands;
This blessed plot, this earth, this realm, this England,
This nurse, this teeming womb of royal kings,
Fear'd by their breed, and famous by their birth,
Renowned for their deeds as far from home,
For Christian service and true chivalry,
As is the sepulchre in stubborn Jewry
Of the world's ransom, blessed Mary's son;
This land of such dear souls, this dear dear land,
Dear for her reputation through the world,
Is now leas'd out — I die pronouncing it —

Like to a tenement or pelting farm.
England, bound in with the triumphant sea,
Whose rocky shore beats back the envious siege
Of wat'ry Neptune, is now bound in with shame,
With inky blots and rotten parchment bonds;
That England, that was wont to conquer others,
Hath made a shameful conquest of itself.
Ah, would the scandal vanish with my life,
How happy then were my ensuing death!

Ben didn't know if he was more impressed by the speech it-self, Isaac's rendition of it, or the tears that were now spilling from his brother's eyes.

"Of course, Shakespeare wasn't talking about leasing out England to the Muslims and blacks," Isaac went on. "But he was talking about preserving the English nation state from outsid-ers."

"Keeping England ethnically English, you mean?" Ben asked.

"Yeah. But now expand England to Europe and any land claimed by Europeans. We want to keep the Eurosphere Euro-pean. That is, white. And this speech is a big inspiration. The 'happy breed of men' and 'dear dear souls' in the 'blessed plot' who are 'renowned for their deeds' are losing their home by leasing it out to those from 'less happier lands'. Any of this sound familiar?"

Ben proposed and rejected two different answers before set-tling on one. "Yes. I just never liked to think about it that way before."

"Why not?"

Ben did a slow-motion shrug. "I don't have a college degree, Isaac. I never made real money till I started in testing. I loved doing it, and for the first time in my life I was successful and had something to lose. I guess I didn't want anything to threaten that."

"Well, it's being threatened, Ben," Isaac said. "Like in the speech, the Eurosphere is too strong to be conquered from with-out, so it is being conquered from within. It's achieving its own extinction."

"And I guess interbreeding with foreigners would only make it worse, right?" Ben said with a mordant grin.

"Then they wouldn't be a 'happy breed' anymore. Would they?" Isaac responded. Ben detected a whiff of a challenge in his brother's tone.

Ben lightened the mood with a laugh. "I never took you for a Shakespeare scholar, Isaac."

Isaac smiled. "I'm not," he said. "I've never even read the play all the way through. Michael just makes everyone memorize this one particular speech when they join. He must have been an English professor or something in a previous life."

"Oh, so it's dogma," Ben said. He regretting saying it almost immediately.

"No, it's 'truthma'," Isaac responded, flashing his brother a sharp, annoyed glare. "I've come to understand that white people have produced things of great beauty and brilliance over the years because we ourselves are beautiful and brilliant. It sounds conceited until you actually live in worlds created by non-whites, especially the Arabs, the Hispanics, and the blacks. You know beauty and brilliance by seeing their opposite all around you. You know there must be an absolute Good, because the worlds these people create, with all the crime and corruption and oppression and poverty, are undeniably Bad. That's essentially why I'm here."

Ben was reminded of cornfields and basketball courts and didn't disagree. "I guess it's like writing items," he said. "There can be only one true answer. Everything else is untrue."

"Yeah."

"So this was an epiphany? You just came to this realization one day?"

"It was a little more involved than that."

"Then what happened?"

Isaac rubbed his shoulder and looked to the floor, seemingly tired of the conversation. "I'll tell you some other time. It's a long story. Anyway, you should be more focused on preparing for the next training camp."

Ben wanted to hear more. He looked away, not daring to act on his disappointment. "Okay. How many days until then?"

Isaac looked at Ben patiently. "Ben, you should stop thinking in terms of days. Start thinking in terms of years. I don't even think about time anymore. There is no time. For what we do, you're either living or you're dead."

"Can you at least tell me what I can do to prepare for training?"

"You'll stay here. In this house. We have a library. You'll start your physical training. You'll study Mandarin and Arabic. We'll work on getting you a new identity."

They remained quiet for a long time.

"Are you afraid you're going to die on one of these…what did you call them?" Ben asked.

Isaac patted his pillow a few times and then rolled onto the mattress. "Agitation raids? Sure, I'm afraid," he said, cupping his hands behind his neck. "I'm even more afraid of being taken alive. But they got that covered here."

"What do you mean?"

"There's a dentist in town," Isaac said, gesturing to his left. "He injects two of your molars with this really nasty poison. Looks like cavity filling. But if you bite down a certain way, you'll release it into your system. Kills you in half a minute. Untraceable. They say it's a really painful death, though."

"What if they catch you alive?"

Isaac squinted, thinking about it. "The Feds? Well, it depends on what they caught me doing. If I'm lucky they'd kill me."

"Come on. Really?"

"Really. And if I'm not lucky, they'll send me to the Supermax. They say the Supermax in Marion, Illinois is the place. Did you know in prisons they used to segregate inmates by race?"

"Yes."

"It helped keep the peace. Because, you know, it gets kinda tribal in there. Not like it gets out here," Isaac rolled his eyes and pretended to laugh. "Anyway, about ten years ago they stopped doing that. They sent all the white prisoners to other prisons. Thieves, rapists, psychopaths, basket cases, all gone. Then they made Marion the home of the American White Nationalist Movement."

"What do you mean, home?"

"Basically, if they had reason to believe you were a White National, they would send you to Marion. You'd be the only gringo there, including the guards. Couple weeks in a place like that would break anybody. And of course they'd promise to transfer you to a better prison if you'd just, you know, play ball, with the FBI, prosecutors, whoever. They say the leads they got in Marion eventually led them to the Culpepper compound."

"Then it was just a matter of time before they got to Wahoo."

Isaac let out a deep, resentful "Yeah."

Ben fell onto his pillow. "Isaac, those folks in Wahoo got killed because they didn't surrender. There were two other compounds, remember? And when they gave up, they went to jail. But many of them are out now."

"What are you saying, Ben?"

"I'm saying that suicide may not be your only option."

Isaac closed his eyes, deciding how to respond. "Do you even know what we do here?" he challenged.

"Yeah, you said you model proteins and go on agitation raids. Agent provocateurs."

"But whom do we provoke?"

"I don't know."

"We provoke Muslims, Ben. That is our primary charge. Other bases target other segments of society, like blacks or whatnot. But with us it's far worse than you can imagine. They're not gonna forgive us that. If you're convicted of acts of violence against Muslims—"

"I know, I know. Religious sensitivity laws."

"After they get done with you in Marion, you could get deported to a Muslim country where they don't give fair shakes to their own people, let alone us. So, yeah. Kill me, please."

Ben thought for a moment. "So that thing in Akron, Ohio. That was you?"

"Not personally. But I was in on the planning."

"Tulsa. What about Tulsa?"

"Same."

"Okay, so you're like an administrator or something, right? You brainstorm, you manage, you—"

"You're forgetting something."

"What?"

"Muncie."

The metal frame in the bed above him had a three-millimeter-wide semi-sharp ridge, and Ben slammed his head into it trying to stand. He cried out and then curled up onto the mattress, whispering profanities as he rode out the pain. "That was you!" he shouted.

Isaac sat up and nearly moved himself to laugh. "I was wondering when you'd figure that out. You okay?"

"I should have known!"

"Look, Ben. Terror is the type of war the Muslims brought to the West. We're just fighting back in kind. Thank God we finally have the stomach for it. And have you noticed that the attacks on mosques have been mostly bloodless?"

"Yes."

"That was on purpose. With such a small body count, it makes it hard for others to sympathize with Muslims when they overreact. And they *always* overreact. With every Allah Akbar and church bombing and beheading we get more sympathy and more recruits."

Ben sat up to face his brother. He checked for blood on his scalp but didn't find any. "Yeah, but these measures are also getting white people killed. Isn't that against your covenant or something?"

"Well, Muslims don't care when Muslims get killed. It's war, Ben. How else are we going to win? Our membership increased by 300% nationwide after the Akron reprisals alone. Reprisals are a great way to get to the point where it is acceptable to hate the enemy, just like how we hated the Japs during World War Two. And better to do that now, before the Muslims have complete control, than after."

"But what if that bomb you left in the Muncie mosque exploded at the wrong time? Your sympathy angle would have fallen apart."

"That wasn't gonna happen."

"Why not?"

"Because I had no intention of detonating it."

"What?"

"It took me weeks to convince the guys to let me do this. I wanted to test my theory that it wouldn't matter if you killed some of them or none of them, Muslims would react the same way. And I was right. It's all psychological to them. Perceived threats make them fly off the handle just as much as real ones do."

Ben remembered those young Muslims taking sledgehammers to that church bell in Chicago. "Last time I checked it was five dead, nine injured," he said.

"Now it's ten and fourteen. Sixteen if you count the delicatessen attacks in Savannah three weeks ago. But that might have happened anyway. We don't know."

"Isaac, I can see this no kill policy is a good way to take the moral high road. But is it gonna work over the long haul?"

"Unfortunately, we'll never find out. We're drawing serious blood next time. There's a giant mosque in Bethesda, Maryland. We're gonna blow it up during a big Islamic holy day next year. We expect maximum casualties. Maybe more than a thousand."

"Oh, boy."

"Michael and Eli got the order from on high. Since I'm only Number Three here, I wasn't consulted. No one's ever done anything this big before."

"Will I be going on this raid by any chance?"

"You? No. You're just going to be an earner. I already told you."

"Then why were you teaching me how to wear an apparition suit?"

"It's part of basic training. Everyone has to know how to use one. We train in a supermarket about four miles from here. At night when they're closed. The manager is one of us. We walk there in these suits. And back. Or run. Depending."

"Why?"

"Well, it helps fulfill our physical training requirements. It's also great practice with the suits and with PVNs. But mostly because we need to be invisible. The enemy knows about us, Ben. I mean, not 'us', as in you and me sitting in Nathan's Ford right now, hopefully. But 'us' as in the rebellion. It places spies everywhere and constantly searches for us via satellite. It's gotten to the point that if a large number of whites meet regularly at odd hours anywhere in this country, the enemy will probably know about it. 'Baby sitter guys', and all that."

"And because self-driving automobiles can be tracked—"

"Not just those. Any vehicle made since the McKinney Act twenty years ago. Motorcycles, buses, airplanes, helicopters, bicycles even. They all have devices in them that allow them to be tracked via satellite. Even when they say they don't."

"I know," Ben said. "McKinney requires older cars to have tracking devices in their emissions filters. They say it's because older cars pollute the environment more. I have to pay a thousand dollars for a new filter each year to avoid paying an additional $1500 in taxes. It's just another way for big government to solidify its power."

"No. That's not it."

"That is it."

Isaac sat up and touched Ben on the arm. "You're not wrong. But you're not entirely right either."

"What do you mean?"

Isaac pointed to his chest. "They enacted that law because of us."

"What?"

"They didn't want any white supremacist types riding around in old jalopies. Because then ya can't track 'em."

Ben stared at his brother dumbfounded as he pondered the logic. "How do you know this?"

Isaac smiled. "The government isn't the only organization with spies."

Ben smiled back. "Nice."

"Yeah. That's why we have a mechanic in town. He has six or seven untraceable early century vehicles for us. He's got 'em running real good."

"Fred's Desktop publishing?"

"The box truck? Yeah."

"Then why don't you use them to get to training?"

"And have a parking lot filled with pre-McKinney vehicles in the middle of the night for weeks on end?" Isaac countered. "Why call attention to ourselves when we don't need to? Instead we follow the railroad tracks. Hoof it across a few fields and we're there. The entire route is unlit. Remember, the point is to be invisible."

"What would happen if we ever become visible though?" Ben asked. "Like here in Nathan's Ford?"

Isaac let his jaw hang slack for a moment. "Another Wichita, I guess."

"Wichita? You mean another Wahoo."

"No. I mean another Wichita."

Ben shook his head. "What happened in Wichita was over drugs, wasn't it?"

"No. The enemy targeted our Wichita base. They wiped us out."

"I heard that rumor. I investigated it on debunk.com. It's not true. The Ear Muffs were running a cocaine purification operation in those houses. They found the labs, the chemicals, the..." Ben trailed off as he watched his brother close his eyes as if falling asleep.

"Shut up, Ben. Why do you argue with me?"

Chastened, Ben couldn't even look at Isaac. "I don't understand. Why didn't you guys say anything? Why didn't it make the news?"

"Ben, we don't exist," Isaac explained, his words now laced with pique. "We're invisible. How many times do I have to tell you that? After the attack we had no choice but to scatter and regroup."

"What? They just bombed you? Can they even do that? At Wahoo there was a siege and law enforcement and due process and Miranda rights, and the whole thing was televised. How could they just—"

"Wahoo was five years ago," Isaac said, as if to keep from laughing. He then took Ben by the elbow. "Come with me."

"Where are we going?"

"I'm taking you into the tunnels," Isaac said. "After that you won't have any more questions about Wichita."

Chapter 19

Peer Gynt, the eponymous character of a play by Henrik Ibsen, claimed to have made a fortune by

A. swindling passengers on a Mississippi River steamboat using a variety of ingenious disguises.
B. buying dead serfs from landowners and then taking out a giant loan against them as collateral.
C. seducing and marrying a wealthy countess by bribing away all other suitors and, in one case, wounding one in a duel.
D. selling Negro slaves along the Trans-Atlantic Slave Trade and then establishing them in a prosperous Carolina plantation. (correct)

A Civil War calendar and an animated bikini model poster had the door hiding in plain sight. Isaac reached for its left side where the doorknob wasn't and waited. A barely audible click, and the door swung open, exposing the knob on the right side as nothing more than a decoy. By the way the door advanced so gradually, so inexorably, Ben could sense its formidable weight.

"Pretty wise, huh?" Isaac said, turning to Ben and then walking through. "And if you actually try to turn the knob, two iron bars lock into the concrete frame around it." Isaac snapped his fingers. "Like that."

Ben was less concerned with the door than with the gaping darkness beyond it. "Is there a light?" he asked, pointing to the black hole into which they were about to descend.

"Nope. Just put both hands on my shoulders and stay close behind me. We walk on the left side, not the right. And keep quiet."

Ben followed his brother and immediately felt the temperature drop. The burka-black darkness rendered his eyes obsolete and induced a swarm of little panics with every step. The soft, springy floor adjusted quietly with their weight like rubber mulch, and the place smelled like the inside of an old, well-kept automobile. Ben couldn't get a feel for the ceiling, but dead reckoned from the sound of his own breathing that the mineshaft was barely wide enough for two. He gathered that Isaac was running his left hand along a string or wire which stretched high along the wall. Ben took guilty solace thinking that if they were to approach anything unawares, his brother would be the one smacking into it first.

After a long while, Isaac turned left. He said nothing and didn't alter his pace, fully expecting Ben to keep up and not tumble. Ben adjusted. Upon reaching a steep decline, he stood as tall as he could, taking it on faith that his head wouldn't get ambushed by something hanging from the ceiling. After a half mile, Isaac started tapping the wall to his left. He found a door and placed his palm in front of it, waiting for it to recognize him. In seconds, light peeped into the tunnel as the door clicked ajar. Isaac pushed it open like a dark gray yawn and yanked a string dangling from the ceiling inside. Sixty watts of light spilled over him. Ben squinted in the meager gleam and followed him in. "Does this mean I can talk now?" he asked.

Isaac smiled at him. "Yeah."

Immediately, Ben knew he was inside an old and exceedingly large automobile. Isaac strode into the gray haze beyond the bulb and turned on three more.

"Holy cow. Recreational vehicle," Ben said, as he took in the cramped cabin around him. The couches and some of the storage space in the living area had been replaced by a dozen or so foldable deskpods which were hanging against the walls. Ben passed without comment what appeared to be at least twenty top-end machine guns, rifles, and grenade launchers all secured against neatly the walls. The remainder of the vehicle seemed almost livable. The kitchen had been left more or less alone minus the stove and counter tops. Fridge, microwave, sink, they were all there. The driver and passenger seats had been turned around to face the fun.

"I had a roommate who owned one of these," Ben said as he explored the vehicle. "We drove to Mexico in it. Had a blast. Wait. Is this whole thing underground?"

"Yep," Isaac said as he slid back past Ben.

"Why?"

"Save money," Isaac said, spinning adroitly into a deskpod.

"We got five of these buried across town. Why build sap-serv space from scratch when you can just buy it third-hand and bury it? Right?" His virtual keyboard stretched out in front of him. The machine shrouded him in blue.

"I guess if you wanted to make a quick getaway you could do a lot worse," Ben said.

"That's the idea."

"Pre-McKinney, right?"

"Yes."

"Aren't you worried about being *visually* tracked in these things?" Ben asked. "I'm sure they're not easy to hide from satellites."

"We've taken precautions for that," Isaac said.

"Roadblocks? All points bulletins? Police?"

Isaac shrugged. "It's a risk. But our experience tells us the government will not likely go there. In order for them to pursue us on the ground, they'd have to get the word out to law enforcement. And at least for now the feds want to keep this war under wraps just like we do. If it becomes known that government forces are indiscriminately slaughtering white people like they did in Wichita, they'll risk open rebellion. There are still a lot of whites in this country, many of whom are not happy."

Ben tapped the wall a few times, "Well, let's hope the government doesn't find out about these. They could bomb you just as easily down here as they could out there."

"Don't make noise," Isaac warned. "We're not far from the surface." He belligerently wiped his nose and then starting tapping text into his deskpod. Ben heard something that made him freeze like startled prey. A snore. Looking up, he noticed the partially bald head of a man sleeping in the bunk above the dashboard. Ben stepped back to his brother without breathing, pointing to the bunk. Isaac flashed a glance in that direction. "That's Ian. Total genius. Invented Fickleskin."

Ben watched Isaac type. "What are you doing?"

"Security we got's sick," Isaac said. "You actually have to type in your password."

"Old school."

"Yeah. My password is twenty-six characters. But it's not just what you enter but *how* you enter it. Here. Does this sound familiar?" Isaac cracked his knuckles and typed his twenty-six characters in a familiar, tiptoeing rhythm.

Ben smiled and hummed along. "Yeah. That's famous. 'In the Hall of the Mountain King'. By Ibsen, right?"

Isaac snorted and almost laughed. "You read too many books, Ben. It's by Edvard Grieg. Ibsen wrote the play. Grieg wrote the music."

"You mean like Gilbert and Sullivan?"

"Yeah, but with fewer dancing pirates. It's called a KSP or key stroke pattern. You have to enter it in a certain rhythm, and the easiest way to do that is by selecting a song and 'playing it' on the keyboard. I picked mine because it was the first song I learned how to play on the piano. Six eighth notes. Quarter note. Two eighth notes. Quarter note. Two eighth notes again. Quarter note again. Twelve eighth notes. Half note."

"Nice."

"If you mess up the notes you still get in, but to a dummy page that has all sorts of bogus information. Un-freaking-hackable."

Ben gave his brother a single, solemn nod. "So why did you bring me back here?"

"You were asking questions about Wichita. So here are your answers." Isaac ran holographic footage and held out his hand to him as if expecting a tip. "I was there, okay? I saw the whole thing."

Ben squinted at the footage. Night surveillance video from the side of a house. Photo-crystal, evidently, since there was no audio. Three men and a woman, hastily dressed and arguing. One could have been Isaac. One man, whom Isaac identified as Keith, was trying to locate a stealth chopper somewhere in the distance with infrared binoculars. Isaac and the other man were preparing to launch an anti-aircraft missile from the man's shoulder. The woman watched on, folding her arms in apprehension.

A rocket from high in the sky punctured the night. It exploded into the home next door before the four principals could even react. The structure melted in a ball of liquid fire, and shockwaves ripped through Isaac and his fellow conspirators. Keith, who was closest to the explosion, made a half-turn towards it and then folded in half, jackknifing into the grass. He was still clutching his binoculars. The woman was out on her feet and pitched towards the house. Her face collided brutally with the drainpipe, bending her neck back at an impossible angle. Partially shielded by the unnamed man to his right, Isaac fell to his knees in a daze. The unnamed man, still with the rocket launcher on his shoulder, spun almost 180 degrees before dropping it and collapsing on his back. One of the shutters on the house dangled by a corner, rocking in the aftermath like a pendulum.

"No way the Redneck Mafia has that kind of power," Ben said.

"No kidding," Isaac said.

"That wasn't a chopper-launched hellfire missile, Isaac."

"No kidding."

"What was the chopper even doing there?"

"Must've been a decoy to make it look like the Ear Muffs did it."

"But that rocket came from outer space. Why didn't the media say the rocket came from outer space?"

"Shh! Watch."

Three men appeared from below. Not bothering to glance at the flaming remains of the house to their right, one retrieved the rocket launcher, while another retrieved Keith, carrying his unconscious body back towards the house. Isaac was stumbling aimlessly until the third man led him gingerly back towards the house as well. Since Isaac was semi-competent and headed in the right direction anyway, the man released him and turned to rescue the woman who hadn't stirred from her grotesque contortion on the drainpipe. Before he could reach her, he stopped as if tugged by a leash. He hesitated for a second and then darted back inside.

"Why'd he leave?" Ben asked. Isaac said nothing. Four seconds later the house began to shake like a washing machine with an unbalanced load. White flashes in the distance coincided with the image beginning to disintegrate. Eventually, it bled black.

"That's what happens when you machine gun photo-crystal,"

Isaac said. "As I said before, Ben, the federal government targeted our Wichita base without warning and wiped it out. Killed over 120 of us."

"Was that other house one of ours?"

"Nope. Family of five lived there," Isaac said, turning to Ben. "They were white."

"But why did they blow up that house and not yours?"

"We occupied three houses in Wichita. Three. They destroyed five. If we occupied a house, they destroyed the houses nearby but only raided ours." Ben rolled his eyes searching for an answer. Isaac didn't wait to give him one. "They wanted to kill the witnesses so no one could see what they were gonna do."

"Which was?"

"Kill everybody they could and plant sophisticated labs in our basements to make it seem like big, bad, whitey was making crack cocaine to sell to poor inner-city blacks and Latinos. And then dress it up like some sloppy ear muff attack."

Ben held out his hand. "How could they even do that? The cops were there in less than ten minutes. That was the main argument from debunk.com."

Isaac nodded at Ben three or four times. But they were such minute nods and the light was so dim that Ben didn't notice. "Watch, Ben. This happened in our basement of the Thurman Street house, where we lived. We had photo-crystal everywhere."

A few keystrokes later Ben was watching more surveillance footage, this time of a large room. Deskpods lined up against walls, and a picnic table stretched along the middle of it. The walls were white, the carpet beige and stained. Three men in black T-shirts played a lethargic game of cards on one end of the table while two others worked on their deskpods nearby. Several high-powered rifles and other weapons were lined up against the wall next to a small pile of unidentifiable technical equipment. Jackets, hats, and bullet proof vests crowded the wall-mounted coat rack. Pizza boxes and soda cans cluttered the unused part of the table.

The men stopped playing and looked towards the door. The men at the deskpods turned as well. Someone was leaning into

the room, shouting at them, throwing his entire weight behind
every gesture. He was a big, powerfully built man whom Ben
found eerily familiar. In seconds, the room swirled with activity.
The men collapsed the deskpods, donned their armor, gathered
their weapons and equipment and withdrew. Isaac rewound the
footage and then paused and enlarged it. "Do you recognize
him?" he asked.

"The one leaning into the room?"

"Yeah."

"I do, actually. Well, no. I don't know."

"That was Michael. That's what he looks like without his
Fickleskin. This was before we even had Fickleskin."

"Was this when the house was fired upon?"

"No," Isaac said. "It's when we first learned about the chopper. It was one of those new stealth ones that make almost no
noise. We really wanted to take one out. Well, Keith did. Michael
didn't. I was stupid enough to go along with Keith. But Michael's smart. He got everyone out fast. Thanks to him most of
the Thurman house survived. That's more than we can say
about the other houses. Thurman only lost six people. And that
does *not* include the innocent bystanders those bastards murdered." The eyes of a wolf shined in Isaac's face as he shook his
head.

"Awful," Ben lamented.

"Here, let me fast-forward a bit."

Ben examined the footage. Nothing was happening. "What
are we—" He shut up when heavily armed soldiers in black
stealth gear swarmed into the room like air into a vacuum. Soon
there were more men than room, all scurrying harmoniously like
army ants. They brought large gray canisters and long blue bags
and hand trucks and dollies and boxes. Within three minutes
they had established a crude cocaine purification lab, with
stoves, flasks, tubs, vats, and other instruments. Everything was
worn, dirty, and make to look like it had been there a long time.
Men tacked handwritten papers and equations and diagrams on
the wall. Others littered the room with debris and garbage and
sprayed the air. At five minutes they began their disciplined departure in teams. By eight minutes, the room was empty.

"How did they get out?" Ben asked.

"Same way we did. Tunnels."

"How did they even know you had tunnels?"

"Mole. Must've been. We can't think of any other explanation."

"Ever find him?"

"Nope. I was absolved since I got my brains scrambled by the blast. Keith would have been absolved too, had he made it. This was Michael's first show. He singled out three likely suspects and took care of them."

Ben tried to get his brother to look him in the eye and failed. "You mean, like, executed them?" he asked.

Isaac clicked his tongue. "Not 'like' executed, Ben. Executed. Execution is not *like* anything. All right?"

Ben stopped breathing and stared.

"What? We can afford prisons?" Isaac went on. "We can afford to let the enemy in on our whereabouts just to swap POWs? Like they give a crap about any one of theirs we capture? We gotta set an example. If you're gonna sabotage the mission, you're gonna pay."

Ben could only offer a stupefied smile. "Wow," he said.

"Wow, what?" Isaac asked, testy and curt. His blue deskpod halo gave him a sinister, otherworldly gleam.

"I just have to remember not to be shocked by how you've changed."

Isaac shut down his deskpod. Blue-black bumps under his synthetic eyes betrayed his exhaustion. "I haven't changed, Ben," he said. "I've always been a racial person. I'm just rooting for a different team now." He looked away and whispered, "Our team."

Chapter 20

What did Constantinople ultimately 'get' from the Turks?

A. modern concepts of freedom, equality, and democracy

B. military protection against hordes of invaders from Asia

    C. mutually beneficial trade relationships along the Silk
       Road
    D. 'the works' (correct)

Apparitions haunt the night. It is their only home. Silent, invisible, armed and armored, they march through forests and fields. To meet. To train. To plan. Their peculiar fears and weaknesses subsumed by a new ancestral brotherhood and a commanding sense of fate. A hasty education bolsters what they already know and rewires their minds with cruel and inexorable logic. Discipline relieves them of the need to think. Their lives are no longer their own. They have no past; only present. They leave the future for others. Ambivalent to religion and ideology as well as to country and soil, they fight for just a notion, the notion that God plays favorites with His children. All men are *not* created equal. They have seen how forgetting this for almost a century has made a fool of the West. It has dragged a great people by its lapel and collar along a veritable Children's Crusade to the brink of the Third World. It has corrupted their genetic strength, diluted their public character, and confused their systematic codes of morals. Glaring across the span of a mere two or three decades is the very real threat of a nascent serieval period, as it were, darkening humanity's brightest lights in a vast miasma of poverty, oppression, and quotidian savagery.

They don't want that to happen. They remember how things used to be. They want to shore up borders that have crumbled, from the Rio Grande to the Caribbean, from Morocco to the Suez, from Asia Minor to the Holy Land. They want to re-draw that once unbreakable line between citizen and barbarian. They want to be the crack troops of revolution, the blood spilled on the beaches, the mortal tender invested in war. They want to retake their natural place at the foot of God. They want their world back, and they don't want to share. Not anymore. The best lessons are the painful lessons, and they know now the follies of racial condescension and promiscuous altruism. There is no going back. Not for them.

***

The produce section of the supermarket on Highway 473 occupied a suitably vast space. Ordinary fruit and vegetable pushcarts populated it during the day between convex glass shelves and impassive refrigerator units and huge sale signs defeating the purpose of the windows to which they were taped. Shiny, checkerboard tiles stretched to their full potential at night when the revolutionaries rolled these pushcarts into a back room. With the delicatessen on one end, and the bakery on the other, the training ground took up over a quarter of the store. Thick blankets covered the doors and windows. PVNs kept the world from listening in.

On the first day, Michael insisted that everyone sit crisscross applesauce around him on the floor for his introductory lecture. There were thirty-six recruits, including five women. Most young, no one past middle age. In his apparition pants, pressure plastic boots, and plain gray T-shirt, he towered over his audience, hands clasped behind his back. Behind him, a voice-activated holographic image supported his talk with presentation slides. His Asian face was red with excitement. Light brown fuzz was sprouting through his scalp. Behind him stood four men, dressed the same way. The recruits were dressed no differently, except that their T-shirts were white and conspicuous bandages covered the sides of their necks. Tight lips and stock-still chins all around.

"We often talk about the odds," Michael began. "For example, what are the odds that one of you here is a mole? You know, a stooge from the government who carries sabotage in his teeth like a pirate's knife." Michael clapped three times as if squashing airborne insects. "That was not a rhetorical question! Does anyone here have a clue?" Michael arched his back seemingly for no other reason than effect.

No one dared offer up a ratio. Michael looked to one of his assistants, a five-foot-three-inch bodybuilder whose square frame and immense chest made him seem like a rook on a chessboard. His legs were bowed almost like boomerangs. "This is Colonel Roland Turk," Michael said. "I'm sure he has an opinion he'd like to share."

"I'd give it sixty percent," Roland announced, his ringing

Southern drawl clearly at odds with his perfect diction. His voice was high but sharp like an electric guitar. He had short, black hair, and his ears jutted noticeably out of his skull. Innocent eyes pleaded helplessly beneath brushstroke eyebrows. "Twenty-five says we have two of them here."

"That's right," Michael said. "And how do we know?" Apparently a rhetorical question since this time he didn't try to intimidate an answer out of his students. He smiled as if holding back on a punch line. "Well, have you heard of the Four Horsemen of the Apocalypse? We have ten of them." Michael held up his hands. Ten fingers. "These men, and only these men, control the revolution. One of them is assigned to us, and he comes from time to time with directives, information, intelligence. And we give him recruits and information and intelligence. From what he says, the enemy can reach us even here. They know of us, and they can reach us."

Michael took a few steps and looked to the ceiling. "If one of you is a spy, we'll figure it out," he said. "We have five weeks to get to know you exceedingly well. In one of our underground RVs, we have about a half-petabyte of data, profusely indexed, containing practically every article, book, magazine, pamphlet, video, hologram and photograph published in the last fifty years. We have engines combing through all of that right now to see if each and every one of you is who you say you are. Like almost everything we have around here, the technology is about ten years old. So it should take a week. If that turns up empty, we have brood sites containing your encrypted data, ready for download. This way other bases can take a stab at you. In case there was anything we missed."

Michael stood still. The students didn't dare look at him, or each other. "And if we do catch you..." He bit his lower lip. "Nothing personal, but we will have to make an example out of you."

"If I may, General," Roland said. He stepped among the students, all of whom made way for him even though there was no need for it. His arms were too muscular to fully extend and hung like anchor chains from a ship. His right fist clenched and unclenched as he spoke. "It is *very* personal. If you're a spy, we will torture you, we will mutilate you. *I* will mutilate you. This won't be any pussy water-boarding bullshit where we're just trying to get information out of you. No. It will be torture for torture's sake, and it will only end in death. After a day or four of agony that will make Christ on the freaking cross seem like an all-expense paid sabbatical in some Amsterdam alligator fuckhouse with a couple of cum-drunk, nympho skanklets taking turns sliding up and down your dripping wet dick like a merry-go-round, everyone will know not to. Fuck. With. Us."

Roland hadn't raised his voice, but, for the prehistoric awe he inspired in the supermarket that night, he might as well have screamed until the pencil thick veins on his neck burst in a spray of gore. He seemed perfectly relaxed but gave the impression that the transition between relaxed and its polar opposite would be like flipping a switch and not nearly as reversible.

Michael let that sink in before resuming control. "Traitors don't just exist here," he said. "They're everywhere. Like cockroaches under floorboards, you can find them but you may have to destroy your house in order to root them out. And just like there are some blacks who truly appreciate whites and have allied with us in our struggle, there is an entire class of educated and influential Caucasians who prefer blacks. Or, really, any race that isn't their own. They are what you call oikophobic — the antithesis of xenophobic. Instead of abhorring what's strange, they abhor the familiar, which is, in this case, anything associated with Western civilization. They see the white race as the ipso facto villain of the world and would consider it poetic justice if all whites — including themselves — were to be go extinct." Michael shrugged and smiled. "I don't get it either. It's insane. It's suicide. These people may have good intentions. They may not. Either way, they are traitors to their race and need killing."

"The white skin on your face is a target," Roland said. "Or, as we like to call it, a badge of honor. Don't ever forget that!" He pointed his finger at the crowd, indicating that what he had just said was more threat than direction. He then smirked and returned to the other instructors.

Michael cleared his throat and continued. "This is war. The time for first and last things. The enemy knows about us, of

course. But do they know where we are, who we are? They may.
They may know right now and are waiting for the right time to
strike. Maybe tonight they're going to cut a wide, bloody swath
through the rebellion and wipe out five or six bases at once."
Michael waved his arm to demonstrate what a swath is.

"For them, small changes are affordable. We can hijack this,
blow up that. And they'll recover. But for us, small changes have
big effects. 122 soldiers were lost in Wichita. That night we lost
not just around a half-of-a-percent of our fighting strength, but
ten, fifteen percent of our security. People read the writing on
the wall and decide to desert or turn coat, or pass on joining us
to begin with. So we — that is, you and you and you and I — don't
have the luxury of living. Our futures dangle over our head like
a Damoclean sword.

"So I'll bet some of you have done the math by now," he
went on. "122 multiplied by two, that's 244. Round up to 245.
That's one percent, making our entire fighting force to be rough-
ly 24,500 men. How can you expect such an anemic fighting
force take on the U.S. army, navy, air force, marines, national
guard, police, various paramilitary government agencies, and
the FBI? That's 700,000 men. Give or take, not to mention the billions of dollars of weapons and materiel and infrastructure and
intelligence they have. So how are we going to beat them?"

The silence eased a cackle out of Roland. "I think they're hoping that that's another one of your rhetorical questions there,
General."

"It was. Don't worry," Michael said. Then he bowed his head
and shot up two fingers as high as they would go. "We have two
things going for us. One, a significant proportion of our people
are on the inside. That's part of our plan. Train young white men
and women. And then have them enlist. In five weeks, when
your training is complete, about twenty of you will be selected
to do just that. And you'll be in good company. I'm sure by now
we have thousands of agents undercover. While the armed forces give special preferences to blacks and Muslims and Latinos,
there's also something ancient about the armed forces. They can
judge a man's worth. And our advantage over all the others is
that we have good men."

The compliment and Michael's ensuing smile caused a lot of easy breathing. A few recruits fidgeted. An older man straightened his leg and leaned forward to touch his toes. One woman cracked her neck. A young recruit held up his hand and, before being recognized, asked, "Excuse me, sir. Where's the bathroom?"

"In your fucking pants, Dickwit!" barked Roland. He marched straight to the unfortunate recruit and punctured his personal space with his head. The recruit had to lean almost to the floor to avoid a collision. "Speak out of turn again and I'll elbow a crater in your face and rip your goddamn head off!" Roland threatened. "You read me?" The recruit knew better than to answer. Roland stared him down for about ten seconds and then left him with a contemptuous little shove.

"You'll get a break in three-and-a-half hours when we're done," Michael told the recruits after Roland returned to his post. "In the future I suggest you take care of your needs before you start training. Clear?" This elicited sheepish nods from the recruits and another smirk from Roland.

"Long story short," Michael went on, "when the time comes to draw swords, we'll have enough people on the inside as well as in our foreign bases to make it abundantly difficult for the enemy. And the second thing we have going for us? We don't have to beat the enemy. We just need to gain control of a few of their nukes. Then we'd have a heck of a chance."

Michael smiled as he watched the crowd shudder and then pivoted to his associates behind him. The tallest one stepped up to meet him. The others joined the huddle and bounced out. Michael and his tall associate then turned to the crowd. This new person had an edge on Michael by at least two inches. Michael clapped him on the shoulder. "And now I'd like to introduce General Eli Humphrey who will go over some more technical aspects of our organization."

Eli took a half-step backwards before stepping in front of Michael to address the recruits. The only one of the officers who sported a full head of hair, he had the allure of a shy college student. Glasses. Uneven facial hair. Chubby cheeks just asking to be pinched. He was at least 275 pounds with ungainly yet powerful legs pressing together at the thighs. Wide hips and a soft, round belly gave teddy bear charisma to this disaster of an athlete which even a bulky chest, clearly the product of many hours in the weight room, could not offset. Dimples in his cheeks turned to creases as he briefly beamed. "Good morning," he began. "I am the medical doctor who oversaw the surgeries in which BREMAT chips were inserted into your necks. I hope the surgeries went smoothly for you.

"BREMAT stands for Bio-REceptive Monitoring And Tracing, and, as General Archer pointed out, the technology is hardly new. Yet we've tweaked it. The device transmits an encrypted electromagnetic frequency to a receiver here in Nathan's Ford. It contains among other information your UID, which is a long alphanumeric sequence that uniquely identifies you in our system. You will be required to memorize yours and those of everyone assigned to work with you. Once it is assigned to a wearer's UID, the BREMAT device cannot be implanted in anyone else. If it is removed, it will kill the wearer by cardiac arrest and then self-destruct. It will also kill the wearer if he moves out of safe-range, which is twenty miles out of Nathan's Ford in any direction."

Sharp, muffled cries and groans were a keen reminder of how green these recruits were. Two women tried to sniff away tears rather than be seen wiping them.

"Obviously, this is the most humane way to discourage escape and betrayal," Eli went on. "But we also wish to prevent potential spies from telegraphing their location to their masters in Washington. Now, while we forbid personal devices and have various means to prevent you from establishing unauthorized contact with the outside, we don't have the technology to scan your entire bodies and declare you clean of all tracking devices. The enemy is clever and can hide them well. But the BREMAT chip will jam whatever devices you do have.

"If you are cleared to leave Nathan's Ford, Michael or I will change the security level of your BREMAT. Once beyond the twenty-mile radius, your BREMAT chip will no longer receive the constant updates from our central computing machines. This means that if you are a mole and you do have an implanted tracking device, a signal could escape. This is why we are so strict in vetting you and why we almost never allow people out of safe-range.

"If that does happen, however, your BREMAT can contact us only through sleep transmissions. These are a series of seemingly random characters that only your device can emit. It's basically an SOS with your fingerprint on it. They're sent over commercial networks that anyone can hack into, so they divulge no sensitive information.

"Any questions so far?" Eli asked. He scanned the group for anything that might propel him along a tangent. He cleared his throat and continued. "Originally we inserted the chips in the ankle like the old house arrest monitors. It worked well until one enterprising young recruit decided to inject his leg with a Novocain-cocaine solution and amputate his own foot. His plan was to escape to Washington by public bus. Fortunately for us, he fell into shock before he could complete the amputation. The tracking device we found later in his ribcage was perfectly operable. Clearly we are being guided by the hand of God in our endeavors to serve Him."

Eli cleared his throat again. "It gives me no joy to share with you this next piece of information. The BREMAT device, we think, may emit low-level ionizing radiation. Alpha particles, to be precise. These are known carcinogens. Just trace amounts, but enough to run the risk of cancer...in the long run. Essentially, the modifications we made to the device may or may not cause the source casing to degrade over time. The revolution is too new for us to have real data yet. We're just going on what we already know about devices like the BREMAT. So far nobody has experienced any adverse effects, and with the Lord's guidance nobody will."

"Sir, will you let us know if that ever happens?" asked a recruit. Male. Solid. Athletic. Not the same person who had inquired earlier about the bathroom. Nor did he seem terribly afraid of Roland, who flashed a sociopath's smile and marched towards him like a juggernaut's lower half. Eli shot an angry look at Roland and smacked him in the chest with the back of his arm, halting him. Completely ignoring Eli, Roland kept his eyes

on the brave recruit who had both hands on the floor and was
ready to spring to his feet if necessary. A crooked nose and cauli-
flower terrain around his ears indicated that he could take care
of himself just fine. By pulling Roland back by the elbow, Michael made sure he didn't have to.

"We will keep our eyes on the matter, I promise," Eli said. He
took a couple aimless steps towards the recruits and then continued. "Okay. Before I hand the floor back to General Archer,
who will formally begin our training, I want to mention that after your training is complete, there will be a battery of tests. The
men who pass them and gain approval from General Archer and
myself will receive another implant, this one in the forearm. This
will serve as your digital Swiss Army knife. We call it the DSAK.
It's a modified personal device which can communicate only
with devices here at headquarters. It includes a range of tools
and a PVN as well as an important stun feature, which will require an additional week of training. Only those going out-
country on missions or raids will have their DSAKs enabled. Unlike with the BREMAT, we cannot enable DSAKs remotely. It
must be done directly either by General Archer or myself.

"When not enabled, the DSAK serves only as a digital identification card and passport, exactly like the forearm devices they
implant in immigrants from China, South Zion, Israel, and other
nations with whom the United States is technically at war. This
device will hold your new identity.

"Finally, I want to say thank you for joining. With every new
wave of recruits, I'm just amazed and overwhelmed with grati-
tude for the sacrifice you all are making. We can't pay you what
you are worth, and we can't promise you anything other than
our undying loyalty and friendship. So, thank you. I also am
heartened by the presence of so many women in this class.
Thank you. Thank you." He walked up to each one of them and
delivered personal, protracted thank-yous, clasping their hands
like distant relatives at a funeral. Like the men, the women were
all young, in their twenties or thirties. Two were tall and athleti-
cally overweight. The others slender, pretty, unimposing.

Eli held out his arms and issued deep like a preacher addressing a vast crowd without a microphone. "And please remember

that our noble Lord, high above all, watches closely and guides us in our crusade to restore His covenant with Man. Our enemy has transgressed the will of God and is bent on remaking Man in Man's image. A twisted, hideous thing that turns its back on eternal providence!" He raised a finger and continued. "The Negro people, the sons of Ham! The people over whom this unpleasantness is being waged! Suffer dearly in the atheistic abyss of the modern world! Freedom to them is poison! Over eight out of ten of them are born out of wedlock. Seven out of ten are born into poverty. They are responsible for over sixty percent of our murders, forty percent of our rapes, and almost one hundred percent of our gang rapes. Drug abuse, prostitution, and abortions are rampant among their lower classes. White collar crime and corruption among their upper classes. When left to their own devices these people become so obnoxious that others must abandon entire cities to them, which only exacerbates their troubles. So let me ask you, are they better off now than before when they were slaves? When the only strife they needed to contend with was in their shoulders and backs after a day of honest labor?

"I say no," Eli whispered, wiping his forehead with a handkerchief. "I say that without the guidance and benevolence of the divine races, these people are doomed to dissolution and misery. This much is manifest. For almost two centuries, we have violated the dictates of God by making racial concessions to the enemy. And as with all concessions, more concessions followed, and more and more until our ranks have become so broken and diluted...that...I don't even want to say it.

"But I have faith!" Eli went on, voice cracking in the drama. "With hard work and the grace of God, we will survive this! We *will* pass this test! We *will* reestablish the natural hierarchy of Man which is ordained by God and bequeathed to us in Holy Scripture." He raised his fist and let it fall down hard. "We *will* smash the sinners! We *will* achieve victory! And we *will* avert the waters of divine judgment so another Great Flood shall *never* threaten the shores of our beloved land!"

The silence that followed was a reverent 'Amen' to Eli's portentous sermon. Solemn nods from the recruits spoke like a chorus of hallelujahs. No one could doubt the power Eli wielded over these young soldiers who were risking their lives to cheat fate of their ancestors' historic blunder. That is, until a muffled snort shattered the atmosphere like a fart. It was Roland. He was laughing.

Chapter 21

A traditional Chinese greeting, 你吃饭了吗 (Nǐ chīfàn le ma), translated into English means 'Have you eaten yet?' What historical event caused this greeting to become prominent in China?

A. The Boxer Rebellion of 1900
B. The Opium War from 1839 to 1842
C. The Tiananmen Square protests of 1989
D. The Great Chinese Famine from 1958 to 1961 in which widespread drought and Chairman Mao Zedong's collectivizing the Chinese economy resulted in between 20 million and 45 million Chinese starving to death (correct)

The hair on Stillwell Cameron's head dangled on either side of his mottled scalp as he pummeled his son on the kitchen floor. His nose was long and thin, his small mouth open just enough to be the receptacle for the sweat dripping down his face. Ben noted the serenity in his father's expression. Stillwell held Isaac's right arm at an unnatural angle behind his back and leaned into him, driving the boy's shoulder into the floor like a pike. Moaning and gurgling, Isaac tried to squirm away. He was long past the point of pleading with his father, long past the point of screaming. He looked at his brother through a prism of tears.

Ben leaped to his aid, but his father merely shoved him off with his free hand and then clocked him in the jaw with his fist. Ben's legs gave way, and gravity did the rest. Fortunately, his head smacked against the refrigerator and slid down, never striking the floor. He couldn't see so well through the blurring motions. But he heard the arm snap. The final blow to the head. The silence. The sirens.

It had started over Isaac's refusal to eat a certain kind of breakfast cereal or something. Stillwell had gotten off the floor as soon as the police arrived. He waved and smiled as they questioned him and cuffed him. The only words they could get out of him were, "A man must stand." He wouldn't even look at his children as the paramedics tended to them or when the police led him away.

"A man must stand."

Ben woke with a shudder and a start, experiencing a strange slowness of breathing. It felt as if something were constricting his chest. His mouth was dry. His hands were shaking. He tried to swallow. He knew what was happening. High decibel pulses of subsonic sound had been blasting through the basement of 310 Garrett Street in Nathan's Ford, his new home and office. They stretched and clawed at his insides, interfered with his breathing, and put him on the edge of a cliff emotionally. Since almost no one can sleep under such circumstance, the revolution leaders decided these sounds would make great wake up alarms, not least because they would keep unsuspecting neighbors from hearing dozens of men mobilizing for the apocalypse every day at five o'clock in the morning.

Ben was confused by the dream. He had had it so many times and so many different ways since reuniting with his brother, he could no longer recall what was fact and what was fiction. Did he really attack his father like that? Did his father really say that to the police? Was it really all about breakfast cereal?

He threw off the fog of sleep with his covers and put his bare feet on the floor. Eighteen other men did the same. Breakfast wasn't for another two hours. He slipped on the same T-shirt and shorts he'd worn the day before and took three steps to his 'desk', which was about fifteen square feet of space along a set of connected plastic picnic tables. Waiting for him was a QTM and a virtual notepad. It was another day.

Ben wasn't fully on board with the revolution until he discovered that he was a pretty good quantum gamer. It was an odd realization, one that he had struggled with for months. Where most men in his class had been placed inside as moles or sent abroad to train as soldiers, Ben was kept in Nathan's Ford as an earner. No doubt, Isaac had a say in that. Nathan's Ford was home to forty-two quantum gamers and engineers, all with Chinese names. Initially Ben had been nursing dark feelings for Isaac and the others for shanghaiing him into this revolution. Now that he was living it, however, and commanding a salary significantly larger than what he'd been drawing at BTC, the Sun began to shine on his disposition. Michael's racialist thought experiments no longer seemed like pretentious exercises in logic. Isaac's persecution anxiety no longer seemed so paranoid. Roland's gruesome threats no longer seemed so threatening. And Eli's sermons about a segregationist God who burns crosses in the name of Christ seemed less and less loony. All because Ben had found a home in the vast and intricate probabilistic mansions of quantum proteins.

Is this how all true believers are? Do all saints and heroes require such positive reinforcement from their chosen profession? And if so, then are they really being heroic? Or does it just seem that way to those who aren't heroes? Maybe Joan of Arc really just enjoyed riding horses?

Ben leaned back from his QTM and stretched his arms. He had been hunched over it for so long his left shoulder tingled. He was contracting for a Swiss pharmaceutical company called Invorne and had been disassembling a cytochrome C protein for the past several days as if it were a mahjong tile structure. His boss expected the job to take two weeks, but after cannibalizing code from colleagues, Ben had gotten it done in a week-and-a-half. It was 11:35, twenty-five minutes till lunch. Like a soldier taking a smoke in a trench, he decided to make those twenty-five minutes his own.

Ben awoke when someone called his name. It was his boss, Major Martinetti. All the gamers were standing at attention, which could only mean one thing: the presence of a superior officer. Ben bolted upright. He didn't dare look to see who the officer was.

"At ease, gentlemen," Eli said. "Go ahead and take your lunch ten minutes early. Be back at one as usual. One-thirty if you're playing basketball. I've been hearing good things about your work here. Keep it up." The men murmured a few jovial profanities while they shut down and headed for the mess hall. Those playing basketball jogged up the stairs. As Ben was about to follow, Eli stopped him. "Lieutenant Cameron! I'd like to talk to you if you have a moment."

"Yes, sir," Ben responded. At that moment he realized that Eli was the only one in the room not in his Fickleskin.

Eli looked towards Martinetti, a well-built, balding man in his late thirties who hadn't yet left with the others. He had a rugged hook nose and wrinkles in his forehead like paper folds. So Mediterranean were his features that Fickleskin could do no better than make him resemble a descendent of Marco Polo who had stayed behind in the East. "That okay with you, Major?" Eli asked. "I hope you can spare him for your basketball game today."

"Sir. The lieutenant here plays basketball like he has a vagina," Martinetti announced through a thin, ironic smirk. "But the Bennett crowd has five vaginas. I think we'll manage without him."

"Outstanding," Eli said. "But Bennett put in fourteen more hours than Garrett last pay period. Not bad for a bunch of vaginas, right?"

"That will be corrected next pay period, sir."

"Excellent, Major. That is all."

Martinetti saluted and then hustled up the stairs. Ben watched him go, hoping to catch another smirk. Martinetti didn't oblige, but shot him a wink for his efforts. Ben looked hopefully at Eli. "Actually, sir, I was looking forward to talk to you."

"Why's that?" Eli asked. A thin roll of fat protruded beneath his chin as he looked down at Ben.

"I think that we can gain more efficiency in using the medical data tabulation repository. We're repeating our efforts with some of the supplementary databanks."

"Hmm. Major Martinetti has told me pretty much the same thing. Did you go to him with your suggestion before coming to me?"

"No, sir."

"Well, follow protocol from now on. Understood, Lieutenant?" he said, clapping Ben on his still tingling shoulder. "But I like the initiative."

"Thank you, sir."

"Let's go upstairs," Eli said. "We'll take lunch on the porch and talk."

Against the flat, banal sky, the intricate shadows of the porch and the assorted stuff residing there made it seem as if they were still inside. Wind chimes and potted plants and hippie art hung from the ceiling along with a decrepit porch swing. Poorly stacked boxes, sporting equipment, and gardening tools caked in clay loitered on the warped wooden floor and rendered the porch unlivable except for the part that Eli and Ben occupied: an empty corner with a glass table and two wooden chairs.

Ben winced as he took bites from his sandwich.

"How's Fickleskin working for you?" Eli asked.

"Well, my face isn't too sore anymore," Ben replied. "Still hurts to eat."

"I can see that. Are you using the compress we gave you?"

"Every night. You know, for a week it looked like bad plastic surgery," Ben said, tenderly rubbing his epicanthic eyes. "But now it's beginning to come together. It looks much more real than I thought it would."

"That's good."

"Yeah, I just wish I were less hairy," Ben said, holding up a sleek, hairless arm. "I've never seen a Chinese person with such hairy arms. I've been using hair remover to get them like this."

"Why? You're an earner. You're not going out-country any time soon."

"In case you ever need me, I could be ready."

Eli sucked down about a third of his glass of iced tea. He wiped his mouth and spoke to Ben in flawless Mandarin. "Ni chifàn le ma, Hu Zhenglong?"

Ben smiled and held up his sandwich. "Chi le. I have eaten. Thanks."

"And how are your language lessons going? Are you making progress?"

Ben struggled through his answers, consciously modulating the correct pitch for each word. As excruciating as his pronunciation was, Ben knew that if he tried to correct it, he most likely would not be understood. Eli asked a few follow-up questions and finished his tea, declining to offer critical assessment of Zhenglong Hu as a native Mandarin speaker. Ben took another bite of his sandwich and enjoyed the breeze blowing through the ripe, musty porch while he waited for Eli to bring up the real reason why he wanted to lunch with him. In the park across the street, the basketball game against the rival address on Bennett had already begun.

Ben noticed his replacement, what seemed like a black guy, with a blue bandana tied around his head. He'd never seen him before, which wasn't surprising given the widespread use of Fickleskin in Nathan's Ford. But wasn't 'going black' frowned upon since 'going back' was nearly impossible? Only people infiltrating the military or the FBI even considered doing that. If it wasn't real, then it certainly was an effective disguise, Ben gathered. The finger-thick lips, the flattened nose, the dark chocolate skin. The dude had some skills too, but not enough to make much of a difference in the game. He was just soft and having a little too much fun out there.

"Who's the coon?" Ben asked.

Eli turned to him sharply and permitted himself a bemused smile. "He is not a coon. He is Curtis Book. He's an ally and a big help around here."

"That's not Fickleskin?"

"No, it is not."

"Wow," Ben said. "Is he stupid, sir? Does he have any idea what we're doing here?" He looked at Eli, hoping for some familiar response, a cozy shrug, an easy smile, something. Instead, he got nothing. An unfamiliar sense of guilt began to wither Ben's insides.

"Don't be smug, Ben," Eli warned. "And don't take your cue from guys like Roland. I don't tolerate that." He twisted his finger near his temple. "Roland has an asshole switch in his head, and sometimes he forgets to turn it off. He doesn't realize that these people are God's people too. Many of them are not stupid. And many, like Curtis, are on our side. Is that understood?"

Ben could tell he was blushing from the infinitesimal pinpricks he was feeling in his cheeks. "Yes. I'm sorry, sir," he whispered, looking away in embarrassment.

Eli placed a meaty paw on Ben's shoulder and gave him an avuncular little shake. "We've all been there," he said. "Hey, did you hear about the earthquake in Memphis a few days ago?"

"Some of the guys were talking about it last night. They said it was pretty bad. Caused a blackout."

Eli released a weary laugh. "Reports are saying that hundreds are dead, many more injured, and thousands homeless. It's probably worse than that, knowing how corrupt the media is. They say it's turning into a war zone, and it's only been three days. Three days! Breaks my heart. Memphis is, like, eighty to eighty-five percent black. These people are too childish and primitive to be able to deal with something as devastating as an earthquake. And here they're suffering and dying all because they don't trust us anymore. They think they can do better. Is this better?" He stared at Ben for a moment. "I'm asking you, Lieutenant, is this better?"

"No. Of course not."

"This is not God's plan for them," Eli whispered, shaking his head. "It can't be…"

Ben said nothing for fear of letting slip another gaffe. Eli stifled a burp and wiped his lips as he stretched his long, fat legs. "Well, Lieutenant, first I'd like to say you're doing a fine job for someone who hasn't gamed before. It's been eight months, has it?"

"Closer to ten, I think."

"Right. And how much do you make?"

"Almost 250, sir."

"Not bad. For ten months' experience in rural Virginia. No, that's not bad."

"Thank you, sir."

"We got another recruitment class coming in soon. Twice as big as yours. The average income here is $350,000. With this new class I'm looking to add over a million to our net by next year."

"That would be great."

"Now, I'm hoping you wouldn't mind a slight change, Lieutenant. You see, Major Martinetti will be taking on an important new role soon, and we need someone to replace him."

"You're promoting me?"

Eli laughed. "No. Martinetti will be going out-country on an important mission in a couple months, and we need someone to take his place full time while he trains for it."

"Okay. What do you need me to do?"

"Well, as you know, we need to camouflage money transfers to certain businesses we run in China and Hong Kong and other places. Gambling businesses, mostly. We have to figure out ways we can reliably lose large sums of money and not be detected. That money funds our armies overseas where $10 million can go a lot farther than it does here."

"Right. I blew several hundred on roulette last night."

"But no one's told you *how* this money gets transferred, correct?"

Ben shook his head.

"Praise God," Eli said, throwing up his hands in a lazy hosanna. "We're doing it through brood sites. Saves a lot of money. They're just dangerous. The government is always on the lookout for patterns, suspicious activity, whatnot. We can't take the chance they'll notice forty-two people from the same town in southern Virginia losing thousands every month on virtual Texas hold 'em. These sap-servs are run by a country that's technically at war with the United States. If the feds notice that, they might investigate."

"Got it."

"So you'll do it?"

"Yes, sir," Ben said. "Oh, my boss at Invorne told me that after I finish this one cytochrome C protein, she wants me to validate a couple more. What do I tell her?"

"Don't tell her anything."

"No. I know...not to tell her about...us," Ben stammered. "I'm talking about my contract with Invorne."

Eli was unmoved. "What about it?"

"We'll have to put someone else on it, won't we? To give me time for this new task."

Eli shook his head.

Ben's expression began to melt. "What? You said this new

thing was full time. I'm already working ten-hour days."

"Then you'll have to learn to game faster or manage your time better," Eli said. "For example, this morning I saw you sound asleep at your desk. You could have spent that time gaming."

Ben looked away, trying to hide his escalated breathing. "Yes, sir."

"We can't afford to lose your income, Ben."

"Yes, sir."

With nothing else to talk about, the two observed the ongoing Bennett-Garrett basketball duel taking place across the street. Michael was leading Bennett like a platoon with organized plays and timely personnel changes and lots of diaphragm-rattling grunts. Garrett lacked the discipline and the stamina to keep up. They may have had more individual talent, but by the latter half of the game, they were relying too much on their outside shooting and were too exhausted to put up more than just token defense.

"Hello," said someone at the foot of the porch steps. It was Isaac. Gray shorts and sneakers, V-neck T-shirt with sunglasses secured at the bottom of the V. He needed a haircut and a shave. An uneven suntan marred the Fickleskin on his face.

"Look who's back!" Eli said.

"Hey, Isaac!" Ben called.

Isaac climbed the steps and shook hands with Eli, completely ignoring his brother. "Did you see my research?" he asked.

"Got done about an hour ago."

"That was over 10,000 words," Isaac said, giving him a playful glare. "You must have been up all night."

"Well, the Lord gave me strength. That, and two Surplex pills."

"Two?" Isaac responded. "You have a death wish? I'm going on ninety-six hours vertical, and I've only had one."

"Well, some of us need our beauty sleep more than others, it seems."

"Why have you been up for ninety-six hours, Isaac?" Ben asked.

Isaac took two sidelong glances at his brother and said,

"Please don't speak until spoken to, Lieutenant." In the shadowy flatness of the porch, Ben noticed Isaac's slack expression and how painfully red his eyes were. "There's a gray 2006 Toyota Corolla parked down the street," Isaac said, still looking at Eli. "Get into it please. I'll join you shortly."

Ben took a moment to gather that Isaac was talking to him, and then did as he was told without a word.

As he climbed into the passenger seat and shut the door behind him, Ben noticed that the car smelled as old as it looked. It was as if the dust in the air hadn't been disturbed in decades. Ben was careful not to make any noise, not that it mattered. The seat had been set for someone much shorter than he, and there were no switches or controls that he could find. He held his breath as he reached underneath for the handle and breathed again as he slid the seat back. Of course, without a key, he couldn't lower a window or turn on the air conditioning. He was afraid to open the door since Isaac hadn't explicitly given him permission to do even that. He was growing intensely aware of the heat with sweat now dripping down his forehead, collecting on his upper lip, and drenching his back against the vinyl upholstery. With his DSAK disabled, he was completely isolated.

After several minutes of twentieth-century tedium Ben looked down to the car floor. Exposed by the recently retracted seat was a pamphlet which proudly displayed a wind-rustled American flag. A strange pattern on the flag however put a split-second twist in his windpipe. He reached for the pamphlet. It was what he had feared. The graphic artist had replaced the fifty white stars in the flag's canton with fifty stylized stars and crescents, the unmistakable symbol of Islam. It was subtle, and the crescent moons were more slivers than anything. But they were there. The flag flew before a golden backdrop of small town America inside a green frame bedecked with interlocking geometric shapes. A young American couple knelt side-by-side on Persian-style prayer rugs — the woman, blue-eyed and fair in her stylish, flowing hijab, and the man, strong, earnest, and impossibly blonde. They were looking to Heaven as if channeling some of its bliss down to Earth. Front and center, the pamphlet read, 'Take Part in the Islamic American Future!' At the bottom, in smaller print, it read, 'Visit the Islamic Center of Bethesda for a consultation today.'

Chapter 22

Sleep deprivation was a major cause of which of the following disasters?

  A. the 1989 Exxon Valdez oil spill
  B. the 1986 space shuttle Challenger disaster
  C. the 1979 nuclear accident at Three Mile Island
  D. All of the above (correct)

The front door clicked open. It was Isaac. Ben didn't know how long he had been watching him or if he had been watching at all. Isaac noticed the pamphlet as soon as he fell into his seat. "You're not supposed to see that," he said. "Where did you find it?"

"On the floor," Ben said.

Isaac reached across for the pamphlet and snatched it. "Don't know how I missed this when I destroyed the others," he muttered. He opened the driver side door and set the pamphlet on fire with his DSAK. He watched with keen interest until the last square millimeter turned to ash. He stirred the detritus with his foot.

When Isaac fell back into his seat and strapped in, Ben asked, "Why can't I look at a pamphlet you leave on the floor of your car?"

Isaac looked at him intently, seemingly with some effort. He was so gaunt that his chin cast a dark shadow on his neck. "Because I said so?"

"Oh, *there's* a good reason."

"Watch what you say to me," Isaac warned. "I'm a colonel. You don't talk to me that way. Even when we're alone. Understand?"

Ben gave him a chastened little nod. "I'm just beginning to feel a bit like a slave here. Eli just doubled my workload without even—"

"I don't want to hear it!" Isaac snapped, shaking his head.

"Keep your whiny bullshit to yourself!"

Ben looked away. "Yes, sir."

Isaac started the old machine, its reluctant engine churning a few times before starting. With both hands on the wheel, he executed an adept three-point turn and headed off at a moderate speed. "I'm sorry," he said. "But you keep breaking protocol. You keep saying my name in public. I don't care if there's a PVN. And you gotta stop asking questions!"

"I know. I'm sorry," Ben said. He held his hand over his brother's thigh for a second and patted it once.

"I'm going out-country again tomorrow," Isaac said, softening. "Thought I'd see you for a little bit before I crash."

"I appreciate it."

"There's also somebody I'd like you to meet. It's kind of important."

"Yeah? Who?"

Isaac's only answer was a coy smile. No amount of needling from Ben could get him to reveal anything until they reached their destination.

The daycare was almost two miles west past the center of town on 473. A nondescript, one-story structure, it shared a block with a Baptist church and boasted a colorful, fenced-in playground, some well-manicured shrubbery, and as many windows as a medium-sized airliner. The Sunny Day Daycare was constructed out of the same brown brick as the church, which suggested that it had once been an appendage of it, such as a school or dormitory. It truly was the edge of town since beyond it, the road stretched down a small hill, crossed a river, and folded into a picturesque pocket of trees.

The parking lot was full, so Isaac parked thirty yards away by the church. This was the first time Ben had been out in public with his Fickleskin. He was obsessively mindful that he'd see someone he'd recognize: Pendergast, that meddlesome female police officer, that horrid drunk Jerome. He couldn't help but look at people and wonder if they could see through him. A young, overweight mother who had just exited the daycare and two Mexican migrant workers sitting on the back of a pickup truck didn't bother. In fact, they all looked away from his Sinosimulated face the moment he sought them out. Ben's lips snuck into a smile as he followed Isaac inside. Invisible empire indeed.

Once inside, Ben paused to take in the three-dimensional jungle scenery on the wall. Antelope, elephants, gazelles, hyenas, lions, and zebras all proudly presented their first letters and invited parents and children alike to partake in a tactile safari of felt ears, trunks, tails, and manes. With the bright Sun and flowing streams and tall, lush grass, it was a beautiful day on the Serengeti. Ben took in the slim, attractive figure of a teacher as she was leading her class out of her room. He was reminded of how he hadn't seen a woman up close since basic training—and how he still missed Ariya, despite the oath they made him take. No sexual relations with non-whites, no exceptions. Ben had taken the oath willingly enough. But did that oath apply to Ariya?

He turned to see Isaac fumbling through a conversation in fake broken English with the brunette behind the desk. No security, no bullet proof glass, no photo crystal. Nothing but smiles. She peeked into the office behind her and then invited Isaac and Ben to enter.

Behind the desk sat an oblong woman with sharp, angular features and stylish hair of varying lengths and colors. Ben noticed her wide hips and flat chest the moment she stood up to greet them. Her tan blouse was confidently unbuttoned almost halfway down her chest, and her eyes glared happily at her two guests. Her worldly snarl of a smile suggested an uncomfortably recent trailer park pedigree. "Perry?" she said. "That you?"

Isaac enabled his PVN and shut the door. "How've you been, Sharon?"

They gave each other a slightly more than cordial hug. Sharon pulled away to look at him. "Aw, man! Haven't seen you in your skin in a long time. Look at you! Fortune cookie dude!"

"Good to see you."

"Good to see you, too. Where've you been, anyways?"

"Just got back from out-country."

"Ain't for me to know. Cool. How you doing?"

"Oh, the usual," Isaac said. "Could probably fall into a coma as soon as I get horizontal. How are you?"

Sharon waved her hand and scoffed. "Don't worry about me. I got it easy. Dealing with rug rats from eight to six and gambling online all night. Who's your friend?"

"This is Zhenglong. He's new here. Just made lieutenant."

"Well, congrats, dude!" she exclaimed, foregoing a handshake for a head-to-toe appraisal. "I don't even remember what I am. What am I? A specialist, right?"

Isaac smiled. "I have no idea."

Sharon ran her fingers through her hair as if that would help her think. "I think I'm like a specialist five or six. I ain't even know they had those!"

"Yeah. Eli dreams up all these rankings," Isaac said.

Sharon raised one eyebrow. "Think he'll ever dream up an officer ranking for one of us girls?" Isaac laughed and demurred. Sharon turned to Ben. "You see, our boss doesn't like women much, or haven't you noticed?"

Ben stammered through a noncommittal reply and smiled.

"It's not that Eli doesn't like women," Isaac said. "He just likes them a little too much. He says that women would encourage 'sinful thinking' if placed alongside men in the tunnels."

"That sounds like something he would say," Sharon said.

"Was he talking about himself or about men in general?" Ben asked.

Isaac mustered enough cynicism for a smile. "Does it matter?"

"What was your name again?" Sharon asked, turning to Ben. "You're new, right? Did they tell you that they only implant DSAKs into men? Women in the revolution can't access the same data y'all do or have the same tools and weapons."

Isaac nodded. "Well, yes. But the fact remains that men in the revolution outnumber women almost seven-to-one. So..."

Sharon rolled her eyes. "Would you say that to a woman who's putting her life on the line for the revolution right now?"

"I would," Isaac yawned. "Anyway, Specialist Craig, I came here to see Melissa for a few minutes. And then get my six hours. So..."

Sharon lifted her hand and flopped it back down again. "Go. You know what room she's in. You don't need to come in here to see her."

Isaac turned to leave. Ben followed with a little wave which Sharon did not return. "Isaac?" she said.

Isaac turned back to her in the doorway, startled to hear his name. Fortunately, he hadn't yet disabled their PVN.

"Just want you to know that I love doing this," she said. "Who'd a thought I'd be good with kids, right? But here I am. I'd do anything for these children, I swear."

"That's great," Isaac said.

"Please tell Michael he did the right thing by putting me here."

Isaac nodded and turned to leave. Ben followed him back into the hall. "What was that all about?" he asked as they passed the last animals on the flatland. "Who's Melissa?"

Isaac ignored him and stopped before a window to one of the classrooms. Two teachers, young, heavyset white women, were folding mats and placing them in bins beneath the cubbies. Children were keeping busy in their primary color playground: puzzles, blocks, dolls, toys. All but two were white.

"Right there," Isaac said, pointing to a little blonde girl in a yellow flower sweat suit who was assembling a shapeless structure with oversized Legos. She still had creases on her face from when she'd been sleeping. Isaac looked at Ben with a semblance of pride and said, "My daughter."

"Wow! How old is she?"

"Just turned three."

Ben smiled. "Congratulations."

Isaac smiled back, and the two shared an awkward ten seconds of nods, averted looks, and shifting postures. "Her mother's dead," Isaac said, touching the glass and looking intently through it.

"What?"

"She was killed. And you don't have to ask too many questions because you saw it happen."

Ben had to keep from shuddering as he remembered the photo crystal footage of the Wichita attacks. The rocket streaking through the street and annihilating a home in an orange ball of power. The revolutionaries caught off-guard. The woman knocked off her feet by the shockwaves, bending her neck at a preposterous angle against a drainpipe. "Oh, my God," Ben whispered. "She was your wife?"

Isaac didn't stop looking through the glass. "Sure," he said. The two stood together, watching children play for another minute. Isaac sighed and took his hand off the glass. "All right. Let's go."

Ben pointed to the room. "Don't you want to see her?"

"She wouldn't recognize me," he said, walking to the door. "I never visit her in my skin. Come on."

Ben hesitated, then followed his brother. The heat from outside shocked the taut skin on his face. He felt sweat amassing in his pores almost immediately. "Wait a second," he said. "Does she even live with you? Where does she stay?"

Isaac stopped, as if about to respond, but then kept walking. "Not here," was all he said until they reached the car. Once they climbed in, Isaac took a long, sober look at his brother. "I brought you here so you will be able to recognize Melissa and know who she is. In case anything happens to me, you will be responsible for her."

"Understood."

"I may not come back from one of these agitation raids. Especially the one that we have coming up. I just want you to know where the daycare is in case you ever need to..."

Ben put his hand on Isaac's shoulder. "Does she even live with you?"

Isaac shook his head. "She was a newborn when Wichita happened. After that we couldn't take any chances. We have certain houses around town dedicated to raising all of our children. Her official address is 401 Hazel, but I know she stays somewhere else. I don't know where. I only see her from time to time at the daycare. She knows me. She just doesn't know I'm her dad."

"Really?"

Isaac looked annoyed. "Yeah. Suppose the feds want to get to us through our kids? Remember, conservatives are subhuman to these people. We have no rights they feel obligated to respect. This is why we run this daycare, to protect our kids. We also have a private grammar school in the back. Just about everyone working there works for us."

"How many kids do we have?"

"Maybe twenty-four in both."

"That's a lot to take with you in an emergency."

"Well, we have tunnels and an RV out here in case they need to make a getaway. Notice how the daycare is at the western edge of town. Away from all the action. Away from us."

"So they would survive another Wichita even if we don't."

"Hopefully."

"But with all the white employees, how do you get past diversity audits?"

"We have allies claiming they work there, on paper anyway."

"Allies like Curtis Book?"

"Maybe. Interesting cat, Curtis," Isaac said. "Eli just adores him. You should meet him. Plays a wicked game of basketball."

"I'll see about that," Ben said. "But what about the black children? Are they allies too?"

"What black children?"

"I counted two in Melissa's room, and at least one more walking in a line with the others."

"What can I say? It's a business. We can't arouse suspicions by turning down the public. Not all those kids in there are ours, even the white ones."

"But what would happen if there were another Wichita? What then?"

Isaac strapped himself in. "Let's hope Sharon has some contingency plans for that," he said. It was more of a mutter, and he was looking at the daycare when he said it.

Ben was about to strap himself in when the call came, so he didn't notice the sudden change in Isaac. He knew something was up when his brother abruptly pulled him from his PVN and started communicating through his DSAK. Ben couldn't hear a thing, but knew something had gone dreadfully wrong. Isaac punched the steering wheel and hunched forward. From his gentle convulsions, Ben had the feeling that Isaac was crying. He didn't want to lean over to see the emotional torment in his brother's artificial face. Only, he did. He had never seen his brother cry as an adult. A stoic hippie, Isaac Cameron had a mind as durable as the soles of his dirty feet. If he could endure repeated pummeling from his father with his characteristic non-chalant optimism, then what couldn't he endure? Isaac punched the steering once more then leaned back in his seat blinking and shaking his head in a futile attempt to drain out the tears.

Ben tapped him on his shoulder. "What's wrong?"

Isaac expanded his PVN. "I just want to sleep. That's all. Just sleep."

"What happened?"

"Turk sent out a sleep transmission."

"Who?"

"Roland! That man-eating asshole. He's in trouble again," Isaac said, nostrils dilating in laid back rage. "In Memphis this time."

"Memphis, Tennessee?"

"Yes!"

"They just had an earthquake there a few days ago."

"Yeah. My orders are to bring you back to Garrett and then head out there and drag him out of whatever trouble he's gotten himself into."

"You have any idea what happened?"

"Yeah. Strap in. We gotta go."

"Don't they know you haven't slept in ninety-six hours?"

"They don't care."

"What?"

A sigh rattled in Isaac's windpipe. "Look. I still have three Surplex pills. I'll be fine!"

"Those things are dangerous, Isaac! You overdose on them and—"

"I can handle it! I've done this before."

"What about weapons?"

"I have the standard issue."

"Do you have an apparition suit at least?"

"Yes, but the battery's dead. Apparition suits wouldn't be very useful on a mission like this anyway."

"Why not?"

"Because I don't have time to answer any more of your stupid questions!" Isaac snapped. "That's why!"

"Isaac, you're clearly in no shape to do this. Why are they sending you when you've been up for ninety-six hours?"

Isaac let his head fall onto the steering wheel with a dull thud. "Because I am the only officer who can get through to Roland, maniac that he is. He doesn't respect Michael and Eli. He *hates* Martinetti. Marek and Ted are out-country, I don't even know where. Ivan is most likely dead. And none of the guys in Turk's crew are trained to go out-country yet."

"Isaac, this sucks."

Isaac inserted the key in the ignition. "Gotta stop calling me that," he said. "Now strap in."

Ben put his hand on his brother's shoulder. "No."

"What do you mean, no?"

"No means no."

"That's an order."

Ben smiled. "No, it ain't. Because I'm driving you to Memphis."

Isaac gave him a slovenly sneer. "Oh, don't be a goddamn hero."

"Hero this," Ben said as he snatched the key from the ignition and stepped out of the car before Isaac could react. He took long, quick strides around the front of the car.

Isaac met him by the driver side door. "Get back in the car!" he whispered, spit flying. "You don't know what—"

"I'm driving," Ben said.

"You're in over your head. This is the shit! You don't have the experience or the credentials—"

"Then this will be a good way to get them."

"They won't let you."

"Yes, they will."

"No, they won't! You go eighteen miles down that road, you'll suffer a heart attack!"

"Not if you tell Eli to disable my BREMAT device."

"He's not going to do that!"

"He will if you tell him. Look at you, Isaac. You're dead on your feet. You're in no shape to go back out-country."

"Your orders are to go back to Garrett Street, Lieutenant."

"I don't care. I'm driving."

"This is insubordination!"

"Uh-huh."

"We can execute you for this!"

"But you won't."

"Give me the key, Ben!"

"No," Ben said, holding it high, above his brother's reach. "And stop calling me by my first name." Isaac leaped for the key, but Ben pulled it away, giving his kid brother the kid brother treatment. He found it easy to sidestep his exhausted brother like a matador.

"I can stun you!" Isaac threatened.

"In public?" Ben shot back. "How often do you see two Chinese guys stunning each other over car keys in a parking lot?"

Isaac stopped. There were four Mexicans now sitting on that pickup truck. Two young mothers with strollers were hurrying into the daycare to avoid seeing more of their altercation. Isaac's DSAK caused him to turn. It was headquarters contacting him again. He secreted himself in his PVN and took a step away from the car to communicate.

Ben slipped past him to the driver side door and hopped in. Isaac was just too tired to respond in time. He tried to lodge his arm in the door, but Ben shoved it aside. He closed the door, locked it, and opened the passenger side door. "Get in!" he commanded.

Isaac glared at him through the window, but Ben only glared back. "Get in!" he repeated. "I'm not gonna lose you! Not again!"

Isaac responded, but Ben couldn't hear since he hadn't been put back in his PVN. "They can hear me!" Ben shouted through the window, pointing to the small crowd now observing them. "Do you really want them to hear me?"

Isaac glanced at the crowd and bit down in frustration before hurrying to the passenger side and hopping into the car. He didn't bother letting Ben back in his PVN as Ben sped west along the two-lane state highway. The ancient engine wasn't suited for fast rides and so churned and whined in protest. Isaac was talking frantically as they approached the twenty-mile safe-

range mark, wherever that was. Ben expected to die at any moment. He knew heart attacks were unbearably painful. He knew
because he saw his father Stillwell suffer and die from one years
ago. He also knew he was going to live. Isaac would not let him
die. Isaac would not let him die.

Twenty miles past the daycare, and he was still alive. He
looked fondly over to the passenger seat where his brother lay in
a deep and well-deserved sleep.

Part 4: Memphis

Chapter 23

According to his interview with *Look Magazine* in 1956, J.
W. Milan murdered Emmett Till because Till

A. spoke fresh to Milan's sister in-law.
B. wolf whistled at Milan's sister in-law.
C. put his arm around Milan's sister in-law.
D. bragged about having sexual relations with numer-
   ous white women. (correct)

A city without a skyline is a hulking thing. Like a graveyard
for an ancient race of giants, its indistinguishable black mono-
liths sit in Neolithic ruin. Not obscured by a forgotten forest or
laying atop an inaccessible ridge, the city is front and center, in
the way, impossible to ignore. I-40 slices through it like a knife
through rotting fruit. It forces travelers to contemplate the pre-
electric dread of fairy tales and fantasy novels but without
torches or lanterns or horse hooves clopping on cobblestones to
suggest that the city still breathes and churns with life.

Three days before, Memphis, Tennessee had been hit with a
7.8 magnitude earthquake in the New Madrid Seismic Zone
which all the experts had seen coming. The black mayor and the
all-black city council had chosen not to act, and doubled down
in the days leading up to the event by neglecting to have a plan
in place to minimize damage and casualties. Then the predictable happened. The quake damaged or demolished over 300
buildings in the southwestern part of town, from South Mem-

phis to Midtown. It was worse than the one in 1895. Nearly two hundred people were killed on the first night, with hundreds more injured. Despite being in a historically active seismic area, most of the buildings had not been designed to withstand earthquakes, and most of the citizenry lacked any inkling of how to prepare. Almost as critically, the quake struck the recently-reopened fossil fuel power plant to the city's southwest. Aside from severe structural damage throughout the century-old facility, the tremors caused several corroded turbine bearings inside the generators to fail. The subsequent fires coupled with damage from the tremors themselves and a shorted-out transmission line made the plant inoperable and severed it from the grid.

Being the city's main source of power, the plant had supplied electricity for thousands of homes and businesses. Other power plants on the grid, from Arkansas and Missouri all the way to Nashville, now had to spin up to handle the massive increase in bandwidth. They couldn't do it. They were already operating at their maximum capacity. With the state of Tennessee over $100 billion in debt, three plants had closed down in the past decade. The extra load bumped the remaining ones off the grid. The tremors began late in the afternoon on a Saturday and didn't let up until close to midnight. So without any warning, nearly the entire city of Memphis plunged into primordial night.

The mayor declared a state of emergency, but it was clearly past the powers of his government to do much more. It had had difficulty keeping streets lit and police paid under normal conditions. Over half of the MPD had been on strike anyway over pension promises that the nearly bankrupt government could not keep. Now, police were almost non-existent except as a full-time guard for the mayor and his cabinet. Many police officers either stayed home to protect their families or took part in the chaos on the streets. The local media had long suspected that the mayor and police department, enmeshed in Mafioso-style corruption, were merely going through the motions of fighting crime. They often recruited from the black and Latino gang populations and would rather bargain with thugs and would-be warlords than actively oppose them. Now that they were forced to break kayfabe and perform out of necessity, the incompetence of the city government quickly floated to the top of the bowl.

Within hours of the blackout, armed gangs took control of the neighborhoods most devastated by the earthquake. Mayhem ensued there and elsewhere. The economic life of the city, such as it was, had been halted and was replaced by something very close to a state of nature. Within two days nearly all whites and Asians had fled. Businesses were either boarded up or abandoned altogether. At least three hospitals had to be evacuated, mostly by school bus since almost two-thirds of the city's ambulances were not functional. An additional couple hundred people died in the chaotic transition. Automobiles were broken into and then flipped or set on fire. Windows everywhere were shattered. Public transportation was non-existent. Supermarkets and grocery stores were raided down to the last shelf. Thieves and looters as young as eight boosted whatever clothing, jewelry, or electronic equipment they could find. They also harassed the populace and served as scouts for the local strongmen who were now preparing to rumble for recently-opened turf. Arsonists lit the night and provided Pulitzer opportunities for photographers, journalists, and documentary filmmakers foolish enough to chronicle such a disaster firsthand.

So chaotic was the city that rescue workers and volunteers refused to enter all but the safest neighborhoods, which were in the northern and eastern parts of the city. Trained technicians also could not be coaxed into entering dangerous neighborhoods to repair the transmission line, a crucial element in getting the city back on the grid. Despite being smeared as racists by the national media, they quite reasonably did not trust the Memphis police and promised to act only if the National Guard could guarantee their safety. That would take another two days, they were told, since the National Guard itself suffered from similar dysfunction, mismanagement, and debt. Law-abiding citizens tried to assemble neighborhood watches in the meantime, but with strict gun-control laws, there was little they could do to curb the turmoil. Anyone not up to no good learned to stay indoors or leave town.

When civilizations convulse in their death throes, they bleed refugees. Nearly 45,000 of them managed to escape Memphis and sorely test the capacity of its suburbs. Ben and Isaac witnessed it twenty miles east of the city after ten hours on the road. It was late at night, and they saw cars streaming out of the city and none entering it. Straining hard in the darkness they could see people escaping on foot as well. They consulted the internet to discover how this earthquake and its historic aftermath was rapidly deteriorating a once-great city into a palsied ruin.

Helicopters hovered in the black sky and burned frenetic inscriptions into the city with brilliant shafts of light. All exits off of I-40 were blocked. State troopers in reflective vests and riot gear stood by barricades of traffic drums, flashing lights, and muscle trucks. When Ben put on his blinker and slowed before one of these exits to evaluate the likelihood of entering the city, an officer marched up to them waving a glowing nightstick. Ben considered speaking with him but was dissuaded by the man's panicked glare. Ben sped away before the officer could smack his car with his stick.

"Christ, they're not letting anybody in," Isaac said, placing both feet onto the dashboard.

"How the hell are we gonna get Roland?" Ben asked.

"I don't know. According to Eli his sleep transmission is still active."

"Do you know where he is? Or how far away?"

Isaac pointed to his window while scrutinizing his DSAK. "Roland is five point two miles that way. Northwest. He's at a Motel Twelve. Third floor, it seems. Pauline and Eastmoreland. Close to midtown. According to this, it's a rough area."

"How rough?"

"Ninety-nine point six percent black. Actually, there's a travel advisory for Asian-Americans, Native-Americans, Muslim-Americans, Hispanic-Americans, and whites warning against passing through that neighborhood."

"Really?"

"Yeah."

"I love how everyone is considered to be a such-and-such American except for whites."

Isaac smiled. "Apparently, we are beneath the dignity of a hyphen."

"I bet aid organizations are gonna take their time going over there."

"That's good for us. Aid organizations could ascertain Roland's identity. The Red Cross has already established a presence in a couple less violent areas. It says they're gonna get started soon in the old hospital less than a mile from Roland. Maybe by tomorrow."

"That doesn't give us much time."

"I know," Isaac said. "And the crime rate in Roland's location is double the Memphis rate which is already almost five times the national average. A person has a one in sixteen chance of being a victim in that neighborhood according to these stats."

"I'll bet the chances get higher at night after an earthquake."

"And when you're Chinese."

Ben laughed. "Somehow I don't think there are too many Chinese people sticking around in Memphis to test that theory."

"All right, what's going on now?" Isaac asked, dropping his feet and sitting up. The traffic up ahead had started to bottleneck, with all cars braking to a standstill. It wasn't sudden, but Ben still had to skid on the asphalt to avoid rear-ending the vehicle in front of him.

Just like that they were stopped.

Being at a standstill longer than three minutes taxed the Corolla's Freon-depleted air conditioning until it became no better than a noisy fan. The air thickened and expanded into a kind of humid soup that seemingly sucked moisture out of the body. After twenty motionless minutes, Ben cut off the engine. "So, this is all caused by one truck?" he asked.

"According to this, it's two," Isaac said, pointing to his forearm. "It seems a truck was negotiating a turn near a damaged road and just toppled over perpendicular to traffic."

"Oh, no."

"Then a second couldn't stop in time and plowed into it. This all happened half an hour ago."

"I take it no one was hurt."

"No. But they're predicting they won't clear up the road till morning."

"What? No!" Ben shouted, gripping the wheel.

"That's what they're saying."

"How can they leave thousands of motorists stranded like that?"

"Because three days ago there was an earthquake," Isaac said. "And all you have in charge of Memphis are corrupt and ignorant blacks."

"What about the state of Tennessee? What about the national guard?"

"Ben, thousands of refugees are coming out of Memphis. There's a real humanitarian crisis going on, or haven't you noticed?"

"Still, moving an overturned truck twenty yards—"

"*Two* overturned trucks."

"Whatever! I can't imagine it's that hard."

"When you're in the kind of hock we are in, it is hard, Ben."

"Fine. But we can't just sit here till morning. What about Roland?"

"He'll have to wait until we think of something."

"I thought this was an emergency."

"It is."

Ben let go an incredulous laugh. "Then why aren't we treating this like an emergency?"

"We are. We just don't have many options right now," Isaac reasoned.

"Yes, we do."

"Like what?"

"Like turning this car around and getting off the highway."

"We can't do that."

"Yes, we can!" Ben said, punching the steering wheel.

"How?"

"Just a few miles back I saw where we could cross the median. We could just get on the shoulder and back out of this and then turn around and find another way into the city."

Isaac snatched Ben's hand and yanked it off the wheel. "We will *not* do that!" he ordered. "You hear those helicopters? We commit a traffic violation, and they're gonna see it. We cannot afford to have state troopers pulling us over and asking questions and wondering why we're traveling with apparition suits and firearms and medical kits and survival gear and all that. It's bad enough we're driving a pre-McKinney vehicle. That's enough to arouse suspicions in some places. So we are not going anywhere!"

Ben sneered through the windshield and said nothing.

"Is that clear, Lieutenant?"

"Yeah."

"Good. And the next time you say 'yeah' to me instead of 'yes, sir' I will include it your report and you will suffer the consequences when we get back. Do I make myself clear?"

Ben waited a beat longer than he needed to before responding. "Yes. Sir."

After an uncomfortable ten minutes, jackhammer knocks on the driver side window shattered the silence. Ben felt his heart skip a beat and then pound frantically as if to make up for the lapse. He looked left to face his latest tormentor.

It was a woman, short, white, and plump. Garish tattoos crept down her breasts and into her skimpy blouse like alien life forms. Ben could see she was not terribly pretty. Gaps between her teeth. A collection of eyebrow rings over her right eye. Prominent nose vaguely shaped like an avocado. She was panicked almost to the point of inaction. Her face was dribbling with tears. A tall mulatto boy with wide eyes and trembling lips held her hand. His afro was blonde.

She knocked again, and Ben lowered the window halfway.

"Please! Are you doctors? Are y'all doctors?" she cried through a trashy Tennessee drawl. "We three or fo' cars ahead! Mah boyfr'n! He a tahp two diabetic! He's havin' a fit!"

Ben remembered his training and responded in his best Mandarin, knowing that this hysterical, simple-minded thing couldn't possibly understand him. He cordially introduced himself, told her his hometown in China, and explained that he worked in Virginia for Bayliss Recruiting.

"Please! You got anythin' sweet? Candy! Juice!" she pleaded. "Yer the third car I ask! We run outta medicine. Please!"

Ben stopped talking. He knew there was still juice in Isaac's cooler. Looking through the windshield, he saw a small crowd pulling a large, convulsing black man out of a beat up, blue

Chevy. His shirttails flapped over his khaki shorts, and a pana-ma hat fell off his head in the confusion. It looked bad. His jerks became violent, and one of his swings struck the woman who was the main support under his shoulders. She was knocked off-balance, and the man crashed to the pavement, head bouncing off of it twice. The woman had to be rescued from his uninhibit-ed flailing.

The girlfriend gasped and then looked at Ben. It was a final plea for help. How could anyone withhold assistance before a scene of such obvious moral imperative? Who could possibly have a heart that insensate? The woman's features sharpened as she took a sidelong look at Ben. Revulsion and disbelief replaced the blind cocktail of hope and panic that had been torturing her up till then. She seemed to be wondering if Ben were really hu-man at all. After her son tugged twice on her arm, she let him lead her back to her stricken boyfriend. Ben raised the window and lowered his forehead onto the steering wheel.

"You did the right thing, Ben," Isaac said.

"Did I?"

"White women like that need to be reminded of their mistake every day of their lives."

Ben turned to his brother. Isaac was biting his lower lip, plac-idly watching the scene unfold. Someone had arrived with a soft drink, but the man was too deep in his throes to imbibe. They tried to pour the beverage between his tightly clenched teeth but only splattered his face with cola. Meanwhile, with her incessant shrieks, his imbecilic girlfriend continued testing the limits of the human throat in both endurance and durability.

"Didn't you date a couple black girls in high school?" Ben asked.

"I was a child," he responded. "I didn't know then what I know now. These people are an older model of Man. They're *Homo sapiens* 2.1. We're *Homo sapiens* 5.7. Why any white woman would want to bed down with these knuckle-dragging savages is beyond me."

Ben shook his head but said nothing. They were finally get-ting some sugar in the man's belly. His convulsions were wind-ing down.

"I understand why there used to be laws preventing blacks from having sexual relations with whites," Isaac went on. "For people who have a racial identity, it's more than just aggravating. Watching your own kind being corrupted like that, little by little, and knowing you have the power to stop it, but you can't use that power. It wears on your sanity. It tempts one to murder."

Ben at first said nothing, hoping that Isaac would either change the subject or stop talking. But then he was possessed by a sudden idea. "Have you considered that interracial marriage is a way of giving blacks some class?" he asked.

"Oh, I'm sorry. Are we talking about marriage here?" Isaac snarked. "I mean, my redneck is a little rusty, but I could've sworn that that toothless road slut just called that stupid ape over there her boyfriend. Close to eighty percent of blacks are born out of wedlock these days. You think those people really care about marriage?"

"I meant to say that perhaps the silver lining here is that we are improving their gene pool as much as they are degrading ours."

Isaac tossed his head back and forced a laugh. "Oh, what a wonderful idea! Creating an entire subclass of people whose lives depend upon racial diversity. Don't you see? If you're half white and half black, you become part of a static electorate. You *must* believe in the equality of the races. No argument, no evidence can sway you, otherwise you'd have to admit your own inferiority. You *must* vote for the party that panders to as many races as possible. You *must* vote for leaders that swear off the racial cohesion of the dominant race. Doesn't matter how disastrous their policies are. What's the national debt now? $40 trillion? What's the unemployment rate? Twelve percent? Our GDP has been shrinking every year for two freaking decades."

"I know. Ever since the Leftists and liberals took over both parties, America has become a second-rate economy."

"And they don't care! They'll just invent more clever arguments to pin the blame on people like you and me, the ones who have had almost no say in what goes on in this country for over fifty years! They've become elements of decline because they'd rather take part in a dying culture than be shut out of a healthy one."

Ben squinted at his brother. "Where did you read that?

"Nowhere. Made it up myself. Just now."

Ben gestured to the diabetic who was still struggling on the pavement. His seizure appeared to have run its course, but now he was twisting in agony for some reason. "So you're blaming people of mixed race for the downfall of the United States?" he asked.

"No. There are many reasons for that. It's just that you'd have a hard time finding people who've contributed to our downfall more eagerly." Isaac stuck his finger in the air. "That, I got from someone else."

"Who?"

"Michael. Of course."

Ben said nothing and decided to focus on the diabetic drama unfolding in front of them. The man had thrown up and now seemed to be choking on his own vomit. People were scrambling to deal with this new emergency. His girlfriend was trying to soothe him, but Ben imagined that her aggressive caresses and hysterical sobs were only making matters worse. The blonde mulatto child was sent to run between the cars, apparently to find more help. The helicopters had finally taken notice and were streaming light on the scene. Isaac noticed that it was all being broadcast live on the internet.

"We could have prevented all this," Ben said, slapping his knuckles against the windshield. "We could have given that guy some orange juice. It's one thing to think about these things, but to do them yourself..."

"I felt that way starting out too," Isaac said, nodding almost imperceptibly. "For about five minutes."

Peering up at the helicopter lights, Ben realized that they illuminated the diabetic and his family like actors on a bare stage. He and Isaac sat safely in the dark beyond the spotlight as if in an audience. He suddenly felt that it was okay to watch. Like everyone else.

"We are leaving this vehicle," Ben announced suddenly.

"What?"

"This is our chance to get Roland."

"What are you talking about?"

"You said this is going to last all night, right? You also said that Roland is only five point two miles away. Well, let's just go there on foot, pick him up, and take him back here. And it's not like the car is going anywhere, right?"

"Wrong. Bad idea," Isaac countered. "They probably already know we're here since this is a pre-McKinney vehicle. They'll be watching us as soon as we step out of it."

"No, they won't," Ben shot back, pointing to the lighted scene before them. "They'll be watching that!" Isaac turned to look. A fourth helicopter was now hovering overhead, shining even more light on the fiasco which was now resolving itself in front of them. The man had finally gotten his seizure and his vomiting and his choking under control. His blonde son had brought back someone who was at least acting like a physician. His girlfriend had gone from hyperactive shrieks to a more soulful, deep-throated wail. No one had stepped up to comfort her.

"We don't have much time," Isaac said as he dove into the backseat. He pulled a military backpack onto his lap and started combing through it. "The apparition I have is out of battery. But we can't leave it here. We have to carry it with us."

"Okay."

Isaac pulled out a twenty-two caliber semi-automatic pistol and placed it in Ben's hand. "Here. Six rounds in the magazine. One in the chamber. Safety is not on."

Ben slipped it into his pocket. "I hope I don't have to shoot anything big with this."

"I hope you don't have to shoot anything at all with it," Isaac said. "Except maybe yourself." The brothers looked at each other. "Remember, I have poison in my molars. You don't. If I die, Ben, and you're surrounded by feds or cops or whoever, please don't let them take you alive. Just..." He jammed a finger into his neck and yanked it away, imitating recoil.

Ben sighed. "Okay."

"Fickleskin dies minutes after you do. They would have to really know what to look for to find it."

"Right."

"Now, take off your shirt. Put it in my bag."

Ben thought to question the order and then reconsidered. He popped out of his T-shirt. Isaac produced a small tub of a gray, waxy material the width of his palm. He scooped a handful and gave it to Ben. "Here, rub this all over you. But not your face or your pits. Those parts of your body produce too much oil."

"What is this?"

"Rubber glass," Isaac said as he applied the goop to himself like soap in the shower. "It's basically silicon dioxide mixed with chemicals that react with water in your sweat. Imagine a shirt made of non-brittle glass that can transmit light around your body."

"It makes you invisible?"

"Eh, not quite. Especially not in the day or when light is directly on you. But at night, it can give you an edge if you're trying not to be found. And it's better than what we were wearing. Don't know what to do about those white shorts, though. Won't be hard to spot those at all."

"Should I put some on them too?"

"Not unless you want glass shards in your ass. It gets brittle if you don't mix it with water soon. It also hurts like hell when you remove it. Pulls out hair, skin. God help you if you have psoriasis." Isaac found a baseball cap in the bag and put it on. "Sorry I don't have a cap for you. But wear this," he said, handing Ben a pair of tinted glasses. "These are night-specs. They'll keep you in my PVN as long as you stay within a few feet of me. They also let you see better at night. And if you slide your finger on the edge, here, they act like binoculars."

Ben put the night-specs on. His vision was almost perfectly clear but was drained of all but the most drab, lifeless colors. Isaac handed him a shiny, cylindrical object about five inches long. "What's this?" Ben asked.

"It's a high-powered death-laser."

"Really?"

Isaac smiled. "No. It's a flashlight. Just a flashlight."

Ben smiled back and put it in his pocket.

"Okay, I assume your DSAK is disabled?" Isaac asked.

"Yeah. Eli and Michael can't enable it remotely. Can they?"

"No, they can't. Now, I've synced the bag to your UID and mine. If we both die, this bag explodes like twenty pounds of TNT. You understand?"

"Yes," Ben said. "How about cash? I got like a hundred bucks. Should I keep it?"

"Sure. It's good that you have it. I'm almost out of petty cash myself."

Ben watched as his brother sealed the bag and strapped it to his chest.

"Are we ready?" Isaac asked.

Ben lifted his chin in a half-nod. "One question. You said you knew what Roland was doing out here. What was it?"

Isaac held out his hands as if describing the length of a fish he just caught. "Roland Turk thinks that one way to combat the enemy is to limit their ability to reproduce. Sexually. So the psychopath trolls police sites looking for young, deadbeat dads, black guys who've had more than three kids out of wedlock. Then he hunts them down, he traps them, and he kills them."

"This is sanctioned by Michael and Eli?"

"Of course not! But Roland used to be in charge in Nathan's Ford. He was the only general there for a while. Then a couple years ago he was demoted by our Horseman for doing some psychopath stuff involving a triple homicide in Mississippi. But when they put Michael and Eli in charge, he insisted on keeping his privileges. So he comes and goes as he pleases."

"How does he trap these guys?"

Isaac smiled contemptuously. "He whores out our women as bait." The brothers stared at each other in breathless silence for several seconds before exiting the car, scared and ready to fight for their murky cause in the thick, savage darkness of a ruined city.

Chapter 24

Which of the following was NOT a lasting accomplishment of Byzantine emperor Justinian I, who ruled from 527 to 565 AD?

A. Rebuilding the Hagia Sophia into a beautiful house of

God with columns of porphyry and verd antique, intricate mosaics backed with gold leaf, and a giant
dome 108 feet wide and 180 feet high
B. Reorganizing the Roman legal system by researching
centuries of legal precedent and codifying over 4650
laws in a twelve-volume document known as the Co-
dex Justinianus
C. Bribing two Persian monks to smuggle silkworm eggs
out of China so Constantinople could breed the
Bombyx mori silkmoth and manufacture silk on its
own
D. Restoring the Roman Empire to its second century
borders through military conquest (correct)

The chatter surrounding the diabetic intensified yet again
now that the seizures had abated. The physician and a few others were insisting he go to the hospital, while the man himself
and his mongrel household were emphatically arguing otherwise. Meanwhile, Ben and Isaac disappeared into the trench beside the highway, burned a hole through a metal fence with
Isaac's DSAK, and removed themselves from the scene.

Moments later a wholly new form of chatter pervaded the air.
Black voices. Shouting. Always shouting. "What could these
people possibly be talking about?" Ben asked as he and his
brother skirted a small field through overgrown woods. He
knew he was using the word 'talking' quite loosely.

"We got cars park on the road out deh!"
"Hah?"
"Yeh, he do!"
"Who dat say wha?"
"Hah?"
"You look over deh! Dem mothafucka stop!"
"We git em! We git em!"
"Hah?"

Apparently, the Memphis denizens had just learned about
the traffic bottleneck and were about to rush the road to see
what advantage they could take at the expense of the stalled motorists. There were maybe forty of them, all under thirty and almost half female. In the dim light of the nearby spotlights, Ben

noticed that the men wore sleeveless sports jerseys, sleeveless undershirts, or no shirts at all. Nearly all wore baseball caps or bandanas. The women were in strapless blouses or bikini tops, mostly, and skintight athletic pants.

The sudden appearance of helicopter lights made even the grass appear white and revealed a corrosion of garish, animated tattoos on almost all of the troublemakers. The increasing proximity of the propeller blades caused them to panic. A few fell over backwards like dumbfounded cartoons, but most beat a disorganized retreat away from the highway. Isaac and Ben were now facing the unanticipated problem of having to outrun some of these people to keep from revealing their presence not only to them but to the police hovering above as well. Isaac was navigating with his DSAK and followed the tree cover thirty degrees to the right, *away* from Roland's location. The woods continued, though they were thinning out. The chaotic hollering of the Memphis denizens held steady behind them. A road soaked in helicopter light was approaching fast.

"Pick it up!" Isaac shouted as he broke into a measured sprint. Ben followed. In four strides the brothers crossed the two-lane road that interrupted their cover. Ben was relieved to see the center of the nearest spotlight about twenty feet to their left. In leafy darkness once again, Isaac called, "In three, ninety to the east!"

On the count, Ben skidded in the dirt and followed his brother's sharp right turn. While this kept them beneath the trees and protected from the helicopter lights, it took them even further from Roland and set them at cross paths with nearly a dozen black Memphians who were still hightailing through the trees. Nothing could be done. Ben kept his head down, picked up his pace, and hoped he would not collide with any of them. A tall, slender Memphian dashed this hope when he slammed into him. Stunned, Ben spun nearly 180 degrees, and then sank to his knees. The man who had struck him kept running. He noticed that he had hit someone but couldn't see Ben in his rubber glass. Isaac waited for a few others to pass before pulling his brother to his feet and leading him out of the foot traffic.

As they approached a four-lane highway, which Ben knew

would be impossible to cross undetected, Isaac spun his backpack to his chest and grabbled through it. He produced a black umbrella. He sat Ben down by a tall tree, mere feet from the curb. Up went the umbrella over the two of them. "Thermoflage," Isaac explained, pointing to his umbrella. "Keeps them from detecting our heat. Hopefully with everyone running everywhere they won't notice us dropping off the grid."

"Looks like a regular umbrella," Ben noted.

Isaac shrugged. "You can use it like one if you want. I mean, why not? Right?" Ben closed his eyes and smiled. Isaac touched his on his knee. "We're gonna have to stay here for an hour or so. Just because the lights are turned away doesn't mean they still aren't looking."

Ben nodded wearily, silently blaming Michael and Eli for sending Isaac out on this dangerous mission without enough sleep. Emerging from the trees about an hour later, Ben and Isaac made the sensible decision to avoid all human contact until reaching Roland. This time they turned left, away from a row of one-story brick homes which were lit by a blazing bonfire. They could hear footfalls and clanging and incessant chatter. Unfortunately, the trees which had provided such excellent cover against the helicopters were nearly useless in camouflaging two East-Asian men from Memphians who were already keyed up from their street party and prowling the vicinity.

The brothers snuck around the corner of a whitewashed brick building and noticed a pair of overflowing dumpsters at the far end of it. Across the street a barrel of black children were running and jumping among the trash as their parents and grandparents sat on porches smoking cigarettes. Someone had lit a fire in a rusted metal garbage can, and the smell of kerosene, rotting food, and excrement hung like fog around them. The road was clearly no longer used as such since it was littered with domestic detritus, most seemingly from the last century: washer-dryers, televisions, exercise machines, microwaves. Ben thought he saw a few motorized wheelchairs and a catheter machine among the rubbish. Down the crumbling road the adults were using wood from an abandoned house to fuel their bonfire. Ben was reasonably sure he and Isaac would not be spotted as long as they stayed where they were. Isaac, however, unfolded a two-foot-long plastic weapon from his backpack and seemed intent on moving toward the action. Ben pulled him back by his shirt. "Hey. What are you doing?"

"Let go!" Isaac said, swatting Ben's hand away. "We need to get to that dumpster."

"Why?"

"Because from there I'll be in range to launch an EMC into that bonfire," Isaac said.

"Embedded Molotov Cocktail?"

"Oh, you remembered your training. How nice."

"Oh, I'm sorry," Ben snarked. "I thought we weren't supposed to call attention to ourselves."

Isaac turned and pointed a finger at his brother. "Idiot! These things have a delay. We launch. We run. It explodes. The helicopters come to check out what's happening rather than wonder why two Chinese guys—"

Ben heard footsteps and a grunt and knew something bad was coming his way, most likely a punch. With an athlete's instinct, he tucked in his chin, and raised his hands to protect his face. The blow grazed off the top of his head. He then twisted in any direction he could to protect himself from further blows, which were now raining down on him from multiple sources. A few found their way to his face and abdomen. They hurt and they knocked off his night-specs, but they were inexpert punches, swung wildly and without the torque that two well-placed feet and strong hips can apply to a moving fist. Ben was more worried about the kicks which felt like baseball bats smacking into his legs and sides. He wanted to fire back punches to create space between him and his assailants but he couldn't afford to take his hands away from his face. And his back was to the building, so he couldn't run away. All he could do was sink down and pray for the beating to stop.

Stop it did. Isaac stunned two of his assailants but not before one of them had smashed his EMC launcher with a baseball bat and left it cracked and leaking fluid onto the pavement. The third assailant continued working Ben over as if nothing had happened. All that Ben could tell in the dark was that he was tall, slender, and young. Finally given a chance to retaliate, Ben stood to his full height, squared up with his man, and pumped two jabs in his face. The first one landed flush and hard. He followed up with a straight right to the jaw which missed. His kick to the groin didn't, however. The point of his toe found the soft spot between his man's legs.

From his assailant's screams, Ben could tell that the person he just beat up was a freakishly tall pubescent boy. He didn't have time to reflect on this, however. He dropped to his knees and began groping for his night-specs. Just as he retrieved them, Isaac pulled him up by the elbow and led him towards the dumpsters. The two fled down the nearest side street not lit by any bonfires. A mist of darkness clouded their furious retreat.

Between the moonlight and the incessant bonfires and the roving helicopter lights they sprinted west through six or seven neighborhoods, each of which looked every bit as bleak and wasted as the one before it. Metal fences became more prevalent, as did abandoned buildings, frazzled undergrowth, empty lots, and front yards made entirely out of concrete. Grass sprouted through the cracks like long, sickly fingers, and dilapidated cars sat rusting on cinderblocks. Squat, brick apartment buildings, fabricated from charmless, tri-color architecture, lurked in the distance.

If not for the civilized distances between dwellings, central Memphis resembled a shantytown with its rows of thin, flimsy homes which appeared rigged rather than designed to stand in all sorts of reasonable weather. The earthquake had demolished almost a quarter of them and convulsed many others into semi-habitable shambles. It left the remaining structures leaning tipsily in their lots. Ben and Isaac tried to stay off the streets as much as possible, but they were still noticed and pursued by malingering Memphians, who apparently knew no bedtime.

After ditching their pursuers, the brothers emerged from a wooded area and were walking among gravestones before they even knew they had entered a graveyard. The graves seemed to be intact and unmolested. A few had recently been decked with flowers. A humble church of white brick stood nearby. They were mere feet from a four-lane highway. Across it stood some kind of abandoned industrial facility, the fences of which were swaddled in blankets of barbed wire. The lot must have stretched nearly a mile and was populated by rows and rows of long, one-story buildings. Isaac motioned that that was where they needed to go.

Just then Ben noticed a strange, orange glow lingering above the highway to the north. An infernal rainbow. Aurora Urbanis. Something. Helicopters clustered above it like mosquitos. "What is that?" he asked. "It's too big to be another bonfire."

"Black people burning the city down," Isaac said with bored assurance.

"Why are they doing that?"

"The correct answer to that question, Ben, is who gives a shit?"

Ben considered his brother's hazy gray profile but didn't have the chance to respond. They heard a car approaching and dove behind the largest grave stones they could find. Isaac started consulting his DSAK. "We still have over four and half miles to go."

"No. We ran more than a half a mile," Ben said. "I know it."

"When I said five point two miles back in the car that was how the crow flies. Now we're talking actual distance on streets."

Ben let his head fall back on the grass. "Isaac, why are we doing this? If Roland is such a loose cannon, isn't he a liability? Wouldn't we be better off just leaving him here?"

"No. Unfortunately."

"Why not?"

"Because, first of all, Roland knows everything. If he were to be caught alive, everyone in Nathan's Ford would be dead in less than an hour. That is not an exaggeration."

"But we are trained not to be taken alive, right? What about the poison in our teeth? What about—"

"Stop!" Isaac interrupted. "Roland is just too valuable to lose. We can't risk it. We also have over fifty people in Nathan's Ford now. I would say half of them follow him and no one else. And a good chunk of these people would take a bullet for him. That's how much loyalty Roland inspires. Michael and Eli are the ostensible leaders, but no one's going to take a bullet for either of them, or for me. If we left Roland to hang in Memphis, we'd have mutiny. Nathan's Ford would be finished."

"Shit."

"Why do you think we have two leaders instead of one? It's because our Horseman wanted extra insurance in case Roland decided to get uppity."

"Wow."

"Yeah, wow. Our recruits *love* Roland. He embodies the anger and the hatred we all have. And he does it so well sometimes even I'm tempted to follow him. I'm really worried he's going to take over Nathan's Ford again someday. Some Beer Hall Putsch or whatever. And then God help us."

More cars were approaching. Ben held his breath. He was too afraid to move, too afraid to look. The cars were close. He imagined he could smell them, the metal, the rust, the lingering, smoky exhaust. He imagined he was almost underneath them as they sped by, his hair fluttering in the fumes. Ben closed his eyes and reflected upon the last ten months of his life. Where he was and what he was doing still seemed so unreal. He had to keep reminding himself that this was his new life and that he could never, ever retrieve his old one...the innocence, the joy, the petty concerns. There was an underground war going on. Didn't he know their odds for victory were slim and that all this struggle and strife was likely futile? Civilizations rise and civilizations fall. It is the immutable law of history. *Why fight it?* White people had had their day. From the cradle of Christendom to the man on the Moon, nearly all lasting developments in science, technology, philosophy, mathematics, and the arts came out of the West, from Caucasians of European descent. So then what happened? How did we let ourselves come to this? How did we lose what we had? And whatever it is, can we ever get it back? Is it possible to reverse the inexorable decline of civilizations?

"Ben!" Isaac whispered. His voice had the deep, diaphragmic rumble of someone making as little sound as possible when he really needs to make a lot of it. Ben peeked above the gravestone like a castle wall. A metal fence stood between the graveyard and the road, but several sections had been warped almost flat by years of abuse. Isaac had stepped over one of them, and now stood by an old sports utility vehicle which had stopped in the rightmost lane. Both front doors were flung open. On the pavement by Isaac's feet were two figures. One was considerably less still than the other.

"What happened?" Ben asked.

"What does it look like?" Isaac answered. "I flagged them down and stunned them! We're stealing their car!"

Ben rushed towards the car as Isaac bounced on his toes and turned to the driver side. Before jumping into the passenger seat, Ben looked at the bodies to confirm what he had suspected. Yes, they were both black. Yes, they were both unconscious. The woman was convulsing like a wind-up toy thrown on its back. He couldn't detect anything more about her except that she was stout and matronly. The man lay on his face mere inches from the two front tires. Ben felt a sharp acidic yank in his gut, not unlike hunger. But he wasn't hungry. Just the opposite, actually. He tried to remember what ever could have possessed him to call Curtis Book a coon. He could not.

"Get in!" Isaac urged from the driver's seat. Ben obeyed, and Isaac gunned it before he could shut the door. With a car speeding up from behind, Isaac had no time for reverse and ran the man over like roadkill. The body thunked like a pumpkin as it was crushed. Isaac made sure the rear wheels got him too. An abrupt rise. An abrupt drop. The car behind them sped past the moment they were free.

"You just killed that guy!" Ben shouted.

"Most likely. He got a good look at me, so I hope I did."

"The woman back there was shaking like crazy, too."

"I know," Isaac said, bearing left with the highway. "The stun feature on a DSAK causes neurons to fire synchronously, among other things. It depolarizes your brain, and usually that's enough to knock you out or put you on queer street for a while. If you're an epileptic, it's the same as a seizure."

"She's an epileptic?"

"Or going to be." Isaac slowed down enough to let another car pass. They were heading north. The infernal rainbow in front of them had lost some of its intense color, but was growing wid-

er beyond the tree line. It resembled the upper lip of some preternatural maw about to swallow them whole. Isaac noticed on-
coming traffic and gunned it before taking a sharp left. An abnormally tall, one-story building towered over them on the left
side. It occupied the entire block. Ivy and weeds were smother-
ing the fences to the right. There were no signs of people anywhere. Ben found strange comfort in the desolation.

"Eli said in training not to leave a trail of bodies," Ben said.
"And that we're supposed to treat enemy fighters and innocent
civilians differently."

"Ben, there are no innocent civilians," Isaac said. "That's
something we should have learned twenty-five *hours* after nine-
eleven, not twenty-five years." He lowered his window to spit as
they sped over railroad tracks.

"Fine. How much further?"

"Still saying another four and a half miles."

"What the hell?"

"Yeah, well, that left we took back there was a detour to keep
from being charbroiled by those apes uptown. What do you
want me to do, Ben?"

They soon found that the road bore to the right, north, towards the fire. Isaac stopped at a stop sign near a small church
and consulted his DSAK. The dim orange sky was picketed by a
chaotic complex of beams and concrete. It was a metal walkway
which teetered over a cluster of railroad tracks to their left. It
had been smashed by the earthquake, apparently.

"Look left," Ben said, pointing to a small, makeshift convenience store across the tracks. About three dozen young blacks
were gathered there, socializing by fires in garbage cans and
playing games in the street as if it were their living room. There
were enough bodies and objects in the road to block traffic. They
hadn't yet noticed Ben and Isaac.

"Oh, great. That's the way we need to go," Isaac said. "According to this, we go about one point three miles west on this
road and then take State Highway 51 north for two-and-a-half
miles to Eastmoreland. After that the motel is just a few blocks
west."

"So, you're saying Roland is northwest of here?"

"Yeah."

Ben pointed to the railroad tracks beneath the dilapidated walkway. "Do those tracks also head northwest?"

Isaac squinted in the dim light. "They do."

"I don't think many trains are running through Memphis after an earthquake. What do you think?"

Isaac smiled and turned left. Just as the moonlighting Memphians noticed them, he took a sharp right onto the tracks. There were four tracks side by side. Two were impassable beneath the rubble of the walkway. Two weren't. They made it to the latter pair with only a couple hurled bottles smashing against the rear of the car. Isaac gunned it on the gravel between the tracks to make their bumpy escape. Several Memphians tried to follow on foot but quickly gave up.

The four tracks soon merged into two, and after about a half mile, Isaac discovered there wasn't enough room to drive comfortably between them. He pulled the passenger side up onto the track on the right, and severely tested the vehicle's shock absorbers against the railroad ties. Every bump felt like an uppercut. Ben couldn't speak without feeling the jarring vibrations just below his chest, and so gritted his teeth and fended off sheer panic in silence. Fifty miles an hour on railroad tracks is mighty fast, Ben realized. But at least they were alone for the time being, surrounded by the black relief of trees against a starless blue-orange night.

Isaac leaned on the horn. He could see something Ben couldn't. Then Ben saw it too. A clearing. Dark, thin figures up ahead. Four or five of them. People crossing the tracks. Isaac did not slow down. "Get down!" he shouted, as he leaned on the horn. "Don't let them see you!"

Ben got down. They didn't see him. Isaac flew through the clearing, and then another before Ben sat up again. "Just people hanging on the streets," Isaac said. "That's all."

Ben swallowed and suddenly felt his fatigue throb. The car's digital clock read one twenty-three. He blinked and rubbed his eyes with his fists until it hurt. Curiously, he couldn't yawn if he wanted to. Isaac looked for the auto-drive function on the car's computer and turned it on. He then unstrapped himself and began searching for something in the backseat.

"What the hell are you doing, man?" Ben asked.

"Getting Surplex pills from the backpack."

"I'll do it! You drive!

"They're in the third zippered compartment," Isaac said as he returned to his seat. He turned off the auto-drive. "Get one for yourself, too."

Ben unstrapped himself and reached into the backseat. He had to brush aside the owner's belongings before discovering the dim, bulging outline of Isaac's bag. He found the zippered compartment which held the Surplex pills. They were in a baggie. There were only three. Just as he zipped up the backpack, however, a streak of light exposed the bag's black fabric and gray trim. The bag then bled a blinding white along with everything else in the vehicle.

"Whoa!" Isaac shouted as he swerved, scraping his wheels jarringly against the tracks.

Ben returned to the front seat and squinted against the light reflecting off the hood of the SUV. The noonday Sun couldn't have lit things more brilliantly. He dropped the pills without realizing. "Where's that light coming from?" he asked.

Isaac gripped the steering wheel and leaned into it like he wanted to rip it out of the dashboard. "Helicopter," he muttered, voice shaking from the rails. "Stay cool. With all the bad things going on in this town, I can't imagine they'll care about us for too long."

Ben tried to look up through the windshield and caught only glare. He then lowered his window and leaned his head out of it to get a glimpse of the helicopter. "Don't let them see you!" Isaac ordered.

Ben fell back into his seat and realized that he hadn't strapped himself back in. Taking two swift breaths, he grabbed the buckle and started hunting around for the lock. By the time he secured himself, the light was gone. The brothers sighed in unison. After taking a moment to make sure the light wasn't coming back, they both relaxed. Their chests heaved and fell, their shoulders sagged, their arms slackened, they shared a look. They smiled. It was the most natural thing they could have done. They made it. They were safe. Isaac gunned it just a little bit just because he could.

Ben felt his stomach plummet. The taste of nauseating fear rose in his throat like bile. Or maybe it was bile? They were falling, Ben, Isaac, car, and all. Just like that. It happened so suddenly that Ben's mind couldn't even process it as sudden. In the split second it all happened he was no better than an animal: acting and reacting to physical things in his environment. He turned to see. The ground was fractured. It was ruptured. It had been twisted and ripped in the vehement birth pangs of a continent. Momentum and gravity were conspiring to change their trajectory. It wasn't personal. It was just physics. Ben had the fleeting idea that there was a science item in all this.

He didn't really think that. That came later. What came then, right before that terrible, deadly impact, right before he blacked out, was the realization that, yes, in fact, there had been an earthquake in Memphis.

Chapter 25

A speeding 2,000 kg vehicle carrying two occupants falls off a cliff for 2 seconds. According to Newton's third law of motion, if it strikes the ground with a force of 20,000 N, crumpling the engine, accordionizing the frame, and killing one of its occupants with unwatchable, gore-splattering violence, what is the force with which the ground strikes the vehicle?

A. 2,000 N
B. 5,000 N
C. 10,000 N
D. 20,000 N (correct)

Ben didn't know why he could feel the hair on his head move. His sweaty face was cold from the breeze. He detected acrid smells of mud and rust. Faint sounds crept in. Cars. Shouts. Horns. Helicopters. Helicopters! His hands felt like they were miles away. He tried to lift one and couldn't. He opened his eyes. He tried to remember. Where was he? What was he doing there? Where was—

"Where's the windshield?" he asked. He recognized he was in a car despite the lack of light. But what kind of car doesn't have a windshield? He could barely tell in the darkness, but it sure seemed like it wasn't there. That would explain the sound and breeze. Beyond it he expected to see sky and stars and trees. All he found was oblivial darkness.

Inside the vehicle, he noticed heavy crumbs of shattered glass and deployed airbags. Why did his neck and forehead hurt so much? And why was his seat inclined back? An impact! It must have been. The car's recline reflex had been activated. It was a safety feature which instantaneously angled seats away from an impact to protect a passenger's head and torso. People complained a lot about whiplash. Ben remembered this. He felt almost like he had whiplash—and he wasn't dead. So an impact it must have been.

"Isaac?" He remembered his brother just as he said his name. He tried to turn, but a stabbing pain in his neck stopped him. He was also aware of an incessant ache in his collarbone and ribcage. He felt his body to see if anything was broken. Nothing was. In moments, simmering panic caused him to wake fully. "Isaac!" he called, now starting to worry. He slapped the empty driver's seat trying to locate his brother. Gingerly he turned his neck and shoulders in hopes that his eyes might be of use as well. Still in his night-specs, he spied legs and part of a torso hanging over the dashboard. Isaac had crashed through the windshield. He had not strapped himself back in. And his right arm, the one now devoid of tattoos, the one he could no longer lift over his head, lay by his side, no doubt unable to protect him the moment he needed protection the most.

"Isaac! No!" Ben called. "Speak to me! Isaac, wake up!" He tried lifting his brother and pulling him back into the vehicle, but couldn't get the leverage. His head and neck and shoulder hurt, and he was afraid he'd do more harm than good by dragging his brother back over whatever broken glass remained on the windshield.

He remembered the flashlight in his pocket.

When he finally shed light on the body of his brother, Ben remembered fully what had happened. They had fallen off a small cliff that had been ripped into being by the earthquake. The tracks had twisted and snapped as the tremors caused the Earth to part. One side of the fracture had gone up, the other down, creating a chasm of about forty feet. Isaac's stolen automobile had launched off the upper end at full speed and crashed into the lower end. Without a seatbelt, g-forces had caused Isaac's body to free fall just a little bit above his seat while they were in midair. Upon impact, the vehicle's recline reflex—which had undoubtedly saved Ben's life—had had little effect on Isaac's trajectory. He had careened headfirst and helpless over the airbag and speared a skull-sized hole through the windshield. The entire windshield had then separated from its frame and folded away from the wreckage, pulling Isaac's lifeless body along with it.

Ben's face collided with the deployed airbag and stuck to it as he passed out.

***

Ben hated being a man. This was not so much Man as opposed to Woman, but Man as opposed to Boy. Knowing that there is nothing between abject failure and the opposite of abject failure, whatever that is, except you and your solitary efforts is unsettling to say the least. Ben wondered how anyone could ever get used to it. It rattled his heart and boiled up from the bottom of his gut. He had to resist the urge to turtle up on the ground and wail.

The very thought that his brother had been cut down before they could truly reconcile and before they could accomplish what they needed to accomplish—before they could win the war, or lose it—sent Ben back twenty-five years. The wall between raw emotion and reason is pretty thin when you're five, when the former occupies much more of your mind than the latter. Ben was spilling so many tears he couldn't see, even with his flashlight, and he knew better than to wipe his eyes with hands now covered in shattered rubber glass. Ben remembered his training. He knew what he had to do. Moreover, he knew he had little time in which to do it.

After exiting the vehicle to make sure there were no witnesses, he labored to extricate Isaac from the scene of his violent demise. At first, he tried to push him back into his seat, but Isaac was more out than in and was lying on a shattered windshield along the hood. Ben was loath to mutilate the body any further. He resolved to lift it through the dislodged windshield frame and pull it free. This required getting much closer to the body than he had wanted. It smelled. If Ben had had food in his stomach, he would have retched. He couldn't afford to be delicate. He didn't have the time. He was forced to shake and yank. The final pull threw him back, and rather than fall with the bloody body in his arms, he dropped it and watched it land in the mud with a liquid, oozing thump. He watched it all with a dry heave and a sob.

Without giving himself a chance to mourn or reflect, Ben raced back to the car in a painful, ungainly shuffle and snatched Isaac's bag from the backseat. He was rifling through it before he placed it on the ground, searching for an anaerobe, another clever invention of the revolution. He knew it by feel, a slippery synthetic sheet folded over several times like a garbage liner, but about ten times as heavy. It was essentially a hermetically sealable bag, large enough to fit five grown men when completely unfolded. When you need to discreetly dispose of a body, you put it in an anaerobe. A remote-control device shrinks it to every contour of its contents and removes all external oxygen before sealing. Then the device initiates a combustion reaction chemically similar to anaerobic respiration, only with reagents that are far more flammable. Temperatures can get as high as 2,400 degrees Fahrenheit. What a traditional crematory can burn in two hours, the anaerobe can dispatch in less than twenty minutes. Its tinted hafnium gel lining traps over ninety-eight percent of the heat without melting and absorbs over eighty percent of the light. There can be nothing identifiable about a body after it is incinerated in an anaerobe.

Ben found Isaac's cap on the ground and put it on. He then inserted his brother into the anaerobe and carried him up a grassy slope on the west side of the tracks where they would be well covered by trees. He initiated the burn sequence after triple checking the parameters on his remote device. The incineration began immediately and lit Isaac a dull, computer blue.

Ben touched the anaerobe by his brother's face. It was cooler than his fingers, despite the heat raging just millimeters below. The Fickleskin was dead, but Isaac's face was now a distended mask. Ben sobbed quietly when he realized that he hadn't seen his brother's true face since that night in Muncie so long ago. He looked hard at this one, the non-fickle one. He could only imagine it resembling his brother's. Squinting didn't help. Moving closer didn't help either. He looked for as long as he could. "You never did get your chance," he said. "Did you?"

He remembered the beatings their father Stillwell had given him. His brother's slender arms were no defense against the thick fists of their father. Even as early as ten, Isaac had liked to wear his hair long, and that only made it easier for Stillwell to keep a hold of him while beating him. Did Ben really come to his brother's rescue like that? Or did he dream it? It was getting so hard to remember. He thought it was true. He hoped it was true. He had never talked about it with Isaac. He had never talked with his brother about a lot of things.

All the blank pages of the mystery that was his brother sent Ben hurtling through a maelstrom of emotions. What pained him the most was the certainty that Isaac had never found peace. Not in his growing up. Not in his chosen path. He had lost a wife. He had lost friends. He had a daughter who didn't know who he was. And now this. This stupid unforced error. Ben couldn't even blame it on the federal government or the roaming Negroes of Memphis. The pitiless, unyielding laws of physics were what did Isaac in, punishing him at the worst possible moment for a very human and understandable oversight. There had been an earthquake, Ben reminded himself. How can you train for a goddamn earthquake?

When the self-pity and guilt began to recede, Ben concluded that Isaac had been done in by bad luck, all because certain decisions he had made, righteous as they may have been, had put him in places where bad luck is likely to snatch victims like fairy-tale villains. All because he stood up for himself. Because he wanted to be proud of himself and his people when the rest of the world would not allow him to be proud of himself and his people. This was it. Ben knew it. This was the crux of it all.

A man must stand.

By the time Ben opened his eyes, Isaac was gone. The anaerobe had diminished him to the size of a small bath towel. Its shriveled, raisin-like exterior was dark from all the ash. Ben set the apparatus to rapid cool, and after ten minutes, reached into the anaerobe to receive two surviving items: Isaac's BREMAT implant and his DSAK chip. The size of rice grains, they were in tough ceramic casings which don't easily burn. They were items Nathan's Ford could not afford to lose to the enemy. They also held aural, visual, and neurological data of a user's final thirty seconds which could be pieced together by a computer to give a fairly accurate accounting of what had transpired up to that irreversible moment when things ultimately stopped transpiring.

Ben scattered his brother's ashes amid the underbrush separating the railroad clearing from one of the more blighted neighborhoods of a now sleeping Memphis. Ben took it in. Two homes demolished by the tectonic ravages and one twisting precariously on its foundation like an old drunk attempting a pirouette.

Ben placed the emptied anaerobe in Isaac's bag and then did the last thing he was required to do before leaving the scene. He took from the bag a time bomb disguised as a golf ball and secured it to the backseat. He set the explosion for two hours. He had about two hours until daylight. It would either blow up then, or whenever anyone tried to remove it from its new upholstered home. Before he shut the door, he remembered the Surplex pills. With his flashlight in his teeth, he searched the floorboards until he found them.

Popping one as soon as he was free, he felt the jittery surges and throbbing temples almost immediately. Fingers trembled. Breathing escalated. Sounds around him doubled, tripled in volume. He wanted to jump. He wanted to run. He remembered his training. He remembered the coma you could fall into if you crash too hard on this illicitly amped up narcotic. He remembered the heart attack you can incur if you exert yourself too much on it. After wiping away the shards of rubber glass still remaining on his arms and torso, he donned his shirt and resumed his clandestine quest on foot. With nerves in his legs firing like motorcycle engines, that part was easy enough. Difficult was envisioning his brother's true face in his firecracking mind. Ben disappeared down the railroad tracks, smiling in desperate anguish and spilling tears into the void.

Chapter 26

In Homer's *Odyssey*, what *really* happened when Odysseus and his men tried to outwit the Cyclops who was holding them captive in a cave?

  A. They got the Cyclops drunk on powerful wine.
  B. They poked out the Cyclops' eye while he slept.
  C. They tied themselves to the underbellies of sheep and escaped from the cave.
  D. They did all of the above and were stomped to death by the Cyclops and a dozen of his pals who laughed at the clever Greeks for employing such a preposterous stratagem. (correct)

The bonfires and noises to the east had finally died down. Even the helicopters seemed to be giving it a rest. The darkness was beginning to lift, and the flora were thinning all around him. Fortunately, Ben was alone. He remembered Isaac's saying to take State Highway 51 north. Beyond that, he couldn't remember except that his destination was the Motel Twelve.

A large garage-like structure on his left and some faint, productive activity within indicated he was approaching an industrial part of town. The air smelled of garbage and gasoline. Squinting, he could see cars parking and people lumbering out of them, going to work presumably. The tracks merged with others, and a brick building with barred-up windows loomed to his left. A vast parking lot stretched to his right. There were more cars, more activity. The good kind. The morning kind. Without any more trees under which to hide, he was out in the open, cloaked in the chilly darkness. He felt safe, despite the crunch of gravel and last autumn's leaves underfoot.

The sky was fuzzing peach. He looked behind him. Dawn.

He took off his night-specs and sat down away from the tracks. Up ahead they went over a bridge which traversed a highway. He was pretty sure that highway was Highway 51. He was voraciously hungry. With wobbly fingers, he reached into Isaac's bag for the last morsels of food and the last swig of water. He also found some painkillers, which he took straightaway. He hoped they would do wonders for the injuries he had sustained in the car crash. He also wondered how they would react with the Surplex pill he had just taken. Three pills to one. Three substantial downers—two more than the recommended dosage—versus one very serious upper. Although his hands hadn't stopped shaking, he felt his mind sway and reality bend. He closed his eyes. He didn't want to witness how the drugs were marring his perception of things. He didn't want to stand in a sailor's disequilibrium, not knowing where and when the ground would rise to meet his knees. Finally relieved of the throbbing torture in his neck and ribs, he understood that all he wanted—all he needed—after all this trauma was sleep. He promised himself he would rest only for a moment. Surely he could spare that. Roland couldn't have been more than a couple miles away, he thought. That's not far. No, not far at all.

Ben felt something nudging him. *Things*, actually. They were smooth, forceful, insistent. They were reaching into his pockets. Fingers! Waking up with a start, Ben bolted to his feet. It was bright and sunny, and his eyes rebelled. At once he saw the culprit: a homeless black man in ragged denim. Ben felt all around. His backpack was still on. The zippers had been synced to his fingerprints, so he knew it was secure. His gun and flashlight were still on him. His eyes raced as he tried to remember what else he had that was worth stealing. His money. Of course! He had nearly one hundred dollars in cash. He felt his back pocket. It was gone. The man was now backing away over the bridge. Ben approached, fists clenched.

"I wuz jus' checkin' on ya. Makin' sho' you won' dead or nuffin'," the man babbled, holding up his hands. The ragged kink-patches populating his face couldn't quite be called a beard, and his filthy clothes had been worn down to different shades of grime. He had a junkie's stupor and was cadaverously thin. Ben couldn't guess his age. Only his blue University of Memphis Tigers baseball cap was relatively new and clean. Ben grabbed him by the shirt and punched him in the chest. The man fell over between the rails. "Come on! I dindu nuffin'. Whatchoo got 'gainst a brutha tryin' —"

Ben pulled out his gun and jammed the barrel under the man's chin. Up close he could see the dust in the man's afro, the congealed yellow film between his teeth, and the insect-trail lines in his neck. Shuddering at the man's pervasive corpse-funk, Ben wondered if he would have smelled better dead than alive. "Give me back my money, or I will kill you," he said. The man attempted to squirm and gave up after several seconds. He patted Ben on the thigh with the purloined wad of cash.

Ben took it and stood. It was all there. The man, still on his back, started to beg for his life as if Ben still had any interest in killing him. There were cars driving sporadically underneath. People were working not terribly far away. "Don' shoot me, man! I jus' need some money for ma dawta. She sick! She got a kidney machine, and we ran outta in-shurnce. Lawd, please!"

"Don't shoot?" Ben repeated incredulously. "If I were you, I'd be begging me to shoot."

"Aww, have mercy! We all bruthas! Come on!"

Ben backed away and pocketed his gun and his money. He comprehended that this man was not repulsed by his own squalor for the same reason a chimpanzee is not repulsed by his. It's all they are capable of making for themselves, so to them their lives do not seem squalid at all. The man sat up. "You ain't gon' shoot me, are ya?" he asked.

"Get up," Ben said, looking in all directions to make sure they were alone. "Wanna make twenty dollars?"

"Ahh, yeah! Uh-huh," the man gulped as he stood, knees cracking.

"How do I get to the Motel Twelve?"

"Motel Twelve?"

"Motel Twelve."

"Ah, that way," he said, waving north. "'Bout a mile-an'-a-half."

"What road is this?"

"This road h'ya? Is Bellevue."

"Bellevue? Isn't it also Highway 51?"

"Yeah. Das right. Fitty-one."

"And is the Motel Twelve on this road?

"Nah, see!" the man said, gesticulating. "'Mile an' a half, take a lef'."

"Left onto what road?"

"Ah ha. I think is Easmawlin.'"

The name rang a bell. "You mean Eastmoreland?" Ben asked, "East. More. Land?"

The man either didn't notice Ben's proper pronunciation or didn't care. He held out his hand, waiting for his payout. "Yeah, das right. Eesmawlin. Take a lef'. Down fo', five blocks onna right. You got it!"

Ben produced a twenty from his wad but pulled it away before the man could snatch it. "Hey now!" the man shouted.

"You steal from me. I steal from you!" Ben said through an unforgiving grin. He stuffed the money back into his pocket and disappeared in the tall grass separating the bridge from the highway below. The man leaned over the bridge's north side balustrade and waited for Ben to appear underneath. "You Chinee chink cracka mothafucka!" he called. "Fuck you! Ya hear me? *Fuck* you! That's my money, bitch! That's my money!"

Ben would have run all the way to the Motel Twelve if he could, health warnings on his Surplex pill be damned. He wanted to sit down and properly reflect on his brother's death without having to worry about being robbed, shot, or stabbed. He also wanted to get Roland home so he could show Nathan's Ford that he was qualified to do this kind of work. Another bridge and some large trees gave him cover, but after a hundred yards or so, he was back in the open with brick buildings on either side of him. It was a breezy, chilly April morning with the Sun still hanging low in the clear sky to his right. The crisp air abraded his lungs.

Two overweight black women in a Japanese hybrid convertible got him to stop running. They were driving south, but pulled into the northbound lanes and cut him off. The driver wore a tight, sparkly top with spaghetti straps and sported a prison cell

of green and orange tattoos on her shoulders. Her hair was perfectly blonde. She leaned out of her car and hollered, "Hey,
white boy! What'choo runnin' in our neighborhood for?
What'choo scared of, bitch?"

She then hurled a large beverage cup at him, complete with
plastic cover and straw. On impact it cracked open and splattered a cold, brown ooze all over his body. It took Ben a moment
to realize that he had just been pelted in the chest with a chocolate milkshake. Livid, he discreetly drew his weapon and advanced upon the vehicle with long, fast strides like an assassin.
This had the desired effect. Shrieking like an obese character ac-
tor, the woman threw up her hands hallelujah-like and fell back
into her seat as she zoomed away.

Ben bit his lip, chewing on his dwindling options. Run, walk,
hide. The neighborhoods were getting more residential, and it
was still early. Few cars were on the road. Ben imagined that
fuel was scarce and people who had somewhere to be at such an
early hour were even scarcer. After an exhausting night of arson
and rioting, he presumed that Memphians preferred to sleep in.
There wasn't a helicopter in sight. With milkshake congealing on
his chest and sweat spilling beneath his backpack, Ben became
ravenously impatient to end this little quest. He wiped off whatever sticky chocolate gunk he could and took off running. A mile
and a half, he thought. In fifteen minutes I can run a mile and a
half.

Ben sprinted for a quarter mile through a disrepaired neighborhood and then slowed down as the road was about to open
up to a large intersection. From the sounds of human bedlam up
ahead, he knew he was no longer alone. What few trees there
had been were now gone. He put his night-specs back on and
zoomed into the looming nexus. Gas stations, fast food restaurants, and a convenience store populated the juncture. Parking
lots sprawled in all directions. Front and center were three overturned cars in the middle of the street. Six shirtless and heavily
tattooed black teenagers were entertaining themselves by spinning one of the cars around like a top while ignoring a medium-
sized gang rumble going down behind them. Others were
lounging on living room furniture in the middle of the street or

walking in and out of the convenience store as if they owned it.

No pedestrian could pass without their knowing. Perhaps that was the point of their presence there. Fortunately for Ben, they were still over 300 feet away and preoccupied. Less fortunately for Ben, however, about a dozen black youths, most likely between the ages of thirteen and seventeen, appeared from a side street behind him. They wore bright sporting jerseys, bore conspicuous bling, and were carrying firearms. They were about 500 feet away and heading in Ben's direction.

Ben knew that he was exposed from the front but was relatively safe for the time being considering the distance between himself and the intersection. He had some cover from behind, but not much. There just weren't very many trees in that part of Memphis. Sunlight slamming into the faded asphalt was raising the temperature by the minute, and the humidity and lack of wind wasn't helping. It was as if God were holding His breath. Pushing forward was no longer an option nor was retreating towards this new threat from behind. And by doing nothing in his treeless pocket of ghetto he was only waiting to be discovered.

A tall red house to Ben's right stood as bloodshot witness to his plight. A solid wooden door occupied the first floor. One window, easily broken into but too high to reach, interrupted the warped siding of the second. Unclimbable wooden fences guarded either side of the structure as if it were a castle. Ben eased up to it, rummaging through his options. First, he tried the door, but it was locked. Its only weak spot was a peep hole well over six feet from the ground. Ben surmised that whoever installed it must have been as concerned about home invasion as he was tall. Attempting to break or shoot his way through would only make noise and invite the entire neighborhood to investigate his little enclave.

Next, he made sure there wasn't anywhere to hide. There wasn't. A small thicket of trees beckoned from across the street, but he would have to walk in plain sight and scale a metal fence to get there. Ben also understood the dangers of hiding. If he stayed in Memphis long enough he would eventually be discovered by the Red Cross or the National Guard who had the technology to discern his identity despite his Asian disguise.

He thought about continuing on and calmly acting as if he belonged there. If he just kept walking with his head down, the people up ahead would hardly even notice him. Or if they did, they wouldn't think to question him. He calculated the considerable risk and rejected the idea as a silly, script-worthy conceit. Nothing more.

He considered devising a ruse — calling himself a doctor or an aid worker. Ben knew that aid organizations would arrive at any point. But did these detention center rejects know that? And, smelling like chocolate ice cream like he was, would they believe him? The rumble up ahead had just taken a nasty turn with a woman being knocked unconscious. No one seemed terribly concerned about her as she was nearly trampled in the confusion. Ben gathered that the omens spoke ill of this gambit.

Alternate routes? Ben didn't see any. Unlike Isaac, he didn't have a device that could tease out such information. All roads led to the four corners of hell up ahead.

He considered drawing his weapon and blasting a path to the Motel Twelve, action film style. He'd look tough and threaten to pump lead into anyone standing in his way. He quickly reconsidered. He had only six bullets, not counting the one reserved for his forehead in the likely event that his cinematic suicide maneuver didn't pan out. He had a feeling there were more than six people waiting for him between where he stood and the Motel Twelve.

Ben shook his head. His ideas were getting dumber and dumber. He estimated the punks were about 400 feet away. So engrossed were they in bragging about this and shouting about that and lacing everything they had to say in the grossest profanities, they still didn't see him. But they would soon. He needed an answer. Other than suicide. He needed not to be undone by a gang of sub-literate goons with an average IQ of eighty and chips on their shoulders the size of their bulging deltoids. He needed to remember every great idea he'd ever learned, every great story he ever read, every great movie he'd ever seen, every great historic episode there ever was. All to come up with a plot, a plan, a ploy. Something, anything. Anything other than suicide.

Ben found his answer. A permanent disguise so he could slip through these people like a virus. He needed how much time? What did Michael say when they held him hostage? Ten minutes! Ten minutes to damage skin cells irreparably. To make them produce enough melanin that you'd never, ever go back. Ten minutes is a long time, Ben thought. Never ever is a long time too, but at that moment ten minutes seemed a lot longer. The barbarians down the street were closing in.

Ben removed his Fickleskin remote control device from the backpack and then ditched the backpack deep beneath some nearby shrubbery. He pressed the remote hard on his neck to sync it with his UID. He closed his eyes as facial images appeared in his mind. Race templates. He thought-scrolled through all the European and Asian features until he landed on the sub-Saharan West African template. His head throbbed violently. He almost selected it. The face was a shiny dark brown. Childlike, wide-set eyes. Broad, simian nose. Squat, powerful jaws. Cheekbones extending almost beyond the ears. Lips thick like bicycle tires. Ben mourned. He could not imagine a face like that belonging to a civilized human being. Could he look like that for the rest of his life? He kept scrolling, afraid that he would run out of templates and be forced to make a difficult decision. He was euphorically grateful to discover an alternative: the much more familiar North American Negro template. Skin a lighter shade of brown. Eyes reasonably childlike. Nose reasonably flat. Lips reasonably wide. The admixture of European genes manifested in the slightly reddened cheeks and angular jawline. This was the only solution.

He folded as much of his hair as he could under Isaac's cap and then selected it. Necessity dictated he opt for the express change option. Ten minutes to simulate 50,000 years of natural selection. The tingling and the twitching started immediately. He had gone through this once before and was dreading the imminent permutations. This was going to be far worse than selecting the East Asian template, especially considering that he had opted for the forty-eight-hour path to become Zhenglong Hu and had taken medication to ease the transition. Skin would itch, and he could not scratch. Skin would burn, and he could not balm. Skin would stretch and bleed, especially around the mouth and eyes and nearly every joint in his body. Then there was the nausea and the fever. Sharp hunger piercing his belly reminded him that he would not be able to keep down food for twenty-four hours after the transformation. He hoped he'd have the strength to endure. He wished he could look in a mirror and say goodbye to the face he had always known, his familiar, handsome, Caucasian face.

But that face wasn't his anymore. His was an Asian, Genghis Khangoloid face, one more at home storming the Great Wall of China on the back of a Mongol horse or sacking Baghdad in a tempest of arrows than braving the mean streets of America. This was the face he had briefly forgotten. His new face. The one that he should have remembered. After a moment, he realized that it didn't matter. Ben Cameron was already gone. He was long gone. The man without a face fell on his back and writhed as he felt the unspeakable ravages coming on.

Chapter 27

Medical professionals have difficulty dealing with viruses such as Ebola in part because such viruses are adaptable to different environments. This is caused by the high tendency of the virus's single-stranded RNA genome to

A. target its host's immune system.
B. mimic the structure of messenger RNA.
C. reproduce rapidly through binary fission.
D. yield mutations during replication. (correct)

The thugs relieved him of his money, his night-specs, and his handgun. They kicked him a few times, wondering what this funny looking, chocolate smelling nigger was doing on the ground bleeding all over himself. One of them joked about taking him to the 'Red Cross crackers' setting up by the hospital up the street. Another urinated on his face. It felt like hot acid on skin that had already been scoured by a steel brush. And moving only made it worse. Ben barely had the strength to protect himself. Fortunately, after five minutes they went to join the

Quickie-Mart melee up the street. They had failed to notice his backpack under the shrubs.

Ben didn't move for at least an hour. A few gunshots punctured the air, precipitating a mass caterwaul and, from the sound of it, a stampede. But he was too focused on not disturbing his brand-new torture cocoon to care. His skin couldn't have been cooked more effectively in an oven, he thought. His lips had become engorged almost to the point of bursting. He didn't know how he could ever smile, talk, or eat again. His nostrils were breaking and bleeding under the strain.

After another couple hours the pain eased slightly, during which time several children rifled through his pockets and poked him with a stick to see if he was dead. All Ben wanted to do was to wrap his head in bandages Elephant Man style to contain the bleeding. He considered whether Isaac kept bandages in his backpack. He eyed it under the shrubs. It was three feet out of reach. He had to squirm like a worm to get to it. It took half an hour, but he did find a bandage. The cool cloth on his face was minimal relief, and he was grateful for it.

He rolled to his side, and, after confirming that he wouldn't pass out, stood up. He kept his eye on the house just in case he staggered into it. Sure enough, he staggered into it. After regaining his balance, he looked at himself, his arms, legs, abdomen. He was darker, all right, but not as swarthy as he had perversely hoped, given his acute suffering. He waited a few minutes for the swirling in his head to subside and then retrieved his backpack. He worked up the nerve to strap it on after ten minutes. Then, as if reaching for invisible bannisters, he stiff-legged his way into the street like a zombie.

Aside from his roasted body and the martyrly torment he endured trying to move it, the remainder of Ben's journey was astonishingly easy. His shambling leper act, enhanced by a trail of freshly-dripped blood and an ICU of grunts and groans, kept the curious well out of his path. The thirty or so useless souls still bickering or loitering at the intersection let him pass without issue. One stumbled in front of him but removed himself in time to avoid a collision. The man even apologized as he got out of the way.

About a half mile past the intersection, Ben saw that he was approaching a camp being constructed by the American Red Cross. A small group of white people in red vests were setting up tables and tents. Police and media swarmed all around. To avoid attention, Ben turned left along a side street which had been agitated into rubble by the earthquake. It was completely impassable by automobile. Three women ignored him as they pushed shopping carts filled with stolen goods up the steep gravelly hill. When the road ended a half mile or so later, Ben turned right to continue his northward trek. After what seemed like a long time, he reached Eastmoreland. He guessed he had to turn left, and again was ignored by the local population. This time it was by five muscular gangbangers loitering by some overturned cars. They were shirtless, heavily tattooed, and had the intimidating presence of criminals making up their own authority as they went along. One of them smiled at Ben and mocked him by playing with his lower lip.

The Motel Twelve was a long, three story structure the color of wild ivory. Ben figured it hadn't been painted in twenty years. He turned the corner and noticed that the earthquake had ripped a gaping trench through the parking lot and front lawn. Three trees had fallen by the motel entrance, and one leaned against the building's side by the external stairwell. Men with chainsaws were cutting up the lumber while others with shovels were clearing a passage through the lot. A short, bearded black man was directing the clean-up effort and promptly exchanged his push broom for a rifle as soon as he saw Ben.

"You get outta h'ya now, y'hear?" he warned.

Even though the man pointed the rifle at Ben's chest and stood only ten feet away, Ben wasn't unduly worried. The man wore a short-sleeved, white button-down shirt, which was tucked in over his sizable paunch. His khakis were clean, but his boots were not. An expensive computing device and a silver cross hung on chains around his neck. He looked a well-preserved fifty. The man's finger rested alongside the trigger guard rather than on the trigger itself. An experienced firearm handler, Ben thought. Another comforting sign. "I need to see a friend," he said, muffling his words through his swollen lips.

"He might be staying here. Third floor."

"No, he ain't," the man countered. "Ain't nobody up there!"

"He told me was. He told me last night."

"You get yo black ass outta h'ya!" the man shouted. The men stopped working and watched with interest in case their boss had any difficulty convincing this interloper he should shove off. The man's finger found its way to the trigger.

Ben held his hands up. "Please," he said. "I've come a long way." He began to worry about what he would do if Roland weren't in the Motel Twelve after all.

A matronly, gray-haired black lady approached from the motel, squinting in shock at the state of Ben's face. The man lowered his gun a few inches. "Boy, what in the worl' happened to you?" he asked.

"Mugged," Ben explained, lips smacking in thirst. "Got gangbangers that way. Look, my friend's in trouble. Just wanna get him and go." Ben noticed the workers still gripping their tools and staring at him as if he were a freak in a cage. He knew he looked black, but he had little experience *sounding* black. He suddenly hoped his fattened lips were impeding his speech enough to obscure this deficiency.

The man didn't lower his gun entirely. "Well, he ain't up there. We ain't got no runnin' water. No heat. Nothin'. All the gues' lef' aft' the earf-quake."

"You sure?"

"I had my maids check all the rooms the day after," the woman said in a sing-songy voice. "We don't break laws here. Law says you can't keep people without running water, so we don't keep people without running water." She appeared about as old as her husband and was as articulate as an educated white person. She wore a nice blue blouse over cleanly pressed slacks. She kept her salt-and-pepper afro in check with a white linen scarf. Ben imagined she had been quite attractive for a black woman in her youth.

"Mind if I take a look please?" Ben asked. "I've come a long way."

The man lowered his gun and looked to his workers. "All right now," he said. That was all he needed to say. The men got back on task without complaint or delay. He then looked at Ben. "Son, you need to head to the hospital right quick and have them doctors look at ya. What happened to your lip?"

Ben smiled painfully through his chapped, bleeding face. "Punch. Several punches."

"Do you need some water?" the woman asked.

"We got 'em on ice in a cooler over there," the man added.

Ben nearly cried imagining his relief. But given his devious reasons for being there and the fact that he was an accessory to murder from the night before, he could not bring himself to accept the hospitality of these people. Not yet. He promised himself he would, however, if Roland proved to be a no-show. Ben shook the man's hand. "No, thank you. Very kind. I'll just..." He left the rest of the sentence dangling as he motioned to the stairwell.

"I'll come with you," the woman said. This seemed to be the cue for the man to get back to business. He nodded at Ben and went back to sweeping away the dust and rubble.

"Don't have to do that," Ben said to the woman as he followed her to the office. The stairwell was immediately past it on the left.

"Yes, I do," she insisted. "If I got squatters in one of my rooms without any running water, I need to know about it."

Ben opened his mouth and then shut it. She was right. But if she went up there with him and saw Roland with his prostitute and his dead black john and his apparition suit and whatever else he had up there, then either he or Roland would have to kill her. With a silent, gastric laugh he realized that revolutions could be quite revolting indeed. He could not let that woman go up those stairs.

"Are you all right, son?" she asked, touching him on the arm. "Let me get you that water. We got some aspirin too."

She turned to go into the front office, and Ben reached out to her too late. He could see the water bottles in the cooler through the window. He frantically began fumbling through all his options, hurling each one of them against the wall in his mind to see which ones would stick. He figured he had twenty seconds.

Which of the following would give Ben the best chance of avoiding disaster?

A. leaving the premises immediately and hoping to return at a later, unspecified, time
B. allowing the woman to accompany him to the third floor and hoping that they didn't find Roland
C. running up the stairs while the woman's back was turned and hoping she or her husband didn't run up after him
D. making up a lie powerful and plausible enough to discourage the woman from accompanying him to the third floor (correct)

"Ma'am," Ben said, articulating as best he could under the circumstances. "I don't think you should go up there. My friend might be infected with the Kibaale virus."

The woman was about to walk through the door. She turned and looked at Ben. "What?" she gasped. She had light skin for a black person, and Ben noticed her face beginning to blanch.

"I didn't mention it before because I didn't want to worry you," Ben explained. "I survived Kibaale recently. That's why I have all these sores on my face. But because I survived, I'm immune."

Petrified, the woman started backing into the office. "I touched you."

"I'm not contagious."

"You shook my husband's hand!"

Again, she was right, but this time she was on the verge of panic. Trapped by his own tactic, Ben could only double down and hope for the best. "I am not contagious," he reassured her. "If I were, I'd be doubled over, rolling in pain, barely conscious. You lose all bladder and bowel function. You've seen the videos. I only look this way because it takes time for the skin to heal. But the infection in me is gone."

"How do you know?"

"I know because I am a male nurse working as an aid worker for the American Red Cross. We're providing disaster relief about a mile and a half down the road. This morning we started treating people. On Bellevue. South of here. By the railroad tracks."

"You're an aid worker looking like that?"

"I was mugged getting here. My red vest was stolen. I was lucky to get through alive."

"Then where's your ID?"

"Also stolen. You know how dangerous it is out there. Why else would your husband be pointing a rifle at me?"

Offended, the woman forgot herself and started waving her finger in a wide arc over her head. "Now, you don't *dare* question how I run *my* business on *my*—"

"Ma'am!" Ben shouted. He didn't want to do it. The skin on his face was not about to forgive him. And he prayed to whatever god that would take him that this woman's husband and his crew out in the parking lot didn't hear. "I'm trying to save a life! There are only ten of us in our unit. We have some injured people down there. They can't spare me more than a couple hours. And since I am the only one in the unit who has had Kibaale, I am the only person who can rescue the person hiding in your motel. Please!"

The woman shook her head. "I don't believe you're an aid worker," she said. "I don't know who you are, but you are not welcome here. You go back from where you came right now. You hear?"

Ben blinked several times. "Ma'am, I am an aid worker. I know what I am talking about. Kibaale is a nasty virus. It's related to Ebola, and it is only contagious through the exchange of bodily fluids, like saliva, mucous, mother's milk. But *not* by standing five feet from someone and talking to them. It's an RNA molecule that infects target cells and transcribes its genes into the cell's messenger RNA. It forces it to replicate, killing the target cell, and then going out to find more target cells to infect. This goes on exponentially. And what makes it so deadly is that the target cells tend to be white blood cells, monocytes, neutrophils. Our own immune system. The body can't defend itself unless it is given drugs to help it tell apart healthy cells from infected cells. Okay? Do you believe I am an aid worker now?"

Ben could tell the woman was smart. She wasn't quite buying it, no matter how many biological terms he threw at her. Ben wasn't quite buying it either. He had no idea if what he was saying was correct. He had written all of one Kibaale item eleven months earlier based on a news article he had little more than skimmed. He knew he was in the ballpark, but his doubts must have weakened his delivery somehow. And his atrocious appearance and impeded speech weren't helping. Ben was not an accomplished liar. The best way to lie is to shovel truth at a person as rapidly as possible until the person gets so tired of listening that their skepticism flags. Therein lies the breach through which trickeries can slip. This woman's primary strength, however, was skepticism. She folded her arms and looked to the parking lot, to her husband, about to call him over to help resolve the situation.

Ignoring his pain, Ben dropped his backpack and opened it. He produced Isaac's apparition suit and presented it to her as if selling a gown. A schoolgirl's expression of awe transformed her face, making her seem ten years younger. "Ma'am," he began, "if my friend is sick with Kibaale, I will put him in this, which is called an RVU, a retrovirus containment unit. It is state of the art. No virus can get through this material. And as you can see it covers a person from head to toe. It doesn't even have holes for eyes. I guarantee you that you will be safe as I escort my friend out of your motel." Ben paused for dramatic effect. "I'm asking your permission. Please."

Ben held his breath and hoped he hadn't oversold his case. He was out of tricks in any event. All he could do was pretend that his heart was not pounding like it wanted to knock him over. The woman softened her eyes and relented. He tried not to let the relief show on his face.

"There's a stairwell on the other side of the building," she said. "Take that when you leave. And don't let me ever see you here again."

She closed the door to the office behind her before Ben could say thank you. He said it anyway and then lurched up the stairs feeling his skin scream with every step.

Chapter 28

In the King James version of the book of Luke, what did Jesus transfer into a herd of swine to cause the pigs to run into a lake and drown?

A. poison
B. viruses
C. bacteria
D. devils (correct)

Twenty doors on either side of the Motel Twelve waited for Ben on the third floor. He sighed, fearing he would have to knock on every single one of them before getting to Roland. He also needed a way to clue Roland that it was him coming to his rescue and not the proprietor checking for squatters. He settled on knocking to the melody of 'In the Hall of the Mountain King' by Grieg. Or was it Ibsen? He couldn't remember. If Isaac shared his key stroke pattern with him, maybe he shared it with Roland as well.

Roland's door was the fourth one down on the side of the building facing away from the clean-up crew. Roland yanked it open before Ben could complete the second measure.

Ben understood instantly that Roland was a brute. A five-foot-three-inch, barrel chested brute. He had the eyes of an innocent babe which his scruff and muscles could not offset. But his inveterate sneer and crooked teeth could and did. Roland wore a pair of tight dungarees, which were not even buttoned at the waist, and nothing over his pale, hairless torso. His massive pectoral muscles resembled shields and seemed to make up a quarter of his body weight. His arms were the sculpted weapons of superheroes. Ben imagined that Roland could easily bench press 400 pounds. A second later he noticed that Roland was not in his Fickleskin.

It occurred to Ben that Roland's ability to recognize him in *his* Fickleskin, dark and darkening as it was, would be iffy at best. They had met once before, months prior, and had never really spoken. To Roland, Ben was just another quantum jockey working in the basement of the Garrett house. Now, he would be just another nigger.

Roland's eyes grew even wider once he perceived that a bloody, bedraggled black man was about to step over his threshold. He immediately activated his DSAK and aimed it at Ben, fully intending to stun him. Ben saw this coming and spoke up in time. "PVN! Put me in your PVN, Colonel Turk. Please!" he pleaded, hands up in cringing supplication.

"What?" Roland said in a thin growl. His gruffness seemed forced, as if to disguise the girlish timbre of his voice.

"Colonel Turk, I'm a friend," Ben whispered. "But I don't know who's listening. So please put me in your PVN."

Roland scratched a deltoid the size of a small coconut and sniffed as he networked Ben in. "Who. The fuck. Are you?" he demanded.

Ben cupped his hand to his chest. "I'm Lieutenant Cameron. Colonel Isaac Cameron's brother. I'm here to rescue you. You sent a sleep transmission yesterd—"

Roland grabbed Ben by the shirt with one hand and yanked him inside like a chimpanzee pulling a banana out of a tree. Ben felt Roland's enormous strength and, in his weakened state, was powerless to resist or to break his inevitable fall. He face-planted on the motel carpet. The rekindled burning made seconds feel like hours. He thrashed instinctively to make the pain in his face go away and then stopped when he remembered that thrashing only made things worse everywhere else.

"Fuck. You," Roland said, after shutting the door. "What the hell took you so long? And why do you smell like milk and piss?"

Ben rolled to his side and was blocked from further movement by his backpack. Trying to remove it without irritating the skin on his arms made him look like a man trying to make do without elbows. He soon gave up and contented himself with sitting partially upright against the dresser. He pressed his hands to his bleeding face as his only form of comfort. "Towel, please," he groaned.

Roland threw his hands back at Ben's audacity. "I don't have any goddamn towels! What am I? Fucking room service?"

Ben heard another groan in the room. A woman was lying on

the bed and seemed to be suffering far worse than he was. He also detected a deep, sepulchral stench wafting out of the bathroom. It stirred the bottom of his stomach like a cauldron. Roland kicked him in the thigh. "Get. The fuck. Up."

Ben dragged himself upright, perversely grateful to Roland for not kicking him a second time. He attempted wiping his face with the sleeve of his T-shirt but abandoned the idea when he ripped the skin on the side of his torso. He had to content himself with blinking the blood and sweat out of his eyes. "Sir, I changed my Fickleskin using the American Negro template only a few hours ago."

"I know that. Asshole!" Roland barked. "Do you think I'm so dumb to not know that?"

Ben decided it would be best not to respond to such a question.

Roland pointed behind him. "I have a beautiful white woman dying just a few feet behind me, and you come whining to me about Fickleskin?" Again, Ben kept quiet. Roland stepped closer, nearly jamming his chin into Ben's sternum. "I don't give a fuck who you are or how you got so goddamn ugly. I need you to help me transport this woman without killing her and without being seen to whatever mode of transport you came here in!"

"I'm sorry. I don't have transport nearby."

Roland opened his mouth and hissed, "How's that?"

"We abandoned our car on I-40 last night. There was an accident. A truck was knocked over. The traffic was—"

"Waitaminute. Waitaminute," Roland interrupted, threatening to karate chop Ben in the throat. "Who's 'we'?"

"My brother Isaac and I."

"And where's Isaac now?"

Ben gulped hard. "He didn't make it."

Roland said nothing. His expression did not change as he waited for more information. Ben had a feeling that Roland would start manually extracting that information if forced to wait too long, and so recounted every detail he could remember from the day before. He told his story dispassionately, without opinion or speculation, as if reading aloud a local news item from another country. He was repulsed by the smacking of his parched lips, but there was nothing he could do.

Ben expected Roland to interrupt him at any moment, but he didn't. Roland wasn't even looking at him by the time he finished. He wasn't looking at anything. "Colonel—" Ben ventured and then noticed something so unbelievable he had to interrupt himself. Tears were popping out of Roland's eyes. And these were not manly tears. Roland's face had morphed into a child's guileless grin as his barbell-hardened chest heaved up and down in anguish. He fell to his knees by the bed where the stricken woman lay and placed his arms on the blanket as if to pray. The sobs poured out of him. Embarrassed and afraid, Ben moved as little as possible, hoping not to be in the way in case Roland's mood were to swing violently in the other direction. Roland wiped his face on the blanket and stood, caressing the woman's brown hair. Ben finally afforded a good look at her and saw clearly that she was in a very bad way. She had been beaten up. One eye was swollen, and so was her jaw. Her bruises were a livid purple. A nasty gash on her forehead had been hastily bandaged. Ben could hear a cracking wheeze every time she took a short, shallow breath.

Ben guessed that Roland's medical kit must have been lost or compromised. All out-country soldiers were required to carry computerized medical kits which not only diagnosed thousands of medical problems but provided instructions and guidance on how to treat them.

"It kills me when we die, Ben," Roland whispered. "When one of us gets killed, part of me fucking dies, man. Why is it like that? Why does it hurt so much? Why does it hurt?"

Ben was so startled he stopped breathing. His heart began to race, and his body and mind were doing unsettling things on their own. He did not like the sensation, and for a moment forgot that he was trapped in a permanent costume of burning skin. It was if he were underwater and swimming upwards for dear life. But there was no daylight, and he didn't know when or if he would ever breathe again. It was a lonely purgatory of suspense, hoping to know, waiting to remember.

Roland resumed his sobs as he stroked the woman's face and then kissed her with pope-like tenderness. "This woman has given so much to our cause. She's a saint. Look at her. Look at her! Saint."

"What happened to her?"

"She was assaulted. Four groids. There was only supposed to be one of them. Fucking baboons. I got here as fast as I could."

Ben understood based on what Isaac had told him the day before. He figured that the four johns were now methane-bloated corpses stinking up the bathroom. "I'm sorry, Colonel," he said.

Roland turned back to Ben with his irreproachable eyes and strode across the room to embrace him. It was more like a football tackle. He pushed Ben into the dresser behind him. One arm hung around his neck, the other around his ribcage. Ben didn't make a sound despite the pain. He could only wait for it to end. He put one hand on Roland's back and kept it there in a show of warmth.

With his bear hug, Roland had spun Ben about ninety degrees to his left. This allowed Ben to look in the mirror above the dresser and see his new self for the first time. He was prepared for the shock, but not for the sadness. His skin was now a dull grayish-brown wherever blood wasn't still oozing from it. It was as if he were suffering from bubonic plague. His nose had been stretched and flattened fairly symmetrically, but his lower lip, still a bright, incongruous pink, had outpacing his upper one in approximating the Negroid ideal. His face seemed stuck in an existential pout.

Roland released him, but kept both hands on his shoulders. "Your brother Isaac was a good man," he assured Ben, tears still streaming. "I loved him, Ben. And I know he loved me. It was an honor to serve with him. He was a great white man who made the ultimate sacrifice for our worthy cause. You should be proud of him. I know I am."

Incredulous, Ben stared and blinked. How could anyone impart such a string of platitudes and expect to be taken seriously? Especially after spewing such vicious profanity just minutes prior? Ben's mind began spinning in epicycles pondering the impossible world of Roland Turk when it finally came to him: the reason why he was startled. "Sir," Ben said. "You remembered my name. How did you remember my name?"

Roland kissed him affectionately on the mouth. "I remember the face and name of every white person that joins our cause. God bless you, Ben. And God bless our cause."

They looked in each other's eyes, and Ben could tell from the childlike emptiness in Roland's that the man had seen the light; or, perhaps more accurately, the light has seen him. He was not of reality. He was possessed by an idea—or something—far greater than he was. It would not let him go, like an evil conjoined twin burrowing through his mind. Ben understood with painful clarity than Roland could kill him just as easily as he could kiss him.

"Yes, sir. Thank you, sir," Ben said, afraid that anything other than strict military protocol would tempt Roland away from his current equanimity.

"Lieutenant, we need to proceed to plan B," Roland said. "My car is a quarter mile south of here. It's a 2018 Dodge Grand Caravan. Black. Just head down Pauline and you'll see it on the street to your left if the groids haven't trashed it yet. I need you to retrieve it and bring it here so we can put our stricken agent in it and head for home."

"Yes sir," Ben said. "Um, sir? If we do that, she may not survive."

"Oh, she's going to fucking survive!" Roland said with dime-flip menace. Again he nearly poked Ben in the sternum with his chin. His hands were lowered, but his fists were clenched. "I don't tolerate defeatist bullshit when there's an agent in trouble! Do you hear me, faggot?"

"Yes sir. I have Isaac's medical kit in my backpack, sir. Perhaps while I am out getting the car you can start treating her. I can tell by looking that she may have a broken jaw and a broken orbital bone. I know with a medical kit we can—"

"Oh, you're a fucking doctor, now?"

"No, but in training, we learned that—"

From the way Roland's head began trembling like an electric toothbrush, Ben had a feeling that he was going to get punched in the gut. The moment Roland shifted his weight to get the torque he needed for a good body blow, Ben expelled all the air in his lungs and tightened up his midsection. The punch landed below the ribcage on Ben's left side. It hurt, of course, but Ben made it seem more devastating than it really was. He fell to his knees and started wheezing and gasping as if the wind had been knocked out of him. The blow also helped loosen Isaac's backpack, which enabled Ben to slip out of it while still on the floor.

"Get up! Get up!" Roland said, hauling Ben to his feet by his armpits. Ben screamed as the backpack slipped off of him. It felt as if Roland had just ripped the skin off from under his arms. He stood, trying not to look this unhinged bulldog in the eye during his next little stare down. Roland then grabbed an old-fashioned car key on the dresser and threw it at him. It bounced off Ben's chest before he knew it was even coming. "I'm gonna tell you again, fuckwit," Roland snarled. "Get the goddamn car!"

"Yes, sir!" Ben said as he bent over to retrieve the key on the floor. More abuse from Roland however tipped him into a rebellious state. He picked up the key and the medical kit from Isaac's backpack. It was about the size of two old-fashioned laptop computers stacked on top of each other. Roland saw what he was doing and tried to swat the kit away, but Ben held it high over his head as if keeping candy away from a saccharine-addled child. Enraged, Roland leaped for it a couple times and then with a shrill roar attempted to throw Ben across the room. Ben protected the kit as he crashed into the lamp on the nightstand between the beds. He stayed on his feet and was prepared to defend himself to the end when the afflicted woman on the bed at last gathered the strength to speak.

Chapter 29

The extremely warlike Jivaro of the Amazon was the only Mesoamerican tribe to successfully resist Spanish encroachment. In 1599, they massacred two Spanish settlements containing 25,000 white people because the whites had tried to tax their gold-trade. After slaughtering everyone in the settlements except the nubile females, they collected which body part as trophies?

A. big toes
B. gall bladders

C. Adam's apples
D. heads, the skins of which they peeled, skewered, boiled, baked, and heated over a fire until they shrunk to a fraction of their original size in order to fit on a string around a warrior's neck and become a euphemism for modern psychiatry (correct)

"Please, Roland," the woman whispered. "Let him treat me."

Roland glanced between her and Ben as if following the flight path of a housefly. "Vera. You're awake," he said, once again kneeling by her side. He spoke to her as if to a two-year-old child. "Are you okay, Sweetheart? How are you feeling? Are you all better?"

Vera mumbled something, but her shortness of breath and the death rattle in her voice made her impossible to understand. Roland moaned as he took her hand with both of his and kissed it. Ben placed Isaac's medical kit on the bed in front of him. "I'll get the car, sir," he whispered.

Ben was about to open the door when he looked back and saw Roland staring passively at the medical kit. He was running his finger over it, trying to find its fingerprint reader. Ben realized at once what was happening. Roland didn't know how to operate it! This explained why that poor woman had been lying there in agony for days. Roland had put her in harm's way but lacked the expertise to save her if things went wrong. Ben was shocked. A leader in the most potent revolt against the United States government in almost 200 years, and he didn't remember his basic training. Ben remembered his, all right. He remembered how strict Michael and Eli were. No one was allowed out-country without knowing how to operate a medical kit. No exceptions. Ben could operate the thing by the fifth night of training, and he was just an earner, not an active duty officer like Roland.

Roland began to blubber and convulse. "I'm disgusting! I'm no good! I'm nothing!" he intoned, as if beseeching the Lord to cleanse his unrighteousness. He began slapping himself in the head. The blows were hard and crisp and reddened the side of his face. "I'm disgusting! I'm no good! I'm nothing! I'm disgusting! I'm no good! I'm nothing!"

Vera tried to restrain him but lacked the strength. "Roland. It's okay."

"Sir!" Ben called. "I see you're trying to locate the kit's fingerprint reader. This is a new model, and the fingerprint protocol has been changed. This is probably why you can't find it. With your permission I can show you."

Roland heard him and curtailed his iambic mantra. He let fly two more slaps and then stopped those too. Ben took a couple tentative steps, reached across the bed, and activated the kit's fingerprint identifier. He then gingerly took the kit and placed it in front of him. Knowing better than to ask Roland for a towel again, Ben wiped his face on the bed sheet and activated the hologram function on the side of the kit. A pin-like light shone up and reflected off of a concave virtual mirror about a foot and a half above the bed. Above it, little light could be seen, but below it, an operating room aura shone down over the patient.

"This syncs the kit to your UID in your BREMAT device," he said, pressing a small, wired chip against the side of his throat. He then placed his hands, one by one, into the kit's slender glove pocket. "This sterilizes your hands and coats them with a synthetic program that's networked to the kit. It's similar technology to Fickleskin. Now the kit can see what you see and feel what you feel. Look."

Ben booted the kit's virtual screen, and a color image of Vera appeared whenever Ben looked at her. It was exactly what Ben saw. It blinked whenever he blinked. Roland did not come over to look. "I know about that," he insisted. "I did know about that."

"That's good," Ben said as he reached back into the kit for adhesive micro-gauze masks. Nearly invisible, they fit over one's nose and mouth and still allowed full freedom to speak and breathe while filtering out any noisome smells. Ben handed one to Roland who thankfully knew how to put it on. "Now, I'm about to examine the patient, and I don't know a thing about medicine," Ben said. "First, we'll need to slide the virtual screen over her so I can look at her and it at the same time. And I will have to keep my head and eyes perfectly still for this to work."

Ben slid the image to its appropriate place, and then, hunching over Vera, used a small controller on the kit to inch the image to exactly where it needed to be. "It's asking when she suffered these injuries. Was it four nights ago?"

Roland nodded. Ben didn't see him.

"I can't look up, so please answer."

"Yes. Saturday. The night of the earthquake."

"Okay. It's saying to remove the blanket now. Here goes."

Ben inched the blanket off of Vera and had to keep from gasping at what he saw and smelled. Her left leg was broken at the shin and engorged like a waterlogged corpse. Cuts and scrapes of various sizes peppered her legs and abdomen. As he trained his eyes delicately across her torso, he caught two large bruises on her ribcage.

"I would kill every groid on the planet if I could," Roland whispered. "I swear to God, Ben, if I had nothing left, if there was no chance and it was all finished, I would strap on a fucking apocalypto bomb like a goddamn dildo and go to the middle of Harlem or Detroit or sand-nigger Mecca or wherever and...put myself in the history books. It would be glorious. Like the fucking Rapture, but opening up the gates of Hell instead. I want the devastation so complete and my name so synonymous the death and destruction that no one would ever name their child Roland again."

In an effort to derail Roland from his genocidal tangent, Ben read the diagnoses on the kit's virtual screen. "Okay, it says here she's fractured her left tibia and fibula. Obviously."

"You know, that's a white thing, don't you?" Roland challenged.

"What's a white thing?"

"Going out like that. Blaze of glory, and all that. The tragic hero sacrificing himself so future generations can sing songs about how he raped Death in the ass. Only white people think like that. Only whites wrote stories like that. Even back in ancient times. Check out the *Ulster Cycle*. Or the fucking *Iliad* if you don't believe me."

Ben knew he didn't have time to believe. He also knew enough about the *Iliad* not to want to argue with Roland even if he did have the time. He put his finger to the digital screen and squinted. "She didn't burst an artery. So that's good. She's got a fever. Low blood pressure. It's not sure if she has, ah, Acute Respiratory Distress Syndrome or something called a neuro, pneumothorax. It's giving me percentages but they're changing a lot, and they're all near fifty. It needs more time to figure it out."

"What's a pneumothorax?"

"Not sure. I'm inferring it's a punctured or collapsed lung."

"Shit! Shit! Shit! Shit!"

"All right. I need to set her leg first. It's not saying why."

"Is that bad?"

"I don't know. First, we have to give her antibiotics and some powerful painkillers, which are also like anesthesia. I am going to insert my hand into the machine's glove pocket. It is going to give me five pills. Roland, can you please administer them?"

Roland nodded like an eager puppy. "Okay. Okay." Vera ingested the pills directly, but with her parched throat and swollen jaw she may as well have swallowed five thumbtacks. Ben watched with humbling awe and endured vicariously as much of her discomfort as he could. He then placed his hands on Vera's lower leg as the kit instructed. His hands had to be exactly placed, so for nearly ten minutes he adjusted them finger by finger, millimeter by millimeter. The machine indicated when it finally had a match. It couldn't have happened too soon since Ben was realizing how uncomfortable it is to hunch over someone motionlessly and not know when it's going to stop. He was also dripping sweat and blood on her, which he knew could not be helped.

"Okay, Vera, you can't move," Ben warned. "I'm going to put the bones back together. And then I am going to set them. It's gonna hurt. And I can't do this quickly. Do you understand?"

Groggy and half-conscious, Vera groaned and nodded.

Roland gaped at Ben with his vulnerable eyes. "If you hurt her, I will murder you," he warned.

"Roger that," Ben said without looking up. "Just hold her down by the left arm and collarbone, please. Okay. Here we go." With the image of his hands directly over his real ones, he fol-

lowed the glacial motion of the arrows onscreen. Vera shrieked
weakly whenever he placed the mildest pressure on her leg and
released bloodcurdling terror-croaks whenever he moved the
bones.

"DON'T YOU FUCKING HURT HER!" Roland screamed.
His threats grew more pornographic the closer bone got to bone.
Still, he held her down. She did not move.

After a grueling ten minutes the bone connections were ade-
quately restored. Ben readjusted his right hand according to the
screen and inserted his left back into the medical kit. The sound
of sucking air filled the room. Ben removed his hand, and attached to it was a thin, prehensile tube. He eased the tube to the
bone juncture, and from it came a shaving cream-like ooze
which quickly hardened into a medicated cast. He moved his
hand around the wound until it was set. He was clearly inexpe-
rienced and used far more ooze than necessary. Much of it landed on the sheet or on her other leg where it also hardened. He
ran out after covering her ankle and half of her foot. It was an
ugly mess, but he hoped that it would at least prevent the leg
from getting worse once they moved her.

Ben closed his eyes and stood to his full height to stretch his
beleaguered back and ease the pain which was wracking his
skin. "Hey, what are you? Taking a fucking break here?" Roland
barked.

"No, sir," Ben responded, resuming his Nosferatu pose over
the bed. Addressing the remaining wounds on the legs and abdomen was simply a matter of applying medicated liquid bandages and letting them self-dry. The kit then recommended a gy-
necological examination which Ben simply ignored. Even if an
obsessively protective Roland could be trusted not to spear his
fists into the back of Ben's mouth for touching Vera like that, the
idea of violating this woman after she had already been violated
repelled him. You'd need a heart of stone to take the Hippocratic
Oath, he thought.

Continuing on to the chest, the kit estimated a sixty-eight
percent chance that her worst troubles were caused by a pneumothorax. Ben swore to himself with vehemence his exhausted
body could not afford when he learned what treating this life-

threatening condition would entail. He looked to Roland. He could not have him around for this.

"Hey, Roland. I mean Colonel Turk, sir," he began. He was going to ask Roland if he had an anaerobe with which to dispose of the corpses in the bathroom. He stopped short when it occurred to him that if Roland hadn't bothered to learn how to operate a medical kit, he may not know how to work an anaerobe either. Ben also didn't think Roland would react seamlessly to directions from a subordinate, however delicately put they may be.

"Yes. What?" Roland said.

"So, how many guys attacked her?" he asked, stalling, trying to think.

"Four."

"Really?"

"Yeah, really."

"And you killed all of them. By yourself."

"I stunned two. Took a bowie knife to one. Killed the last one with my bare hands."

"Wow. Right here?"

"Yeah. You know, that's the point."

"What's the point?"

"Why Vera and I do this. We trap these fuckers, make them think they're going to get laid. Vera pretends she's a whore. Groids love them some snow bunny snatch. They know they never get it so good at home."

"Isaac told me all about it."

"You know, they never learn? When they hear they can get cheap white pussy they turn into cartoons. I mean groids are fucking priceless! They *hate* it when we characterize them as stupid, hormonal children, but when we dangle a cooz-oozing ginger cunt in front of them, they come following their rock-hard dicks like metal detectors."

"Well, what are we gonna do with them, sir?"

"You know, I've killed forty-seven groids? Personally."

To keep him on task, Ben pointed to the bathroom. "Including them?"

Roland re-did the math. "Make that fifty-one. Fifty-one deadbeat dads. Fifty-one losers who have kids and don't take care of them. You know the illegitimacy rate among groids is around eighty percent, right? A couple hundred guys like me, and we can have that number down ten percentage points in less than a year."

"But what are we going to do with *those* groids?" Ben asked, pointing to the bathroom.

"With who? Oh. The bodies?"

"Yes, sir. The med kit is saying I have about another half hour of work, and then we'll be okay to travel."

"I've got an anaerobe."

"Oh, good."

"Bet you were wondering why I didn't use it by now," Roland challenged. "I bet you were wondering. How much do you want to bet?"

Ben glanced at a quietly-suffering Vera. "Tell me," he said.

"Because I didn't know if I was going to need it for her. Pretty smart, huh?"

"Yes, it was," Ben said. This useless conversation was only making him more aware of Vera's condition and his exhaustion and how his Fickleskin was still feeling like burning hot plastic wrap on his skin. Ben had nothing more to say to Roland Turk. Roland squeaked like a rubber bath toy and sauntered towards the bathroom to clean up his linoleum killing floor. He twisted his wrists in anticipation. Ben shuddered with disgust when Roland left the door wide open behind him.

"Vera," Ben said. "I need you to listen carefully." He had to repeat himself a couple times before Vera, in her enervation, could acknowledge him. "It's saying here that you have a collapsed lung. Air is getting trapped in the space around the lungs. That's why you have shortness of breath. When your diaphragm pulls down and expands your lungs to bring in oxygen it stops short because the air around your lungs prevents them from expanding. This is why you're light headed and have shortness of breath. It's reducing your oxygen supply and putting pressure on your heart. The kit is saying we need to do something now or you might pass out and die. Do you understand?"

Vera blinked and nodded.

"Okay. I have no idea what I am doing, but the med kit wants me to insert a small, sterile tube between your ribs to allow air to escape. Okay? It's gonna hurt, and if I mess this up, I'm sorry."

Vera smiled and then turned away. Ben inserted his hand into the glove pocket and came out with a six-inch plastic tube. There was a short, hollow needle on one end and a suction device on the other. Also on his hand where two tiny napkins: one for sterilization, the other for anaesthetizing the insertion point. The kit warned that both napkins needed to be used within ninety seconds because they consisted of chemicals that degrade when reacting with air.

Ben stopped as Roland reappeared carrying one of his distended murder victims. An afro and soul patch dangled over one of Roland's arms, and two long legs dangled over the other. Smooth brown skin stretched everywhere in between. Stark naked, the man resembled a casualty in the Zulu War.

"Look at this shit!" Roland boasted. "This fucking gorilla. I caught him in mid-rape! He swatted my knife away and thought he could get me down and pound me out. I choked him to death with his own T-shirt. God! Look at the foot-long, Rasputin crotch monster on this guy. What a buck! I'd like to cut the dick off of every groid I kill and keep them as trophies. Stuff them and put them on my wall. I mean, look at it. Look at it! Fucking beautiful."

Grinning like a kid posing for pictures on his birthday, Roland clean and jerked his most dangerous game to a more comfortable position over his shoulder and then headed back to the bathroom. Ben was stupefied as he watched. Roland had taken off his jeans. He was entirely naked. And this time, he shut the door behind him.

***

Unlike Ben's journey to the Motel Twelve, their escape from it never deviated from design. Ben's chest tube insertion brought Vera out of immediate danger. The kit instructed him to attach it to her side with surgical tape and apply the suction device periodically. He then left the room to retrieve the minivan, which was where Roland had said it was. The passenger side window had been smashed in, but that was the extent of the damage. By the time he returned, Roland was ready to transfer Vera, and the anaerobe was doing its thing in the bathtub. Roland had packed Ben's medical kit in his bag along with his own. Ben found it odd, but was too exhausted to ask questions. Ben then told Roland about his plan to disguise him and Vera as Kibaale victims, and Roland donned his apparition suit. They shrouded Vera in her bloody bed sheet to help convince the locals that she had died from the virus. That would probably keep their curiosity in check. It worked. The proprietor and proprietress and their small crew watched from a safe distance as Ben and Roland loaded Vera into the back of the minivan and took off.

Roland said he knew a back-road exit from the city which would subject them to minimal scrutiny, and Ben trusted him utterly with their deliverance. He was too exhausted not to. Roland gave him one of his knives and taught him how to slit his own throat in case that decision proved to be unwise. Of course, in such a circumstance he'd have to slit Vera's as well.

Ironically enough, they escaped by driving over train tracks to traverse a river and circumvent the city to the north. Seven hours later, they were driving east on I-40 through the Appalachian Mountains, finally free from the clutches of a dying Memphis. Night was falling in a purple mist over the claustrophobic pines and craggy terrain all around them. The Moon had not yet come up, and the sky was clear and clean. Long branches overhead seemed to reach for them. They were always too late.

Part 5: Nathan's Ford

Chapter 30

How did Joseph Stalin gain supremacy over the Soviet Politburo after the death of Vladimir Lenin in 1924?

  A. He won the first general election in Soviet history by a landslide.
  B. He had been appointed by Lenin on his deathbed as the nation's new leader.

C. He was Lenin's first-born son and acquired power
through the right of primogeniture.
D. He isolated his opponents through a combination of
deft political maneuvering and hardline tactics and
later tried them on trumped up charges and executed
them in purges collectively known in the 1930s as the
Great Terror. (correct)

Dude's moves were wicked. Crossover dribbles, head fakes,
step back jumpers, fadeaways, slick drives. His game was all
about deception. Leading his opponent to be where he had no
intention of being, or, if the bluff were called, going there anyway. He was so quick he always had time. Ben noticed how he
never showed any of these skills in that scrimmage against Bennett. Curtis Book. He could have had a noteworthy college
hoops career and perhaps even made the NBA, but standing only five feet, eight inches tall must have made it a little too hard
for him. His eyes were bright and clear. His mouth seemed a
couple sizes too large for his face, and would break out in an
electric grin whenever either man scored. The lines on his face
were deep, healthy crevasses. As chocolate as a candy bar, he
wore nothing but a pair of sneakers, black socks, and black
shorts even though it was in the low-fifties and windy. In their
games of one-on-one, Ben was content to stay a step behind but
make him work hard for every point. He also made the most of
his three-inch height advantage on rebounds and managed to
swat away shots whenever Curtis got a little too cute. It had
been two weeks since Memphis. Ben was finally healed and as
comfortable in his new skin as he was going to get. He'd been
hoping that by looking like a black guy he could start playing
like one too. Curtis was only too happy to toss a soaking wet
blanket on such aspirations.

In their first game, Curtis beat him twenty-one to fourteen.
The second game was worse: twenty-one to twelve. In the third
game, however, Ben's physical training and stamina began to
pay off as Curtis lost some of his explosiveness and grew less
inclined to contest rebounds. Most importantly, he missed more.
Ben was losing only seventeen to sixteen when they saw Major
Martinetti walk out of the Bennett house garage. He was about

two hundred yards away and on the other side of a hilly, grassy field. Behind him on Bennett Street were a few more cars than usual. Black kids in ill-fitting clothes were one-upping each other on their self-go skateboards nearby. It was a bright, cloudless day with a bite of winter still in the breeze. Beyond the edges of the hemmed-in Appalachian sky they could hear the highway with oblivious vehicles zooming past.

Ben and Curtis stopped playing and waited. The old basketball court had once been part of a middle school playground but now stood alone near a swing set. Tall grass stood where the school had been. Thick, gray shrubs riddled a dusty baseball field nearby. Two soldiers in full Mandarin guise sat playing chess at a picnic table near the court. As soon as they noticed Martinetti, they squashed their cigarettes and collected their pieces. No instruction or communication was needed. Ben knew enough about the rules of chess to know that these two had not been playing chess. Kings moved like queens. Bishops moved like rooks. Pawns moved any which way. They played on a cheap, foldable, checkerboard with red and black squares. The square in the bottom right corner for each player was black, when it should have been white—or red. They were Roland's men, everyone knew. It was time to go.

Ben and Curtis followed them down to the Bennett house. "Thanks for the game, Curtis," Ben said, pumping fists with him. They walked slowly, exaggerating their strides in the tall grass to give the two men before them a growing lead.

"Yeah, man!" Curtis said. "You got a nice shot." His speech was quick yet partially mumbled through a thick piedmont drawl.

Ben turned to him. "So, Curtis, I gotta ask you—"

Curtis leaned back. "Aww, here it comes!"

"What the hell are you doing here, man?"

"Shit. All y'all wanna know that. Y'all's like, 'Is that Fickleskin you wearin' or what?' And I'm like, 'Naw, man. This shit's for real!'"

"I know it's for real," Ben said, pinching the skin on his own face. "This, on the other hand, is not!"

Curtis bent over in a cynical snort. "Ain't that the truth. You

boys might as well put on the ol' blackface with big red lips
singin' 'Mammy' n' shit." Curtis then stopped and, with one
hand on his chest and the other in the air, began a credible — and
shamelessly loud — rendition of 'Mammy.'

"Knock it off!" one of the men called back without looking.

"Who sang that?" Ben asked. "Nat King Cole?"

"Nah. Al Jolson."

"Who?"

"White cat. Hundred years ago. Used to dress up in black
face in the movies. Only honky they ever let party in Harlem.
Ever see *The Jazz Singer?*"

"Missed that one," Ben said.

"Well, I 'magine that Jolson was real glad he could take off
his makeup every night. Unlike you." Curtis punctuated his sentence with a sharp, pitiless guffaw. Ben sullenly said nothing.
"Welcome to the club, Bro," Curtis said behind a tall, picket
fence grin.

They were now close enough to Martinetti to end their conversation. Ben's curiosity about Curtis would have to wait. Michael and Eli had been reviewing his case for the past week, and
Martinetti's appearance from the garage indicated that they had
finally ended their deliberations.

"Court-martial proceedings require your presence again,
Lieutenant," Martinetti said, looking at Ben. He had an odd, self-
composed smile which Ben found reassuring. Still, the words
'court-martial', absorbed so insouciantly by the afternoon
breeze, nudged his stomach the wrong way. Was Martinetti trying to tell him something? He liked Martinetti. Tough, quiet,
self-confident, always looking for an excuse to say the word
'vagina.' Ben hoped that Martinetti liked him as well.

"Yes, sir," Ben said as he slipped between Roland's men. He
gave Curtis an optimistic good-bye nod and followed Martinetti
through the treacherous congestion of tools, toys, and farm machinery in the musty Bennett house garage. They could hear the
rumble of subterranean chatter before they even reached the bottom of the stairs to the barracks. Together they looked to the
door at the far end of the room. Roland and his men were making noise in the tunnels. Martinetti sighed, irritated. "They're not

even using a PVN," he said.

Stepping past Ben, Martinetti reached for the side of the door where the knob wasn't and waited to be identified. After a barely audible click, they were inside the dark tunnel, feeling their way with the string above them. After ninety-four steps, they stood outside the room where Roland was holding court with his men. It was the physical training room, the one with the nautilus machines and the treadmills and the 400 square feet of rubber floor mats used for mixed martial arts. Roland was regaling his audience with stories of his travels to Portland, Oregon. Big laughs all around did not relent when Martinetti opened the door.

"I lived in that rat's nest for six months and in Gresham off and on for two years," Roland declared. "You absolutely have to go to this book store I know in Hazelwood. What a commie nuthouse that is. Animated graphics of bin Laden and the Black Panthers everywhere. The bathrooms had wallpaper of that painting of Jesus covered in elephant shit. Just being there gave me a raging, fascist hard-on I wanted to go beat some hippies to death with."

The room was a blue rubber dungeon with a drooping seven-foot ceiling. Ben's head would have scraped it had there not been two steps leading down into the room. Fluorescent light strips illuminated everything with sitcom clarity. Fifteen men in various shades of Fickleskin sat on benches or on the floor. They were in their workout gear, sweaty and healthy and focused on Roland who faced them with his back angled obliquely to the door. His massive arms hovered on either side of him like bodyguards. Thick, black sweatpants could not hide his radically bowed legs. Ben imagined that Roland could stand at attention and still fit a grapefruit between his knees. He kept looking to his audience as he addressed Martinetti. "Afternoon, Major."

"Sir, do you know we could hear you from the stairs?" Martinetti said.

Roland rolled his eyes and winked at his audience. "Sorry, Major. The boys and I got a little carried away. Won't happen again."

Amid a swirl of importunate snickers, a few of the men took

up the chant: "Number Three! Number Three! Number Three!"
Roland did nothing to quiet them down.

"Are you going to leave the door open so the whole world
can hear us, genius?" Roland asked, this time deigning to look at
Martinetti. Martinetti smirked defiantly back at him and didn't
move. During the insolent delay, Ben began to sweat and felt his
heart thump. Looking at Martinetti's cool, confident stance however, he had a feeling that Martinetti's heart was doing just fine.

"No, sir," Martinetti said finally.

"Then shut the fucking door, shitwit!" Roland commanded.
Murmurs of approval rumbled from the crowd. Martinetti again
tickled Roland's wrath with an order-following moratorium.
This one was even longer. "Yes, sir," he said as he finally started
backing out of the doorway.

And that's when Roland noticed Ben. "Oh! Look who we
have here! Isaac Cameron's kid brother! The man who saved the
day in Memphis!"

Pretending that this unwelcome attention was not unwelcome at all, Ben smiled and waved to the crowd. He could hear
Martinetti sigh in annoyance as he stepped aside so everyone
could get a clear view of Ben.

"Come here, son!" Roland said, waving him over. "It's okay."

Without risking a glance at Martinetti, Ben took the seven
steps he needed to stand next to Roland before the boisterous
throng. Roland clapped a hand over his shoulder. "This man,"
he began, "at great risk to himself, infiltrated the groid population of Memphis and walked miles through hostile territory to
rescue Vera Barry and myself. Good job, Ben!"

The crowd clapped and whistled to show their appreciation.
Being closer to them, Ben got a look at the men who were clearly
so supportive of Roland. He could tell they were tough, serious,
athletic. He saw black eyes, swollen lips, missing teeth, cauli-
flower ears, and bloody bandages. It reminded him of his disastrous tryout for the wrestling team sophomore year in high
school. The line between civility and violence was pretty thin
with some of those guys. Here it was even thinner. Their mouths
hung open. Their bodies were tense and still. Their truculent
eyes glistened as if longing to cross a stretch of no-man's land.

They were waiting only for their fearless, fanatical leader to give the order.

"Thank you, Colonel!" Ben said in an appropriately chipper tone. This was the first time Roland had spoken to him since the Memphis rescue.

Roland gave him a couple brotherly shakes which Ben imagined looked ridiculous given their stark difference in stature. "No, thank *you*, Lieutenant! You did the white race proud. And you made yourself go full-groid to do it, too. Permanently. Now, that's sacrifice!"

The men laughed and clapped and hollered. Embarrassed, Ben felt himself blushing but knew no one could tell by looking at him. He decided the best course of action would be to smile and say nothing, an option Roland, apparently, would not allow. "So what do you have to say for yourself, Lieutenant?" Roland asked. "Any words?"

Ben shook his head in an easy, bashful motion. "Noooo," he demurred. "I did what any one of us would have done under the circumstances."

"Sir," Martinetti said. "I was instructed by generals Archer and Humphrey to lead the lieutenant back to his court-martial—"

Roland turned to Martinetti. "Shut the fuck up, Major. That's an order."

Insolent smirk gone, Martinetti stood there, looking at no one and registering as little emotion as possible. Ben felt his breath escape. He was on his own. "Come on, Lieutenant," Roland said. "Anything you want to say to the guys?"

"Sir?"

Roland pointed a finger at Ben, his tone considerably less brotherly than before. "Hey, I have a great idea! Why don't you explain to the men what went down that afternoon!" Ben looked at Roland for further clarification. "In the motel room. How we saved Vera's life. You remember. Don't you, Lieutenant?"

"Yes, sir," Ben said, knowing that the time for hesitation was over. He also finally discerned Roland's purpose. Roland Turk was the belligerent fool who took an agent on a dangerous, inessential, and completely unauthorized mission and nearly got her killed because he did not remember his training. This was the truth, and Roland was egging Ben on to say it because to say it would clarify things politically to say the least. Telling the truth would incite nothing short of indignant rage from Roland. He would naturally be forced to denounce Ben as a slanderer, and, by extension, Michael, Eli, Martinetti, and the rest of the movement's brass for propagating such an insidious lie. Ben knew that this would only edge the base in Nathan's Ford closer to civil war, which could only benefit Roland. Ben also did not want to contemplate the immediate effects of such an admission. He was currently in Roland's wheelhouse with the man's full strength on display. Why provoke a lion in his den? On the other hand, *not* telling the truth would ingratiate himself with a man he feared and despised while alienating the very people he felt were the movement's most competent leaders.

In a flash he saw Roland Turk as a political genius and deadly adversary. In one move Roland consolidated his fearsome power while inviting those who would stand in his way to disorganize and blunder. Ben had no illusions about what such a blunder would cost.

"Basically, Colonel Turk's medical kit had been damaged," Ben began. "That prevented him from treating Vera—I mean Agent Barry. So when I got there, he took out my medical kit and used it to save her. Just like that. I assisted him, but my biggest role was fetching the minivan. Colonel Turk couldn't do that because he was tending to Vera. Also, if he went out there himself, there were good chances he wouldn't survive in a hostile black environment because he's white."

Ben offered a smile and a nod as his conclusion and hoped it would be enough. Roland offered no response, not even body language, for nearly six seconds, each exponentially more excruciating than the one before it. Suddenly he started beaming. "Couldn't have said it better myself!" he declared. While this eased the tension in the room, Ben didn't think he could hate a human being more than he hated Roland Turk. Outwardly, however, he smiled and shook Roland's hand to general and fervent applause. During this time, Martinetti had the sense to close the door.

Then Ben had an idea. Roland's power could be his power too, if only he could say the right things. "I gotta go get court-martialed now!" he announced, pumping his fist in the air. This elicited a volley of boos and jeers. "You think I deserve a court-martial?"

"Hell, no!" the men shouted amid a wave of pornographic profanity.

"I can't hear you! Do you think I deserve a court-martial?"

The men clamored their negative replies at top volume.

"That's right! I rescue Colonel Turk and this is how they reward me? Hell, no!"

"Hell, no!" the crowd responded.

"Say it again! Hell, no!"

"HELL NO!"

"HELL NO!" Ben repeated.

"HELL NO!" came the response.

Ben folded his arms and held out his chin like Mussolini as the crowd gave him the vociferous response he'd been hoping for. He considered jumping among the men for some shoulder thumping and high-fives, but refrained as he imagined how ridiculous he would look getting manhandled by these bruisers. Instead, he pointed to a few of the more energetic ones and put his fist back in the air. Then he did what he wanted to do all along: he stepped back to the door. "That's right! Gotta go fight the good fight! Wish me luck! Thank you! Thank you!"

His support was unanimous and enthusiastic with the lone exception of Roland. Roland was smiling at Ben, but you couldn't tell from his placid, unadulterated eyes. He was clapping, but he wasn't making a sound. Ben afforded a friendly, one-second glance at his nemesis. Any longer and Roland could have construed it as a challenge. With something this dangerous, Ben wanted to leave behind as much doubt as possible.

In the tunnels a safe distance away, Ben heard Martinetti chortle as if coughing up hairballs. "Wish me luck! Thank you! Thank you!" he mocked. His imitation of Ben was passable, and Ben was deliriously grateful for the opportunity to laugh.

Chapter 31

Which African-American leader encouraged Southern blacks to accept segregation and Jim Crow laws in return for basic public education, due process, and Northern funding for black enterprises?

A. Marcus Garvey
B. W. E. B. Du Bois
C. Frederick Douglass
D. Booker T. Washington (correct)

Ben stood alone in the middle of the thin, windowless room with his hands behind his back. The walls, ceiling, and floor were made of concrete, and had various rugs and quilts and things hanging in all places to absorb sound. Fluorescent strips on the ceiling resembled upside-down runway lights. It was always cold and dank in those tunnels, but with the ventilation system not working properly, the three rooms under the Garrett house which Michael and Eli used as headquarters were especially cold and especially dank. The engineers responsible for their upkeep belonged to Roland. Last anyone heard, they were going to get to it any day.

Michael sat crossed-legged on a folding chair at an old, torn up card table with a bottled water and a legacy e-reader device. Head tilted, he listened to Eli read their decision. He wore black boots, jeans, and a blue sailor's jacket buttoned up so high that Ben couldn't tell if he had a shirt on underneath. As usual, he was in his Fickleskin, but not anymore to appear Chinese. His skin was bronzed and his cheeks puffed to affect an overall roundness of face. Ben guessed it was one of the central Asian or Arab templates, which made sense given that Michael would be leading the upcoming raid in Bethesda. Ben had wondered why their Horseman would allow one of their generals to lead such a risky raid. Rumor in the tunnels had it that Michael had forcefully insisted. Beneath his nose was the shadow of an incipient mustache.

Eli stood on the other side of the table and addressed Ben directly. He wore hiking boots, multi-pocketed trekking pants, and a blue sweater which did little to flatter his cheese curd physique. Glasses made him seem even less threatening. As usual, he was not in his Fickleskin. Also in the room were five bookish officers seated at deskpods and Major Martinetti, who stood. That was it. That was the extent of Michael and Eli's strength, Ben feared. He knew there were others. Eight more gamers, still green from their recent training. Five engineers. Ian and his small group of techies. Three MDs. Four officers who were still out-country. About two or three others, older men, whom he had seen but did not know. And then there were the women. Could any of these be counted on to resist Roland if he were to make a move?

"First of all, Lieutenant, we finally played the composite video constructed from your brother's neural chip," Eli began. His voice was thin and close to trembling. Ben had never seen Eli so distraught. "The events seem to have transpired as you described. Colonel Cameron died simply because he removed his seatbelt and drove off a cliff. The cliff had been caused by the earthquake, and we agree that at night it was impossible to see until the last moment." Eli paused and shook his head as if to lament the atrocious luck of it all. Michael, on the other hand, remained perfectly still. "As a result you will not be charged with negligent homicide."

Eli paused again, this time removing his glasses to wipe tears from his eyes with his massive wrists. He motioned to Michael, and, without even bothering to gauge his reaction, sat down. Michael took the hint and stood.

"We would also like to commend you for your valor and your sacrifice, Lieutenant," Michael began in a much steadier voice. "Your resourcefulness, your conscientious adherence to protocol, your successful rescue of Colonel Turk and Agent Barry all weigh in your favor. We also applaud your decision to adopt the North American Negro template when applying your Fickleskin. You were made fully aware of the risks during training and you took them anyway so as to not compromise the integrity of this imperative mission. General Humphrey informs me that with your Fickleskin permanently deactivated you may expect a slight depigmentation—over time—as long as you stay out of sunlight and apply the appropriate dermatological medications, which, unfortunately, we do not have at present in Nathan's Ford."

Michael stopped. Ben's only response was to swallow. "We would also like to again extend our condolences for the loss of your brother, Colonel Isaac Cameron," Michael continued. "He was one of our best officers, and he contributed perhaps more than any one man to the cohesion of the group in Nathan's Ford."

Ben bit his lip and bowed his head.

"With that out of the way, we have decided to sentence you to three months in the minimum security north tunnel holding cell for deliberately disobeying orders to return to the Garrett house. We are not equipped for proper incarceration, as you know. The holding cell is reserved for minor offenses committed by offenders we know we can trust. So your punishment will be brief and lenient. You will work under the supervision of General Humphrey on camouflaging money transfers via brood sites."

"Basically, you will be doing the same work you did prior to Memphis," Eli said. "You'll just be sleeping in the holding cell instead of your bunk. We've also told your boss at Invorne that you've had a death in the family, which explains your unexpected absence. We'll give you the details before you start tomorrow. You'll also be free to leave your cell under guard between 1500 and 1600 hours every day for exercise. We'll have three meals sent to you every day. Understood?"

"Understood, sir," Ben said.

"General Archer, permission to speak," said an officer. He took being ignored by everyone as a 'yes' and continued. "Right now, Lieutenant Cameron is pretty popular with Colonel Turk and his crew. So perhaps three months might be too long to incarcerate—"

"Excuse me, Captain," Eli interrupted. "It's *our* crew! Not Turk's!" Suddenly annoyed, Eli stood and threw his hands in the air. "Okay, everybody out! Except for you and you," he said, pointing to Ben and Martinetti. Michael seemed even more clueless than the others. After the room cleared out, Eli glowered at

Ben. "If there ever was a time for you to be honest, Lieutenant, it is now."

"Of course, sir," Ben said.

"I have a hard time believing that Colonel Turk, by himself, used your medical kit to save Agent Barry," he said, fat bulging beneath his chin. "Did he?"

"Well, in my report—"

"I know what's in your report, Lieutenant. I want you to explain why it was your fingerprint that activated the kit and not Roland's."

"Because it was my kit. Or Isaac's, really. And when I took it out from my bag I naturally activated it. But then Roland insisted that he take over from there."

"Yes. It's too bad that Agent Barry was unconscious during this time. We have no one but you and Colonel Turk to corroborate this."

"That's what happened, sir."

"Don't you find it curious that the kit was damaged while you were gone? Roland claims he dropped it in the room's bathtub while he was disposing of the bodies."

"I wasn't there, sir. So I—"

"You see why I'm asking you this, don't you?" Eli said, pointing a pudgy, powerful finger at Ben. "Because the machine was damaged, we have no record of whose BREMAT device was synced to it. Are you sure you don't know how the kit became damaged?"

"No. When I got back, the kit was already packed in Roland's bag."

"Did he even mention that it had been damaged?"

"No. The first I heard about it was a couple days after we got back. After Roland filed his report."

"Did he at least tell you *why* he packed both medical kits in his bag?" Eli asked. "Why didn't he give you back your medical kit so you could stow it in your bag?"

"I don't know, sir. I did think it was odd at the time."

"And you didn't think to ask him."

"No, sir. We were focused on getting out of there as quickly as possible."

"So shortly after you activated your medical kit, he told you to get the minivan while he took care of Vera."

"That's right, sir."

"And how long did it take for you to find the minivan?"

"I don't remember."

"Why don't you remember?"

"Not to sound disrespectful, sir, but I didn't think to time it."

"Well, how far away was the minivan?"

Ben took a breath and gambled that it didn't make him seem like he was hesitating. This was a detail of the story he never included in his report. If he had, he would have been forced to lie. And lies, he knew, have a way of unraveling over time. He remembered Roland telling him the minivan was a quarter mile south of the motel. In reality, it was slightly less than that. Even in his enervated state it took Ben all of thirty minutes to get there and drive back. If he had put Vera in the hands of Roland as soon as he arrived and then left to retrieve the minivan, there wouldn't have been enough time to jibe with his reported account, which said that Vera was in stable condition with her left leg in a cast and a catheter lodged in her ribcage by the time he returned. Ben had hunched over her for well over an hour saving her. So over an hour for him to travel less than a quarter mile and back? No way Eli and Michael miss a plot hole that big, he thought.

"I don't know, sir," Ben said. "It felt like it was over a mile."

"Over a mile?"

"I really don't know. It seemed far."

"Did Colonel Turk tell you how far away it was?"

"I—I don't recall."

"In Turk's report, he said the minivan was a lot less than a mile away."

Ben didn't know what to say other than, "Yes, sir."

"Quarter mile to be exact."

"I was unaware of that, sir."

"And Pauline doesn't go south much more than a quarter mile from your motel anyway."

"Sir, I—"

"Excuse me, General," Michael interrupted. "Doesn't Pauline

cross a highway and then turn into a different road south of it?"

Eli flashed an exasperated look at Michael. "So what?"

"Well, maybe Ben here did walk a little further than you think."

"First of all, Roland said the minivan was a quarter mile away. And secondly, even with the new road it still doesn't add up to even a half mile."

"Okay," Michael said, leaning back and surrendering the point.

Eli turned back to Ben, brimming with impatience. "So, Lieutenant, was the minivan only a quarter mile away or not?"

Ben shifted his weight and placed his arms behind his back. "It seemed a lot farther than that, sir."

"Well, it would have to be, Lieutenant. I saw Agent Barry when you returned to Nathan's Ford. It would take a very long time for an untrained hand guided by a medical kit to treat her the way she'd been treated. Definitely over an hour." Eli cleared his throat and considered Ben for a moment. "So how is it that it took you over an hour to fetch a minivan that was only a stone's throw away? Were you detained by locals?"

"No, sir."

"Did you pass out along the way?"

"Not that I'm aware."

"Then why?"

"Sir, with all due respect, you've read my report. You know what I had been through. I was in such bad shape with my Fickleskin transformation that every step was murder. I was moving very slowly. It was all I could do to walk in a straight line. I was lucky I didn't collapse on the curb."

Eli sat down and pursed his lips. "Ben, I think you're a very good fibber," he said. "I have a hard time believing your story. I don't see how one minute you're clever enough to convince a complete stranger that you're an aid worker looking for Kibaale patients, and then next minute you're wandering cluelessly on the street unable to tell a quarter mile from one."

Ben hung his head. There was no way he was going to cop to the lie. Not to these two. Aside from ruining his credibility forever, reversing himself would force Eli and Michael to take action against Roland. And given his cadre of testosterone-addled henchmen, this would not bode well for the movement. More importantly, Ben had no fear of Michael and Eli. They were civilized. They followed rules. If either of them wanted to execute him, they would have done so already, and not without a real trial. And all the niggling and caviling over a quarter mile here, a half hour there belied their petty, managerial methods, not to be mistaken for real leadership. Roland, on the other hand, was a real leader. He was sexy, decisive, dangerous, insane. He did a good job of masking the insane part in a brilliant display of profane passion and race patriotism. Of course, Ben had no intention of stagediving into the churning mosh pit that was Roland's camp. He just knew better than to challenge the most powerful man in Nathan's Ford on his home turf without first ascertaining where all the pieces stood on the board. It was a showdown that he, surprisingly enough, was not exactly dreading.

"General Humphrey, have you ever applied the Fickleskin North American Negro template to yourself?" Ben asked. An insolent question since the only possible answer would be no.

"We ask the questions here, Lieutenant. Not—"

"Sir, I was in agony," Ben interrupted. "I was moving like a zombie. The slow kind, you know, from the old movies. It killed me to bend my knees and ankles. Every inch of my body hurt. I was hungry. I was tired. I hadn't slept. I was feverish. I was light-headed. I kept my head down, and I moved very, very slowly. Maybe the van was a quarter mile away. Maybe it was a mile away. I don't know. I don't remember." Ben raised his fists to his chest in a non-threatening show of frustration. "I'm sorry I cannot give you better information. But it's all I have!"

Ben wished that Eli would have taken at least some time to consider what he had just said before responding. He didn't. "What you don't seem to understand, Lieutenant, is that we're being generous for not incarcerating you longer than three months. This generosity can be easily revoked."

Ben nodded respectfully and otherwise had nothing more to add. Michael broke the ensuing silence by tapping Eli on the knee. "Look, I understand your concern, but I think there's reasonable doubt here."

"Reasonable doubt!" Eli scoffed.

"Yes. Everything Lieutenant Cameron has said so far is consistent and plausible," Michael said. Eli turned away as if looking at Michael would only tempt him to say what he really wanted to say. "I also think you're overreacting a little bit," Michael went on. "You're trying to get Ben to admit to saving Agent Barry in order to trump up a charge of negligence against Roland."

"I think Colonel Turk lied in his report," Eli said. "I don't think he knows how to operate a medical kit."

"Then why don't you place one in front of him and prove it?" Michael challenged.

Eli grimaced seemingly in anger. "Because we all know there are political reasons why we shouldn't do that," he said almost under his breath. An astonishing admission, even though Ben was not terribly astonished. He saw it clearly. Eli was *afraid* to put the question to Roland. A leader afraid of his subordinate. Clearly, Eli wanted to take this to Roland. But without corroborating evidence or testimony he wouldn't dare. Ben didn't know whether to disdain or sympathize with Eli for this.

"I guess that means we have no excuse not to promote him," Michael suggested blithely.

"You think we should make him Number Three?"

"He is next in line."

"He's a hothead."

"We could really use him in Maryland."

"He's a menace."

"Now I think you're being hyperbolic, General," Michael said. "You see that, don't you? It's not like he'll be put in charge of Nathan's Ford. There's still you and me. I've also worked with Roland. He's a good soldier. He can be trusted to hold his own under fire. He was also incarcerated after Culpepper and kept quiet, so that counts for something."

Ben looked sharply at Michael. Culpepper had led up to Wahoo. He remembered Isaac telling him about it, but he never said that Roland had been involved. Could it be true?

"Roland also has something that many whites today don't have, even here," Michael continued, "and that is complete hatred for the enemy. Of course, we all know who the enemy is, but precious few can muster the consummate and resolute enmity that Roland can. And that's useful. In fact, it's instrumental to our survival. The men certainly recognize it. It would be foolish for us to pretend that they don't."

"Oh, so blind hatred now dictates policy?" Eli challenged. "We are to acquiesce to our basest, most animalistic impulses?"

"Of course not," Michael countered like a patient college professor. "But in times of total war it has always been considered honorable to love your friends and hate your enemies. The ancient Greeks knew this well. Euripides, Xenophon. Even Plato in his *Republic* averred that justice is giving good to friends and evil to enemies."

Eli leaned back in his chair and waved his hand as if to swat away Michael's argument. "Ah, so you're telling me that the Sermon on the Mount never happened." Michael sighed and fidgeted, awaiting the tiresome arguments he knew were to follow. Ben was almost entertained by the standoff: the preacher versus the lecturer. "Michael, whether you believe in God or not, we must always strive for the divine," Eli went on. "We must know that what we do now will be judged for eternity. And please do not think your Greeks and Romans did not know that. With or without religion we must hold ourselves to a high, even an impossibly high, moral standard because that is the only thing that separates us from animals. That is the only thing that makes civilizations great."

"Not the only thing," Michael said. "Keeping the polis free of barbarians is another."

"We've had barbarians in this country since its inception. African blacks and aboriginals. Did that ever stop America from being great? And, yes, I do think, for our survival, we should temporarily hate our enemies. But our true enemies are the small cohort of academic atheists, racial Leftists, and radical Muslims now occupying Washington. Colonel Turk, however, believes that anyone who isn't white is the enemy. *All* blacks. *All* Arabs. *All* Hispanics. He hates the people, not just their wicked leaders."

Michael leaned forward and rested his chin in his hand.

"Don't the people bear responsibility for the totalitarians they elect into office?"

"Yes, but when led with a firm and wise hand, these people have done and still can do a lot of good! We need to return to that."

"But we already tried that approach, General. We tried living with these people and governing them and protecting them from their own devilish natures. Look how well it turned out."

"We failed because we lost our racial confidence," Eli insisted. "We need to regain that confidence and remember what's in our hearts. Only then will they respect us again and accept the reasonable controls we place on them. In the early twentieth century, for example, most blacks accepted these controls and were much better behaved and productive than they are today. I think this was the case up to about 1960 which ended a golden age for them and for us."

"What was wrong with 1860?"

"Excuse me?"

"While I disagree with Roland on a lot of things and am not comfortable with his lack of control, I think he's basically right," Michael said. "These people have to go. All of them. Either that or we enslave them again. And I say this not because of some evil impulse but because it has been historically proven that large proportions of inferior, tribal races in a free and open democracy must eventually lead to the kind of totalitarianism that we have today. This is why democracy never originated in Africa or in the Mesoamerican or Arab worlds. These people are violent and tribal by nature and necessarily will promote leadership that is also violent and tribal. Maybe Roland sees blacks, Hispanics, Arabs and other inferior peoples as an existential threat."

Eli scoffed. "Roland doesn't even know what the word 'existential' means!"

"Sophistry," Michael chided.

"He sees them as a threat because he's xenophobic."

"Tautology," Michael chided again, this time lilting the word into song.

"And he's xenophobic because he's a psychopath."

"And that's an ad hominem attack," Michael said, pointing

his finger to the floor.

"No. It's a biological fact," Eli asserted. "I studied psychiatry in medical school, General. It is my professional opinion that Colonel Turk suffers from a mental illness, perhaps caused by a combination of paranoid and antisocial personality disorders and exacerbated by the stress of the revolution."

"I bet you'd feel the same way about Alexander the Great or Augustus Caesar," Michael challenged. "Isn't that right, Doctor?"

"Put them on my couch and I'll let you know," Eli shot back.

Ben couldn't tell if that was some cute in-joke or nasty retort between rival colleagues. He also wasn't terribly interested in finding out. "Uh, Generals?" he began. "Are we done here? Can I go now?"

They both looked at him. He was both out of line and not. Michael gestured to Eli, giving him the floor. Eli cleared his throat. "Have Major Martinetti escort you to the holding cell at eighteen hundred hours," Eli said. "It's almost fourteen hundred now, so you have a little time for yourself."

"Thank you, sir," Ben said, saluting both men, and then exiting. Just as he and Martinetti walked through the door, he overheard Eli telling Michael, "I cannot be cruel to him."

Moments later in the tunnel, Ben felt Martinetti's hand on his shoulder, stopping him. Ben turned to peer at him through six inches of fusty pitch. Martinetti activated his PVN. "I understand why you said what you said in there," he said. "I don't think those two really comprehend what Roland is capable of."

"I don't think they know how crazy he is," Ben said. "I've seen it up close."

"Me too. But tell me, honestly, did Roland operate the med kit by himself? Did he really?"

For the first time since his brother's death Ben felt he could possibly have a friend and ally in this terrible rabbit warren war. He felt his eyes moisten thinking of all things he'd like to share with Martinetti but couldn't.

"Yes," Ben said, compelled by his own mendacity. "Yes, he did."

Chapter 32

A rare form of dwarfism called diastrophic dysplasia is a genetic disorder which is inherited recessively. A child MUST be affected with diastrophic dysplasia when

A. one parent has a copy of the mutated gene.
B. both parents have a copy of the mutated gene.
C. one parent passes the mutated gene to the child.
D. both parents pass the mutated gene to the child. (correct)

"I'm definitely in it for the pussy," Martinetti deadpanned through his characteristic smirk. "That's why I signed up."

Ben took a swig of beer and nearly spat it out laughing. "Gonna have a hard time finding that around here."

"The worst thing is getting used to having no women around. This place is such a hard dick convention you can't even beat off without bruising the head of your cock on the bunk above you."

Ben kept laughing, feeling the pleasant, buzzing effects of his beer. He was halfway through his third one. "But you keep doing it, don't you?"

"Of course."

"Dedication."

"Ya gotta make sacrifices."

"But if you ever find yourself fantasizing over Humphrey's man boobs, you'll probably need to switch hands or something."

"Fah! I'm almost forty," Martinetti said. "They got me beating off like I'm ten."

Ben frowned facetiously. "You were beating off at ten?"

Martinetti winked. "Well, more like eight."

Ben kept laughing until he coughed.

They sat in a long booth in the Last Gasp Bar and Grill in Nathan's Ford. Despite being devoid of customers, the place was perhaps not quite as dingy as it sounded. It was a well-kept, nostalgic diner with turn-of-the-century memorabilia on the walls: posters of elderly NFL and NBA stars in their primes, stills from *The Lord of the Rings*, *Harry Potter*, Marvel Comics film franchises, and animated screenshots from a few vindictively violent video

games. They even converted a handful of giant-sized iPads into
table tops so children could manipulate them with their fingers
while eating pizza and ice cream. Still, from the torn, vinyl tablecloths to the plastic-covered menus to the gunk-covered salt and
pepper shakers, an astute diner could size up this restaurant's
middling quality before taking a bite of anything.

Martinetti took a long pull from his beer. "Sometimes I wonder why I joined this turkey outfit."

"Really?"

Martinetti sighed and plopped his elbows on the table. "No,
not really."

"Was it bad?"

Martinetti hung his head. "Yeah. Pregnant wife and daughter
walking to their car in a supermarket parking lot outside of Boston. Flash mob. Six niggers with pipes and baseball bats. That
was it. Not terribly interesting. My daughter died right away.
My wife lingered in critical condition for about a week before
she passed. 'Course the baby didn't make it either."

"Sorry to hear that," Ben offered, lame but honest.

Martinetti's smirk grew into a disingenuous smile. "Me too!
What was interesting though was that three of those animals
had serious priors. Like armed robbery and assault. But we had
these new laws that made it harder to put blacks in prison and
keep 'em there for long stints, you know? It was some bureau-
crat's genius idea to make everybody equal, I guess. So they
were set free after, like, six months when it should have been
five to ten years. And within a couple weeks of getting out they
murdered my family."

"That's what brought you to Nathan's Ford, huh?"

Martinetti drained his beer and wiped his mouth with his
sleeve. "Well, not right away. My dad owns an auto repair shop
in Milton. He inherited it from his dad. My family had been in
Milton since the Great Depression. I got roots there, you know?
Anyway, Dad knows people in the local government, and we
tried to sue the city for negligence. But our lawyer said that we
had no case. Technically, the city was following the law. Well,
we sued 'em anyway. It became a bit of a cause for a while, but
we still lost."

"I remember hearing about that! So that was you."

"Yeah. And I'll never forget how happy it made the local blacks. They cheered like crazy in the courtroom the day we lost. They heckled us throughout the trial. One of them spat on me when we exited the courthouse. There was a whole crowd of 'em jeering at us. Like my murdered family meant nothing." Martinetti shook his head ruefully. "That's when I knew the system was broken. It can't be fixed as long as these people are a part of it. So, I knew a guy who knew a guy who put me in contact with another guy. And here I am."

"Still bitter?"

Martinetti's face lit up ironically. "Yeah. But I think the leadership here has it right. You pick your fights. You go after them little by little, and then you disappear so they don't know what hit 'em. You raise money and build up recruits." Martinetti opened up into a coarse grin. "But make no mistake. If all was lost, and it was just a matter of time before they whack us with rockets like they did in Wichita, then I would take my weapons and I would kill every goddamn nigger in this town—man, woman, and child—until one of them figures out how to kill me." Ben nodded sympathetically and ignored the powerful impulse to look away. "What do I got to live for?" Martinetti asked. "As far as I'm concerned, I'm already dead."

Ben shook his head. "You'd think you can become inured to all this. Like, with experience it would hurt less. But it doesn't." Ben took a long swig from his beer. It tasted good.

"So, you're the only one here who isn't a volunteer, right?" Martinetti asked. "You were shanghaied."

"More or less."

"But you're on board now, right? I mean that was a pretty dangerous mission you volunteered for with no experience. It's impressive what you pulled off, despite what happened to your brother."

"Well, I'm convinced we're the superior race," Ben began. "Over the Hispanics and Arabs. Definitely over the blacks. I used to work in educational testing. All that plays out statistically. I've seen thousands of data. For any given item, seventy-five percent of the Asians would get it right. Seventy percent of the

whites would get it right. Sixty percent of the Hispanics and Arabs would get it right. And, like, forty-five percent of the blacks
would get it right. I used to think that these were just numbers
that didn't mean anything. Then I started to work with blacks,
and I realized that they did."

Martinetti nodded with an ironic smirk. "Oh, that's good. Ya
figured out we got one up on the moulinyan. Next thing you
know you'll be taking off your training wheels and riding your
bike all by yourself."

"Well, I'm not entirely comfortable with it."

"Comfortable with what?"

"Race," Ben said. "I never got into this racial rah-rah stuff."

Martinetti choked back a laugh. "So you don't 'embrace the
race'?"

"No, I do. I just wish we didn't have to. But I recognize that
pretty much all the other races do it. So we have to do it too for
our survival."

"Maybe that's not so bad, though," Martinetti suggested. "Ultimately, it's about who do you want in charge, us or them.
Blacks act like they have the moral high ground, but they want
power as much as we do. Sure, neither side is perfect, but when
blacks are in charge what do you get? Corruption. Oppression.
Poverty. Crime. I mean real stupid shit. Same thing with the Latinos, the Muslims, the Arabs. But when whites are in charge, we
build great countries."

"Yeah."

"You know, my wife was half-Chinese," Martinetti said.

"Really?"

"I don't tell anybody that around here. Most likely, it
wouldn't be a problem. But you never know."

"Yeah, well, all this racial business is a mess," Ben said. "I
guess the most important thing to remember is that while you
shouldn't judge a person by his race, you should judge a race by
its persons."

Martinetti forced a smile. "Cute. But we're way past that
point, Ben. This is war. Until the bastards surrender and go back
to Africa or Mexico or wherever, I'm judging every fucking one
of them by their race."

"Even guys like Curtis?" Ben asked.

"Well, guys like Curtis are honest. They don't mind being second-class citizens once we win the war and go back to the Jim Crow laws we used to have before this country lost its mind."

Ben squirmed in his seat and bit his lower lip.

"Gotta take a dump, do ya?" Martinetti asked.

"No. I just don't like it," Ben said.

"I don't like it either, Ben," Martinetti argued. "But laws have to reflect how we are, not how we want to be, you know? And since the blacks are on the bottom—intellectually, morally, and every other which-freaking-way that doesn't include a basketball—we should have laws that reflect that."

"You know, Isaac used to refer to them as an older model of human," Ben said. "We're *Homo sapiens* 5.7. They're like *Homo sapiens* 2.0."

"Did Isaac ever tell you what happened to him and why he joined us?" Martinetti asked, smirk suddenly gone.

Stunned, Ben would have blanched if he could. "No."

"No?"

"Tell me, please," Ben whispered.

"It's a hell of a story."

Ben leaned forward, mouth open like an infant breathlessly awaiting his food. Martinetti pressed his hands together and began. "Five years ago Isaac used to work as a technician in some genetics lab at a university. Now, DNA has two strands connected by chemicals, right?" He separated his forefingers to demonstrate strands.

"Yes. Nucleotides."

"Right. A long time ago, in the 1980s, a couple of scientists wanted to figure out who was more closely related to humans, gorillas or chimps. So they took a human DNA strand and a gorilla DNA strand—"

"And merged them together," Ben interrupted. "I read about that. But because they weren't the same species, the bonds they formed between the strands were imperfect. Then they heated the hybrid DNA until the bonds broke. And since they needed more heat to split apart the human-chimp DNA than the human-gorilla DNA, they deduced that humans and chimps had more genes in common."

"Right!" Martinetti said, pointing his finger. "But the genius thing was that they next wanted to see who was more closely related to *chimps*, humans or gorillas. They used the same process—"

"And they found out it was humans."

"Yes."

"But what does that have to do with Isaac?"

Martinetti was beginning to flush from the beer. He had already polished off two and was starting on a third, waving his hands as he spoke. Ben could tell he got a bit more exuberant when encouraged by alcohol. "Well, the scientist running Isaac's lab was doing a similar experiment, looking at the genetic differences between humans and chimps," Martinetti explained. "Only he had more exact equipment. He could measure heat to a finer degree than they could in the 1980s. And when he did his experiment he discovered—to his surprise—that there were not one but two benchmarks for DNA differences between chimps and humans."

Ben scratched his head and considered this for a second. "One for blacks and one for whites."

"Bingo."

"He needed more heat to separate black-chimp DNA than he did for the white-chimp DNA," Ben said.

"Just a wee bit. But it was enough to prove scientifically that those spear-chucking porch monkeys who murdered my family are more closely related to chimps than we are."

Ben thought for a moment and finished his beer. "What happened after that?"

Martinetti's smirk once again crept across his face. "Well, the scientist of course wanted to publish his results. Problem was, Isaac was some hippie communist at the time. He actually believed all that Kumbaya racial equality shit. He tried to talk his boss out of publishing. But the boss said no. It was going to make his career. See, the boss was Korean. He didn't give a crap about political correctness and Left-wing stuff. He'd seen it up close and knew it was bullshit. He knew a study like that would never see the light of day here, so he was going to hop a plane to his homeland, redo the experiment, and publish it there.

"Only Isaac intended to stop him. And he did what any young communist in that situation would have done."

"He called the police," Ben said.

Martinetti shook his head. "The FBI."

"What?"

"He was expecting them to lean on his boss, confiscate his equipment, or maybe get him discredited or fired. But instead, they just shot the boss dead. And his two graduate students."

Ben's face lit up. "I heard about that! That was at Northwestern. They never found the killers. They couldn't even establish a motive."

"Well, I got a motive for you right here," Martinetti said. "And you know what? They wanted so bad to keep it under wraps that they tried to kill Isaac too. They sent someone to his apartment to make it look like a robbery gone wrong. They thought Isaac was home. But he wasn't. But he was such a skinny little hippie back then with the long hair that from behind he looked just like his girlfriend, who was home. So they broke in and killed her by mistake."

Ben put his hands to his mouth. His father's funeral. Isaac and his girlfriend kneeling at the casket. They were nearly indistinguishable from behind. Martinetti's account could only be true, he realized. Now he knew why Isaac never wanted to talk about why he joined. Four innocent people dead because of him. Ben's breath grew choppy as he contemplated the massive guilt that must have been crushing his brother. He clenched his teeth until his jaw hurt. The sudden, skidding friction of violent emotions was almost more than he could endure.

"You okay?" Martinetti asked.

Ben ventured a tired smile. "No wonder I could never make him laugh."

"He made us laugh. He used to sing these songs. Ever hear 'em?"

Ben's vision drifted out of focus for a moment as he remembered. Satirical music. Isaac played piano. 'In the Hall of the Mountain King' by Ibsen or whoever. He said he wanted to be songwriter. "No," Ben said.

Martinetti scanned the empty dining room before searching
for a file on his DSAK. "Yeah. Funny songs. He'd take popular
songs and change 'em around, make 'em relevant. Check this
out. It's one of our favorites. That slight hiss you hear is because
we recorded inside a PVN."

A slant-view holographic image appeared, laser pixeled to be
visible only from intimate angles. Both Ben and Martinetti
leaned in to watch. Before them was Isaac, sitting at a virtual
keyboard under the streaky fluorescence of the tunnel mess hall.
He was in fatigues and a tank top. The footage couldn't have
been terribly recent since his body was still thin and doughy and
lacked the wiry musculature that Ben had grown accustomed to.
A crowd of about thirty stood around him, anxious and cheering
the impromptu concert. There was a Vibratobox attached to
Isaac's throat.

Isaac noodled a bit before addressing his audience. "This next
song was considered pretty edgy when it was written in the
1970s. Supposedly it made fun of bigotry. They didn't know
what bigotry was in the 1970s. But I've changed it around. Now
it belongs to us."

With slight variations throughout the song, Isaac played the
same three chords with his right hand like a pulse. Quarter note,
quarter note, eighth note, quarter-plus-eighth note. With his in-
dolent left, he slapped notes and intervals in pairs, linking the
measures and adding a funky hiccup to the song's lazy rhythmic
shuffle. He started singing each measure after the downbeat,
and that little pause coincided with the bursts of languid glory
from the bass keys. It gave the impression that maybe one
shouldn't take this song too seriously. After all, if this lumbering
little ditty couldn't wait for its own singer, then what could it
wait for? Isaac smiled broadly as he sang.

Black people got no reason
Black people got no reason
Black people got no reason
To fail

They got great big hands

Great big minds
We'll never let them
Fall behind

They got welfare checks
Help 'em pay their rent
They got Head Start service
From the government

They got race audits to
Discriminate
They got full time jobs that we
Allocate

They got college placement
Don't need no test
For equal rights you better
Acquiesce

Well, I
Just want more Black people
Just want more Black people
Gotta have more Black people
'Round here

Black people are just as smart
As you and I
(Racist am I)
All men are equal
Until the day we die
(It's a wonderful lie)

Black people got nobody
Black people got nobody
Black people got nobody
To blame

They got gangsta rap
And crack cocaine

They like to whoop and holler
And drive you insane

They got basketball
And football too
They practice boxing
On me and you

They like to sing and dance
And fornicate
Make us forget about
Their murder rate

They got ghetto English
And lockdown graces
They call you cracker because
You're a racist

A double standard, yeah
Ya gotta try it
But if you do, you know they'll
Start a riot

Well, I
Don't want no black people
Don't want no black people
Don't want no black people
'Round here.

Well, I
Don't want no black people
Don't want no black people
Don't want no black people
'Round here.

By the second appearance of the chorus the crowd had
caught on and were swaying together and bellowing out the lyrics as if in an Irish pub but without all the booze and bonhomie.
They were still singing after Isaac had stopped playing. But

where Isaac had sung the lyrics with a detached irony, the crowd was taking them very literally and turning them into a rallying cry, an insistent, impatient, menacing call to arms.

DON'T! WANT! NO! BLACK! PEOPLE!
DON'T! WANT! NO! BLACK! PEOPLE!

A few were clapping to the beat, but most were stomping to it. Deep, masculine voices shattered the song's moderate tempo, metalizing it, weaponizing it. The atmosphere had reversed itself. It was no longer about the music. The music, now, was about it. Isaac seemed to understand this as he watched the song take a life of its own. He did nothing to discourage the transformation. Was it approval? Or was it a sham?

Ben knew his brother and his seemingly soft support for radicalism. The young Isaac Cameron would often endorse cold-blooded realpolitik with shocking, if gentle, candor. But Ben had always assumed this was more fetish than praxis—Isaac's way of projecting the classroom into life rather than the other way around. In the past Ben couldn't imagine his brother actually having the stomach or the discipline for the righteous path. That would force him to fight, and fighting is never pleasant. What kind of hippie jams and drug-induced love-ins can one hold in a foxhole? Ben knew that life would always be harsh to the true believer.

Ben also knew that the new Isaac must have opted for that foxhole at some point. But the question now was not whether he would fight, but the degree to which he would fight. Is it for political victory and a favorable change in the status quo? Or is it to start history over again from scratch? Ben imagined he saw his brother shifting from the former position to the latter when he stood on the dining table and raised a fist. He led the men twice through the hidebound chorus with veins bulging from his neck as if they were feeding his new belligerent countenance. This was not the face of a person who takes prisoners. This was a war mask worn by the shock troops of history. Muscles clenched, teeth bared, eyes sparkling, he pumped his fist in the air with the chorus, and then ended the song by turning quarter notes into half notes before repeating the chorus. He doubled the denominator once more for the final line and let the song trail off to riotous applause. His math was perfect.

Chapter 33

In 1933, Adolf Hitler cited the alleged arson attack on the Reichstag Building in Berlin as his reason to do which of the following?

A. reform Reichstag fire safety regulations
B. increase Germany's firefighting budget during the Wannsee Conference as the 'Final Solution' to Reichstag fires
C. appoint Leni Riefenstahl to direct educational films promoting fire safety with the slogan 'Only YOU can prevent Reichstag fires!'
D. establish an emergency government which greatly limited the civil liberties of citizens and imprisoned thousands of Hitler's political enemies thereby giving the Nazi Party and their allies a majority in the Reichstag. (correct)

Ben noticed someone tap Martinetti on the shoulder. It was Michael. He was wanting in on their PVN. Martinetti gave it to him, and slid towards the wall to give him room to sit. Still unaccustomed to seeing his superior as a mustachioed Arab, Ben tried his best not to stare.

"Sir," Martinetti and Ben greeted him.

"At ease, gentlemen," Michael said. "You know, I was there in the audience that night."

"You mean with...?" Ben said, pointing to the paused image of Isaac still hovering over the table.

"Absolutely. Look at approximately one minute and twelve seconds in. You'll see me in the front pumping my fist in magnificent sync with everyone else."

"Nice," Ben said.

"Let me once again offer condolences for the loss of your brother, Ben," Michael said. "Quite frankly, he was the glue that kept us together. It was things like this that made Isaac the obvious choice for Number Three. He wasn't a charismatic leader, and he had a dearth of empirical knowledge of modern revolutionary tactics, but he was popular. He nearly went out on his shield at Wichita. He had a real sense of urgency about everything we do. No one was more committed to the cause. And being the closest thing we have to a rock star certainly didn't hurt. He helped keep Nathan's Ford together because everybody liked him. Especially Roland's crew."

"Roland's crew?" Martinetti challenged as he turned off the hologram. "I coulda sworn I heard Eli telling us that they were our crew, not Roland's."

Michael smiled. "That was on the record. This isn't."

"I take it then that making Roland Number Three is also off the record," Martinetti said.

"No, it is not," Michael said. "We will make it known to everyone tomorrow at oh-seven-hundred." Martinetti leaned back and glanced shrewdly across the dining room sucking food particles from between his teeth. "What were our alternatives?" Michael reasoned. "Make an unpopular decision and risk mutiny?"

"I think the men would have gotten over it," Martinetti muttered.

Michael rubbed his fledgling mustache. "Well, making him Number Three really simplifies things for the Bethesda charge. If he's not, then someone else would have to be. And that someone else would have to lead Roland's men and Roland himself on that mission. Now, would you want to do that, Major?"

"Aren't you leading the mission, sir?" Martinetti asked.

"Half of it, yes. It will be an especially perilous and multifaceted agitation raid with many moving parts. That's why we are assigning two teams of five men to it. The Bethesda Ten we're calling them. And we need someone to lead the second team. Marek and Ted are still out-country. The only other choice was you, Major."

"I know."

"Roland has led these kinds of missions before, though. And you haven't. And he's also shown competence in the field, for example with saving Agent Barry's life recently in Memphis.

Don't take this personally, but he does possess the more proven track record."

Ben took in a wisp of air and let it out as smoothly as he could. He prayed that neither man would look to him for further confirmation of his earlier lie.

"He's also a proven lunatic," Martinetti said.

"No, he's not," Michael countered. "He served with distinction in Culpepper and he did not crack once during his four weeks in the Marion Supermax."

"Roland did time at the Supermax?" Ben asked. "That explains a lot. Did he ever talk about what they put him through?"

Michael shook his head. "He doesn't have to. We all know what happens to white prisoners over there. This is why I think he'll do fine in Bethesda. His focus and loyalty are beyond question."

Martinetti waved his hand in weary dismissal. "Yeah, but appointing someone as Number Three just for one mission—"

"It's not just one mission, Major," Michael interrupted. "It is *the* mission. This mission is everything. If it goes successfully then we are going to kill in a matter of seconds over a thousand Muslims in a mosque while they pray on Al-Isra Wal Miraj. That's the Muslim holy day celebrating Muhammad's supposed trip to heaven. It takes place in two months. So I need to ensure we have the best people on board for this. And I'm sorry for you, but that includes Roland."

"Am I going on it at all?" Martinetti asked with a blank expression.

"Yes, but you'll be on my team. I won't have you answering to Roland."

Martinetti waited a few seconds before giving his superior a curt "Okay," signifying the enigmatic end of the discussion.

"Excuse me, have we war gamed the inevitable backlash from this attack?" Ben asked both men. "I'm sure the sizable Muslim minority in this country let alone the federal government won't take this lying down. It's likely they'll use this attack to go full-bore fascist on us."

"Well, we don't expect a whole lot of backlash here where there are few Muslims," Michael said. "If all goes well, we'll all be back home a day and a half before the mosque blows."

"And...?" Martinetti asked.

"And after that, I'm not sure. The directive came from on high. Our Horsemen must already have a plan."

Martinetti smirked. "They better."

"Any idea what that plan is?" Ben asked.

"I have my theories," Michael said. "But that's all they are given that our Horseman has no obligation to tell us anything. And he shouldn't since the less we know the better."

"I see," Ben said.

"But you know who has a way of sniffing out these things?" Michael said. "Roland. He was involved in the movement before any of us, and was in command of Nathan's Ford before General Humphrey and I were assigned here."

"But he's not in charge anymore," Martinetti interjected. "Not for a while. So how would Roland know anything?"

A man holding a plate of hot food dropped it on the table next to Michael with a quick, obnoxious crash. Ben's heart clenched like a fist, and shards of sweat seemed to stab their way through his cheeks and forehead. Michael and Martinetti were just as startled. It was one of Roland's men. Chuck. Muscle-bound athlete showing off his sculpted guns in a tank top despite the cool weather. Ben recognized him from the physical training room earlier in the day. He was naturally thick of body, so his muscles didn't jut out much. But the strength was there. Ben could sense it. Chuck's tight crew cut flattened the top of his head with military pretensions. Like Michael, he was on his way to becoming a ruddy-faced Arab complete with bulbous nose and jowls. He was handsome, with equine jaw muscles and a thin, confident smile that could have been written on his face with a pencil stroke. Ben pegged him at five feet, seven inches and 190 pounds. He smelled like a gym bag.

Chuck nodded to Michael indicating that he wanted him to scooch over. It was a tight fit. With three men now in the booth, Martinetti was pressed up against the window with his elbows practically pinned to his sides. He kept his irritation admirably to himself.

Behind Chuck appeared another man with a plate of food

who sat down next to Ben. Ben had always hoped that Gideon Sneed was not part of Roland's crew and was now disappointed to learn that he was. Gideon was a quiet, aloof lieutenant with blonde hair, a receding chin, and braces. His droopy eyes were too close together, and his facial hair grew in splotches around his jaw. Of average height and build, he certainly wasn't one of Roland's able-bodied epigones. He was also not in his Fickle-skin. Without waiting for anyone, he hovered his head over his bowl and started spooning heaps of chili into his mouth like he was going to miss the bus.

"And how would Roland know what?" someone asked. It was the truncated man himself. He was holding two double decker cheeseburgers and a sloppy mound of fries on a plate in the reddened fingertips of his right hand. In his left was a root beer float in a tall fountain glass. He put the food down with hardly a sound and then improvised a throne at the head of the table with a free chair from a nearby table. The vinyl cushion squeaked as he plopped down.

"You know, any nutless flunky who reads lips can under-stand every word you fuckers say," Roland said. "Now, are you going to let us into your PVN, or what?"

Chapter 34

In 1898, when Spain ceded Cuba to the United States after the Spanish-American War, it demanded the United States also assume Cuban debts. The Americans refused, claiming that such debts were imposed on the Cubans against their will and were contrary to their interests. In international law, such debts are referred to as

  A. abominable.
  B. preposterous.
  C. bone-chilling.
  D. odious. (correct)

"I got it!" Roland announced, cheeks bulging and greasy with meat. He clapped his hands and pointed to Ben. "You have a reputation of being a real brainiac around here. You used to write the SATs, right?" Roland gulped down his food like a pelican swallowing a fish. "Well, here's a test for you."

Despite his revulsion against Roland's gluttonizing and resentment for the way he'd co-opted his conversation with Michael and Martinetti, Ben was momentarily excited by the challenge. Trivia had always been his thing. He had found at least two girlfriends during trivia nights in various San Diego bars and once led a team of trivia hounds to win the city-wide San Diego Trivia Challenge. He still had the trophy in his condo somewhere.

"Have you ever heard of a famous book from a hundred years ago called *Black Like Me*?" Roland asked. All eyes turned to Ben. His stunned expression indicated that he hadn't. Profane and violent thoughts swirled in his mind as he wondered how a muscle-bound meathead like Roland could trump him on the topic of twentieth-century literature. This had *better* be an important book, he thought.

"I guess it wasn't that famous," Chuck snarked. Gideon dropped his spoon and guffawed along with Roland. Even Michael mustered up a chuckle. Only Martinetti failed to find the crack amusing.

Roland took a deep breath before continuing. "So there's this fucking white pinko journalist who thought he could sell some books if he disguised himself as a groid and tooled around the segregated South, writing down all the quote-unquote indignities he faced for pretending to be part of a stupid, oversexed, ape-like species that's threatening civilization just by being there." Roland had expelled nearly all the air from his lungs during his little exposition and needed to take another deep breath before continuing.

"So he publishes it, and everybody fucking loves him. *Black Like Me*. Meant to show how raaay-cist and eee-vil honkies are. They even made a movie about it. But they never corroborated it. They never interviewed the whites he interacted with. They never tried to tell the lies from the truth. They just accepted it because it was what they wanted to hear."

"What's your point?" Ben asked.

"Well, now that you're a groid, Ben, you should do the same

thing!" Roland waited a moment for his bomb to explode among his confederates. It didn't. "You're a gamer now, right? According to Eli a pretty good one. And you obviously don't have the stomach for agitation raids. So why not? Instead of wasting your talents here, why don't you get a job at some pharmaceutical company? We can set you up with an identity. In fact, I will personally set you up with a groid identity. That's a promise! I think I can pull strings to make you some Rastafarian reject from Jamaica."

Ben nodded blandly, understanding this to be a ploy to get him out of Nathan's Ford. Roland clearly wanted to purge the town of witnesses to his own incompetence. Ben also chafed under the claim that he lacked the stomach for agitation raids. After Memphis, he was feeling just the opposite.

"You're one of a kind, Ben," Roland continued. "You're a groid who can do quantum gaming. You're like an endangered species. I guaran-fucking-tee you that everyone's going to sit on your dick and grind on you until you get tired of jizzing. And it'll be even better if you tell them you're a fag! Then after you get all the promotions and money you can handle you can write all about the special privileges you get today when you're black!" Roland slapped the table, startling everyone except Gideon. "You can call it *Black Like Me Too*! Get it?" he said, holding up two fingers. "It'll be the fucking sequel!"

Chuck laughed and clapped approvingly while Gideon looked up from his chili long enough to say, "That's funny."

"Noted," Michael said drily. "When we go from the business of instigating insurrection to publishing satirical literature we'll give this idea solemn consideration." Michael hadn't even finished speaking when Roland dove into his second burger. He had been seated for all of five minutes and his fries were almost gone. He slurped ruthlessly from his root beer float.

"Why do you eat so much?" Martinetti asked him.

Roland finished slurping, masticated twice, and responded, "I like to shit."

"You like lying, too?" Martinetti challenged. "Like how you supposedly read our lips just now? I say you can't read lips. I say you got some secret device in your little jock strap that lets you listen in on other people's PVNs."

A hack Hollywood screenwriter couldn't have blocked Roland's reaction any better. He kicked his chair back and stood. Silverware and plates clinked against each other. With both fists clenched he made as if he were about to leap over the cluttered table to get to Martinetti. Chuck stood and blocked him mostly with his left shoulder as if he didn't dare raise his hand to his boss. He whispered calming things into Roland's ear as Roland bristled at Martinetti like a mustang in a cage. Roland issued a series of sexually explicit threats which evoked striking images from his favorite genres of porn and revealed a preoccupation with vibrators and other sexual paraphernalia typically used by middle-aged women.

Martinetti hadn't even bothered to get up to meet Roland's predictable tantrum. He just sat back, smirked fearlessly, and kept saying, "Any time. Any time." Michael stretched out his arms between them and, by alternately cajoling and ordering both men, prevented escalation.

Ben looked to the front of the restaurant to see who was watching. The manager, who supported the cause, was ushering the frightened waitresses into the kitchen. He was stout and didn't look terribly healthy with his baggy eyes and wrinkled skin sagging from his neck like theater curtains. He locked the front door and then flipped the 'Open' sign to 'Closed'. With great effort he began closing the blinds in the dining room.

Turning back to the impending brawl at the table, Ben noticed that Gideon held a steak knife in his left hand. It was partially obscured by his plate and napkin, but Ben saw the tight, murderer's grip with which he held it. Gideon was staring at Martinetti as if waiting for him to bet or fold in a game of cards. That knife could just as easily be for me, Ben thought.

"What we wanted to ask you, Colonel," Ben said, "is what our Horsemen intend after Bethesda." All stopped and looked at Ben. "General Archer says you might be in the know." Ben really wanted to keep an eye on that knife in Gideon's hand, but forced himself not to.

After a moment, Roland nodded. "That's right," he said, taking his seat. Chuck followed suit, and the mood at the table began to relax. "But some people here believe I am a liar. So why the fuck should I say anything?" Ben felt that the best thing he could do was to keep quiet and hope that Gideon didn't stab him in the ribs for his impertinence.

"Well, Ben here has proved that you're not a liar," Michael offered. "That's not nothing."

"Oh, yeah? You know what else is not nothing?" Roland countered. "This!" He bolted to his feet again and preposterously dropped his pants and underwear. Between the height of the table and his lack of stature he couldn't reveal much more than his milky white washboard stomach. He then stood on his tiptoes and cupped his scrotum with his left hand, jiggling it for all to see. His uncircumcised member was a respectable length but otherwise unremarkable.

"I got your anti-PVN device right here, Martinetti, you pig-fucking dago!" he taunted. He let his scrotum lay on the table for about two seconds before collecting it back into his underwear. "You try to embarrass me again and I'll skull fuck your eye sockets, you understand?"

Martinetti looked back to Roland with a widening smirk and folded his arms comfortably across his chest. Ben saw that Roland's threat, credible as it was, meant nothing to Martinetti. Martinetti really was dead. For a moment, Ben wondered who was crazier, him or Roland.

"Enough!" Michael ordered. "I've had it with this internecine bickering! Whoever makes threats like that again makes them to me. And I can handle any one of you. Is that clear?" Silence. "I asked you a question!" Michael said, now showing his teeth like an angry animal. The group murmured its affirmative response. He turned to Martinetti. "You were out of line with your accusation of Colonel Turk."

"Yessir," Martinetti said.

"Apologize now."

"Yessir. Sorry sir."

Michael turned to Roland. "We made you Number Three and we can unmake you Number Three. Don't forget that!"

Roland nodded, overselling his contrition. "Yes, sir! I will never forget, sir!"

"You also have to remember that we are in public," Michael went on. "Anything we do or say can be seen, heard, or recorded, despite our precautions."

"Permission to leave, sir."

"Go," Michael said with a terse wave.

Roland shoved his borrowed chair aside to make room for Chuck to exit the booth. Gideon poured what was left of his bowl of chili into his mouth. As he was wiping his chin on his sleeve, Ben stopped him. "Wait," he said, and then looked to Roland. "Before you go, can you tell us what our Horsemen plan to do after Bethesda?"

Roland looked to Michael and then back to Ben, saying nothing.

"My guess is that we have several Bethesdas planned," Michael said. "And after the government tries to crack down on whites, the revolution can begin in earnest."

"What then?" Ben asked.

"Our moles in the military will alternately defect, bringing as many weapons and as much personnel and materiel as possible with them, or they will remain undercover to perform espionage—or terror—as needed."

"Yeah, but what's to stop the feds from hitting us with robot bombs or apocalyptos?" Martinetti asked. "Last we heard, it was going to take years before we get control of those."

"Something's changed," Michael said. "I don't know exactly what, but I can say that our Horsemen are not exactly worried about that anymore. And that can only mean one thing."

"What?" Ben and Martinetti asked.

"China," Michael said. "China's got our back. That's the only thing I can think of that could potentially deter the U.S. government once it realizes it's facing tens of thousands of domestic hostiles for the first time since the Civil War."

Roland sat back down, listening carefully.

"The Chinese must be getting sick of us giving them a hard time in South America," Ben said. "So that's what we're promising them in return? Scrapping the Monroe Doctrine and giving them free reign down there?"

"I'm sure they will also want us to repay our debt to them,"

Martinetti said. "It's over twenty trillion now."

"That's not our debt," Gideon said. "That's Washington's. Why should we pay that?"

"Yeah. It's not like they're borrowing to help whites," Chuck said.

"I don't think the Chinese will care in either event," Michael said.

"Why not?"

"Because they can afford not to. In return for their assistance in this upcoming war they will ask for Alaska and Hawaii. Because they can. And we will give it to them. Because we must."

"No shit," Martinetti said.

"And that will absolve us of our debt. To the Yuan."

Roland closed his eyes as if he were about to fall asleep and laughed. "Oh, that's nothing."

"What?"

"I said that's nothing," Roland said. "They're not going to stop there."

"Then where are they going to stop?" Michael asked.

Roland cracked his neck and said, "California."

Chapter 35

In the late 1960s, some scientists began to suggest that IQ differences across races results mostly from heritable genetic differences rather than from environmental factors. Although this claim has been vindicated in recent years, many scientists vehemently opposed it at the time. Some of the most prominent and powerful critics included Jerry Hirsch, Stephen Gould, Leon Kamin, Richard Lewontin, and Steven Rose. What do these five guys have in common?

A. They were all Virgos.
B. They were all left-handed.
C. They all had the middle name Jay.
D. Come on. You're not going to make me say it, are you? (correct)

"The whole left coast. Gone," Roland said. "What are we going to do? Say no? Without those slanty-eyed fucks we're screwed."

"I'm from California!" Ben exclaimed.

Gideon chuckled. "Not anymore, you're not."

Michael shifted in his seat and squinted for a microsecond at Roland. "How do you know this?" he asked.

"I have my sources," Roland said.

"Are these reliable sources?"

"No worse than yours."

"We cannot give them California," Ben said.

"Why not?"

"Because it's ours!"

Chuck and Gideon laughed, slowly at first and then joining into a gentle rumble. It was as if they were laughing at a child. "And the spics say it's theirs," Roland said. "So the fuck what? It's ours only if we can keep it."

"But ceding such a large swath of land to a powerful rival is dangerous," Ben said. "Something as inexact as the Rocky Mountains are going to be the border between the United States and China? If history is any indication that's going to lead to more warfare as the two powers contest over the land."

"First things first," Michael said.

"Yeah. Let's take back our country from the muzzies and the groids," Roland said. "Then we can take out the Chi-coms."

"No," Ben countered. "They'll be taking us out." Gideon snorted while Chuck and Michael both shook their heads and murmured their dissent. "They outnumber us five-to-one!"

"So what?" Chuck said. "We have a huge technological edge over them in robot bombs and laser weapons and TF-70s. And our ballistic shield is impregnable. Once we win the present war and root out all the corrupt elements from our military and bring back the draft, we'll have the best trained armed forces in the world again."

"But the Nazis had better technology and better soldiers than the Soviets, and they still lost," Ben argued. "The Soviets had more manpower, and they were able to close the technology gap during the war."

"Yes, but the Soviets had thousands of miles of land they

could retreat on. They were supported by an indigenous population. They also had the Russian winter. The Chinese in California wouldn't have any of that. And the fighting will be on our turf, not theirs."

Ben quickly remembered that Chuck was one of the few people in the movement who had actually served in the United States Armed Forces. He was considered the military expert in Nathan's Ford and was not one to contradict on such matters. Ben grunted a couple times thinking of a counter-argument and then stopped, realizing how silly he must have looked.

"Uh...uh...uh," Gideon mocked. Cornbread crumbs were muddling his ugly face. Ben decided that he really didn't like Gideon. He took a quick peek at that steak knife and resolved to snatch it if things got out of hand again.

"Ben, it's not so bad," Roland said. "What do we have in California anyway?" He held up his hand to count along. "Commies. Fags. Spics. Chinks. Hollywood. Think of how strong we'll be without 'em! We win our war with the government. We take back our country. Every yellow, bucked-tooth fucker will flee to the west coast. We *annihilate* the Muslims. We ship whatever groids we don't kill off to Jamaica or Haiti. We put all the Mexicans on a train back to Mexico. And we go back to how the Founding Fathers wanted this country to be. We'll put it right there in our Constitution so we don't make the same mistakes twice. We only give the vote to white men. We outlaw communism. We outlaw Islam. We end all immigration except for white Caucasians. We outlaw interracial marriage. We outlaw abortion of white babies. In fact, we should have tax penalties for every able-bodied white between twenty and forty who isn't married and having kids."

"You mean, basically become another South Zion," Martinetti interjected.

"Yes. Maybe we even entice the SZ to come here. The European Defense Leagues. The Nordic Nationalist Front. Any racially conscious whites would be welcome, especially if they have experience killing muzzies and groids."

"You're forgetting one thing," Michael said. "The reason why South Zion is failing in Africa."

"Because they only have like a quarter million people and they're surrounded by millions of black Africans?" Martinetti answered.

"That's not it."

"That is it," Martinetti insisted. "They didn't get the support from whites they thought there were gonna get. After the UN declared them a rogue state, they expected funding and arms from white Europeans and Americans like us. They were hoping we'd go there and hunker down with them too. And it just didn't happen."

"And why didn't they get that support?" Michael asked.

Martinetti groaned through his hand. "Not this again. Everybody knows they didn't get support because of what they did in that city."

"You mean the city of Beira?"

"Yeah. They killed all those Chinese and Indians. They shouldn't have done that."

Michael pointed his finger at Martinetti. "First of all, a lot of those people weren't loyal. They were colluding with the blacks and were responsible for a good deal of terror and sabotage. Furthermore, we warned all foreigners to leave Beira before the killing started. It's not our fault they didn't listen."

"Well, that's what the SZ are telling everyone," Martinetti offered, clearly losing enthusiasm for the argument.

"Oh, I get it. They're lying," Michael snarked, sticking up two fingers. "White man. Speak with forked tongue. Right?"

Martinetti waved in surrender. "Okay. Okay."

"The reason why South Zion failed is simple," Michael announced. "They put the Star of David on their flag."

"What?" Ben said.

"That's right."

"That was their saving grace! That's why they've lasted this long."

Michael wagged a finger at Ben. "No, it wasn't. They were doomed to fail the moment they decided to be a second homeland for the Jews."

"But it was their denunciation of anti-Semitism that got the UN to recognize them at all," Ben argued. "I paid close attention to this when it happened. They wouldn't have had a legal basis to form their country if they hadn't used Israel as a precedent."

"For all the good it did them," Michael scoffed. "Leave it to the hypocrisy of the Jew to astound. They take land that wasn't theirs *by force* so they can claim their own shitty little country. But when *we* do the same thing, when we try to carve a homeland for ourselves in a hostile environment, what do they do? They lead the charge against us. Because *we're* the ones who are racist!" Michael pounded the table, rattling everything on it. "These people, the Jews, are tribal. In every country they occupy they outlaw all tribalism except their own. And with SZ, we made *overtures* to them! We offered them a place in our home! And it didn't matter. Didn't matter!"

Ben hunched forward and brought his arms in front of him as if keeping warm in the cold. He suspected Michael didn't have the whole of it. He somehow felt that what Michael was calling Truth was really a miscreation of selected facts. Ben had studied the Jewish question, both while researching social studies items and on his own. Having personally dealt with so few Jews in his life, he felt he could address the issue with minimal bias but also with minimal experience. But would that be enough to offset Michael's arguments? Ben had a hunch that the right thing to do was to find out.

"Well, I say the SZ had to include Jews," he said. "They had to show the world they weren't the second coming of Nazi Germany."

Martinetti smiled and patted Ben on the arm. "I've tried this line with him. He ain't gonna buy it."

"Oh, so South Zion insisting on freedom of speech and limited government and free markets wasn't enough." Michael responded, spewing sarcasm. "Because the Nazis were all about *The Federalist Papers* and Friedrich Hayek, obviously."

"Then what about Tal Youngman and Bert Cohen and that South African casino magnate donating practically their entire fortunes to South Zion?" Ben challenged. "What about the Silicon Valley refugees? Many of whom were Jewish. They practically set up South Zion's IT infrastructure during a three-front war, not to mention ran their PR campaign. What about the eight hundred Jewish soldiers from the U.S. and Canada that fought and died for South Zion? What about all the war tech smuggled out of Israel by sympathetic Israelis? What about the Israeli advisors who helped model their entire military strategy on Israel's wars with the Arabs? Are you going to say that none of that happened?"

"No. But it wasn't enough, was it?" Michael countered. "South Zion is still losing. They're under siege. Sooner or later they're going to surrender. But if they had made it clear from the outset that they would never be friendly to Jews they would have received more support from white nationalists the world over. Instead of thousands emigrating they would have had millions. That would have enabled them to defeat their enemies and deal with the international resistance, which was going to come regardless. South Zion has thoroughly demonstrated that no white nationalist movement can afford philo-Semitism."

Ben squinted in bafflement. "So basically whites hate Jews so much they'd rather fight over land with Muslims who want to kill them than share land with Jews who don't?"

"That's not what I'm saying."

"Okay. Then admit that it was a good thing the SZ included the Jews. Because I don't believe they would have lasted a year without them."

Michael smiled mirthlessly. "Oh, so what you're really saying is that Jews are just superior. They're so indispensable they should just willy-nilly be given license to lead the one true Aryan nation on Earth, even if it means they will eventually destroy it through communism or multiculturalism or degenerate, unfettered capitalism, like they always do. Admit it!"

Ben shrugged in disbelief. "What—the hell—are you talking about?"

Michael slid his hand on the table towards Ben. "Come on, don't pretend," he said with a knowing grin. "It's all about control, and Jews have to have it." He slapped the crook of his arm. "They're like addicts. And they do it through liberalism. They founded the NAACP and the ACLU, didn't they? They were behind the Civil Rights Movement and the ANC in South Africa. They were the founders of the Frankfurt School, which ruined the university system in this country. They masterminded the New Deal—AKA 'the Jew Deal'—which extended the Great Depression. They were behind much of the Soviet espionage in the U.S. during the Cold War. And they were and still are instrumental in weakening our genetic strength by promoting immigration, homosexuality, feminism, and abortions.

"And then there's communism, which we all know is a Jewish phenomenon. From Marx to Trotsky to at least half the top Bolsheviks not to mention their Jewish financiers in America and other places. The Soviets were responsible for the deaths of over fifty million people. The Orthodox Old Believer Christians, the Kulaks, the Holodomor in Ukraine, countless Russian dissidents, the Gulag Archipelago. These people were all killed, starved, or worked to death. And Jews, like Kaganovich, Berman, Yagoda, that despicable shit Mekhlis, and thousands of others were in large part responsible. And many of the ones who weren't Jews, like Molotov, *had Jewish wives.* For every Hitler or Goebbels, I can give you half a dozen Jews with just as much blood on their hands. In fact, I will go so far as to say that the Jewish Holocaust, which did happen, was perfectly justified. It was payback for the atrocities of Jewish Bolshevism. And in my opinion not a moment too soon.

"So don't *talk* to me about the Jews!" Michael concluded, pointing his finger at Ben. "There is not a single positive thing these people have accomplished in the political sphere of history. Not one!"

"What about funding the American Revolution?" Ben offered. Michael tried to interject but Ben ignored rank and wouldn't let him. "No. *My* turn!"

"Okay. Let's hear your bullshit," Michael said. Giggles from Gideon and Chuck and a half-hearted chuckle from Martinetti.

"As far as the Bolsheviks go," Ben began. "Stalin was the prime killer, not the Jews he moved around like pawns. And he had gentile support as well. No one's going to say that the Politburo or the Communist Party was one-hundred percent Jewish. It wasn't. It never was. Lenin, Stalin, Khrushchev, Beria. These were all gentiles. So, your blaming the Jews alone for Bolshevism is a little disingenuous."

"Solzhenitsyn himself said how the Jews remained faithful to Stalin up until the very end, even when he was plotting to annihilate them all."

"So? You're forgetting how anti-Semitic the Czars were. They forced the Jews to live in the Pale. And when the pogroms came they never really bothered to protect them, did they?"

"Not true. That's a myth told by Jews who like to embellish their suffering. And the Pale was necessary since Jews impoverished ordinary Russians through usury and alcohol!"

"Guys! Guys!" Martinetti called out. "This is a fucking pissing contest! Can't you see that? Muslims and niggers have taken over our government. We've practically ceded a quarter of our country back to Mexico. We're about to give up California to the Chinese. And you two are arguing about Jews?"

Michael held his hand in the air. "Fair enough. But my original point was germane. The Jews are a separate race. They have their own priorities and agendas, and they don't care if these priorities and agendas ruin any nation that hosts them.

"My father used to tell a story about the day he stopped loving Jews. It's when he read about a meeting that prominent Jews held in Washington, DC a few years before I was born. Liberal Jews, conservative Jews, moderate Jews, whatever Jews. They were discussing the decline of America due to non-white immigration and how Jews need to position themselves vis-à-vis the rising tide of color. It was astounding. It was like they were acting out *The Protocols of the Elders of Zion*. But it wasn't a forgery. It was reported in a Jewish source! It really happened. They initiated America's decline by pushing for non-white immigration for over a century. They pushed for the dispossession of whites. And when that finally started to happen, there they were conspiring over how they could ally themselves with non-whites in order to finish the job. These people have no loyalty but to themselves. They're like parasites, and when they begin to notice that their host is flagging, what do they do? They start looking around for another host to prey upon.

"History has shown they've been doing this for centuries now, and I don't want it to happen again in South Zion, which, aside from America, is the last, best hope for the white race."

Michael let his hand fall. "That's all I have to say."

All eyes fell on Ben, who shrugged and said, "He's not wrong." Martinetti let out a soft gasp which was drowned out by an incredulous snicker from Gideon. "Look, as agents of communism and Left-wing causes throughout the last century, the Jews have caused a lot of damage," Ben went on. "We all know this. They were the biggest champions of anti-white multiculturalism which has put us in the predicament we're in right now. Of course, not all Jews are like this. Most aren't. But almost all of the ones *with the will to power* are. And these people tend to be very smart, very wealthy, and very influential. That's why Jews are such a problem."

"So you're agreeing with me now?" Michael asked.

Ben made a show of hesitating. "Eh. You're not wrong, but you're not entirely right either. We *have* benefited from Jewish advances in science, medicine, and a ton of other fields. It may not seem obvious to you because your legs aren't warped by polio, but it's still true. You can't just look at the bad and conveniently ignore the good. And there is a lot of good."

"Your argument is weak," Michael said, not without empathy.

"I don't think so," Ben countered. "You want to bring up family? I can do that too. My mother was a nurse in San Bernardino before she married my father. She told me about an old physician she once knew. An oncologist. And he was so brilliant, so imaginative, so free with his mind, that he revolutionized the way we diagnose and treat tumors. People around the world practically worshipped the guy and would consult him constantly. He saved countless lives. But you wouldn't know that unless you work in his field because everything he does was under the hood. He only wrote technical papers.

"And, of course, he was Jewish. A great man. But a Jew. This is why we call it the Jewish Question and not the Jewish Answer. There have been hundreds maybe thousands of guys like that. That has to count for something."

"Like what?"

"I don't know. But I'm sure it can be quantified. Have you heard about the body count propaganda coming out of Israel?"

Ben asked.

Michael nodded and responded with growing civility. "Yes. The supposed hundred thousand Americans who died once most of the Jewish doctors fled for Israel ten years ago. I have no reason to believe that figure wasn't doctored somehow. But in any event, your argument is well-taken but misguided because the Jews suppressed our racial identity, which made us vulnerable to multiculturalism and the genocide we're facing today. And that cost us far more than one hundred thousand lives."

Ben nodded confidently. "I agree. But perhaps all our problems stem from *diaspora* Jews and not the ones doing their thing in Israel. That's why I'm always a little distrustful of hardened anti-Semites. I can understand when they complain about Jews here. But when they refuse to give Israel a break and stand opposed to Jews as *folk*, and especially when they shed crocodile tears over how the Jews treat the Arabs who want nothing more than to kill us, that's a little crazy on our part, don't you think?"

Michael defiantly shook his head. "Just self-preservation. If not for Jewish, Zionist meddling, the Arabs wouldn't be wanting to kill us."

"Like in Vienna, September 11th, 1683?"

"Those were Turks, not Arabs. And yes, the Ottoman Empire was infested with Jews back then as well."

Ben sighed. "Okay, fine. But this just leads back to my original point. Now that the Jews, or really, the Israelis, have been forced to nurture something as precious as a state, they've shifted more to the Right. They've become more hawkish against their enemies, who are also *our* enemies. They've become less problematic for *us*, don't you see? And with the vast majority of them in Israel now, and not here, it doesn't make sense to keep hating them."

Michael leaned back into his seat, the cushion of which poofed under the weight of his broad back. He looked at Ben as if he were having a hard time seeing him clearly.

"Yeah, I have to agree with young Ben here." It was Roland. He appeared uncharacteristically serene as he reached across his chest with his right arm to rub the bulging triceps on his left. "We should just lose the whole Jew thing. In fact, the only Jews I hate are the black ones." He paused to wipe his nose and give Chuck and Gideon time to laugh at his joke, which they did. "And the Israelis do a bang up job of keeping them in the jungle where they belong. And I *love* it when they kill muzzies."

"Fuckin' A," Gideon slurred through an illiterate drawl.

"I'm afraid this is all Old-World bullshit, Mike," Roland went on. "Fifty years ago I would have agreed with you. But now, who gives a fuck how many Shylocks or Fagins there were? Who still cares about the Rosenbergs or Noam Chomsky or George Soros? We're not a Zionist Occupied Territory anymore. The Beast is dead. Over ninety percent of Jews live in Israel now. Whatever bullshit they pull, they're not going to hurt anyone but themselves. Your gripe against the Jews is starting to smell like stale dick sweat. You've got to get over this obsession. It's unhealthy."

Martinetti whistled in disbelief. "And what would Turk the Jerk over here know about unhealthy obsessions?"

"Enough to know that I'm still going to skull fuck you."

"What does a guy have to do to get skull fucked around here?" Martinetti implored, hands in the air. "Look at this guy! He's all talk and no fuck!"

It must have been something in Martinetti's delivery because Roland didn't lunge across the table to commence intercourse with his eyeballs as promised. After an affront like that Ben was fully expecting an all-out, revolution-ending, how-are-we-going-to-explain-this-to-the-local-constabulary-not-to-mention-the-doctors-in-the-ER kind of brawl. He was mightily relieved when Roland simply started laughing. Chuck and Gideon joined in, and so did Martinetti. Roland reached over to clink his nearly-empty root beer float with Martinetti's beer bottle.

"You're a fucking dead man," Roland warned.

"Not as dead as you're gonna be, pal," Martinetti responded. Still with the smile, Roland kept his arm outstretched as if he were deciding whether to dump his beverage on Martinetti's lap or beam him in the face with it.

"Ah, excuse me," said a voice quavering with age. It was the restaurant manager. He was standing by the table with his hands clasped respectfully behind his back. "Would it be okay if we open for business again? We've had to turn a few people away at the door. It's okay if the answer is no. I was just wondering."

Michael smiled warmly and rapped his knuckles on the table. "It's fine. We have to leave anyway. Gentlemen…" The men got up from the table like obedient schoolchildren. Michael looked at Ben and smiled not so warmly. "And you, my friend, need to start your sentence."

"Yes, sir," Ben replied, wondering if his defense of the Jews was going to land him in even greater trouble. Michael gave no indication as they were shuffling to the door. Instead, he slowed down and put his arms around Roland and Martinetti. The others stopped and turned honest eyes to their leader. They could feel a speech coming on.

"Men, I would like to express how much I appreciate your openness with me," he began. "We should all remember that the society we wish to forge from the wreckage of war must be a free one.

"Things could not be darker now than they were after the Roman defeat at Cannae. 70,000 legionnaires lost in a single day, in one battle. The Italian peninsula was occupied by a large invading force comprising a barbarian hodgepodge which shared a deep enmity towards Rome. Led by one of the world's greatest military geniuses, this force posed the most dire threat to Western Civilization up to that point in history. There was panic in Rome, and the enemy was enticing several Italian city-states to join their cause."

Michael released Roland and Martinetti so he could enhance his oration chironomically, *à la* Cicero. "Why fight when defeat is eminent?" he asked. "Why court more death and destruction? Why not just give in to the inevitable and cease the bloodshed?" He remained quiet for a moment but was not waiting for a response. "The answer is the same now as it was then. Because the promise of what we are fighting for is greater than anything our enemies can offer. Hannibal's armies consisted of paid mercenaries and disparate tribesmen. What were they fighting for? To become enfranchised citizens of Carthage? No. They were fighting for hate and plunder. The Romans, on the other hand, fought for freedom and the *res publica*. They fought for the singular *idea* of civilization and their natural rights to partake in it, to own land and govern their own affairs and be protected by law.

"And we, each and every one of us, are fighting for the same thing against an enemy which only wants to oppress and strip these rights away. In the ancient world, the Greeks and Romans noted how barbarians always centralized control and oppressed their people. The Huns would never have tolerated the give and take we had moments ago. There was no public accounting or audit of generals in ancient Egypt. If this were ancient Persia, I would have had you all beheaded for daring not to worship me. Instead, however, I listened, because we all understand that leadership is in part consensual. And as citizens you have the right to take part in that."

He looked to Ben. "You may be correct, Lieutenant, about the Jews. I don't think you are. But I admire your candor and courage in standing up to me." He waved his hand between himself and Ben. "This is why we discuss and debate. The Greeks bequeathed this to us as dialectic. The Socratic Method. To our enemies, this seems like senseless squabbling, but really we're winnowing out Noise to get to Truth. That is what civilized people do."

He looked about his audience. "But tell me, do any of you see that with our current enemies? Now that the blacks and the Latinos and Muslims have taken over this country, we're seeing something else entirely, something eerily familiar. We're seeing the same thing the Greeks and Romans saw in *their* barbarians thousands of years ago: the consolidation of absolute power and the complete removal of rule of law. What we're facing is, in effect, one-party totalitarianism with socialist trappings. The president, with his use of executive fiat, has made Congress irrelevant, not that that corrupt body of bureaucrats couldn't have been bought off or stuffed with partisan shills easily enough. He wages improvised wars, he terrorizes his own citizens, he takes their land, criminalizes speech he doesn't like as 'hate speech'. He quarters SWAT teams and DEA agents in private homes. The first president to actually violate the Third Amendment." Michael rolled his eyes. "I didn't think that was even possible. But our autocratic liberal leader found a way.

"But what's most astounding is how he dispenses with people in his own party who oppose him. Once upon a time, they would just label someone a racist and ostracize him. Then it grew to IRS audits and harassment from the press. And when that wasn't enough they resorted to trumping up charges and trying people in kangaroo courts. Now, it's just murder. The second liberal critic of the president has turned up dead. For the moment they're trying to make it seem like random killings, but soon they won't even bother with that.

"Now, how is this any different from the barbarian hordes the Greeks and Romans faced?" Michael asked. "How is this different from the primitive, tribal chiefdoms in Africa or the bizarre, cannibalistic theocracies in Central America or the greedy, autocratic satrapies in the Arab world? It's as if half a millennium of exposure to Western Civilization has done nothing for these people. We used to think that it was our superior cultural and political institutions which gave us our advantages. These were based on ideals such as liberty, democracy, reason, and capitalism. All the barbarians had to do was accept these obviously wonderful things and they could shed their savagery in some exhilarating, life-affirming catharsis. And make no mistake, this did happen. But only with the *European* barbarians or with some Central or East Asians. Not with the Arabs, not with the Hispanics, and certainly not with the blacks. Now that these people have accomplished through immigration and multiculturalism what they could not accomplish militarily, they've essentially gained control of the West. So, I ask you, have they changed?"

"No. Fuck no," Roland answered.

Michael bit his lower lip and shot breath hard out of his nose, flexing his entire upper body. "That's right! Or not nearly enough of them have. This is not just our war. This is also the war of our ancestors, men who fought to bring order to chaos, men who subdued superstition with reason, men who, not without great pain and sacrifice, handed civilization down to the present generations. And remember, this civilization was *theirs*. It was not copied from any society outside of Europe. Societies outside of Europe copied us! This is why we have more at stake than our enemies. Civilization belongs to us, not them! Fix your eyes on the great European civilizations at their best. Renaissance Italy, Western Europe of the Enlightenment, the vast commercial British Empire, the science and music of Nineteenth-century Germany, the innovative and freedom-loving United States. Look at these civilizations and fall in love with them! Love them and remember that they were established by men of courage, honor, and genius.

"It is incumbent upon us to rival what they have accomplished and defend what they have achieved. This is going to be a great, terrible war. But wouldn't you rather fight and suffer and join your ancestors in Elysian oblivion than buy a meager and temporary reprieve on Earth through weakness and submission? How else can we better serve their memory as well as ensure that our children venerate ours?"

Michael took a moment to look his men in the eye and touch them one by one like apostles. Roland was weeping in a flood of tears, his face twisted in an artless scowl. Martinetti was giving Michael his solemn, smirk-free attention. Chuck was nodding almost after every sentence. Gideon seemed somewhere else entirely, focusing on a spot inches in front of him with half-closed eyes and a half-opened mouth.

"Take heart, gentlemen!" Michael said, squeaking his shoes against the tile floor in a kind of vigorous two-step shuffle. "We are in a good place right now. This may sound like blasphemy, but Wahoo was the single best thing that could ever have happened to us. Before Wahoo we had a name, 'The American White Nationalist Movement.' We had telephone numbers and websites and sap-serv space and PO boxes and tax returns and physical addresses you could easily look up online. You could knock on our door and say hello. We were targets and like dupes we were easily found. It seems so absurd now because we've learned our lesson. The massacre at Wahoo forced us into a much deadlier vantage point—into the shadows, into anonymity where we can strike like death and then strike again.

"In two months we are going to initiate a war to reclaim civilization. We will target the thieves and savages and interlopers

who have hoodwinked it from us and hounded us from its do-
main. And we will not forgive. Our victory will be complete. All
we have to do is take it!"

Not even flushed or breathing heavily after concluding his
speech, Michael signaled to the restaurant manager to open the
door.

"Yeah! That's a white man!" Roland proclaimed. "A white
man just said that!"

After high-fiving Roland, Michael led the men outside into
the chilly Piedmont air. All except for Ben, who lingered in the
restaurant, watching them leave. His mouth was slack and dry,
and from it came a feeble, creaking wheeze. He couldn't swallow. The muscles in his shoulders hunched him like an old man.
He knew he wasn't sick. He understood clearly the origins of
these sudden, debilitating symptoms. It was dread, the kind that
tastes like death and dampens all sense of panic and flight. "You
are doomed," it tells you. "There is nowhere to run. Now, don't
you wish you didn't know that?"

Of course, Ben knew. But it couldn't be, he thought. It *couldn't*
be.

Chapter 36

Which famous twentieth-century supernatural thriller movie
produced the catchphrase "I see dead people"?

A. *The Phantom of the Opera*
B. *The Cabinet of Dr. Caligari*
C. *Nosferatu, a Symphony of Horror*
D. *The Sixth Sense* (correct)

Ben soon discovered that being a prisoner in Nathan's Ford
was a lot like not being a prisoner in Nathan's Ford. Work hours
were longer, and no one took care of your laundry. Basketball
was forbidden as well. But that was about it. The four feet between his thin, lumpy bunk and his desk became Ben's entire
world. With his doubled workload for Invorne and Eli's money
transfer project, he had grown accustomed to sixteen-hour
workdays and five hours of sleep a night. There was no upper

bunk, so Ben was wide open to the lodes of photo-crystal on the ceiling. The toilet was relatively clean when he first encountered it. The presence of a vile, shit-flecked brush on the floor next to a plastic bottle of bleach indicated that it was his job to keep it that way. The room smelled like garbage and pond scum. The unpainted plasterboard on three plywood walls must have been the only thing protecting him from the naked earth outside. The fourth wall contained a common wooden door leading to the rest of the compound. It had a handset and a deadbolt lock.

His first week comprised mostly the shock of internal exile and settling into his demanding new routine. A few books and a jump rope took care of the little free time he did have. Either that or the occasional vagina dialogue with Martinetti over dinner in the mess hall. The prophetic dread he felt after Michael's speech in the restaurant eventually receded but never went away. How could a blazing ball of emotion result in any kind of action unless accompanied by memories of real events? As with the images of his father's abuse of Isaac and his own subsequent heroics, Ben was not even sure if his breakdown had been triggered by memories or by dreams. But what memories? What dreams?

Despite being entirely removed from sunlight, his gray-brown complexion never changed. There was no mirror in the cell, and without an enabled DSAK he couldn't project one. This made shaving his face difficult and his head nearly impossible. He cut himself numerous times on the former and gave up with the latter after one try. The thin, rippled reflection from his concave QTM screen showed that his lips were beginning to attenuate back to their natural Caucasian form. It occurred to him that the Fickleskin template must have also permanently altered the cartilage in his nose since his appendage remained wide and flat like a prizefighter's. From this battered visage however arose a masculine aura of strength and resilience which his previous countenance, for all its Vitruvian symmetry, simply lacked. The change was not entirely unwelcome. Ben figured a flat, less obtrusive nose might be an asset if he were ever struck there again.

One morning, while disassembling a particularly thorny protein for Invorne, Ben matched its behavior to the medical database and was shocked when he encountered a world so unreal as to become risibly tragic. Pregnant men, acromegalic infants, hummingbird heart rates, bowling ball BMI's. Most insidious were the lab results. After an hour of investigation, he deduced the cause. In several central European test sites, decimal points entered as commas had been naively construed as commas by the computing systems. Perfectly healthy levels of 1,1 mg/dL for, say, total bilirubin or creatinine had been converted to positively lethal levels of 1,100 mg/dL by the time they reached Ben. He laughed, realizing that he had been wading hip and thigh through a binary river of dead people who survived their cases of allergic rhinitis and post nasal drip only to be metaphorically massacred by an unsophisticated data cleansing interface. The poor patients never stood a chance.

His first visitor arrived during his fifth week of incarceration, three weeks before the Bethesda launch. It was almost noon. His guard, one of Roland's men, arrived and took him through the main tunnels and up the stairs of the Bennett house to an unshaven Eli who was chugging iced tea at the kitchen table. Standing next to him was Sharon, the Sunny Day Daycare manager, in a striped lavender blouse and jeans. Her hair was blonde this time with pink and red highlights. A pair of sunglasses perched atop her head like a translucent tiara.

"Well, howdy, Ben!" she called.

Ben said nothing. He recognized her from the daycare but had completely forgotten her name. He remembered her questioning the role of women in the movement and insisting that she loved working with children. He couldn't imagine why she had said that or why Isaac had taken it so well in stride.

Eli smiled brightly at them. "I believe you two know each other."

Ben's face lit up. "Of course," he said, offering her his hand. "From the daycare."

She took his hand. "Lookit you. Can barely recognize ya!" She turned to Eli with a whip of her lithe upper body. "You don't suppose you can fix this boy up after all he's done for ya. Huh, Doctor?"

Eli shot Ben a weary look and a wink. "Not unless you can get your hands on some Eclumenicib. The generic version of that compound runs at about $1300 an ounce. We're not a pharmacy, sweetheart."

Sharon sucked some air between her teeth in annoyance. "I don't know how anybody can stand this man," she said as she took Ben by the arm. "Come on, Ben."

"Where are we going?"

"You have an orphan niece," she told him, revealing her fat gums. "As one of the earners here who has custody of a child, you need to be made aware of our contingency plans at the day-care in case of another attack."

Ben hesitated and looked to Eli. "But right now I'm being held—"

Eli waved once. "Go. I approve. So does Michael. It's a cloudy day. It won't hurt you or your skin to get some fresh air. And Ben, be back within two hours, okay?"

Two men, whom Ben recognized in their mandarin guises as Alan and Doug, the group's young explosives experts, appeared from the basement and sought an immediate audience with Eli. Their bodies hadn't yet had time to accumulate the solid muscle mass that Ben was accustomed to seeing on men in the tunnels. But their eyes were sharp and alert. They spoke with such terse urgency that Eli switched his PVN to them and initiated what appeared to be a pointed interrogation. No doubt this concerned the Bethesda job, Ben thought. He was pretty sure those two were part of Michael's team and were expected to rig the bombs under the great mosque.

He looked to Sharon who was now motioning him towards the sliding glass door. Behind her was a deck, and beyond that was an impenetrable phalanx of foliage comprising wide, sturdy oaks, irregular loblolly pines, various thick shrubbery, and one majestic American chestnut tree which reached over the roof like the hand of a benevolent giant. Maximum privacy, Ben thought. And why not? They could never be too invisible for what they were trying to do. Knowing that his not-so-fickle disguise would most likely ward off scrutiny like a talisman, Ben stepped outside for the first time in over a month. He made Sharon wait while he leaned against the deck railing, relishing the idyllic view and breathing in the fresh spring air.

Once they entered her car, a late model self-driving Toyota, Sharon brushed hair from her face, pursed her lips, and took a long look at Ben. "They really messed you up, didn't they?" she said. "You must be like the first guy here who went totally black. I hope they had good reasons to make you do that."

"You know I can't talk about it, even in a PVN," Ben said. He had been hunched over his desk for so long that his left shoulder tingled. He began rubbing it as the car lurched into motion.

"Here, let me get that for ya," Sharon said, taking over the massage and eliciting groans of relief from Ben. "I appreciate what you boys do, don't get me wrong. But Eli is just too much. 'We are not a pharmacy, sweetheart.' What a condescending shit. And lookit how he tells *you* to make it back in two hours when I'm the one who's responsible for ya." She slapped him three times in the shoulder indicating the end of the rubdown. They were nearing an intersection, and Sharon needed to give the automobile some of her attention.

Ben rolled his shoulder in relief. "Thanks. I think Eli's all right. He's the only leader we have who makes sense most of the time."

"Now that your brother's gone. You know, I really miss him."

Ben nodded ruefully. "Me too."

"But you're sayin' basically that Michael don't make sense, if I'm readin' ya right."

"I just don't understand him," Ben said, letting his hand fall on his thigh. "I don't get why he's so chummy with Roland."

"Well, Roland is crazy," Sharon said after some consideration. "But the good kind. We need people like that."

"He's a menace."

"Maybe to our enemies. I was here when he ran the show in Nathan's Ford. He won't so bad. He sure let more of us girls in on the action than the fat preacher man we got now."

"But shouldn't you look past judging the inclusion of women as an inherent good? Shouldn't we simply ask if it makes us more effective at waging our underground war?"

"Roland wasn't in charge long enough for us to know."

"Okay. But I know he' reckless. I also know that Eli and Michael run a tight ship and are very effective. They've initiated twelve out-country missions so far and lost only two men, including Isaac. Since they've taken over, recruitment is up 250%, and profits and productivity are up eighty percent."

Sharon rattled out a sigh, indicating her fatigue with the argument. "Well, I agree that Roland gets a little too passionate. And he is…strange."

"How?"

"I don't know. Sometimes he comes across like he's gay."

Ben turned to her. "No! Really?"

Sharon took her hands off the wheel as she let the car drive itself again. "You never see him with women. He only talks about them in the abstract. I mean, it's nice he puts white gals like myself on a pedestal and all. But he never laid a finger on any of us when he was in charge. It was weird. He said he had a girlfriend before he got involved. But who knows?"

"Maybe he's like Johannes Brahms, preferring ladies of the night to regular ladies. He certainly talks a good game about it."

"Who's Johannes Brahms?"

Ben shook his head and resisted the urge to sigh. Why be part of a white liberation movement if you don't know the great accomplishments of the people you're liberating? "Classical music composer," he said.

"How you know all that?"

"I used to write test questions in social studies and history. It made me read a lot. I also know that Adolf Hitler once proposed to Richard Wagner's daughter-in-law."

Sharon laughed. "Ree-card who? I don't know who that dude is either! Gah! I'm so ig'nernt!"

"German guy. Wrote operas in the 1800s," Ben said. He then hummed the famous melody to 'Ride of the Valkyries.'

"I know that one! They play it in video games!"

"Just picture fat ladies in chain mail and Viking helmets belting 'em out onstage. And that's Wagner." Sharon snorted into the steering wheel. "But speaking of gay," Ben went on, "I thought that if you were going to say that about anyone here it would be Michael."

"Michael?"

"Yeah. With all that intellectual talk. All those big words. Why use a word with two syllables when six will do just fine?"

"Well, just because he's all hoity toity don't make him gay. I don't get that from him, anyway."

"Really?"

Sharon thought for a moment as she resumed control of the car for a sharp turn. They were only about a minute from the daycare. "Yeah. He behaves himself, all right. Keeps his hands to himself. But I can tell he's straight by the way he interacts with me and the other girls. He comes across like he's married. It's nice, actually."

"What do you know about him?"

"What do I know about him? He was there at Wichita. As was I. He led the evacuation. Lotta folks woulda died if not for him."

"I know. He just worries me."

Sharon pulled into the daycare lot and parked. "Why?"

Ben ran his fingers through his hair, grasping for an explanation. "Something just doesn't feel right about him. For someone so smart to not notice how insane and dangerous Roland is."

Sharon seemed to point her chin at him as she eyed him cautiously. A network of blue blood vessels peeked through the bags under her eyes which were disguised imperfectly with makeup. "I think you're frettin' over that big job coming up I'm not supposed to know about. Am I right?" Ben hung his head as if the weight of all this futility were too much to bear and then nodded. Sharon's face softened, and she started again on his shoulder. "I'm sure Michael has a reason for everything he does. He's our leader, and we gotta trust him. He's gotten us this far. You've said so yourself. Anyway, you've been cooped up for weeks. And you just lost your brother. If it was me I'd be batshit crazy right now."

Ben pretended to laugh. Maybe she was right, he thought. He put on a bright smile and presented it to her like a new bowtie. "There you go, see?" she said. "Now let's go inside."

The daycare hadn't changed since he had last seen it: pretty brunette secretary to the left, three-dimensional felt jungle to the right. The gazelles and elephants and antelope and hyenas were still smiling cheek-to-cheek, teaching us the alphabet one letter at a time. Sharon discussed business with the brunette for a few moments, during which time Ben was hoping the brunette would mention Sharon's name. She did not.

Sharon then put Ben in her PVN and ran him through the evacuation protocols of the daycare. It began in the men's room where the toilet served as a functional prop. After turning off the water and flushing, she pressed the old-fashioned flush button in a certain rhythmic sequence. Ben smiled, recognizing the opening notes to the Rolling Stones 1971 hit 'Brown Sugar.' A curious choice for a keystroke pattern by White Nationals, he thought, given the salaciously miscegenetic nature of the song.

The entire lavatorial apparatus folded silently upwards like a vampire's coffin. The base of the toilet took enough floor along with it to create a man-sized hole to the tunnels beneath. Ben peered into it and noticed ladder rungs embedded in the rock wall. Sharon pointed to the flush button. "You press this again and everything goes back to how it was."

"And what's underneath? More tunnels?"

"Yes. And remember, what I'm gonna show you we only show to parents or guardians of our children. Even Eli, Michael, and Roland have never been down here."

Ben pointed to the closed bathroom door. "If it's so secret, how come you only have a handset lock?"

Sharon smiled. "We don't hire men. This room is hardly ever used. Come on. We won't be long."

After about ten feet Ben landed on dirt. The tunnel was not nearly as well ventilated as the tunnels under the Bennett and Garrett houses. There was no light source other than the two six-ty-watt bulbs from the bathroom ceiling above. This starkly ac-cented Sharon's angular features and cinemagraphed a demonic simulacrum of the woman whose name Ben had hopelessly for-gotten. Her highlights came across as deep black in the gleam. Sharon enabled the flashlight on her personal device and lit the room. It was a ten-by-twenty rocky pocket with six tunnels lead-ing outward like a snowflake.

"Look up," Sharon instructed, illuminating a silver speck among the fuzzy dirt on the tunnel ceiling. "When you press that button, the commode upstairs shuts and disables. Got that? This lil' trap door can never be opened again unless you bring lots of firepower."

"That button is kinda high, isn't it?"

"Yeah, it's high. You'll need to use the stepladder we keep in the northeast tunnel there. Or stand on someone's shoulders."

"Why?"

"So it's really hard to hit. So no one does it by mistake. It can only be pressed once, and that's only after the children and teachers are down here, and the government's blowing up shit up there. Got it?"

"Yeah. So which tunnel do we go down?"

Sharon gave Ben a wide, clever smile. "None of 'em. They're decoys. They spread out about a hundred yards, and we planted big fuckin' daddy-ass landmines at the end of each one." She directed Ben's attention to a space between two tunnels. "If you use your DSAK, you'll see this wall is due west," she said. "There's a door here that opens up like a super-wide filing cabinet. It takes you down some stairs into another tunnel that stretches to the RVs. They're sittin' under a barn off a dirt road a couple miles off. Lotsa tree cover. We scoped it out real good."

"How many RVs do you have?"

"Two. So we can split up if we need to. Thirty-two kids died at Wichita. It ain't gonna happen again."

She knelt down, banged a spot on the wall once with her fist, and got out of the way. An amorphously shaped wall slid open on grooved rails like the mandible of a gigantic robot. The tunnel beyond it led down and out.

"That opened easy," Ben said.

"Well, it's not locked. We figure if you get this far you'll be strapped for time."

"Does it lock on the other side?"

"Yeah. Like a submarine hatch. It should be pretty obvious. And the wall was designed so you can't tell from this side unless you have a lot of light and you really know what you're lookin' for."

Sharon tapped the moveable wall once more, causing it to silently close. It was now practically invisible, its capillary edges camouflaging themselves among the natural imperfections of the rock around it. Knocking on it didn't even produce an echo.

She stood and occupied a little more of Ben's personal space than he was accustomed. Having been without female company for so long, the sight and smell of her, even in this dank, putrid hole, sent blood flowing to all the wrong places in his body. He did not want to be aroused by her, borderline attractive as he found her to be. He knew a relation like this at a time like this would violate protocol as well as muddle his thoughts. Women have a way of making men say and do stupid things, he knew. He was suddenly grateful for Eli's distaff ban despite all the lonely nights. And not remembering Sharon's name certainly didn't encourage him. Mostly, however, he still hadn't overcome the ineffable dread from the restaurant. His mind would default to macabre, cataclysmic fantasies whenever he let it. He imagined everyone in Nathan's Ford as ghosts—not realizing that they were already dead and twitching out the remainder of their short lives in circular busywork. Ben was not a superstitious person. He knew he was never one to panic or lose control of his emotions. He knew he had a pretty good grasp on reality. How else could one write test items for a living? There could only be one answer just like there could only be one Truth. So then why was he *feeling* something without also thinking that very same thing? Never before had he had such dreadful feelings without at least being able to plumb them with an anchor of reason. But this time, he was afraid they were too deep. This time, he was really afraid.

Ben smiled politely at Sharon and stepped aside, allowing her clear access to the ladder. She smiled back just as politely and led the way back up.

Chapter 37

"'Tain't no sin—*white* folks has done it! It ain't no sin; glory to goodness, it ain't no sin! *Dey's* done it—yes, en dey was de biggest quality in de whole bilin', too—*kings!*"

The above quote comes from which Mark Twain novel?

A. *The Gilded Age*
B. *The American Claimant*
C. *The Adventures of Huckleberry Finn*
D. *Pudd'nhead Wilson* (correct)

Sharon led him to the same classroom that Isaac had taken him to weeks ago. Together they watched his niece Melissa and a little boy put together a dinosaur puzzle on the floor. She wore pink tights and a black T-shirt with the word 'love' spelled out with building blocks. A rubber band held her frizzy hair back in a ponytail, but enough had escaped to make her seem as if she were conducting mild currents of electricity. Ben had almost no experience with children and was secretly dreading his introduction to Melissa. Fortunately, she herself had made that nearly impossible. When presented with a large, scruffy black man squatting before her, she ran to her teacher and hid behind her skirt. Her mouth remained locked in a cartoonish pout until a bemused Ben assumed a tight, self-conscious grin and left the room.

A sheet of sunlight overpowered their eyes as they stepped out of the daycare. Sharon lowered her sunglasses, which were almost taller than they were wide, and suddenly appeared as if she were hiding from the paparazzi. Laughing at Eli's weather prediction, Ben could only shield his face with his hand until his eyes adjusted. As soon as they did, however, he encountered an approaching figure which was too close to ignore. Curtis Book.

They addressed each other simultaneously.

"Wassup, Doo!" Curtis said, offering his hand in a modified high-five.

"Hey, man!" Ben said, taking it and transposing it into a manly half-hug. He noticed Curtis wore a pair of athletic shorts and an NBA tank top. With immaculate high-top sneakers and conspicuous bling, he seemed like an overgrown man-child with money. Ben liked Curtis and dearly hoped that the homeboy getup was merely a disguise. He was still irked that Curtis had beaten him two-zip in basketball and knew that had the third game continued he might have worn him down and won.

As glad as Ben was to see Curtis, his composure popped like

a water balloon when he noticed whom he had standing next to him. It was the stocky, light-skinned black police officer, the very one who had arrested him on his second day in Nathan's Ford. She wore a white V-neck T-shirt and blue shorts. Kinky hair afro'ed out the back of her baseball cap. She was pushing a dozing toddler in a stroller. Ben smiled stupidly and waited for Sharon or Curtis to save him.

"Miss Craig, I'd like ya to meet my girlfriend LaKendra," Curtis said, attempting to steer her away from Ben. "LaKendra, this here is Miss Craig. She runs Sunny Day Daycare. Jus' the lady we need to talk to."

"Well, hello! Nice ta meet ya!" LaKendra said, sticking her elbow out at a right angle and offering Sharon a firm, manly handshake.

"Nice to meet you too," Sharon responded.

"We're actually here to see if you have room for little Chelsea here."

"We just might. Lookit you! Cutie pie!" Sharon said, squatting down for a chance to nudge the child playfully on the tummy. "How old is she?"

"Thirteen months," LaKendra said. "Do you have time to meet with us right now?"

Sharon stood. "Well, I'm thrilled you wish to join the Sunny Day family. Please go on inside, and our secretary Kim will be glad to take all your information and tell you about our services. But right now, I'm sorry, we're about to get lunch. I should be back in less than an hour. Is there something you need to discuss with me personally, or—"

"Nah! We can handle it inside," LaKendra said, flashing her mischievous, chipped-tooth smile. "But I appreciate your time!"

"Not a problem! It was nice to meet you," Sharon responded. She then squatted once again to say goodbye to Chelsea. "I'm sorry you're asleep right now, Chelsea. I would have loved to talk to you. Maybe next time!"

After Sharon stood to exchange final pleasantries with Curtis, Ben started to inch away from the conversation. He had growing hopes he could escape without a reintroduction to the intrusive lady cop who had poked her face so painfully into his life nearly a year ago.

"And who might you be?" LaKendra asked, looking at Ben with her devilishly uninhibited smile. Comic book villains might smile like that when they have you where they want you, Ben thought. He opened his mouth before he knew what he was going to say. He coughed to buy some time and then said, "Isaac. Nice to meet you." He offered her his hand and she shook it studiously.

"Nice to meet you too," she said. "Isaac who, if I may ask?"

"Benjamin," he said, tilting his head with a disarming smile.

"Oh, I don't know any Isaac Benjamins in Nathan's Ford."

Sharon gave him a tight squeeze around the waist. "He's my new boyfriend. We do the long-distance thing. He came into town last night."

LaKendra's eyes lit up. "My!" she exclaimed. "Isn't that innerestin'. Curtis, how did you say you know this boy?"

"We played pickup basketball by the old Garrett Middle School this morning."

LaKendra then turned to Sharon and pointed her finger above her own ear. "And is this the first time—"

"Come on, Baby. Why don't you just lay off the questions, huh?" Curtis said. "These good people got things to do, y'know?"

"Of course! I'm so sorry," LaKendra went on. "I'm just nosy. You know me. We'll just go on inside now. Sorry for disturbin' ya!"

Sharon put her hand on her chest in friendly protest while backing away. "Oh, no problem!" she said.

"It's all good," Ben chimed in.

"It's just that..." LaKendra said, turning away from the stroller and looking straight at Ben. "You look so *familiar*. I know I musta seen you before. You say you just got in town last night?"

"Baby, that's enough. Come on," Curtis urged. With LaKendra's back still turned, he gave little Chelsea a hard bump and woke her. The child's gurgling cries had no effect on her mama who was still honing in on Ben.

"Kin I as' you a question?" she drawled.

"Sure," Ben said.

"How you get yer hair so straight?" The question was so un-expected that no one moved or made a sound except little Chelsea. "Such a good lookin' brotha such as yerself, ya gotta share your secrets. I used chemicals and fancy shampoos. Taken pills. Done radiation. Even once broke out my gramma's ol' flat iron. And my hair just keeps getting damaged and hard to deal with. So how you do it?"

"I don't do anything," Ben said. "This is the way God made me." He then turned his profile and smiled like a fashion model.

Curtis and Sharon tried to laugh, but LaKendra's expression didn't change. She leaned in even closer, still baring her broken fang. "I'm askin' 'cos, well, you do look *real* familiar. I'm a police officer here in Nathan's Ford, see? Officer Dobbs." She projected the 3D image of her badge from her personal device. "A while back I remember we arrested a white boy...looked kinda like you. He was in town lookin' for a lost brother or somethin'. After the judge let him go, he disappeared. Now we been hearin' rumors that STGs, Security Threat Groups, y'know, might be operatin' 'round here somewhere. So we been told to keep on the lookout. Report anything suspicious. And I hope you understand, but seein' a black boy lookin' kinda like a white boy we arrested a while back who disappeared alla sudden. That's pretty suspicious, don't ya think?"

Stripped naked to such a withering question—from an officer of the law, no less—Ben understood with burning clarity what an amateur he was. He suddenly had the fervent conviction that someone should scrawl a scarlet letter 'C' across his forehead with a permanent marker—'C' for Chump—and then slap him in the face several times for good measure. Why did he stop shaving his head? Because there wasn't a suitable mirror in the holding cell? What a ridiculous excuse that was. Why didn't it seem ridiculous before? Why did he wait until now to realize that a Negro with wavy brown hair walking around as happy as you please might also seem ridiculous? And why didn't anyone bother to assign him an identity more in line with his new pigmentation? Why hadn't he insisted upon it? Zhenglong Hu? Zhenglong Who was more like it given that this expensive and carefully crafted cover was now more a liability than anything else. Idiot that he was, he never even deleted the images of Zhenglong's phony identification card and passport from his DSAK. All this inquisitive woman had to do was sync her device to his, and he along with everyone in the tunnels could meet with annihilation within hours. Make that minutes if LaKendra were really an enemy agent rather than some chubby hick cop who couldn't keep her hair straight.

Remembering that he still had no poison in his molars, Ben shoved the urge to panic back down his dry, constricting throat. He also resisted the childish urge to imagine he could go back in time and undo his jamboree of blunders. He knew both moves would lead to disaster. More importantly, however, he was offended that he was about to get checkmated so easily by someone who had nothing going for her other than a chipped tooth and a pathological disregard for the privacy of others. No. His cause was too important and he had suffered too much to let something like that happen. He resolved to take this travesty well beyond its absurd finale if he had to.

Both Sharon and Curtis of course laughed and acted like they couldn't imagine such a farfetched thing happening in little old Nathan's Ford. Why, people would just as soon ride to work on the backs of dinosaurs every morning. And they kept pouring it on thicker and thicker, waiting for Ben to solemnly proclaim his innocence. But while grateful that Sharon and Curtis had jumped to his rescue, Ben had no intention of doing what they expected.

"No. I know *exactly* what she's talking about," Ben said through a chipper grin. He watched the color drain from Sharon's face like a cheap special effect. Curtis just looked at Ben as if he'd started speaking in tongues. Even little Chelsea shushed up, as if sharing in the shock.

"Oh, do you now?" LaKendra said.

"Sure. You see, in this country, Officer Dobbs, white people are oppressed," he began, leaning over her to accent his genderial height advantage. His smile was maliciously long, and he meant every inch of it. "Maybe you haven't noticed, but standards are a lot higher for whites than they are for blacks. I'm talk-

ing professionally, academically, and morally. Especially morally. Affirmative action has changed from some benevolent out-
reach effort eighty years ago into a state-mandated, rights-
depriving quota system that looks to empower blacks at the expense of whites. Have you noticed how difficult it is to fire black
people but how easy it is to fire whites? Have you noticed how
blacks can now get away with a lot more misbehavior and criminal activity than whites can? Have you also noticed how whites
get sued or arrested and get their reputations ruined over trivial
things, like having racist thoughts? Yes, it's *Nineteen Eighty-Four*
all over again and thinking something is a crime. Of course, if
you're white there's never any presumption of innocence. Ever
since we turned our backs on the First and Second Amendments, being white is like walking on a tightrope without a net.
Do or say or think something the authorities don't like and
you're condemned as a racist. And from there it's a long fall.

"Now, where I come from I know a lot of white guys who get
that operation. They go black and they never go back and maybe
I did too! Does that satisfy your curiosity, Officer?"

Raging on the inside, Ben knew that if his precious grievance
screed didn't inhibit LaKendra from asking for his digital ID, a
straight right to the jaw certainly would. Then he and Sharon
would have to trust Curtis with the baby as they took the unconscious police officer underground where Eli and Michael would
figure out how to kill her without triggering whatever implants
she had inside her body. And then everyone might just have to
leave Nathan's Ford. All because Ben didn't think to ask for a
mirror.

He saw the doubt in LaKendra's eyes as she pulled away
from him. Her mouth contorted into a smile's ugly opposite,
pulled downward by the protruding tendons in her neck. Relief
flooded Ben's entire body. Maybe she wasn't undercover after
all? Maybe she was just a curious cop who likes to act on rumors
and hunches?

"I guess so," she said.

Ben smiled devilishly right back at her and said, "Then have
a nice day." He turned and headed towards Sharon's car. Sharon followed him after exchanging apologies with a mortified

LaKendra.

Even though their PVN was activated, neither said anything until Ben noticed that Sharon was not taking him back to the Bennett house. "Where are we going?" he asked.

"Is she really a police officer?" Sharon asked. She startled Ben because she asked it in broken Mandarin. She was angry, keeping her mouth shut as much as possible and breathing audibly through her nose. "And don't answer in English please. If they're tracking us or following us, then they're probably reading our lips right now."

"Yes. She is a police officer," he responded in his stilted Mandarin. "She arrested me about a year ago for traffic violations. Before I joined. But I don't think she knows about us."

"Well, she might after what you said to her. Why couldn't you just fuckin' deny it?" Her profanity came out in English, which forced Ben to reconfigure his mind to process his native language and then back again for Mandarin. The resulting mental whiplash befuddled him for a moment. "I said, why couldn't you—"

"I don't know!" he said in English. "I just got fed up with her, okay?"

"What?"

"Look. She was pushing me on the defensive. Not for the first time, either. I get the feeling she really likes to do that. And she's good at it."

"So the fuck what?"

"So I pushed back! She certainly wasn't used to that. And I didn't do anything wrong so she couldn't arrest me."

"You don't know that."

"Well, I acted like I did nothing wrong, all right?" Ben snapped. "If I started denying everything and making stuff up on the fly, the questions would have kept coming and coming. I know how this woman operates!"

Sharon took control of the car and turned left towards downtown Nathan's Ford. She then turned onto a gravel road. The Last Gasp Bar and Grill, wide, gabled-roof tavern that it was, was up ahead on the left. It was painted gray, had portholes for windows, and a purely cosmetic bell tower on top. The tower had a gabled roof as well. Sharon parked in its nearly-empty parking lot.

"Why are we here and not underground talking to Michael and Eli?" Ben asked, remembering his Mandarin this time.

Sharon took her purse and opened the car door. "Because I'm taking you to lunch, remember?" she said, also in Mandarin. "You're my boyfriend now. Start acting like it."

Sharon slammed the door and left Ben behind as she started hiking to the restaurant. Her high heels provided unsteady support in the gravel parking lot. Ben caught up with her with heavy strides and put his arm around her waist like a boyfriend.

"Are you afraid they could be watching us?" Ben asked. "Is that why we're here?"

"This is so fuckin' stupid," she said, again retreating into English for her naughty word of choice. "A black guy who can speak Chinese. Like that's not at *all* suspicious. Like they could never figure out what we're sayin' anyway. Fuck!"

"What do you want me to do"?

She stopped and said in English, "Just hug me."

"Okay," Ben whispered. He combed his fingers through her technicolor tangles and pulled her to his chest. She smelled like shampoo and soap.

"Look away from the street," she said.

"Okay."

Sharon reached under his arms and squeezed him tight by the shoulders. "Sway with me," she commanded.

He obeyed. "What are we gonna do?"

She took a few seconds to respond. "I don't know yet. Neither of us have clearance to contact anyone through our devices. We have to get you underground with nobody watching."

"It's possible nobody's watching."

"Can we take that chance?"

"I don't know. I just can't believe Curtis is dating a police officer."

She pulled away and shushed him on the lips with her finger. "I got it. When does Garrett play Bennett in basketball?"

"Oh, right about now. Lunch time. Drop me off there. Perfect."

She found his hand with hers and led him to the restaurant. "Yes, they'll tell you what to do. But let's get something for ourselves first," she said, again in Mandarin. "Just in case someone is watching."

Twenty minutes later, in the gravel lot next to the courts between the Garrett and Bennett houses, Sharon asked for a kiss. Despite sweaty men playing a rough, physical game of basketball not fifty feet away, Ben gave it to her. It was a hot one, heavy with desire. He ran his fingers along her jawline. She gripped his collar in her fists and then encircled his neck in her arms. After pulling away and exiting the car without saying goodbye or thank you, Ben gave her a look which said he was sad for not being able to stay. He felt like a complete cad for not remembering her name.

Chapter 38

Which of the following men coined the term 'involuntary memory' which describes how sensory input such as smell and sight can trigger hidden or forgotten memories?

A. psychologist Jean Piaget
B. psychologist B. F. Skinner
C. psychologist Sigmund Freud
D. author Marcel Proust (correct)

The apparition suit Ben wore during his two-mile trek through the woods to the rendezvous point still lay on the floor beside him. It was Sharon's. He relished being out of it. But after nine hours of fresh air, he found himself resenting having to live like a coal miner again. As soon as he arrived in the tunnels he was taken directly to the same thin, windowless room in which Michael and Eli had sentenced him five weeks before. Same concrete, same rugs, same fluorescent light strips. Ben surmised that Roland's engineers must have finally gotten to the ventilation system since the room was warmer and less dank than he remembered it. He was also seated instead of being forced to stand. Both were welcome changes but did little to offset the near hostile interrogation to which he was being subjected.

Several card tables were arrayed against him in a subtle arc. Seated facing him were Michael and Eli, front and center. Flanking them were Martinetti, Chuck, Gideon, Alan, Doug, and several soldiers standing by the door. Also facing him was an empty chair. It belonged to Roland who, at that moment, was pacing behind the others as if stalking his own shadow.

"This is why we should never work with groids!" he thundered. "Fucking Curtis! He shacks up with the NFPD, and he doesn't even tell us? We should stick a spit up his ass and roast him!"

"Enough, Colonel," Michael insisted, waving the back of his hand in Roland's direction. "This is bad. We all know it."

Roland flexed his upper body and leaned back as if undergoing some quasi-scientific comic book transformation. His scream was an angry, ragged groan which reached a girlish falsetto at irregular intervals. The men for the most part expressed boredom with his histrionics.

"Of course, we cannot have you act on any of these threats, Colonel," Michael warned. "If that woman is at all unsure about Curtis or Lieutenant Cameron, Curtis's subsequent disappearance would remove all the doubt. They would start with Specialist Craig. Then it would be only a matter of time before they start sweeping the tunnels."

"Also, we can't forget what Curtis has done for us," Eli added. "Having him and several other black allies in Nathan's Ford has allowed us to move more freely above ground as well as gather intelligence. He's helped us a lot in the past despite his lapses in judgment."

"Yeah, he's a real Huggy Bear," Martinetti said. "But he should never have addressed you in public like that, Ben. That's a clear protocol violation."

"I addressed him too," Ben admitted.

"That's why you're in trouble again, Lieutenant," Eli said. "But this time I think it's only fair that General Archer and myself take some of the blame. We should never have let you out looking as you did. We should also have been more proactive about finding you a new identity."

"I agree," Michael said. "However please keep in mind that

Ben is just an earner. He's not had the extensive training Curtis has had. Curtis has no excuse for saying hello to him like that."

"Yep," Martinetti agreed. "Curtis really screwed the pooch this time."

"I'd like to screw him!" Roland said. The subsequent awkward lull in the conversation indicated how seriously the men took Roland's comment.

"Gentlemen," Martinetti said. "We have to assume he's been fuckin' her, okay? We also have to assume he knew all along she was a cop. Just the fact alone puts his loyalty in question."

"Hear, hear," Michael said, pretending to raise a glass in Martinetti's honor.

Eli turned to Ben. "Lieutenant, you did say that she seemed genuinely surprised at your explanation. Do you think that she—"

"It doesn't matter, General," Michael interrupted. "Even off-duty cops are equipped with cameras. They are going to find images or videos of Lieutenant Cameron and match them with what she captured today. Ben, I'm assuming you or others have posted images and video of you on social media. Is that correct?"

"Sure," Ben said.

"And have you ever been televised?"

Ben considered this carefully. "Probably not since my high school basketball days. I was in a few bar bands in San Diego after college. There might still be some footage of that floating around."

"Anything more recent?"

"I was at that Patriot Press conference in San Diego seven years ago. Remember the one where those Lefty moles hurled photo-crystal and started a riot?"

Michael's face sharpened as his eyes thinned. "You were there?"

"I was," Ben said, feeling his stomach tighten.

"Glad I wasn't," Martinetti said. "Lotta people lost their livelihoods over that."

"I was at the previous conference," Eli said. "In Murfreesboro, Tennessee. No issues at all."

Michael hadn't stopped looking at Ben. "I know they ask for donations at those functions. Did you contribute anything on credit while you were there?"

Ben sighed. "I think I did, sir."

Michael nodded pensively and looked into the faces all around him. "Well, the Fickleskin may buy us time, but not much. They will take a template of your face, black as it is, and run it everywhere. I predict they will find a match in less than twenty-four hours. Heck, it would take us only twice as long. And our face recognition software technology is at least ten years out of date."

"So what?" Eli countered. "Okay, so they peg him as Ben Cameron. And now he's black. Many people undergo race change surgery. And Ben gave Officer Dobbs his rationale. Why is there any reason for her to suspect more?"

"She is not 'Officer Dobbs'," Roland snapped. "She is a groid bitch who needs to get her badge ripped off her goddamn tits!"

Eli stood and faced Roland, fists trembling. Before he could speak, however, Michael stood and restrained him. He held his hand out to Roland, who was now being flanked by a rush of soldiers including Chuck and Gideon. Behind Eli stood only Martinetti and the two techies.

"Got a problem, General?" Roland challenged.

"I have a problem," Michael said, approaching him like an angry father. Chuck and Gideon tried to intervene, but Michael simply stood over them menacingly and brushed past them. Michael looked down at Roland, and whispered, "These outbursts must end now. They are anger for anger's sake. They indicate you do not possess the requisite self-control to carry out agitation raids. Such behavior jeopardizes not only individual missions but our very existence here in Nathan's Ford." Michael held a finger over Roland's forehead as if he were about to anoint him with oil. "One more outburst, and you will be court-martialed."

Roland said nothing, neither chastened nor recalcitrant.

"This is your last warning. Do you understand?"

With his ocean-blue eyes looking up at Michael as if pleading for rescue, Roland tightened his lips enigmatically and said,

"Yes, sir."

Michael spun around to the group as if anxious to be done with Roland. "Everyone sit! Please," he said. "You too, Colonel."

The men breathed easily again, and this helped soothe Ben's guilt for not peeking over Eli's shoulder while he was facing down Roland's hordes. Ben just did not think the time was right to play his hand against Roland. Martinetti shot him a wink as he sat down.

"Worst case scenario!" Michael called out.

"That police officer is really an enemy agent," Roland said, now being curiously cooperative. He clasped his hands over his right knee which was crossed over his left. "And she's on to us."

"Best case scenario!"

"There isn't any," Martinetti said.

"Yes, there is," Eli said. "If she really were an enemy agent, she would have no reason to announce to possible suspects that Nathan's Ford is a hotbed of...what did she call them? STGs? Why even say that? Why tell this to someone who is a suspect?"

"Because she wanted me to panic," Ben answered. "She wanted me to backpedal and make up excuses and ultimately contradict myself in the heat of her questioning."

"It's good you didn't do that," Martinetti said.

"Yes, but it's not really about Lieutenant Cameron," Michael said. "In other words, best case scenario, worst case scenario, it doesn't matter what this police officer intended or whether she's an enemy agent. What matters is that somebody in Washington figured out that we're here. They may not know about the tunnels or Fickleskin. They may not know about Bethesda. But they know something. And that's what worries me."

"Yeah, and the fact that this secret war might not be so secret anymore," Martinetti added. "Maybe the feds are ready to go public if they're willing to tell local cops about us."

Eli waved his hand in the air, almost as if to be recognized and permitted to speak. "Well, we don't know how much they've told local police, Major," he said. "For all we know, the FBI has listed hundreds of towns in Virginia that might be hotbeds for STGs. Maybe..." he looked directly at Roland "...*Officer Dobbs* was just following standard operating procedure by questioning Ben."

"After Wichita, is that a bet you wanna take, sir?" Martinetti asked. "They could blow us up from space. We wouldn't even see 'em coming."

Eli compressed his lips. "Well, as in all wars, we have to choose between uncomfortable alternatives. I will have to confer more with General Archer, of course, but I say that the most prudent measure for at least the short term would be to put our wheels on."

Heavy sighs from the men. Ben noted how their heads shook and how exasperated smiles tightened their faces. Their breathing obfuscated the sounds of the functioning ventilation system. Ben knew that 'putting wheels on' meant that the men, all fifty-four of them now in Nathan's Ford, must live and work in their RVs. Ben had done it for two awful days during training. He remembered the close, almost suffocating quarters. The bad breath, the body odor, the humorless farts. They had enough food and water stored away to last months. Ben prayed that Michael and Eli would have the foresight to segregate Roland and his men in their own vehicles. If not, he knew the ensuing confrontations would lead to existential and irreversible changes in their chapter of the revolution.

Michael raised a finger. "And if we abandon Nathan's Ford we do not do it until after Bethesda." Long, slow nods from the men made it clear they accepted this order more readily. "Major, how's the tech team training?"

"Well, we've taken apart and put together the bombs several times now," Martinetti said.

"In the dark?" Eli asked.

"Ah, not yet," Martinetti demurred. "The team mastered the Black Mollies. And one of the Purple Ninjas. Captain Larson went over the Red Beamer with about half of us. That's the most complicated one of the bunch. It's going under the mosque entrance."

"Why hasn't the entire group done it?" Eli asked.

"Well, we weren't scheduled for that exercise till next week."

"What about tomorrow?" Michael asked.

Shocked, Martinetti scanned the other faces for a second

opinion on what he had just heard. "Excuse me, sir?"

"What about tomorrow," Michael repeated. "Your exercise. Can you do it tomorrow?"

Martinetti's mouth fell open. "We have seven bombs. It took us two weeks just to be able to construct them with the lights on. We haven't even gone over our black bags yet."

"Answer my question, Major," Michael pressed. "Can you train your men to disassemble and reassemble your bombs blindfolded in the next twenty-four hours? Or do I need to find someone who can?"

Martinetti looked down for a moment and then back at Michael. "Yes, sir."

"Good. Colonel Turk, how about the security and communications team?"

"We're ready to rock and roll at the drop of a fucking hat, sir," Roland said with ostentatious chin swag. "We've war-gamed Plans A through C and contingencies one through four including the last resort bit about how we convert our apparition suits into fucking HPF40-fucking-MOAB-Apocalypto bombs. That mosque is going down. We've bludgeoned the redundancy, sir. My men and I know every step we have to take, and we won't have to say a word in the field."

"How about the urban camouflage?"

"They'll never find them," Roland said. "One bomb takes the place of a few ladder rungs. One is the entire manhole ten yards from the east side entrance. All we have to do is give them a longer countdown since we're putting them in early."

"Excuse me, sir," said someone. It was one of the techies, Alan. He was speaking to Roland. "The suicide bomb mechanisms still need a going-over with the team. Nothing too major."

"You can handle it tomorrow?" Roland asked.

"Was planning on it. Yes."

"Good. And the radio?" Michael asked.

Alan looked at Roland who fielded this one. "Yes, sir. We have the underground ultra-faint short wave with precision broadcast ready. You will get a noise-coded blow-by-blow of the action in real time." He then looked to Martinetti. "And we can take the broadcast kit apart and put it back together in the fucking dark."

Martinetti registered no response at all despite how everyone turned to him to see how he would react.

"Outstanding," Michael said, rubbing his hands together. "Okay. Given that we may be subject to missile strikes at any moment, it has become imperative that we hit the enemy while we are able. Yes, it is important that we escape with our lives and our weapons and data. But this attack in Bethesda is what our very existence hinges upon. A bumble bee may die when separated from his stinger. But he will sting." Michael consulted his DSAK. "It is almost twenty-three hundred hours now. In thirty hours we move. Oh-five-hundred hours. Wednesday. Any questions?"

Eli cleared his throat and took a moment to speak. "General, I agree with your assessment, but your plan is problematic. With tomorrow's greatly accelerated training, the will men need more sleep time before initiating the raid."

"We have Surplex pills," Michael said.

"We *abuse* Surplex pills," Eli responded. "We all know how these pills affect your judgment and your body. They keep you awake, but at the cost of some of your self-control, to say nothing of the short-term health risks. Over half your team has been taking them all week. They are going to need at least six hours of natural sleep before leaving."

Michael considered this and nodded. "Fair enough. Thirty-two hours then. We embark at oh-seven-hundred."

Eli crossed his massive legs on the second attempt. "Not so fast. My only other concern about leaving so soon is that while these men may have passed their technical training, we're scrapping their social training. You're not giving them time to learn any Arabic or how to impersonate Muslims. You're also not giving us time to furnish these men with plausible identities. They're not Chinese anymore."

"Perhaps that's a risk we will have to take," Michael said.

"But it's a tremendous risk," Eli countered. "Foolhardy, even. If any one of these men gets captured—"

"Then they will release the poison in their molars," Michael said flatly. "They were informed of the risks when they joined."

"Well, aside from your nonchalance about the lives of our men, General —"

"Excuse me, General," Michael interjected. "Please don't accuse me of nonchalance. I'm going on this mission as well. I insisted upon it, as you very well may remember. There is no risk these men are taking that I refuse to take. I'm willing to die for each one of them, and that does not entail leading from the rear. As Julius Caesar correctly pointed out, 'The gods of war hate those who hesitate.' And I have no intention of diverging from that dictum."

"Well, that's brave and noble of you, General," Eli countered. "But I am sure even Julius Caesar would not have ventured forth against the Gauls without proper training for his troops. I propose we give them four more days to prepare. Give them time to learn how to imitate at least native-born Muslims. Without the ability to slip in and out of the general population, they will stand out to the enemy. And with their DSAKs offline, we wouldn't be able to contact them if something goes wrong."

"The point is for nothing to go wrong."

"That leaves us with no margin of error."

Michael squinted at Eli in testy patience. "And every moment we argue about this, General, the odds increase that the enemy will obliterate our margin of error from the stratosphere."

"Why? Because one black female police officer has some suspicions over Lieutenant Cameron?"

"Why not?" Michael argued. "They have photo-crystal everywhere. If they stare at it long enough, they might be able to put two and two together." He turned to Ben. "Lieutenant, did you not say in your report that when you and Isaac entered Memphis on foot there were helicopter spotlights upon you?"

"Yes, there were. For a short time."

"Is it also true that there were helicopter spotlights on you when you were riding along the train tracks in your stolen vehicle?"

"It is, sir."

"And did you not also say that at one point you lowered your window, stuck your head out the window, and looked at the helicopter?"

Ben hung his head and nodded solemnly. "I did, sir."

"Therefore, there is an excellent chance that they recorded your doing so. Is that not also correct?"

Ben sighed in the face of such relentless logic. "Yes, sir."

Michael leaned back and threw his hand up at Eli with a victorious "Ah."

Eli took a deep breath, but his exhale was choppy and broken. He also looked askance at Martinetti before responding. Ben felt this made him seem almost shifty. "I don't...I don't ascribe such competence to our enemy, General," he said. "To say that within twenty-four hours they will piece together footage of Ben from a Pat-Press conference when he did not have Fickleskin, to Memphis when he was Chinese, to this afternoon when he's black, and then conclude that he's part of a revolution taking place in Nathan's Ford, all on the suspicions of one lone police officer is a stretch. And it is no reason to jeopardize this agitation raid!" Ben winced. What Eli intended as righteous anger may have come across as mere petulance.

Michael smiled as if Eli's objections were so self-evidently silly they refuted themselves. He glanced at Roland who was all too happy to remind everyone who the most prepared scout at the campfire was.

"General Humphrey," Roland said. "I have high confidence that we can infiltrate the sewer system, plant the fucking bombs, and return within two days. I also have high confidence that the bombs will remain undetected until the moment we blast thousands of these towel-headed sand-niggers into Hell with their pedophile prophet where they belong."

Eli treated Roland to a miniscule squint, unimpressed and unconvinced. "Major Martinetti?" he asked.

Ben had a feeling that the entire mission hinged upon Martinetti's opinion. With Martinetti behind him, Eli could conceivably wield the clout to delay the attack. The look of saggy-eyed, skeletal exhaustion on Martinetti's face told Ben he was not going to stand behind Eli on this one. No soldier is going to turn away a challenge which tests his readiness and devotion to the cause, no matter how imposing it may be.

"We'll make it," was all Martinetti cared to say. It was

enough for everyone in the room. Eli shook his head and grunted, surrendering the dispute. Michael then ordered training to commence immediately and dismissed the group.

"What about me, sir?" Ben asked Michael amid the hubbub of the adjoined meeting. "Do I stay in my cell? Or do I put wheels on too?"

As Michael turned around to face him, Ben felt the return of the wordless dread he had been feeling since that afternoon at the restaurant. His heart tried to punch its way through his sternum, and again, he had a hard time swallowing. He could sense Michael's annoyance with him. But there was something deeper. Something violent and familiar.

"You stay in your cell," he commanded. "Given that this is all your fault for addressing an ally in public and not keeping your head shaved, I find it only fitting that you be the last person on the RV when the time comes."

Ben didn't respond right away like he should have. He didn't respond because now he understood. He finally understood the source of the dread which had been haunting him for the past five weeks. And if there ever was a time to hate knowledge, this was it. There was a traitor in Nathan's Ford. Every hair that stood on the back of his neck told him it was so. Ben remembered everything now. The Patriot Press conference. The Poway High School gym. The square-jawed, shabbily-dressed muscle man who sat next to him. The way the man suddenly glared at him with primeval malice. The way he and his cohorts disrupted the event with photo-crystal. "Racism must perish!" he proclaimed. "Even if we must all perish with it!" Ben remembered the ensuing riot and the curious two-step the man performed before being subdued by stun guns. It was the same little jig he performed at the restaurant, anticipating the glorious future of the revolution. Ben knew that such a man could never be a friend of the revolution. He could only be a spy leading it to its destruction. Ben saw the man up close and ugly years ago, back when he was honest. He knew who it was now. He knew with stupid, sub-literate certainty. It was Michael.

Chapter 39

Most non-lethal weapons known as stun guns cause uncon-
trollable spasms because they emit electric pulses which interfere with those used by

A. adipose cells.
B. parietal cells.
C. epithelial cells.
D. nerve cells. (correct)

Ben had plotted it out so many times in his cell he could have
written a flowchart from memory. If Michael was a mole, it's
likely Washington had no idea where he was. The BREMAT implants took care of that. They jam any signal produced by other
implants. They kill you if you step out of the tunnels or venture
twenty miles in any direction outside of Nathan's Ford, depending on your security level. They could even detect if you were
using a personal device, or even an old-fashioned smartphone,
to contact anyone outside of Nathan's Ford. BREMATs were
equipped with Voice Recognition Language Translation — or
VORLAT — software which triggers death if it detects verbal
communication which could endanger the movement in Nathan's Ford. Of course, not knowing exactly what would trigger
the software further inhibited wearers from being mouthy. It
essentially reverted one to eighteenth-century standards of
communication. It was still technically possible to mail a letter,
but possession of postage stamps or metered envelopes was
punishable by death in the tunnels.

The BREMAT's one weakness, however, involved the twenty-mile radius around the base's central computing machines.
Inside that radius, the BREMATs received regular updates
which enabled them to jam the constantly changing signals from
the implants. Outside that radius, they did not. This meant that
if a person were a mole and they crossed that twenty-mile mark,
it would only be a matter of time before a signal would escape.

Everything now made sense. *This* was why Michael never
removed his Fickleskin. *This* was why he disregarded Eli's
common-sense precautions. This was *also* why he insisted on

leading the raid in the first place. Most importantly, this explained his leniency with Roland. For Michael, Roland's psychotic behavior didn't matter. He had no intention of ever even entering Bethesda. He would simply tip off Washington of his whereabouts shortly after traveling those twenty miles and then wait for the helicopters to swarm.

After a while, Ben cried thinking about it. He knew pounding on the door would be useless. The cell was in its own wing of the tunnels, and no one would hear — or care if they did. The entire organization was either furiously prepping for the agitation raid or furiously putting their wheels on. They had missed bringing him breakfast and lunch. It was four o'clock in the afternoon, and he'd been sustaining himself all day on sink water and snack food.

Dinner was late. Twenty-one hundred hours. A cold fried egg on a plain supermarket bagel and an apple. To Ben's tremendous relief, the young guard who brought it to him was not one of Roland's men. He was a new recruit. Ben pegged him at five-and-a-half feet tall, thirty-inches around the waist, and not much more at the shoulders. In the past, two beefy guards delivered Ben's food and were under orders to stun him if he caused trouble. With the entire movement feverishly gearing up for action however Ben suspected that this greenhorn was all they could spare for such a low-priority task. He was willing to gamble that the kid's DSAK had not yet been enabled.

The moment the kid handed Ben his meal, Ben burst out of the cell. The tunnel was barely wide enough for two, so a quarterback sweep was out of the question. Brushing past the kid, as unpleasant as that sounded, was the only option. The kid dropped the food tray and tried to push Ben back. He was strong for his size and managed to regain his footing and impede Ben at the same time. "Hey! Stop!" the kid shouted.

"I'm supposed to get an hour of freedom a day!" Ben said as the two wrangled in the tunnel. Ben had little difficulty making progress against this kid but preferred reasoning his way out of the predicament if he could.

"Orders are you stay in your cell at all times!"

"Whose orders?"

"General Archer's."

Ben shoved the kid away from him to get a moment to think. "What? That wasn't my sentence!"

"It is now," the kid said as he tried to push Ben back into his cell. "Archer said so!"

Without so much as a thought, Ben caught his would-be captor coming in with a short left hook. It landed hard and flush on the jaw, and the kid took a seat on the floor. Dazed from the blow, all he could was wobble to his knees. Ben was gone before he could get a foot on the floor.

Ben knew he couldn't run, but he also knew he had to hurry. The kid would contact his backup as soon as he could, and Ben would then be corralled back to his cell by Roland's musclebound henchmen who were probably taxed past their point of patience from having to transfer data and equipment all day. It was a monstrous job, Ben knew. Would they use violence to keep him in his cell? And why was Michael ordering him to stay put, anyway? Did he recognize him from the Pat-Press conference? Did he suspect that he was on to him?

Ben forced these questions from his mind. He needed to find Martinetti and had only the vaguest idea of his friend's whereabouts. Cooped up in his cell as he had been for the past five weeks, Ben had not been privy to any of the Bethesda preparations. Before that, he had spent most of his time gaming in the Garrett basement. So the tunnels, pitch black mineshafts that they were, still held quite a few mysteries for him.

He knew he was heading south and that Garrett was west and Bennett east. He knew much of the Bethesda training was taking place in the east, close to Bennett. With his left arm raised and his fingers sliding along the wire high up the wall, Ben waited for what seemed like an eternity for a left turn. He found it, and right away heard footsteps approaching up ahead. Two pairs. Either they're after me, or they're not, he thought. He decided to maintain the same pace regardless and hold his breath as he walked past so they wouldn't hear his stuttered, nervous breathing.

They passed him by without issue. Ben took three steps and knocked his head back as if to let his tears fall back into his eyes.

He called to them, "I'm looking for Martinetti!"

"Sigma Room!" one of them called back.

Ben had no idea where the Sigma Room was. "That's two doors down, right?" he asked.

"Four. On your left."

Ben turned without saying thank you, and began speed-walking and counting doors with his fingers. Soon he could hear those two soldiers meeting up with the guard whom he slugged just moments ago. They were talking. They were shining a light his way. They were coming. He was busted.

At the fourth door, Ben found it locked. Dispensing with all self-control, he began screaming for Martinetti and kicking and pounding on the door as if he wanted to smash it to splinters. If the revolution were to be saved, it would have to happen now. Just as the guard grabbed his arms and tried to twist them behind his back, the door opened. Two men, Chuck and Gideon, appeared. Eclipsing the fluorescent light behind them, they seemed little more than silhouettes. These two were the *last* people Ben wanted to see.

"The fuck is happening here, soldier?" Chuck demanded.

"Prisoner's getting restless, sir," said the guard. "Taking him back now."

"No!" Ben screamed, now in full panic mode. "I need to talk Major Martinetti! Please!"

"He's too busy," Gideon said.

Ben couldn't believe his bad luck and hoped that by screaming loud enough, Martinetti might hear him. "It's important! I need to talk to Martinetti! He will talk to me!"

Chuck looked to the guard. "Shut him up, and take him back." He went back inside, but Gideon lingered with a cruel, thin-lipped leer to watch the soldiers overpower Ben.

Ben knew what 'shut him up' meant. It could only mean one thing. Ben had been stunned once during training and he remembered what it can do to a person. After a heavy bolt to the brain stem, all appendages debone. Hands become mummified paws. Bladder and bowel release simultaneously. Drool spills from the mouth like from a hungry dog. And even after the victim regains consciousness, things move too rapidly for him to react. It's as if he processes only one second out of every five. Such torpor could last upwards of an hour. Ben did not have an hour.

Knowing that the stuns would come from the forearms, Ben flailed and kicked at the soldiers as they approached, screaming ceaselessly. The guard was trying to stabilize Ben's arms behind his back as Ben writhed and squirmed for a more defensible position. Ben managed to get a hand free which he used to hold off one of the soldiers who was rushing him. The tunnel's darkness and lack of room effectively blocked the third soldier for several seconds, which Ben used to call for Eli. The guard then kicked Ben's feet out from under him, causing the back of Ben's head to crash against the floor. Fortunately, the bouncy playground mulch lessened the impact and allowed Ben another two or three seconds of screaming.

This, apparently, was enough since Eli appeared from a room three doors down. "What is going on?" he whispered fiercely. The floor absorbed his heavy strides, but Ben could hear him coming anyway. The other men had ceased trying to subdue him, and Ben got to his feet just in time to see an enraged Eli, hair and glasses askew, looking voraciously for someone to blame for this disturbance. He put everyone in his PVN and then raised his voice as if smiting demons from the pulpit. "This God forsaken pandemonium may be what you imbeciles deserve, but not the rest of us! I swear to the Lord Almighty if any one of you makes a rumpus like that again I will have you stunned and tossed in the holding cell!"

Ben swallowed in an attempt to squash his nervousness. "Sir, I apologize, but I need to discuss something with you urgently. Just one minute. Please."

Eli's eyes adjusted as they fell on Ben. "You. Why are you not in your cell?"

"Because something has happened. General, please. I have to—"

"Sir! I opened his cell door to give him dinner, and he escaped," the guard said.

"I never got my hour," Ben said. He looked to the guard and then to Eli. "I'm entitled to it."

"General Archer revoked that," the guard said.

"He did?" Eli asked, seemingly surprised.

"General, please," Ben begged. "I just need a minute of your time."

"I don't have a minute," Eli said flatly. "Corporal take the prisoner back to his cell. You two, what were you doing?"

"Parnassus is not taking the encrypted Garrett data," one of them said. "Odin-Three says there's a corrupted cumulus holding up the multithread. We were headed to Delta Three to investigate."

Ben noted that these two didn't seem like Roland's men either. Too articulate. Too comfortable with technical details.

"Go, then. You too," he said to the guard. Eli turned to walk off when Ben twisted his own arm to break the guard's grip and ran after Eli.

"Sir!" he called. "I know why Michael wants to leave tomorrow! And it's not the reason he's giving you. I also know why he made Roland Number Three!"

Eli turned, interested. "You do?"

"Yes, I—"

A thumping tingle in Ben's lower back turned off the muscles in his legs. His arms thrashed like the wings of a dying bird and then shut down as well. In less than a second, he was no better than a vegetable and didn't even register himself going into free-fall. Something hit the floor. Maybe it was his head. It bounced. He remembered that it bounced. He remembered blinking and drooling and trying to keep enough drool out of his mouth so he could breathe. He saw Eli. Eli saw him. Well, at least he thought it was Eli. It was mostly in silhouette, so he couldn't be sure. Whatever it was, it reached for him. Ben did not know why.

***

Hypnotized by the fluorescence and ensconced in the coziness of his own private spot on the floor, Ben didn't overcome his stupor for about an hour. His great awakening amounted to realizing that he was lying on his side with his back against a wall. He was in a room. A cold room. The smell of archaic automobiles and mildew told him that he was somewhere familiar.

The silence at first felt like wads of cotton in his ears. Then he began to register the buzz of the lights and the hum of the ventilation system. All he could see was the underside of a table about three feet away.

Wanting to find out where he was, he struggled to sit up, but his brain objected and rocked violently inside his skull. Vertigo set in as soon as he was upright, and he craved lying back down again in a comfy swoon. Somehow he knew that was out of the question too. He groaned and blinked and felt something around his neck. It was a bib. A blue, plastic, foot-long bib. It was wet, he noted. Wet with drool.

Ben thought about this for a while. The coldness of the room eventually interrupted his ruminations. He comprehended that it wasn't so much the room that was cold, but him. He was cold. And wet. Especially in the groin and inner thighs. Held hostage by his angry, throbbing headache, he knew looking down would be impossible. So he used his hands. His underwear felt dry enough, so where was the cold and wet coming from? And where were his pants?

Overruling the objections of his now raging brain, Ben looked down and immediately recognized what he saw. A diaper. He was wearing a diaper.

"Why am I wearing a goddamn diaper?" he mumbled.

He heard manly laughter and chairs sliding against the floor. Looking up, he saw Eli and one of the techies and an older man he had never seen before. There were a couple others behind them. The thought that he must have looked ridiculous flitted across his mind.

"I wanted to talk to you. That's why," Eli said as he handed him a bottled water. "Here. You're dehydrated."

With fuzzy hand-eye coordination, Ben took it and struggled with the cap. Eli opened it for him and poured some water into his mouth. Ben had never tasted anything so good. Its effects were immediate. He opened his eyes as wide as he could and scanned the room. He knew he had something important to say to Eli and was trawling his mind to remember. "What happened?" he asked.

Eli smiled. "You tried to escape from your cell and were

stunned. But you piqued my interest with something you said, so I wanted keep you here until you recovered." Ben tried to stand, but Eli pressed him firmly back down by the shoulder. "Not yet," he said. "Give yourself a few minutes."

"I'm fine."

"No, you're not. A stun issues a combination of supersonic sound and a special kind of magnetic pulse. Enough to incapacitate a gorilla."

Eli's hand pressed on Ben's shoulder. Ben took it with both of his and climbed up Eli's arm, one hand over the other. By the time he reached his shoulder, he whispered into Eli's ear as faintly as he could, "Michael Archer is a mole."

Ben then let go and fell like a dead body onto the floor. Michael *was* a mole. What more could he say? He didn't even look at Eli to gauge his reaction. He was mostly concerned now with not pissing himself again. He had done his part, made his sacrifices. He determined that if Eli were stupid enough to disregard him at this point, the revolution deserved to fail.

"What did he say?" one of the men asked.

Eli stood, straightened his glasses, and faced his men. He clenched his teeth and spoke as if through a broken jaw. "Clear the room. Now." Once alone with Ben, Eli put him in his PVN, and squatted close. His knees clicked like a bag of marbles.

"They gone?" Ben asked.

"Yes," Eli said. "How do you know this?"

Ben sniffed and cleared his throat. "Michael sat next to me at that Pat-Press conference. He's the one who threw photo-crystal in the air."

"That was him?"

"Yeah."

Eli kneeled before Ben to get more comfortable. "How do you know?"

"I recognize him."

"Are you sure?"

"Yes."

Eli shook his head a few times. "But it was seven years ago. And he's always in his Fickleskin. How can you be sure?"

"He wasn't wearing Fickleskin at Wichita. Isaac showed me

photo-crystal footage. He's also not Chinese anymore. Whatever template he's using now is closer to his original face. Help me up, please. I'm getting better." He got a little lightheaded as Eli obliged. Ben felt the man's strength as he practically carried him to the nearest chair. "Water, please," Ben asked.

Eli gave it to him. "Drink up. You still have your bib, so don't worry about making a mess."

"I'm more worried about a mess on the other end."

Eli aborted a chuckle and smiled. "What footage did Isaac show you?"

Ben took in more water than he should have and spat some out over himself. He felt his energy return more quickly than he could control it. "Some room in the Wichita tunnels. The room where they put all the meth equipment. It was right before that. Guys were playing cards. Someone leans in through the door and tells them they're under attack. Isaac told me it was Michael. He asked me if I recognized him, and I said yes. But then I was like, 'I don't know'."

"Was the image at least clear?"

Ben coughed but then continued drinking. He shook his head, no.

"Then how can you be sure?" Eli asked.

Ben finished the water and felt him shake all over. His fluttering jaw made it hard for him to speak. "Because he looked at me at the conference! Right at me, okay? It was fucking terrifying. I will never forget it. And he did this weird jerky dance move right before they stunned him. He did the exact same thing at the restaurant."

"What restaurant?"

"Last Gasp. Month ago. He gave a big speech."

"Chuck took video. I saw it. It was brilliant. The men are still talking about it."

"He always makes these obscure literary allusions," Ben complained. "And he acts like he's *so* much smarter than everyone else, like *no one else* reads books!"

"What are you talking about?"

"At the Pat-Press conference, you know what he says? You know what he says?" Ben screwed up his face to mock Michael's stentorian style, and added a lisp for effect. "'Racism must perish! Even if we must all perish with it!' I mean, who talks like that?"

"Lieutenant, you need to calm down and get to the point."

"The point is that Michael is a pretentious twat!" Ben raved, now beyond self-control. "He was then and he is now! At the Pat-Press conference he was ripping off these nineteenth-century Spanish anarchists who said the same bullshit. 'Evil and injustice must perish!' Bleh bleh bleh!"

"How do you know that?"

"How do I know anything? I looked it up! And then...and then! You know what he does? You know what he does? He has the grapefruit cantaloupe watermelon *stones* to rip off Thucydides! That speech you think was so goddamn brilliant? He stole it from the Funeral Speech in the *History of the Peloponnesian War*! Thu-fucking-cydides! Like I wouldn't know!" Ben punched himself in the chest. "Like I wouldn't know!"

"Lieutenant, you are hysterical."

"Can't help it!" Ben said in a fit of coughing. "Sorry."

"Hysteria is typical for a person recovering from a stun-induced stupor. It's one of its side effects. You'll be fine."

"I just can't believe he's screwing us like this!"

"Try to make yourself relax."

After one bile-heavy dry heave Ben understood that relaxation was a bridge just a little bit too far. He fell off his chair just in time to extrude a vile cocktail of water and snack food onto the floor. He was too embarrassed to even look at Eli. "I'm not making a strong case, am I?" he said.

"Not really."

"It's the same guy. Find the footage of the Pat-Press conference. Compare it to the footage Isaac showed me. You'll see."

"Can't. Sap-servs are down. Parnassus, Smolikas, Pelion. All down. Odin-One and -Four are offline. Three's doing a back-up. Our devices, even the deskpods, are constrained to the tunnel intranet."

"Isaac showed me the Wichita footage on his deskpod. Maybe it's still in the buffer."

"Could be. But regarding anything beyond what we have on

our hard drives, we're pretty much paralyzed until we get our wheels on."

"So we're supposed to just use the internet in the meantime?"

"That's too dangerous. If they already know we're in Nathan's Ford, then bald internet searches for your Pat-Press conference will draw suspicion. They can even tell if a machine is underground."

"Well, how long until we get our wheels?"

Eli shrugged. "Three hours if we're lucky. Two days if we're not."

Ben sat back up. "What? What time is it now?"

"Almost midnight. They leave in seven hours."

"We can't let them go."

"Sure we can. We have no evidence. Just your word. And if that's all we have, it's not enough."

"Do you believe me?"

Eli thought for a moment. "A small part of me wants to. It's an elegant explanation. I've always wondered why a man as brilliant as Michael could have a blind spot for a psychopath like Roland. And if what you're saying is right, then now we know."

"Then letting them go is out of the question."

"No. Because I don't believe you, Lieutenant," Eli told him. "This is just too crazy. I know Michael, and he has an excellent reputation in the movement. We've run extensive checks on everyone and continue to do so. Plus, his heroics at Wichita are impossible to deny." Ben tried to interrupt, but Eli stopped him. "Keep in mind that if you're wrong and you keep pushing this, you will be court-martialed. You cannot level that kind of charge against a general the night before an agitation raid. Especially now when our backs are to the wall."

Eli's DSAK got his attention, and he signaled to Ben that he needed to deal with something urgent. He removed Ben from his PVN and walked back to the table deep in conversation.

Ben first made sure he could stand, which he did with trembling knees. With one hand on the wall to keep steady, he removed his bib and then did what he could to clean up his mess on the floor. He signaled to Eli that he needed his pants, and Eli pointed to a chair on the opposite end of the table. Ben was still getting dressed when Eli brought him back into his PVN. "I have to take care of a bunch of things," he said.

"What do I do?"

"You need to find that Pat-Press footage."

"But I'm a prisoner."

"I will commute your sentence to time served. Now, go to the epsilon room on the south end. Get an old-fashioned laptop computer, pre-2010, and a two-gig flash drive, also pre-2010. Then just sit yourself down in the kitchen of the Bennett house and start surfing. As soon as you get the video or images, save it on your flash drive, shut off the machine, and come back here to the Theta Room. We'll run our face recognition applications on it. If it's a hit, we don't let them leave. If it isn't, this never happened."

"I thought you said surfing the internet was too dangerous."

"The government may not detect the laptop since it's so old. But it will be slow. The more time you spend searching, the greater the chances of detection. So search smartly."

"And if I do get detected?"

Eli shook his head in a woozy circle. "We can't afford to think about that right now, Lieutenant."

"Yes, sir," Ben said, aware that he was already out of Eli's PVN. He saluted and turned to leave but stopped at the door. "Sir? Now that I'm out, what about my DSAK? Can you enable it?"

Eli took a seat at the far end of the table. "That depends," he said, lifting an eyebrow. "Tell me. Was it you who really operated that medical kit in Memphis? Did you lie to us about Roland?"

Ben hoped he could disguise his visceral shock at fielding such a penetrating question. He took a moment to respond. "No, sir," he said.

Eli's eyebrow dropped. "Well, then, Lieutenant, that's your answer."

Chapter 40

According to legend, Galileo had difficulty convincing other scientists and members of the Catholic Church to look into his telescope and confirm that Jupiter has moons. They resisted Galileo because his ideas contradicted the centuries-old teachings of

A. St. Paul.
B. Copernicus.
C. Jesus Christ.
D. Aristotle. (correct)

Things were not coming easily for Ben at this stage in his life. Finding the Pat-Press footage, however, did. Despite the sluggish, worn-out laptop and the legacy search engines, he was able to hit the link on his third try. Apparently, Michael's 'Racism must perish' pronouncement had been quite the meme for a while.

As the video was downloading, Ben stood and looked around the Bennett house kitchen. Such a tidy little place, he thought. The sink had only one basin, and there wasn't even a microwave over the stove. The dishwasher had buttons like that of an old car radio. Walls painted a garish green separated Formica countertops from chipped wooden cabinets. The stainless-steel refrigerator could not have been any later than 2010, Ben thought. From it, he took a store-bought burrito which he didn't bother to heat. He ate ravenously.

Afterwards, he stepped out onto the deck where the trees seemed to yield like a beaten army. Although they were legion, not one of them obstructed the purple, intimate night which made the view so splendid. Stars woke you from happy dreams like the points of spears. The Moon was the beaming face of a loved one, a spy, a killer. And the darkness. With creeping, evolutionary certainty the darkness had been the only refuge for men like him. It took about one hundred years, but now even the darkness was dying. Soon there would be no more places to hide. Only those on which to fight and die. Ben laughed because it all seemed so peaceful.

Eli had retrieved Isaac's deskpod by the time Ben returned to the Theta Room. Next to him at the table was the older man he had seen before. Ben could tell that Eli had told him everything.

The man had a face like an ancient cliff, with crags rather than wrinkles surrounding bright, paranoid eyes. Gray-blonde hair splayed across his tall forehead. His chin was a pugnacious bulge. "This is Ian," Eli said as he took the flash drive from Ben.

Ben opened his mouth to say hello, but Ian halted him with a question, "What's your brother's KSP?"

"What?" Ben asked, looking at Eli.

"Keystroke Pattern," Eli said. "We have his password. And it would save us time if we had his keystroke pattern."

"People usually use their favorite songs," Ian said.

"Right," Ben said. "It's 'In the Hall of the Mountain King' by Henrik Ibsen."

"You mean Edvard Grieg," Ian corrected him as he began rapid-typing the melody into Isaac's deskpod. "Edvard Grieg wrote 'Hall of the Mountain'. 1867, I think it was. Yes, I think it was." His response was muttered so quickly and matter-of-factly it was if he had been expecting Ben to make that very mistake. This afforded Ben a glimpse of the man's immense intellect. Ben also suspected something was not right with him since he had yet to initiate eye-contact and would not stop babbling. Eli looked down at Ben with a condescending smirk.

"What?" Ben said, striking a defensive posture. "Ibsen wrote the play. Grieg wrote the music. Honest mistake."

Eli nodded, still with the smirk. "I'm sure."

"Okay, we're in," Ian said, flashing an artificial smile to both men. Ben looked back at Eli, and the smirk was gone.

What Ian accomplished in the next two hours astounded Ben, not least because Ian was barely paying attention to what he was doing. He seemed more focused on reciting dialogue from popular internet comedy programs which apparently he followed obsessively. Ben caught a distinct whiff of body odor from him and suspected he hadn't changed his flannel shirt and corduroy pants in days. Ben also noticed that Ian was in his slippers.

Although most of Ian's whitehat legerdemain was over Ben's head, the basics he understood. Ian uploaded the Pat-Press photo-crystal footage onto Isaac's deskpod by hacking into whatever security applications Isaac had on his machine. He did this by launching a worm and three separate bots into the pod's AI interface. These binary entities somehow exposed the bug in the software that Ian was looking for. This bug resulted from less-than signs appearing in code where less-than-or-equal-to signs were required. Once compromised, this code enabled Ian to copy Ben's dark and grainy Pat-Press video onto Isaac's hard drive.

Ian then asked Ben to locate Michael amid the thousands of found footage faces now on Isaac's machine. A daunting task, given that the crystals closest to Michael had been the ones he himself threw in the air and afforded only non-descriptive shots of the tops of their heads. In the wild, parabolic perspectives from the other saboteurs, Michael and Ben appeared as little more than blurry daubs in a throng. Ben did his best, but by one-thirty in the morning, doubted he could continue. He was tiring and had nothing with which to prop up his consciousness. Coffee was forbidden in the tunnels because its aroma could escape through the ventilation system, and Surplex pills on the eve of an agitation raid were scarce. After another hour of fruitless searching, sleep began to take on Sisyphean dimensions. Every time Ben blinked, his eyes wanted more and more to stay shut. He speculated that the bouncy, playground mulch near his feet would make an excellent bed. He spent the final half hour elbow-slouching in the deskpod and scrolling through image after redundant image until he finally zeroed in on what was most likely Michael. He reasoned it had to be Michael because he was pretty sure he saw himself standing next to him.

Ben called for Ian, who, after a minute of eyeballing both images, jammed his palms onto his ears. "This is bad. This is bad. This is bad," he repeated, rocking back and forth in his seat.

Eli shooed him away and sat down to investigate the images. He shook his head with such ferocity that tiny beads of sweat flew from his forehead. "That is not Michael," he announced.

"It is him," Ben insisted.

"No. It looks nothing like him."

"You've never seen him without his Fickleskin," Ben argued. "How would you know?"

Eli's eyes darted in several directions, but not towards Ben and not towards the deskpod images. Fear flooded Ben's gut and made him feel ten pounds heavier. He was about to lose Eli. And without Eli all was lost. At some point Ian swapped his 'this is bad's for an equally persistent stream of 'very bad's as he paced urgently nearby.

"What do you mean, how do I know?" Eli flailed. "It's not him!"

"It is him!"

"But you yourself said that you've *also* never seen him without his Fickleskin. How would *you* know?"

"Because I was there. I sat next to him at Pat-Press. Look!"

"...Very bad. Very bad..."

"But that was seven years ago!"

"So? We have the Wichita footage to compare. Look at it, General. Look at it! Tell me there's no resemblance!"

Eli gritted his teeth and refused to look. Instead, he honed in on Ben with an uncharacteristically carnivorous glint. "You know, Lieutenant, I think *you* might be the mole."

"Me?"

"...Verrry bad. Verrry bad..."

"Yes. You're trying to interfere with an agitation raid by framing one of our leaders."

Ben blinked a few times in shock. "If that were true, I could have contacted the enemy in Memphis," he said, desperate to stay calm. "On the other hand, Michael has never left Nathan's Ford."

"So what?" Eli said, folding his arms like a patient bully.

"General, it's almost four in the morning. We don't have time to argue. We have to run the face recognition software now!"

"We run nothing," Eli said. "We're done here. Get back to your cell, Lieutenant."

"...bad bad bad bad bad bad..."

"I can't believe this!" Ben said, now irreversibly shrill.

"I said get back to your cell."

"But we lose nothing by running the facial recognition software!"

"We could lose you," Eli said. "If we run the software you could face execution for bearing false witness against someone of impeccable standing in the revolution. Now, I have been your friend and benefactor since we found you. I think you are a smart guy and a crack gamer. I have fought for you many times behind closed doors. But my ability to protect you has limits. Men will come to take you back to your cell," he said, now contacting soldiers on his DSAK. "Cooperate or you will be stunned again."

"...bad bad bad bad bad bad..." Ian babbled, still pacing uselessly in circles.

Ben let his hands flop to his sides and stepped back as if to take in a vista as wide as the world. He could see it all. The future of the great North American white nationalist movement now depended entirely upon a pig-headed Christian clinging to his pleasing preconceptions and a childlike genius trapped in some Aspergian feedback loop. Ben could not let it end like this. He stepped in front of Ian and took him by the shoulders.

"...bad bad bad bad bad bad..." Ian kept babbling.

"Why is it bad, Ian?" Ben asked, fishing for eye contact.

"Why is it bad why is it bad why is it bad..."

"You're repeating what I say."

"You're repeating what I say. You're repeating what I say. You're repeating—"

"Fuck," Ben said.

"...fuck fuck fuck fuck fuck fuck..."

Fending off a powerful urge to slap Ian in the face, Ben thought as fast as he could. He knew that Ian knew that the faces matched. Otherwise, why would he be melting down like this? It was Ben's job to get Ian to tell this to Eli. He had seconds. Watching Ian flail, Ben had the idea that Ian's misprogrammed mind was somehow susceptible to suggestion.

"Ian, do the faces match?" he asked.

"Ian, do the faces match," Ian repeated.

"*Ian...*" Ben said, stretching out his name as if warning to a child. Ian said nothing. Good, Ben thought. He knows his name. He knows that tone of voice.

"Do the faces match?" Ben asked again.

"Do the faces match," Ian repeated.

"Do the faces match? Say yes, Ben," Ben tried, nodding his head.

"Say yes, Ben. Say yes, Ben."
"Do the faces match? Yes, Ben."
"Yes, Ben."
"Do the faces match? Yes."
"Yes."
"Do the faces match? Yes."
"Yes."
"Do the faces match?"
"Yes."
"Do the faces match?"
"Yes."

Ben hauled Ian towards Eli by his moist armpits. "ELI!" he called. "Tell him, Ian! Come on! Tell him! Tell Eli!" he commanded.

"Tell Eli! Tell Eli!" Ian babbled.

Ben slapped the table with both hands. "No! Tell Eli the faces match! Tell him the faces match!"

"The faces match! The faces match!" Ian repeated, looking directly at Eli.

Eli stood, still engrossed in his device. He turned to Ben and Ian the moment three soldiers, all Roland's men, entered the room. Ben knew what they were going to do and at last succumbed to the panic tsunami that had been threatening to blow him over all day. He retreated and stuck out his arms as they advanced. "No! NO!" he screamed. The soldiers perhaps shaved a day or two off of Ben's lifespan the way they stabbed psychosomatic needles of fear into his brain. Ben fell on the floor near the wall so he could use his feet as well as his hands to ward off the inevitable. He was *not* going to get stunned again, revolution be damned.

Amid all the screaming and jostling, Eli yelled, "QUIET!"

Mere inches from oblivionizing Ben, the men stopped and obeyed. So did Ben, who noted that Eli's face had grown paler and sweatier in the seconds since he had last seen it. Eli turned back to Ian. "What did you say? The faces match? Did you say the faces match?"

To the excruciating suspense of everyone, Ian picked this time to finally keep quiet. Eli seized two handfuls of flannel and pulled him close enough to kiss. "Do the faces match or not?"

"The faces match. The faces match."

"Did we need to run the software?"

"Definitely need to run the software," Ian babbled. "Gotta run the software."

Eli let him go. "How do you know they match if you didn't run the software?"

Ian took a moment to compose a suitable answer. Ben could tell he had finally jumped off his emotional Mobius strip and landed in a more rational aspect of his mind. "Eyes. Same number of pixels apart. Error margin small. Nose is similar. Could be same jaw. Could be same neck. Definitely same sized neck."

"What?" Eli yelled. He shoved past Ian to look at the faces again. He studied them intensely for ten seconds and then stood and pointed to the footage. "These are not the same people!" he proclaimed.

"I don't know. I don't know," Ian fretted.

"Are you saying these could be the same person, Ian?"

"I don't know. Gotta run the software. Don't have much time. Gotta run the software." Ian was now reaching for the deskpod, but shirked his hand away before touching it.

Eli released a vigorous sigh as if to purge himself of all the exasperation welling up inside of him. "Fine!" he barked. "Run the damn software! It's not going to matter anyway." Without a word, Ian jumped to the deskpod and began doing what he was told. Ben let his head fall on the rubbery floor and his entire body relax. It felt good. He opened his eyes and felt tears spilling down the side of his head. Despite the irritating tingle, he could not be bothered to wipe them.

"Sir?" began one of the men. "What should we do with him? Bring him back to his cell?"

"Yes," Eli said. "Wait. No, it's okay."

The men stepped back. "Yes, sir."

"Thank you, gentlemen. You may go. I'm sure there's a lot that still needs to be done before this morning's raid."

The men saluted and left.

"Do you believe me now, General?" Ben asked.

"No, I do not."

Ben didn't care. It was the apathy of the exhausted. He was prepared to dive into a dream right where he lay. A heavy slap on the shoulder shook him out of it. It was Eli. Somehow he had traversed the entire length of the Theta Room in a split second. Ben recognized that he had been ensnared in the web of perfect sleep. He wanted nothing more than to return to that soft, cozy matrix.

Eli yanked Ben's torso upright and kneeled down to speak to him. "I'm sorry I gave you a hard time," he said. "But I need you to leave right now. Men are coming to this room to make some final preparations. Go across the tunnel into the Iota Room. You can sleep there."

"Is Ian running the face comparison software?" Ben asked, still reluctant to shake off his grogginess.

"Yes," Eli said, helping him up.

"What time is it?"

"Four-thirty.

"How long's the software gonna take?"

"With all the sap-servs down, Ian says it could take hours. The images are real small and grainy. We'll get you when it's over."

Eli led Ben to the door and pointed to Iota, which was thirty feet down to the left. As soon as Ben stepped into the dark artery however he was pushed from behind by three Surplex-addled soldiers who were headed there anyway. A man peeked from behind the door and waved them in.

Chapter 41

Which Left-wing terrorist organization arguably began the phenomenon known as suicide bombing in 1881 when one of its members detonated a bomb killing both Tsar Alexander II and himself?

A. The Party of God
B. The Islamic Jihad Organization
C. The Liberation Tigers of Tamil Eelam
D. The People's Will (correct)

Like every other room in the tunnels, Iota reeked of oil pans, sweat socks, and mildew. It was an oblong, corridor-like room, fifteen feet long and not even seven feet wide at its widest. It reminded Ben that architecture is a luxury for builders not constrained by twenty tons of soil in every direction. A man Ben recognized as one of Roland's was lecturing on the topic of suicide vests, something the Bethesda Ten were required to master before embarking on their raid. He was short and bald and wore a sweat-stained white T-shirt and black fatigue pants. A mess of scruff unsuccessfully hid his receding chin. Ben sat down against the wall with the others as he took in the man's virtual slide presentation. He was asleep in seconds.

"The breakdown of a suicide vest is barbarically simple," the man said. "I mean if the fucking Arabs can build one, you can count on some of our grade schoolers to write a book on the goddamn thing. Ya got a battery. On it is a detonator, which is wired to your explosives. All you have to do is slap it twice. Beyond that, you have your shrapnel. That's four things. Battery. Detonator. Explosives. Shrapnel. B.D.E.S. Got that? Now, I'm sure this point is a little too subtle for you mouth-breathing Neanderthals to comprehend. So here's a way to remember it so you'll never forget. Big dicks ejaculate semen. B.D.E.S. Got it now? It's all electronics 101 after that.

"The battery consists of eight double As. We've already connected the intercom wire to your power source so you troglodytes don't have to. Now, the feds, if they're even looking for this sort of thing, are gonna expect, I don't know, AI, or some kind of fancy neural chip interface or even wireless to control detonation. But the old-fashioned way, with toggle switches and nichrome wire and alligator clips just might go under their radar as long as you footie-fleeced turd burglars don't trip over your own dicks on the way to the party. The only thing modern about our setup is that the entire apparatus is placed in a sleeve of the same material we make apparition suits out of. You give it the right input parameters and it establishes a modified Faraday's cage which will hide its contents and itself from any traditional metal detector.

"After that, you got your typical C-7 plastic explosives in the lining of the vest. And twenty pounds of ball bearings for shrapnel. Don't worry if you think that's not enough. Your bones, your boots, your fucking belt buckles will turn into shrapnel too. Your ugly heads will turn into cannon balls, which is really all they're good for anyway. Your kill radius will be about thirty feet. Remember, the payload on this thing is a motherfucker. The beauty of it is that aside from the apparition sleeve and the C-7 you can get all the materials for ninety bucks. And your apparition suits have C-7 in them already. We even uploaded coded instructions to your implants, so in case you ever get stuck in enemy territory you pussies will have no excuse not to blow up a mosque or two. And, dickheads, remember, you only do this in Bethesda if you *can't get the bombs off.* Try to stand at least sixty feet apart from each other when you decide to splatter. You drooling retards are pretty useless as it is, and you'll be even more so if all you do is blow each other up and not the goddamn muzzies. Understand?"

***

Ben felt a hard nudge in his hip and understood right away that it was a boot. He felt it again and woke up. It was Eli. He didn't hold back with his kicks. "100% match! Move!" he shouted, yanking Ben upwards by his collar. The moment Ben reached his feet, Eli turned and bolted from the room. Ian, who'd been pacing in circles with his hair in his fists, followed.

"What happened?" Ben asked, and then regretted asking such a stupid question. He followed Ian into the tunnel and into the Theta Room where Eli was already seated and lit blue from his deskpod. His glasses cast a diabolically curved shadow on his forehead, giving him the eyebrows of a glowering demon. He was frantically communicating with at least three people. Three other men were doing the same, pacing and colliding into each other behind the table. No one had bothered to establish a PVN, which put the room in a whirl of cacophonous panic.

On Isaac's deskpod, Ben saw the result of the comparison. The Pat-Press and Wichita images were confirmed identical with over 99% accuracy. The actual figure had enough nines to the right of the decimal to become irrelevant. "Why didn't you wake me sooner?" Ben asked.

"Why did you fall asleep?" Eli asked.

"I'm sorry," Ben said, not knowing what else to say.

"It's all right. We should be apologizing to you, Ben. You were right all along."

"Thank you."

"I believe this is the work of God. He wanted us to move and arranged for you to meet that black officer woman. If not for that, we wouldn't have had time to put our wheels on. Now, we can leave in minutes with all our data, hardware, weapons, everything!"

Ben nodded in appreciation. "What about the raid?" he asked. "Did they leave yet?"

Eli finished the last of his correspondence and shut down his deskpod. "Yes. Five minutes ago. And you are going to fetch them."

"What?"

Eli took Ben by the collar and tried to haul him towards the door. Ben resisted and threw Eli's hands off of him. Eli responded by shoving Ben into the wall and jamming a cudgel of a forearm into his throat. Ben felt the man's brute strength and opted to comply with whatever Eli had in store for him.

"In two minutes a car will be waiting for you outside the Garrett house," Eli said. The deep, hypnotic timbre of his voice made him sound like he was enticing Ben to step away from a ledge. "You drive it to I-95 North. You will overtake the Bethesda Ten in a truck that says 'Fred's Desktop Publishing' on the side. Do you understand? Nod for yes."

Ben nodded. Eli sunk his fingers into Ben's shoulders and shoved him through the door. Ben had to hug the wall to keep from being overrun by soldiers hustling in both directions. "Coming through!" Eli bellowed, and the men made room. He pushed Ben and followed him into a blind sprint toward the Garrett house. Eli activated his PVN. "I've enabled your DSAK and disabled your BREMAT security! Do whatever you can to keep them in safe-range! Either way, contact me, and then get back to Nathan's Ford to evacuate the children and staff of the daycare and school! You will be responsible for them!"

"Then what?"

"Go to Lebanon, Kentucky!"

"Where?"

"The nearest base west of here! Get on Fairgrounds Road. There's a clearing in a forest the shape of a cross. Check your GPS. You will meet agents in the center of it. I will tell them you're coming!"

"Is that where you're going?"

"No! We can't afford to tell anyone where we're going in case one of us get captured! We'll regroup at a later date and reunite with the children!"

"Got it!"

"Listen! If Michael gets out of safe-range, he will contact his superiors in Washington, and the Garrett and Bennett houses will be hit from space within forty-five minutes!"

"No way to reactivate their devices, sir?"

"What?"

"I asked if there's a way to re-enable their devices! So we can contact them!"

"Their DSAKs *are* enabled. They're just offline! Michael told me he gave me sole authority to put the team's DSAKs back online in his absence. But we just found out that he lied! We have no way of stopping them except by force!"

"Can't we re-enable Michael's BREMAT security? It would kill him!"

"No! He's a general! Only our Horseman can do that! And we can't reach him in time!"

"Then why did you let Michael go on the raid in the first place?"

Eli tried to respond, but stopped once he realized where they were headed. "Right turn! Right turn!" he shouted.

Since Ben was leading, he overshot the turn, forcing Eli to snatch his collar and rein him back like a horse. Throttled by his own shirt, Ben's feet shot up in the subterranean pitch. He crashed onto the rubber mulch, rear-end first. "Follow me!" Eli shouted as Ben got back to his feet. "Keep your hands on my shoulders and keep up!" The incline was growing steeper, so Ben knew they were almost at the Garrett basement. "You're right!" Eli called back over his shoulder. "It was my mistake to let Michael lead the raid! We shouldn't have trusted him. I'm sorry!"

Despite appreciating the apology, Ben said nothing until they reached the basement, which was every bit as dark as the tunnels, although less cold and dank. "Okay, if anything goes wrong, go in person to our Horseman," Eli ordered. "Tell him everything."

"He's in Nathan's Ford?"

"Yes. I uploaded the address to your DSAK. I also uploaded a hologram of myself and Ian showing evidence of Michael's duplicity. Show it to the men when you reach them."

"Yes, sir!"

"And whatever you do, keep Michael alive!" Eli said, thumping up the stairs. "He probably has a wealth of information we can recover!"

"Yes, sir!"

They entered the shuttered kitchen where the visibility went from impenetrable black to penetrable gray. Their eyes still needed a moment to adjust. Ben opened the door to the garage and groped for the garage door opener. He stepped into the garage as the door slowly lifted. He turned back and watched the sunlight rise up on Eli who was standing in the doorway. Inch by inch, it exposed Eli's clumsy legs which were connected at the thighs. It exposed his wide, soft belly and potato physique which stretched the black fabric of his T-shirt in unflattering directions. It exposed his face, round, pale, and honest. The light banished the bear-like preacher he was in the tunnels. He was no longer defiantly upholding an antiquated creed to justify an apocalyptic race war. Standing before Ben now was a vulnerable, hulking wallflower, the kind sullenly resigned to the fact that pretty girls could never take him seriously. Eli must have been that person not terribly long ago, Ben thought. He figured he'd never see Eli again and vowed to remember him as he saw him right then and there. "Why are you sending me?" Ben whispered.

"Because you're resourceful," Eli said, adjusting his glasses and squinting in the streaming daylight. "And I can't spare anyone else." Ben understood. It was the smart move. The revolution comes first, and in Eli's case it would either keep him afloat or drag him down. "May God be with you, Ben," Eli said as he turned back inside.

Chapter 42

What heavyweight boxing champion successfully defended his title by knockout despite suffering a long and deep cut on his nose which bled profusely throughout the fight?

A. Joe Louis against Buddy Baer, May 23, 1941
B. Muhammad Ali against Bob Foster, November 21, 1972
C. Lennox Lewis against Vitali Klitschko, June 21, 2003
D. Rocky Marciano against Ezzard Charles, September 17, 1954 (correct)

As soon as his eyes adjusted to the light, Ben realized that the vehicle in which he was about to save the revolution was a burgundy, mid-1980s Chevrolet Caprice Classic station wagon complete with fake wood paneling and luggage rack. He was pretty sure it would have been a piece of junk when it was new, let alone now. It suffered from a dearth of style, as if its designers had ignored whatever they knew about aerodynamics, and their idea of aesthetics hadn't developed much past the Ford Model T. It seemed like the kind of car the Soviets would have designed if they wanted to get a little fancy. Ben feared it couldn't reach sixty inside of a minute. Still, he couldn't have been too disappointed. The Caprice Classic predated the McKinney Act by almost half a century and had a full tank of fuel. It started on the second try.

With an eight-to-ten-minute handicap and a finish line twenty miles away, Ben intended to floor it and ignore any cop trying to stop him. He would run the Bethesda Ten off the road or halt them in a fiery collision if he had to. He reached I-95 North without incident and gunned it until he was breaking eighty miles an hour. The engine seemed like it was stuck in low gear by the way it shook and whined. He was actually scared to go

any faster lest the prehistoric machine explode. The power steering fluid was low, Ben could tell, so steering amid the light
morning traffic proved difficult. Fortunately, the other vehicles
on the road were mostly auto-drive machines, so the prospect of
crashing into one of them was fairly remote. Ben looked at the
digital clock. It was 7:09 in the morning.

Ben pounded the steering wheel in triumph when he finally
saw Fred's Desktop Publishing cruising at a moderate speed only thirteen miles out of Nathan's Ford. It was the same dusty, 6-
wheel box truck — smaller than a semi, larger than a pickup —
that he had seen when last heading north on I-95. It had taken
him longer than he had hoped, but he pulled up alongside of it.
Gideon was driving — Ben's first sign of bad luck. He stiff-armed
his horn and swerved frantically, to no avail. Gideon wouldn't
even look at him. Ben's next idea was to lower the passenger
side window and call to him. But the truck's chassis was so
much higher than the Caprice's, he would have had to lean past
the center of the car just to get Gideon to see him. Ben mentally
prepared to do just that when he discovered, to his bemusement,
that the Caprice was not equipped with power windows. He
would have to reach across to the passenger-side and literally
roll down the window — and if the Caprice was anything, it was
roomy. Ben had never rolled down a window in his life, let
alone while speeding along the highway.

The odometer reminded Ben he had a little over five miles in
which to act. He wasn't even sure where in Nathan's Ford mile
zero was. For all he knew it was already too late. He noticed the
familiar Country Route 421 bridge up ahead. Exit 27 was coming
up quickly on the right. Nathan's Ford was Exit 12, he knew.
This was all too close to call. He gunned his automobile and
swerved directly in front of the truck. He banged into it twice
and braked when the truck braked. This forced the truck onto
the exit ramp and Ben partially on the grass in front of it. Both
vehicles stopped. Gideon, however, jammed it into reverse to
back out onto the highway. Ben backed up as well and stayed
parallel with the truck, forcing it either to move forward along
the exit ramp or backwards into the thick grass on the shoulder.
Gideon tried several times to escape Ben's blockade, but Ben

stayed with him. Gideon's last strategy was a good one: race up the exit ramp, cross Highway 421, and return to the highway via the entry ramp on the other side of the bridge. And if Ben moved ahead to block him, back out into the highway like he tried to do originally. It would have worked, too, had two cars not turned onto the exit ramp behind the truck exactly when Gideon shifted into reverse. Fred's Desktop Publishing was trapped in the resulting traffic jam and had to wait for the cars to pass before it could escape.

With the two cars and a third now rubbernecking past, Ben took his chance and jumped out of the Caprice. He showed himself before the truck, hands waving. He saw Roland in the front seat unstrapping his seatbelt. Gideon tried to hold him back, but he shoved him off and leaped out of the truck. Roland's wide eyes sparkled murderously as he marched up to Ben. Gideon exited the truck too, but was too far from Roland at that point to stop him.

Ben took a few steps back, activated his PVN, and played Eli's recorded hologram message from his DSAK. "Stop, Colonel! Eli sent me!" he shouted.

Roland responded with punches. The first landed on Ben's shoulder. The second slammed into his nose. It was a hard, straight shot thrown with maximum force and precision. Ben felt the blood and snot spill. He saw the stars shooting into his head. He felt the fleeting tug of gravity in his knees. When he regained his legs, he knew two things. He knew that Roland had small fists, which meant that he and his modified Negro nose could take his punch. He also knew that if Roland ever tried anything like that again he would kill him. He would rip out his throat with his teeth if he had to. Gideon arrived and restrained Roland long enough for them to start paying attention to Eli's hologram. Ben didn't bother to watch and instead tended to his injured nose by shoving wadded ends of his T-shirt into his nostrils to stanch the bleeding.

Ben looked up and caught the conclusion of the hologram in which Ian demonstrated in incomprehensible detail the nearly perfect match between Michael's Pat-Press and Wichita facial images. Eli then instructed the men to return immediately to Nathan's Ford. Roland and Gideon ignored the instruction, and instead, replayed Ian's technical exegesis. Cars were driving past on the exit. They didn't care.

"Who discovered this?" Gideon asked.

"I did," Ben said. "That was me standing next to Michael at the Pat-Press conference."

"And you wait till now to tell us"?

"Michael was always in his Fickleskin. I didn't recognize him until he switched templates."

"It took you this long?" Gideon asked, brimming with anger.

"The Pat-Press thing was seven years ago. That's a long time to remember a face!"

"But why couldn't you have told us yesterday, motherfucker?"

"I was in a jail cell! Motherfucker!" Ben shouted back. "You're lucky I got out here at all!" Despite his injured nose, Ben prepared himself for a violent encounter with Gideon, the prospect of which he found himself relishing.

Roland got between them, tears brimming. "Gideon, stop," he said. He looked to Ben, again with the blue, childlike eyes which seemed to beg for help. "You're a beautiful man, Ben. A beautiful white man. I'm sorry I punched you!" Roland collapsed onto Ben's chest and bear hugged him in a torrent of sobs. Ben patted him twice on the back in a listless 'there, there' gesture. "I'm sorry! Sooo sorry!" Roland wailed.

Ben looked to Gideon to share the embarrassment. Gideon did briefly, but it was just too much truth for him to take. He looked away, cursing and muttering. All three then noticed the truck shake. Someone was exiting from the back. It was Martinetti. They knew better than to meet him in the open and instead met him in the shadow of the truck, out of sight from the exit ramp and under decent tree cover.

"What the hell is going on?" Martinetti demanded. He double-taked when he saw Ben. "What are you doing here?"

No one seemed anxious to answer. Roland removed one arm from Ben but kept the other wrapped around his waist. Uncomfortable as he was, Ben felt the need to reciprocate. From a distance they looked like lovers on the strand. Ben put Martinetti in his PVN. "Get General Archer out here now," he said.

Martinetti shifted his disposition at such an unmistakable order from a man of lower rank. "Come again?"

"You heard him!" Roland barked. "Get Archer out here!"

Martinetti smirked before obeying and returned with Michael moments later. Roland, Gideon, and Ben formed a grim semicircle around him. Gideon leered at him hatefully, while Roland's face was an inscrutable mask marred by sporadic blinking.

"What is the meaning of this, Colonel?" Michael said. He noticed the hostile postures all around him and became enraged. "What is going on here? Everyone go back to the truck now!" He waited for his order to take effect. It didn't. "Now!" he repeated.

"You're a mole," Ben said.

"*What?*" both Michael and Martinetti responded.

"I said you're a mole, General," Ben said. "We have evidence."

"Damn your evidence! I'll arrest you myself!" Michael charged towards Ben, forearm first, but Gideon stopped him with his. "Step back, sir! I will stun you!"

"This is mutiny!" Michael shouted.

"What's going on?" Martinetti demanded. "What evidence?"

Ben replayed the hologram message. Martinetti stood before it, his hand slowly rising to his mouth as the information sunk in. "General Archer was at that Patriot Press conference in San Diego," Ben said. "Weren't you, General?"

"This is outrageous!"

"I sat next to you. I think you remember. You threw photocrystal in the air, didn't you?"

"I have no conceivable notion of what you are talking about!" Michael thundered, shaking his fists.

"So you're saying that's not you on the hologram? You didn't sabotage the Pat-Press conference? Here. Have a look."

Michael looked. His expression began to change in hesitating spurts. "That's not—that's not me!"

"Ian's software says it is."

"How would it know? I'm always in my Fickleskin!"

"But you weren't when you were in Wichita," Ben said. "We

have footage of that too. Ian ran the comparison."

Michael blinked and looked pleadingly into the empty, une-quivocal faces of the men surrounding him. "No! There must be some kind of mistake! Please understand! I am innocent!"

"Is that why you had me locked in my cell against orders?" Ben asked. "Is that why you lied to Eli about giving him sole authority to put our DSAK's back online? He tried to do that this morning to keep you all from leaving safe-range. But he couldn't because you didn't do what you said you did!"

That was obviously Ben's trump card, and the stunned looks from the others proved it. Michael had no coherent response. He grunted and stuttered and groped pathetically for something to say until Martinetti decided he had had enough. Issuing vile, guttural threats, he shoved Michael into the truck and swung the toe of his boot as hard as he could into his groin.

Remarkably, Michael did not collapse like any ordinary man would have, and instead took the blow like a beast, hunching in silent pain. He would have absorbed more punishment from Martinetti had Ben not gotten in the way. He placed a hand on Michael's shoulder and remembered how this man once knocked him out with a single punch and tortured him in a jail cell with a garrote made of dental floss. Ben felt a pleasurable rush which he hoped he could ignore long enough to get the answers he needed. "If you cooperate, General, we will give you a merciful end," he said.

Michael shook his head and spoke with his characteristic clar-ity. "You're wrong. I am not a mole. I gave Eli full authority to reactivate our DSAKs. He must have made a mistake."

"Unlikely."

"Then perhaps it was a technical glitch. We have them from time to time, especially when we take sap-servs down."

"Has that ever happened before?"

Michael thought for a moment. "In Wichita."

Ben gave him an ironic nod. "None of us were at Wichita, General."

"Then I don't know what happened!" Michael snapped. "But I do know that I am innocent. You can't say there isn't reasona-ble doubt about that!"

Ben sneered back at him. "That was you at the Pat-Press conference, wasn't it?"

Michael jutted out his jaw and shuddered. "Yes, it was."

"Then why didn't you tell us?"

"I was afraid to," Michael said, holding his chin high and gesturing to the paused hologram. "But what you see there is not me. I was different then. I was young and stupid. And I have changed. I have embraced the race. Like many of us have! You have to believe me!" It sounded more like an order than a plea. Michael clenched a fist by his waist and shook it.

"You ruined thousands of lives," Ben said. "You realize that, don't you?"

Michael took a deep breath and exhaled slowly. "I know," he said. "I'm sorry."

"Sorry is not good enough, sir. You should have told us."

Michael looked to Ben as if there were no one else watching and whispered, "I'm not releasing the poison in my teeth, am I? If I were a mole, I would do that."

"What?" Ben asked, realizing that he had understood him all along. He was also quite certain that no one else had. They weren't close enough. Ben blinked and spent a moment considering what Michael had just said when he heard someone behind him say, "Step aside, Ben."

Everyone turned. It was Roland. At once, Ben apprehended that all his pretensions of power were flimsy illusions. He'd been able to cross-examine Michael only because Roland had allowed him to. Now that Roland seemed intent on acting, there was nothing Ben could do to stop him. With swift, inescapable purpose, Roland stepped up to Michael, produced a semiautomatic pistol from his back holster, and discharged a bullet into his head.

Ben knew immediately that the shot was fatal. Michael's body folded by the neck, knees, and hips like a puppet cut loose from its strings. As the gun's muffled report subsided, the men looked to each other to determine what to do next. All except Roland, who remained focused on Michael as if he were waiting for him to rise so he could kill him again.

"We gotta get back to base!" Ben said. "I'll contact Eli!"

"Let's get the body in the trunk of the wagon!" Martinetti shouted, starting to drag Michael over to it. "Roland, give me a hand!" Roland hesitated. "Now, Roland! Any second a cop's gonna find us!"

"Right! Right!" Roland said, scooping up Michael's legs.

"Gideon, back the car up so we're not in the open!" Martinetti ordered. "And pop the hatch!"

Ben was communicating with Eli when he felt a hard shove in his shoulder. It was Gideon. "Gimme the fucking car key!" he demanded with typical caveman candor. Ben handed it over and then walked to the rear of the truck to focus more on Eli. He heard the Caprice back up and the hatch open. He heard the body being dumped into the wagon's cargo area. He heard the hatch close. He heard the car drive off. Then he heard gunshots. Gunshots?

Spinning around, he saw Roland emptying his pistol in the direction of the Caprice, which was speeding north past the Route 421 bridge. Martinetti was shouting and attempting to drag Roland back to the truck. Ben discerned what had just happened more quickly than he could exclaim his shock. There could only be one explanation. Gideon Sneed was a mole too! He had just taken off with Michael's body, and in five miles would be out of safe-range. That meant in five minutes, give or take, he would be in direct contact with his superiors in Washington. The revolution in Nathan's Ford was approximately forty-five minutes from extinction. And so were the lives of a few dozen innocent white people for good measure. Ben felt the blood drain from his head and the strength give out in his knees. Roland couldn't have hit him hard enough to send him to the brink of unconsciousness like this. He put his hand against the side of the truck to keep from falling.

Martinetti and Roland were coming close to blows. Martinetti was struggling to pull Roland back to the truck, while Roland cared only to imprecate abominations upon the head of Gideon Sneed from the gods of porn and prostitution. Cars were rubbernecking past, most likely taking video. An intolerable situation. It was a miracle the police hadn't arrived yet. Ben activated his DSAK, walked up to Roland, and stunned him with it. Just like that, Roland's conniption ceased. He dropped to the ground and squirmed like a man drowning in air. Stunning a superior officer was an act of high treason in the revolution. Ben didn't care. Better that than no revolution at all.

"Thank you!" Martinetti said in an exasperated rasp. "That little gorilla was grappling with me so close I couldn't activate my DSAK!"

Without need for instruction, the two men lifted Roland and carried him to the back of the truck. Ben opened the sliding door while Martinetti slid Roland inside. "Gideon and Michael are moles!" Martinetti told the surprised men inside. "They're gone! We have to get back to base! Take care of Roland!"

Martinetti ran to the driver side, leaving Ben to close and secure the door. When Ben made it to the truck's passenger side, he found Martinetti punching the steering wheel and swearing. "What now?" he asked.

"Gideon took the keys!"

Ben slapped his forehead. "Of course he did! He's the enemy!"

"Do you know of any spares?"

"No. Do you?"

"No! Gideon was the one who got the truck. He was driving!"

"Brilliant!" Ben shouted. "We're dead. We're so dead!"

"No, we're not," Martinetti said as he reached into the deep pockets along the sides of his pants. "I got this."

"What're you doing?"

"Getting my tools. I never go anywhere without my tools."

"You're gonna hot wire the truck?"

Martinetti produced wire cutters, two screwdrivers, and a flap-hammer from the patch pocket of his cargo pants. "My old man runs an auto shop. He did a lot of repossession. I've done this lots of times on old vehicles. And this is a very old vehicle."

Ben swallowed. "Hurry."

"Break out the owner's manual from the glove compartment!"

"Yes, sir!" Ben said. He found the manual and watched with guileless wonder as Martinetti set to work. After pulling the seat back, he hammered the flathead screw driver into the ignition with such force that Ben was afraid he'd damage the steering column. It took seven rapid blows. Martinetti's left hand had been exposed beneath the tool's meager handle, yet he never hit it. He tried to turn the screwdriver, but it wouldn't budge. Next, he unscrewed the plastic paneling around the steering column and pried it open. He got on his back beneath the ignition and stretched his hand to Ben. "Manual!" he called.

Ben handed it to him and watched as he flipped through it. "Here it is," Martinetti said. "Power wires red, starter wires brown." Martinetti kicked Ben in the thigh. "Take my boot off!"

"Okay."

"My rubber gloves are in my kit and we don't have time to get 'em," he said, now cutting and stripping the power wires with the insulated wire cutter. "These pants are a special fabric. Can act like rubber. Cut 'em off beneath the knee. And don't cut me!"

Ben activated the laser blade on his DSAK. Given the urgency, however, he couldn't be too discriminating where or how he sliced. Twice he struck more than fabric, causing Martinetti to cry out and utter a few choice comments about Ben's sister's vagina. Ben sleeved the makeshift glove down Martinetti's leg and handed it to him, whereupon Martinetti used it to twist the exposed power line ends together. The lights and other electrical systems in the cabin turned on.

"Awesome!" Ben said.

"We're not done yet," Martinetti muttered. He handed Ben back his pant leg scrap. "Cut this in half and do as I tell you!"

"All right."

"I'm gonna cut and strip the starter wires. When I touch the ends, the engine will start, but they'll shock you pretty bad if you touch them. So I need you to wrap the fabric around each end without killing yourself. Understand?"

"Yeah!"

"Then you will hold on to them until we get back to Nathan's Ford."

"Got it!"

"Did you cut the fabric?

"Yeah!"

"Okay. Here goes," Martinetti said. He touched the ends and the engine turned and turned for the longest six seconds of Ben's life. It finally started, and if the men had souls, they flew halfway to heaven and back in the time it took for them to celebrate their success. "Take this and wrap it," Martinetti instructed, handing one of the ends to Ben. "And hold on to it since we don't have any electrical tape."

"Can I weld it?"

"What?"

"Our DSAKs have a welding function."

"That's right! Sure. Do it! Are you done? Okay, here's the other. Be careful."

Ben worked as rapidly as he could, wrapping and welding the fabric onto each end with only a little bit of redundancy. He looked at Martinetti, who had just climbed back into the driver's seat and was unlocking the steering mechanism with one of his screwdrivers. "Are we good?" Ben asked as he shut the driver side door.

"My boot!"

"Oh, right!" Ben hopped out and retrieved the boot, which was lying on the asphalt. He handed it to Martinetti as soon as he got back inside.

"Okay, let's go!" Martinetti said.

As they turned back on the highway and sped south under the white sky of morning, Ben knew that if he was going to die that day, he couldn't have picked a more solid and competent man than Martinetti with whom to do it.

Chapter 43

Christian military leader Charles Martel checked the Muslim invasion of Western Europe in 732 AD by defeating a Muslim army at

A. Toledo, Spain.
B. Pamplona, Spain.
C. Guimarães, Portugal.
D. Poitiers, France. (correct)

"What's your analysis say?" Martinetti asked as he sped south on I-95.

Ben consulted his DSAK. "16.2 miles to go," he said. "If we average seventy-five miles an hour, we'll be there in just under thirteen minutes. I figure Gideon will be contacting Washington any minute now. That gives us around forty-five minutes if they torch us from orbit like they did in Wichita."

"How far away is the daycare again?" Martinetti asked. "16.2 seems kinda low."

"Well, the daycare is about nineteen miles out. But you gotta drop me off at 100 Bennett."

Martinetti turned sharply towards Ben. "What? Why?"

"Orders from Eli. I need to tell our Horseman what's going on."

"Our Horseman's in Nathan's Ford?"

"Apparently. You know how it is with Horsemen. No electronic contact. Just vox." Martinetti shook his head and muttered hatefully under his breath. "It's not far out of your way," Ben said. "In fact, you can drop me off at Donald Street. You need to turn there anyway."

Martinetti's face lit up like a clown's when he perceives his foot has been stepped on. "Oh, yeah! Like I don't know that."

"Then what's wrong?"

Martinetti darted his pelican beak towards the back. "You're leaving me alone with those lunatics. Before, I had Michael to help keep 'em in line. Now, I got nothing."

"Not all of them belong to Roland."

"You mean Alan and that other techie Doug?" Martinetti scoffed. "Just what we need, a pair of vaginas to control Roland and his goons."

"I'll get to the daycare as soon as I can," Ben promised. "All right?"

Martinetti nodded a few times, placated but not relieved. Neither said anything until they reached the corner of Bennett and Donald. Martinetti offered Ben his hand by way of goodbye. Ben shook it and wouldn't let it go right away. "If I don't make it back to the daycare, head to Lebanon, Kentucky. Fairgrounds

Road. There's a cross-shaped clearing in a forest. Agents will meet you in the middle of it!"

Ben jumped onto the curb not bothering to gauge Martinetti's reaction. He liked Martinetti and preferred not to have to say goodbye.

He sprinted down Bennett, eyeing each building for number 100. He noticed the stifled expressions on the white citizens of Nathan's Ford as he whizzed past. A young and shabbily dressed black man running for his life on the main street of their town. How could these good people *not* suppose he were up to no good? But like denizens of a conquered city, they kept their reservations to themselves and scattered like lethargic pigeons. Ben was grateful since that helped clear a straight shot to his destination.

100 Bennett Street. The one-story gray concrete police building. It just *had* to be the one-story gray concrete police building. Ben's disbelief overlapped with his newly-discovered appreciation for cold slab irony. Their Horseman was a cop. All Eli's note said below the address was 'Blake' as if someone named Blake had written the note himself. Ben hopped up the steps three at a time making sure not to skin his knee again. There was no sign of Officer Dobbs, although Ben was half-expecting her and her chipped tooth to burst at him nightmare-style through the doors.

The lobby hadn't changed. The same cream-colored concrete bricks. The same photo-crystal on the ceiling. The same square-shaped bullet proof window. The same overweight black officer thwacking dents into his old-fashioned keyboard. That wart on his cheek had been replaced by a large, flex-fab Band-Aid. It was brown and matched his skin perfectly.

"Kin I he'p ya?" he asked, raising his puffy, amblyopic eyes at Ben.

Ben had planned to ask for Blake right away but then thought better of it. "Can I talk to Officer Pendergast, please?" he asked, frantically affecting nonchalance.

"Potenintowa?" the man muttered.

Ben replayed the word several times in his mind until he was sure he had never heard it before. "Excuse me?"

"Wha ya wanna see 'im fo'?" the man drawled, beginning to

get a little testy at Ben's hard of hearing.

Brick-walled by the question, Ben stared at the man stupidly and imagined the clock ticking down on those kids in the day-care as absolutely nothing came to his mind. Irritated, the officer punched a button on the wall. The door buzzed, and with a consumptive snore he ambled aggressively through it. He took Ben's left arm as if he were a misbehaving child and tried to wrangle him out of the building. "Nigga, you get on! Git!" he said.

Cataclysmic exigencies aside, Ben found it offensive that this overweight, mouth-breathing blood pressure bomb would *presume* he was capable of moving Ben if Ben did not wish to be moved. Ben twisted his arm free and uncorked a nasty right cross onto the man's jaw. The man's marshmallow neck could not provide adequate resistance to the blow, and he collapsed unconscious against the wall.

Ben entered, remembering exactly where Pendergast's office was: down a thin, diagonal hallway on the right past the glass cubicles. He turned to the Yankee transplant secretary to his right and said, "Here to see Pendergast," and kept walking. He didn't bother to look behind him, but he knew that men were sliding their chairs away from their desks in their cubes. Soon they would be coming after him. He knew Pendergast's office was up ahead on the right, last one on the corner. He lengthened his strides and felt sweat spill from his feet and armpits. They still hadn't put poison in his molars. It's hard to remain calm in a situation like this, he reminded himself, when you don't have poison in your molars.

"Excuse me! You can't come in here!" the secretary called.

Ben reached for Pendergast's doorknob as if it were about to run away. The door was unlocked, but the room empty. On the desk Schlong of the South was recapitulating the resurgence of the U.S. Confederacy, but thankfully at low volume. Looking back, he saw the secretary pointing at him and three officers approaching fast. He had seconds to find Pendergast. Fortunately, Pendergast made it easy.

"HA!"

Ben followed the familiar high-pitched cackle to the men's

room, which was towards the back of the building on the left. He burst through the door. Past the sinks stood a line of urinals to the right and three stalls on the left. Pendergast was in the handicap stall at the end. He was talking college hoops with someone on his personal device. "Officer Pendergast!" Ben called. "I need to talk to you, sir!"

Ben stopped in front of Pendergast's stall and kicked open the door. Seated Buddha-like on the toilet and eclipsing all things porcelain was Pendergast himself. His pink, sweat-stained shirt draped down past his knees like a carnival tent, and vast swaths of dark pant fabric lay in a pile at his boat-sized feet. Ben did a double take after noticing the long, semi-automatic pistol that Pendergast was aiming at him. Pendergast was pressing his finger white against the trigger. A long, oozing fart then emitted from Pendergast's nether regions. It hissed and fizzed for a good two seconds before discharging. Given the circumstances, however, neither Ben nor Pendergast could afford to act as if it had even happened.

"Please, don't shoot!" Ben pleaded, holding up his hands. At that moment, every able-bodied police officer in the building burst into the bathroom and began ordering Ben to surrender. Ben presumed they had their guns drawn, just like Pendergast.

Pendergast straightened his arm and put Ben unnecessarily in his sights. "I'd do as they say, son," he warned.

"Sir, I'm Ben Cameron," Ben whispered. "You met me last summer. I was looking for my lost brother. I need to talk to Blake!"

Pendergast lowered his weapon onto his massive lap and squinted at Ben. "Now, Bennie, why in hell didn't you say so in the first place?" he scolded. Seeing Ben hesitate, he waved his gun at him. "Go on. Get on your knees. Put your hands behind your head. Let's get this over with."

Ben complied and was cuffed and Mirandized in seconds. "Take him to the holding cell with Jerome," Pendergast told the officers. "Let him cool off for a while."

"What? No!" Ben shouted as they dragged him off. "I need to talk to Blake! It's an emergency! I need to talk to Blake!"

"And close the goddamn door!" Pendergast bellowed. "I still

got some business to attend to. Shit fire!" Despite the labyrinth of limbs forcibly restraining him and the general hubbub of his departure, Ben heard another fart and another distinctive "HA!" as he was led down the hall.

It was the same boxing ring-sized jail cell they had taken him to before. Same canary yellow concrete walls. Same bench on one side. Same seatless toilet on the other. The place smelled a lot better than Ben remembered it. Bleach and ammonia scrubbed his insides every time he breathed, but the under-smell of sweat and vomit lingered like a shoplifter waiting for his chance.

Sure enough, Jerome was snoozing flat on his back near the toilet. Old paint on his gray mechanics pants seemed ready to float off of him like dust. Miraculously, his blue collared shirt was still tucked in beneath a pair of black suspenders. His potbelly stretched it further than Ben believed any normal shirt could go. Ben waited until the clicks and clacks of the officer's shoes receded before dropping himself despondently on the bench. All he could do was wait for his world to explode. He was sure he'd be able to hear it, even from there. He looked at Jerome's belt and chuckled, imagining that it was so long he'd probably crash to the floor before he could successfully hang himself with it.

Deep, almost lazy, footsteps echoed though the jail. Only a man with long, heavy legs could make such authoritative sounds. Ben prayed it was Pendergast. He darted to the bars and was gratified to see that it was. "Officer Pendergast!" he called. "Please hurry! I need to talk to Blake! I—"

"Yeah, yeah," Pendergast interrupted, initiating a PVN. He was carrying a large bottled water and a bucket. "Now, is that really you, Bennie? That's one helluva suntan they gave ya."

"Yes, it's me, damnit! This is Fickleskin."

"I know about that. And I know it's secret too. I instructed everyone back there that I needn't be disturbed with y'all."

"Y'all? Who's y'all? Do you mean Blake? Is he coming?"

Pendergast unlocked the bars and strolled into the cell. "Yee-up!"

"Where is he?"

Pendergast sniggered, and his belly jiggled as he pointed to Jerome. "Got yer Horseman right there. Ha!"

Ben looked from one man to the other and back again without moving his head. He didn't allow himself to be shocked. He didn't have the time. It all made sense once he realized that the feds would suspect a wino of running a revolution from a jail cell as much as they would Chinese gamers of building bombs underground. So, that's what Jerome was trying to do back the Q, Ben thought, protect the revolution by encouraging me to leave town. Ben stepped back and considered his third drastic paradigm shift of the day. He watched Pendergast lower himself before Jerome, one overburdened knee at a time. Ben decided he could trust him.

"Sir, we think General Michael Archer was a mole," he said. "A lieutenant named Gideon Sneed was also a mole. Archer's dead. Sneed escaped with Archer's body about thirty-five minutes ago along I-95 north."

Pendergast looked at Ben. "You don't say."

"I do say."

"Well, then ya might as well get over here and help me get ol' Jerome awake and sober. If anyone'll know what to do, it's him."

Ben sprang to Pendergast and helped him fold Jerome upright. "Hold on, now," Pendergast said, reaching under Jerome's shirt. He pressed a switch of some sort, and Jerome's potbelly began to shrink like a balloon leaking air. "Quick! Get the bucket!"

Ben did and placed it down range from Jerome's mouth, which was opening for regurgitation. Seconds later, fluid vomit sprayed into the bucket like water from a thumbed garden hose. It reeked of beer and bile. "This is how Uncle J. can drink any man under the table," Pendergast said, waving the smelly air in front of him. "He's got his own booze repository right here."

Jerome was now awake but groggy as flabby jowls hung from his face like an old hound dog. Pendergast made him swallow three pills and then half of the bottled water. Jerome's eyes lit up as if reacting to smelling salts. At first, he gazed with innocent wonder at Pendergast and his surroundings. Soon however the heavy wrinkles in his face perplexed his expression. His blue eyes contracted suspiciously on Ben.

"Charlie, I thought I told you to wake me up after I got home," he said. "I spend enough time in this place. I don't wanna wake up here."

"We got a situation, Uncle," Pendergast said, looking to Ben. "Tell him."

"We suspect that General Michael Archer was a mole," Ben said. "We have a holographic message from General Humphrey showing proof. Archer was killed on the way to Bethesda while still in the Nathan's Ford safe-range."

"Who the hell are you?" Jerome asked without moving his lips. "Ah, never mind. I know who y'are."

"Unfortunately, a lieutenant named Gideon Sneed was also a mole," Ben added. "He escaped with General Archer's body about a half hour ago."

Jerome shook his head long and slow. "Well, butter my butt. We had two of 'em. Looks like we gonna have to reassess our vetting algorithms. Wouldn't you say, Charlie?"

"Sir, they're gonna be attacking us from space any minute," Ben said.

"Nah. They ain't that fast," Jerome said, spitting into the bucket. "See, this is a secret war. They won't be blastin' ya from outer space unless it's night time. They gonna bring in stealth choppers. Make it seem like domestic terrorism or some nonsense. See, Ear Muffs can't get ya from space, but they *can* get ya with choppers. Lemme see where they comin' from." Jerome motioned to Pendergast who handed him a personal device. Soon Jerome was lit blue in correspondence. "Well, Charlie, the boy's tellin' the truth. My FBI guy's sayin' they picked up one of their spies on I-95 just now." Jerome adjusted his posture, clearly suffering from back pain. "Say, boys, he'p me up. I need to set on that bench over there."

Pendergast and Ben lifted a much lighter Jerome to his feet and led him to the bench lining the wall. "Did he say anything about choppers?" Ben asked.

"Yeah. They comin' from Norfolk," Jerome said as he plopped down, re-ensconced in the blue aura of his device. "Three of 'em. They'll be here in 'bout fifteen minutes to blow your houses sky high."

"General Humphrey has already escaped in the RVs with everyone," Ben said. "Data, weapons, equipment, everything."

"Did he say where?"

"No."

"That's good. We got vehicles stashed everywhere from here to Orlando to Dallas. If Humphrey follows protocol, he might even make a clean getaway long as this Sneed feller don't know where he's headed."

"I don't think he does."

"Welp. Not gonna matter," Jerome said. "I've started the deactivation override for his BREMAT chip. He'll be dead in three minutes. Enemy's gonna know about Fickleskin, though. No helpin' that. That's gonna change a few things."

"What about the choppers?"

"We'll handle the choppers," Jerome said, still communicating with his mole in the FBI. "As for you, best thing is to stay put. We'll take care of ya."

"Can't," Ben said. "We got guys evacuating the school and daycare as we speak. I'm supposed to meet them there."

Jerome looked up from his device. "I thought you said Humphrey took off with everyone."

"Everyone except the Bethesda Ten. Or, Eight, now. They're gonna pick up the kids and teachers and hightail it from the tunnels under the daycare. We have a place mapped out for us in Kentucky."

"You know they'll be firing missiles at that daycare too."

Ben nodded, feeling the muscles in his abdomen tighten. Jerome harrumphed and made himself more comfortable on the bench. "Charlie, arrange for a ride to take Mr. Cameron here to the Sunny Day Daycare on the high."

"Yes, Uncle," Pendergast said.

"Meanwhile, I'll call in the cavalry."

Ben smiled. "We have cavalry?"

"Shoot, we gonna catch them Yankees somethin' stupid," Jerome promised, chuckling to himself as he corresponded on his device. "Reckonin' ya ain't got the technological edge ya thought ya had? It's a bitch."

"What do we got?" Ben asked.

"Well, our chopper ain't as fast as theirs. And it don't have the firepower," Jerome said, grinning greedily. "But it's got enough. Likewise, it's invisible. Made of rubber glass. They ain't never gonna see us comin'."

"Ben, your ride's almost here," Pendergast said, clearing his throat. "Lemme take ya out back."

"They done fuelin' the choppers," Jerome told Ben. "Start your clock. They'll be in the air in ten seconds." He offered him his hand. "Thank you for your sacrifice and for being a patriot to your race."

Ben took his hand. "Thank you, sir," he said, and then let Pendergast lead him out of the cell. Beyond Pendergast's broad shoulders, Ben could see little. He knew he was being led down a thin hall past more cells. Pendergast waddled as he walked, which Ben presumed was his way of hurrying. Winded by the time they got to a thick metal door, Pendergast needed seven seconds to unlock it as he leaned heavily on the frame with his left hand.

"What are you gonna do now?" Ben asked him.

"Well, Jerome'll probably still be a Horseman," Pendergast said. "Me, I'd join you. But I ain't got the body for it. I think I'll just stay here. Help out any way I can. Wish I could do more."

Pendergast opened the door for Ben, and sunlight flashed hard in their eyes. A beige Ford Taurus idled in the parking lot. Ben could not see the driver. "Thanks," he said.

"You go on now," Pendergast said. His chubby features seemed to fold over his eyes as he squinted in the sunlight. "And kill as many of those Muslim fucks as you can. I swear to Christ this used to be a great country."

Chapter 44

The Battle of Palmetto Ranch, fought in Texas on May 12–13, 1865, is considered the final battle of the American Civil War and a Confederate victory. The Union major general who tried to prevent this battle through negotiation went on to achieve fame by

A. inventing the folding cabinet bed.
B. inventing the coal-powered motorcycle.
C. inventing the leak-proof fountain pen.
D. authoring a bestselling novel, dubbed 'the most influential Christian book of the nineteenth century,' which sold over 50 million copies, was blessed by the Pope, and was adapted into a major motion picture which won 11 Academy Awards, was one of the highest grossing films of all time (adjusting for inflation), and saved MGM Studios from financial ruin nearly a century after the Civil War. (correct)

Ben recognized Curtis Book behind the wheel of the car. His gold chain reflected light from the Sun which was already high in the sky despite the early hour. He wore a gray T-shirt and black basketball trunks. He gunned it as soon as Ben slammed the door and then set it to auto-drive. "Don't start on me, man!" he warned. "How was I to know you was gonna be there?"

"Why didn't you tell us you were dating a cop?" Ben asked, enabling his PVN as the car's computer steered through Nathan's Ford at the maximum legal speed. It estimated the trip would take seven minutes.

Curtis clicked his tongue in annoyance. "I just met her three days ago."

"So? We had to put our wheels on!"

"You gonna blame me for that?" Curtis argued, his voice warping with spite. "How was I s'posed to know you and LaKendra had a history?"

"You shouldn't have said hello to me like that!"

"You said hello to me!"

"And you shouldn't have taken her to the daycare!"

"I didn't take her there! She was goin' there anyway!"

"You still should have told us immediately."

"I was gonna!" Curtis insisted. "I was planning on tellin' Humphrey today."

"All right, Curtis. Out with it. Now!"

"Out with what?"

"Why are you here? With us?"

Curtis sighed. "It's what I tell all y'all. I just hate niggas, all

right? My father left me, and my step-mom neglected me. You
know she went to a basketball game in Charlottesville, put my
twelve-year-old sister in charge of me. I was seven. I burned my
hand real bad on the gas stove. People who showed me crack
was niggas. My cousin got shot by niggas. We all been robbed
by niggas. In fact, the only people not doin' that shit to us is
y'all. And I'm supposed to call y'all the bad guy? 'Cos shit gone
down 200 years ago? Fuck that!"

"What about Roland?"

"Roland's crazy. We all know that. But he only one guy. You
think them niggas marchin' us up and down the street ain't crazy? You think them niggas tellin' us to look the other way when
we rob and kill and rape our own. You think they ain't crazy?
We got lots of them."

"I agree."

"And with all them Arab Muslim motherfuckers we got tak-
in' charge of this country, ain't no surprise blacks are runnin'
back to the party of Lincoln."

"That's true too."

"But don't fuckin' blame me because LaKendra recognized
you! I didn't know she arrested you last year, and I didn't know
you was gonna be at the daycare!"

Ben held up his hands. "Okay. I won't blame you."

"All right."

"But you still should have told us."

"Aww, man! Let it go!"

"No. Because had you told us the night you hooked up with
her, you and I would have been given different protocols. Like,
for instance, being reminded to not say hello if we see each other
on the street!" Curtis shook his head and muttered peevishly
under his breath. Ben realized that this was the closest thing to a
concession he was going to get.

A throbbing explosion upended their tenuous equanimity.
"Oh, it's started," Ben said, "And early, too." He felt all the familiar signs of panic and dread spawning in his head, stomach,
and chest. He leaned back in his seat and wondered how much
more of this he could take.

"Quick! Get it up! Get it up!" Curtis urged.

Ben showed the live, photo-crystal feed on his DSAK. The Bennett house was a fiery shambles. Missiles were hacking divots in the ground the size of school busses and sending firecracker explosions of earth and rock hundreds of feet into the air.

"*Damn!*" Curtis exclaimed.

"They're getting the tunnels," Ben said. "The bastards knew exactly what to hit."

The Garrett Street house was still standing, but in thirty seconds, it too was obliterated. What looked like a brilliant, glowing sky-needle struck it with an order of magnitude more force than necessary. The Bennett house had been on a two-acre plot, so neighboring structures were more or less safe from the blast. Not so the Garrett house, which occupied maybe a quarter of an acre. Two neighboring homes were wiped out. Ben knew by sight the families that lived there. Both were white. One had young children. He could see a burning body crawling out of a second story window.

Ben felt the rhythm of the engine adjust as Curtis shifted out of auto-drive. They were finally at the daycare. Curtis pulled up within inches of the doors, barely giving Ben room to exit. "They hittin' this place next!" he warned. "Hurry!"

"Get out of here!" Ben screamed as his feet hit asphalt. Curtis was reluctant to leave, but zoomed off after Ben smacked his car. Ben regretted not being able to thank Curtis for who he was and all that he had done.

He could hear the pandemonium in the daycare before he could see it. And when he could, he recognized immediately the unique difficulty his cohorts were facing: trained soldiers corralling a tumult of small children who were melting down into red-faced, screaming little monkeys. Martinetti and two of Roland's men, Colton and Ryder, were maintaining a bucket brigade, passing one kid after another to someone in the men's bathroom. From there Ben surmised they were stuffing them down the toilet tunnel where they were given a face full of chloroform or something to shut them up for the great escape. Sharon, whose name Ben still could not remember, was doing what she could to keep the panicking tykes from running off. Two little girls had just managed to escape and were heading for the door when Ben entered. He figured if they were insisting on being scared, he would give them something to be scared about.

He raised his arms, stretched out his fingers like claws, and roared like a hungry beast looking to scrounge up a few living morsels. He knew nothing could be more terrifying to a child than a large black man descending upon them in a state of aboriginal rage. One girl fainted. The other wept in impotent terror and ran back to Sharon who snatched her up and placed her back in the human chain. Ben hoisted the other girl up and handed her to Martinetti. Sharon went to help corral the remaining children as Ben took his place in the human chain.

"Good to see you, Ben," Martinetti said.

"Likewise. I say we have less than sixty seconds."

"I know. We saw Garrett go down." As soon as the last child made it to the men's room, Martinetti clapped his hands. "Okay! Ladies next!" Sharon gave Ben a quick squeeze on the arm as she darted past. She was gone before Ben could reciprocate.

"All right, Ben! You're next!" Martinetti ordered.

"No! I'm going last! Let the others go!"

Martinetti tried grabbing Ben by the arm, but Ben shook him off, noticing someone by the front door. It was a young white mother pushing a toddler in a stroller through the doors, completely oblivious to the circumstances. From Ben's perspective, she was little more than a silhouette, but he could tell she was more curious than fearful about the frenzied action forty feet in front of her.

"No!" Ben screamed, charging at her. In seconds he was shoving the woman back through the glass doors. The stroller toppled over, toddler wailing. With thuggish efficiency, he hurled the woman into the parking lot. She was briefly airborne and landed painfully on the pavement. Stepping back inside, he righted the stroller, wheeled it through the doors, and sent it hurtling towards the young woman.

"Get out of here!" he screamed. Looking up, he noticed three dark spots in the sky hovering just above the tree line. Choppers. "Shi-i-i-i-t!" he shuddered as he sprinted back inside.

Martinetti was alone by the bathroom door, waving him on

like a third base coach. Ben turned the corner and didn't argue when Martinetti insisted on being last. Ben saw the folded-up toilet and the tunnel beneath it. Protecting his head tightly with his arms, he dove in. Colton, still on the ladder three feet below him, broke his descent. Martinetti came tumbling down seconds later, just as the missiles struck. In less than a second the structure above them was pulverized in a blinding tsunami of wood, metal, and fire. The shock sent Ben and Martinetti plunging into a pile of bodies on the dirt floor. Between the heat, the sound, and his concussive landing Ben wasn't sure what was happening other than the temperature in the catacombs was rising fast. His mind was swirling like water down a drain. An incessant flatline was ringing in his ears.

Someone dragged him from the opening and hoisted him on his shoulders. It was Ryder. Ben's head pounded with every jostle and bump. He could see Sharon and one other person escape through the secret portal. Colton had an equally groggy Martinetti on his back and followed swiftly. Ryder then went with Ben, and the warm, orange illumination of the center chamber gave way to the dank, putrid darkness of the tunnel. They passed Sharon who closed the hatch and locked it.

Ben was coming to his senses moments later when a rumbling explosion shook the earth and caused everyone to fight for their balance like sailors in a slanting gale. Ben's back scraped against the wall as Ryder swayed to his right and fell to his knees. Ben let go and rolled to the ground. They had gone maybe two hundred yards. Lit by their DSAKs, Ben, Ryder, and Sharon all instinctively looked at each other, sharing their dread as if that would ameliorate it somehow.

"What the hell was that?" Ryder shouted.

"I don't know, but it was close!" Sharon shouted back.

"They're going after the tunnels!" Ben said. "They did the same thing with Bennett and Garrett!"

The next explosion was even closer, and the tunnel shuddered in tectonic shock. Clouds of dust and dirt filled the air like car exhaust. The three took off running, with Ryder speeding out in front.

"They don't know where the tunnels are!" Sharon shouted.

"They're guessing!"

"How do you know?" Ben asked.

"Gideon has never been down here!"

The moment Sharon said this an explosion many yards behind them lacerated the tunnel with end-of-times violence. The resulting ball of fire lit the tunnel like day, and shock waves struck Ben and Sharon in the back like the fist of God, flinging them forward almost ten feet. The tunnel was now stripped naked for anyone in the troposphere and beyond to see. While this gigantic breach prevented smoke and other toxic fumes from flooding the passageway, it also revealed that the chopper had hit a vein. Ben knew it was only a matter of seconds before it hit pay dirt.

He rolled over to his back and, with tremendous effort, sat up, determined to squint into his fiery doom. He hadn't quite recovered from his mild concussion from before, and this most recent blast only further befuddled him. He couldn't move his limbs without the concentrated effort of a weightlifter. After a moment, he realized that it wouldn't be worth it anyway and let his arms fall. Fate was fate. At least this way death would be painless, he thought. And quick.

The next explosion helped revive Ben from his defeatist stupor. It was further away, tinnier, insulated by over a mile of atmosphere. Following forthwith was the whine of a giant engine plummeting to its death. The uneven thwaps of helicopter blades suddenly became audible, and the chopper crashed a safe distance away, its still-spinning blades cutting a trench into the ground like an electric saw.

Ben turned to Sharon. "The cavalry!" he said. "The cav—" He noticed that she was lying face down in the dirt and not moving. In the combustive haze, Ben couldn't tell if she was unconscious or dead. Suddenly, she was moving. Someone was dragging her away and then hoisting her in the air. It was Martinetti.

"Come on!" he bellowed. He threw Sharon over his shoulders like a sack of coal and didn't pause to see if Ben was following. Head still swirling, Ben rolled to his feet and kept leaning on the tunnel wall as he stumbled his way to salvation. Another explosion rocked the atmosphere, and another helicopter whined to its death. Ben stopped to bring up the photo-crystal feed on his DSAK and then continued on. As he approached the end of the tunnel he was able to witness Jerome's invisible cavalry take out the final government chopper, converting it into a yellow blast of shrapnel. There was no whining of the engine this time, no cadaveric spasms of the helicopter blades. This was a direct hit. The first domestic military victory against the United States since May of 1865. Ben didn't pause to ponder the dire ramifications of such a victory. He paused to celebrate it. "Yes!" he exulted. He fell to his knees to give himself room to raise his fists like a victorious athlete. "YES!"

A door opened, and Martinetti appeared. "You coming or what?"

"We got 'em!" Ben said, getting to his feet. "We got the choppers. All three of 'em!"

"Yeah, that's great. We saw," Martinetti said, throwing something slick and thin at Ben. It was an anaerobe. "Take care of Ryder for me, will ya?"

"What are you talking about?"

Martinetti pulled Ben by the shirt through the door and into a squalid little antechamber which led to the buried RVs. The room was built like the opening of a coal mine but without rails on the ground. Skeleton sets of wooden beams supported the walls and ceiling, making one wonder why tons of earth didn't just spill between them. The backdoor of one of the RVs was flung open. In it, Ben could see light, plastic ration boxes, and the periphery of action. Chatter and sobs emanated from inside. Twenty feet beyond the RV, daylight peeped over a large mound of rock and dirt. Ben surmised it was where the other RV used to be. He was grateful for the fresh air but was too flabbergasted by what lay before him to dwell on it.

Ryder lay slumped between two vertical beams with his head leaning against one of them. Below his nose was a mangled mess of blood and bone. Ben could not discern the existence of a mouth or jaw. Blood was spreading in a perimeter around the body.

"Oh, my God!" Ben shouted.

"Keep it down!" Martinetti warned. "We're not underground

anymore."

"What happened?"

"Roland shot him."

"What?"

"Fuck it. I'll wrap him myself," Martinetti said, retrieving the anaerobe and kneeling before Ryder's body. "Help me get him in this, okay?"

Ben gulped and overcame his aversion to freshly murdered human flesh as he waited for Martinetti to get the anaerobe ready. "Why did Roland do this?" he asked.

"He wanted to leave without you. He put Ryder in charge of driving the RV with all the daycare people and the kids. But Ryder didn't want to leave without you and wasn't shy about it. So Roland got mad and shot him."

Ben squinted his eyes shut to contemplate the insanity.

"You know, he was there," Martinetti went on, finally enabling the anaerobe. "In the PT room when you gave that bullshit speech about Roland saving Vera Barry."

"Who was?"

"Ryder. That's why he didn't want to leave you here. You're a hero for what you did in Memphis."

Rather than respond, Ben shook his head and began helping Martinetti stuff his deceased benefactor into the anaerobe, limb by bloody limb.

"That was bullshit, wasn't it?" Martinetti asked.

"What was?"

"The story about Roland operating a med kit to save Vera."

Ben's head fell in a resigned nod. "I swear to God, Mart. I thought he was gonna kill me. He threatened me enough times on the way back from Memphis."

"I believe it."

"I'm sorry."

"Forget it. I figured you were covering your ass. I shouldn't have asked in the first place."

"So, you saw it happen?" Ben asked. "You saw Roland shoot—"

"Yeah. I mean, I was still buzzed from the blast. We were all standing right here. It happened about five minutes ago. Then he took off. Only me and the two techies Alan and Doug decided to stay and wait for you."

Shocked to the point of lightheadedness, Ben looked at Roland's grotesque handiwork stuffed haphazardly into a bag like a derelict toy. "He was probably still hysterical from being stunned."

"He shit his pants, you know," Martinetti said as he sealed the anaerobe.

"What? You mean, like, literally?"

"Oh, yeah."

Ben sighed. "Does he even know where to go? Does he know about Lebanon?"

Martinetti began fishing for the remote in his pants pocket. "Well, I sure didn't tell him anything. But he used to be in charge here. He knows people. So who knows what he knows?"

"Maybe the feds will track his RV. You said yourself this war might not be secret anymore."

"You better hope that if the feds get anyone, it's him. He was pretty fucking mad at you. All right. Let's cook him."

"You think he'll court-martial me?"

Martinetti initiated the burn and then looked curiously at Ben. "Either that or he'll do to you what he did to this guy."

"I'm not afraid of that man-eating midget," Ben said.

"Me neither," Martinetti said as they lifted the burning body into the RV. "But he has serious backup. In fact, it might be good he killed one of his own. That means there's only four of them. And there's four of us."

Ben smiled through a pained expression as he contemplated the odds. Roland aside, Chuck and the other two, Jackson and Colton, may as well have been the starting defensive line for a junior college football team. They were also very experienced soldiers. He did not want to cross them if he didn't have to. "You mean that, Mart?" he asked. "When you say 'us'?"

Martinetti looked at Ben and nodded. "Yeah, I mean it. I'm goin' down with you, brother. Or we'll bury all four of them in Lebanon. Fuck it."

Alan, a young, slender, Eagle Scout of a soldier appeared in the rear of the RV. His tightly-cropped hair was dense like rainforest grass, and his neck was abnormally long. "All set, Sir?" he asked, pulling the body inside.

"Yeah," Martinetti said. "Is Doug behind the wheel?"

"Yes, sir. We're ready."

"Okay. Hop onboard, Ben. Let's go."

Despite what could be waiting for him in Lebanon, Ben did not hesitate. He hopped onboard.

Chapter 45

What scientific term describes the facial schema that includes a large head, large eyes, chubby cheeks, a tiny chin, and a button nose?

A. Cheiloschitic
B. Esotropic
C. Microtic
D. Cute (correct)

When the revolution's leaders purchased their early-century, Class A RVs, they replaced the antiquated stove tops and furniture with enough reclinable deskpods, e-screens, and hologram stages to serve twenty-five men. They replaced the generators and water filtration systems with less cumbersome current models. They made sleeping space out of the basement bins. They left the bathrooms and the bunks above the cabin and some of the kitchen fixtures alone. Eight deskpods took the place of the bed in the master bedroom and could convert into hammocks if necessary. The ceilings they converted into weapons and materiel storage except where they installed a small hydroelectric conning tower and periscope. The RVs were armed with two solid fuel, S-900 junior anti-ballistic missiles, two Chinese miniature surface-to-surface missiles, and a swiveled machine gun equipped with over two thousand rounds. In the cabinets they crammed enough dry high-protein food to last a month. On the roof, they disguised the vehicles with Apparition fabric and rubber glass. To a pedestrian or motorist, the RVs seemed perfectly ordinary. To satellites and aircraft, however, they would be invisible at night and devilishly difficult to spot during the day. A small compartment in the rear beyond the organic muffler converted exhaust into a spray of black ice which chemically bonded with the pavement as the vehicle passed over it.

Reclining in a deskpod, Ben felt safe enough to sleep. He was told the trip to Lebanon might take thirty-six hours since they were avoiding major highways and were stopping at predetermined hiding spots during the day. One of the women had given him food and water, sedatives, and a painkiller for his injuries. Someone had given him a baseball cap, the visor of which he placed snugly over his eyes. For twelve hours, his sleep had been dreamless. When he awoke, he wasn't hungry, he wasn't tired, he wasn't even worried or afraid. He was just happily cradled in the gentle bump and hum of 2000 revolutions per minute. He stayed in that blissful limbo for another hour or two, dreaming only good dreams as if he were back in the arms of God where grief and loneliness defy the laws of nature, and you never have to fight to survive.

He got up when he felt he had to pee. He removed his cap and stretched and rubbed his shoulder which still hurt from the falls he'd suffered in the tunnels. It was almost dawn. Martinetti was asleep. Ben could see that the women had bandaged the wounds on his calf where he had cut him with his laser blade. Alan was watching a 3D movie in a deskpod close to the front, and beyond him was the apparition curtain which separated the cabin from the rest of the RV. It was Doug's turn to drive. The same apparition material curtained the windows, so they had to rely on thin, cheap fluorescence for light, just like in the tunnels.

Behind Martinetti were the sedated children, from toddler age to about nine or ten. They slept two to a deskpod. Ben counted twenty-four of them and six women. The only one who didn't have a child sleeping on her shoulders was Holly, a pretty, thick-set brunette whose hair fell in waves over the back of her white tennis visor. She stood as Ben walked past. Confronted by such a big, husky girl, Ben found himself sizing her up as if she were a man, despite her pretty face and feminine qualities. She was almost as tall as he was.

"Hi, Ben," she said.

"Hey."

"Are you feeling okay?"

"Yeah, I'm fine. Thanks."

"Would you like to see Melissa? She's right here."

Ben sighed and hung his head to hide his annoyance. He had completely forgotten about his niece. If there was anything that could slip between his spokes, it was children. He never knew what to say to them. He never understood the charm of incipient people. Isn't childhood just a passing phase? If so, then why adore it? Ben knew that there was more to it than his callous argumentation. But still—always with those two words. *But still.* There was nothing he could do. Melissa was Isaac's daughter, and he was now responsible for her. He owed her things. Even worse, he owed her *time.* He shook his head. Maybe one day. Maybe one day after all of this. But still…

"It's okay," Holly said. "She's asleep. They're all asleep."

Ben looked and saw a frizzy blonde mess over closed eyes and puckered lips. A pink shirt, flower print jeans, and lavender socks with no shoes in sight. He smiled, appreciative of the work these women did behind the scenes, effectively raising these children so the men could engage in the deadly business of revolution. It occurred to him, however, that the women probably didn't see it that way. These children *were* the scene. How else to surmount the challenges of the future? How else to survive? Ben patted the girl on the head. "Thanks," he said to Holly, and then headed to the bathroom.

When he stepped out to return to his seat, he noticed that the master bedroom door was shut. He then remembered that Sharon, the woman whose name he had hopelessly forgotten, was not in the main compartment of the RV. Nor was she in the kitchen. Ben lifted his hand to knock but then supposed she might be in the cabin with Doug, out of sight behind the apparition curtain. He took tentative steps towards the cabin. Alan smiled mildly as he passed. Peeking behind the curtain, he saw Doug at the wheel. A thin, scruffy kid in wraparound sunglasses, he was enjoying earsplitting grind-metal on the radio. There was no one in the passenger seat.

Ben passed his deskpod on the way back and decided to investigate. Holly stood up before he could reach the bedroom.

"She's sick," she said.

Ben saw three other women standing behind Holly and another to his left, all looking at him, waiting to see what he would do. "Really?" he said. "What's wrong with her?"

Holly kept her eyes on Ben, but two of the women behind her swapped underhanded glances before self-consciously studying the floor. "I'm not sure," Holly said. "She just said she didn't want to be disturbed."

Ben pointed to the ceiling. "We have medical kits," he said. When the women didn't respond, he began to look at the problem differently. "Wait a minute. She was already screened with a medical kit. We all were."

"I don't know," Holly said. "She said—"

"She told me she still had a headache from the blast," said another woman. Raquel. Older than the others. She had short, auburn hair and brilliant eyes marred by droopy lower eyelids.

"But we gave her painkillers," Ben said.

"She'd been knocked unconscious, Ben," a third woman said. She was younger and shorter than the rest. A skinny, blonde with ordinary features. Ben could hardly see her from behind Holly.

"I know. I was there when it happened," he reminded her.

"She just wanted to rest in the bedroom," Raquel said. "She said it was too bright out here. That's all."

Ben looked from Raquel to the bedroom and back again. "Bright? It's not bright out here." He then studied the tense faces of the women. No one was saying anything. He decided not to waste any more time on them and brushed past them for the bedroom. He heard one of them muffle a gasp. He knocked on the door. After five seconds he knocked again. "Can you open the door, please?" he called. Embarrassed that he still could not remember Sharon's name, he continued knocking. Knocking quickly became pounding. The women grew nervous and scolded him for making noise where children were sleeping. Ben sensed a disturbance to his left and noticed Martinetti approaching.

After five consecutive pounds on the door, Ben heard something he didn't expect: a child crying. The cries were hoarse, lusty wails and were definitely coming from the bedroom. It seemed like an older child, and not small. He could also hear Sharon trying to calm the child down. By this point, Martinetti had parted his way through the women. Two of them had returned to their deskpods to attend to children who were now waking. Naptime in the RV was officially over.

"What's going on?" Martinetti asked.

"You hear that kid screaming in there?" Ben asked, pointing to the bedroom.

Martinetti leaned forward. "I think I hear two."

Ben placed his ear to the door and concurred. This new child must have been a toddler. Its cries were more like hiccupped croaks. Ben looked at Martinetti. "How many children we got? Twenty-four, right?"

"That's the number we counted yesterday."

Ben pointed to the deskpods. "Twenty-four are out there, right?"

Martinetti wasn't sure, so he counted. "Yeah. Twenty-four."

Ben pointed to the bedroom. "Then that can only mean…"

"Oh, shit!" Martinetti exclaimed.

Ben pounded the door as if he wanted to knock it down. It hadn't been designed to withstand such abuse; he could feel it beginning to give. Not wanting to break down a perfectly functioning door, he resorted to the kind of threat his father used to give. He took a step back and shouted, "If you don't open this door by the time I count to three, I will kick a fucking hole in it! One! Two!"

Sharon opened the door, first by a crack and then all the way. At this point, nearly all the children in the RV had woken up. Amid the confusion, Ben could barely hear what Sharon was trying to tell him.

"Everything went so fast, Ben!" she explained, gripping his arm in wet-eyed panic. "We didn't know when we were going to get bombed. Their mothers weren't responding to our calls. What else could we have done? Leave them in the parking lot? We had no time! We had to escape! The girls and I were planning on leaving them right where we kept the RVs, but they bombed the tunnel. I'm sorry! Please don't hurt them, Ben! Please!"

By this point, Ben had sunk into a putrid pit of regret. He knew exactly what she was talking about. So did Martinetti. They pushed past her, not looking at her, ignoring her pleas, to see for themselves what she had been hiding in the bedroom all along: three terrified black children from the Sunny Day Daycare.

Chapter 46

In every human society, men have a stronger tendency to dominate than women. As a whole, they are more aggressive, more willing to make sacrifices for power, and have a greater need for the hierarchical status that dominance brings them. This universal truth is the result of

A. not yet overthrowing traditional societies which encourage dominance in men but not women.
B. not yet eradicating all concepts of gender inequality through compulsory and universal social engineering.
C. not yet finding a primitive, stone-aged tribe in some isolated area of the world which exhibits true signs of matriarchy.
D. testicularly-generated hormones impacting the male central nervous system in utero by greatly maturing brain structures which make the male hypersensitive to the presence of endogenous hormones such as testosterone which boost the need for aggression and dominance. (correct)

They arrived on the outskirts of Lebanon just as the Sun was beginning to set. Ben had been sitting in the front seat next to Martinetti for the past hour and witnessed the sunlight die in its blood orange throes as they headed due west on Route 150 out of Danville. They had left the Appalachian Mountains and the rolling plateau behind and now were cleaving through scruffy grasslands where sparse tree life appeared like shrubbery beneath a giant, swirling sky. Only the occasional mailbox, farmhouse, or barn indicated that humans lived this far beyond the city.

They were careful to leave the main road as soon as possible.

With little tree cover this close to Lebanon, both Ben and Martinetti grew nervous. They still had the dark, but under the stark moonlight they stood out like scarecrows amid the sprawling, uninterrupted farmland. Eventually, the forest crept in as the road began to wind, first on one side, then the other.

They reached the center of the cross on Fairgrounds Road amid a dense forest and recognized that they were in the open. Martinetti backed the RV and parked along the northeast crossbar where there was reasonable tree cover. Both men breathed deep, seemingly oppressed by the wet, heavy air.

"Well, let's do this," Martinetti said.

"Wait—" Ben said.

"No wait!" Martinetti said. He unstrapped himself and brushed aside the apparition curtain to storm the RV. Ben heard the women objecting to his purposeful appearance almost immediately. Children were crying. The RV shifted right and left with the ensuing tug of war. It was inharmonious. Ben did not want to wait for Martinetti to call him and followed him back there to see what he could do.

Martinetti held one black child by the waist. Clearly unconscious, the boy dangled head and foot over Martinetti's forearm like a towel. With his free hand, Martinetti was contending with Holly over another black child, the bigger one. This child was clearly not unconscious and not willing to be dragged out of the RV.

"No! NO! You can't do this! Stoppit!" Holly pleaded, latching onto the boy's torso with one of her long, motherly arms. She pounded Martinetti's shoulders with the other. Being the big, powerful girl that she was, a one-armed Martinetti was fully occupied keeping her off of him. Sharon, Raquel and two other women were trying to come to Holly's aid, but were held back by Alan and Doug. Alan also held the smallest black child, and so could only do so much in assisting Doug.

After unsuccessfully attempting to wrench the child from Holly's meaty grip, Martinetti held up the sleeping child in his arm and looked to Ben. "Take this kid!" he ordered. "Now!"

"Ben! No!" Sharon begged. "No!" Ben could not refuse Martinetti. Not after what they had been through. Not after Martinetti's allegiance in the face of Roland's Posse Comitatus. He took the kid.

Martinetti then thrust his boot into Holly's midsection and wrenched the older child away from her. It was a cruel blow. Holly rattled out a deathly cough and fell back into the crowd behind her. Two of the women crashed into the deskpods, and an untold number of children locked in the bedroom began wailing in shrill terror. Without looking back, Martinetti opened the door and walked down the steps with the child.

Weeping out of sheer helplessness, the child seemed to have an idea of what was about to happen to him. "Miss Howwy! Miss Howwy!" he blubbered, bug-eyed through a sheet of tears. Despite her obvious pain, Holly stood to her full five feet, nine inches and charged vindictively after Martinetti. Ben recognized that the iron fierceness of this girl could be on Olympic levels. She roared like a mama bear and took hold of Martinetti's shoulder before he could step outside. She punched him full force in the back of the head. Finally angry, Martinetti turned towards his men. "Put her down!" he commanded as he stepped out of the vehicle.

Ben knew right away that he was not going to do a damn thing. Stunning an unarmed woman trying to save the life of a child? Only a gun to his head would make him move on such an order. Hypocritically, however, he felt a cathartic relief when Doug stepped in with his DSAK.

Reacting to the stun like a wildebeest to a tranquilizer dart, Holly lurched up in a macabre pantomime of shock and then collapsed face first on the steps. The loud thwock of her skull striking metal resounded dishearteningly throughout the RV. It surpassed the predictable shrieks of the women and rang in Ben's ears. Her ham-sized thighs blocked the entryway to the RV like fallen logs.

"Alan and Doug! Full gear and weapons now! Get mine too!" Martinetti ordered. "Ben, take the other babies, and come with me!" Ben realized Martinetti must have forgotten that he was now outside the RV's PVN. His orders were loud and public. Alan stepped past Sharon and Raquel, who were assisting the prostrate Holly, and shoved the unconscious, drool-splattered

baby into Ben's chest. He then bounced towards the back of the
RV with Doug to retrieve the gear.

"Ben, no. Please! No!" Sharon pleaded. She tried to bar his
way but knew she was powerless to stop him. She clutched his
arm as he squeezed past Holly on the stairs. "You know this is
wrong, Ben," she urged. "You *know* this is wrong!"

Ben looked back at her, wholly sympathetic. But he carried
the two sleeping children outside anyway where he knew they
would most likely meet their silent demise. "You can't let this
happen, Ben!" Sharon insisted as she followed him onto the
grass. "You can't let this happen!" She wasn't begging anymore.
She was demanding. She was invoking a kind of ancient moral
authority which stood against the *malum in se* which he and
Martinetti were about to contrive. Supported by centuries of
common law predicated on a very civilized revulsion against
atrocities, she became bold. She spun Ben around by his elbow
but said nothing. Even in the dim haze of night, he could see she
wasn't crying. She just looked at him, and he looked back. He
finally caught a glimpse of the primeval beauty of this woman, a
descendent, no doubt, of the original white settlers of America
who broke the land on the frontier and served as buffers against
aboriginal hostilities. These were tough people, and this was a
tough woman. He wondered why he could never remember her
name.

As he followed Martinetti into the forest, Ben reflected on the
powerlessness of women in the revolution. They had no say in
their political futures. They made few if any important decisions.
What rights they did have depended solely on their subservi-
ence to men...or, more accurately, to the soldiers and officers of
the revolution who outranked them. And only a trivial smatter-
ing of women outranked men in the revolution. Their influence,
such as it was, came mostly from raising children, or from their
abilities to nurse, whore, and spy. In rare cases did women become quantum gamers. The invisible empire that was the revolution enforced this masculinist imbalance simply by not im-
planting DSAKs into women. Written statutes prohibited it. If a
woman dared challenge a man as poor Holly had just done, the
man could, with customary justice, dunk her into spasmodic

oblivion for an hour. She would need the gritty determination to live like an outlaw for the rest of her life to resist. But wasn't she already doing this by defying the gargantuan federal government to arms? It made sense for women not to anger or annoy the men who protected them. Curiously, though, they rarely objected to their second-class citizenship except in the most circumspect and courteous of terms.

Ben suspected that white men initially allowed feminism to flourish in the late nineteenth century because few credible threats to Western Civilization existed at that time. The Ottoman Empire, that scourge of Christendom for over half a millennium, was in noticeable decline. The Indian Wars on the American frontier were winding down. And most other external dangers remained localized in faraway imperial domains or in the Styx of sub-Saharan Africa. What major threats that did exist took the form of other Western nation states. Since these states were more or less equally feminized to begin with, white men felt they could afford the weakness incurred by enfranchising women. Nations that respected the rights of women would surely respect the rights of conquered foes and perhaps would engage in wars less often. Women have always been a tremendous civilizing and pacifying influence on men, Ben knew.

It wasn't until the first quarter of the twenty-first century when a critical mass of white men began to comprehend that through large-scale Islamic immigration, Western Civilization once again faced a dire threat from a foreign and entirely masculine adversary. These men of Islam intended nothing less than to seize control of the West from the Westerners under the rainbow cover of multiculturalism and other prevailing tenets derived from that bitch's brew of white guilt, radical Leftism, and the New Testament. One cannot remain hobbled by feminism when fighting a war against such a loathsome foe. One must be confident of one's moral and intellectual superiority and not hesitate to be ruthless if one wishes to win. One must remove the flowers in one's hair, exchange theory for practice, and double down on force. Although Ben was grateful that Sharon seemed to understand this, he knew that didn't mean she was wrong.

Martinetti found a suitable spot in the woods and stopped. It was a small clearing, still within view of the RV. He released the whimpering child and summarily stunned him. "You comin' or what?" he called to Ben.

"Activate your PVN," Ben said as he came into the clearing. He laid the two children respectfully down next to the first.

"Right," Martinetti said. "We gotta wait for Alan and Doug to bring shovels from their kits. Can't afford to waste an anaerobe if we're not retrieving an implant."

"Mart, this is crazy. We can't kill these kids."

"Aww, fuck you! How can we not?"

"We just don't."

"Ben, you picked the worst time to grow a vagina. You know that?"

"Come on. I'm serious."

Martinetti pointed to the three sleeping children. "These kids are old enough to know who we are. The middle one is three. If the Feds get a hold of 'em they can possibly identify all of us!"

"After only one bus trip?"

"Ben, you're black, remember? Me and Alan are Arabs. And Doug's a central Asian Uzbek or whatever. If these kids start mouthin' off about what a diverse group of characters we are, it won't take long for the Feds to figure out how we've been hiding under their noses for so long."

"Who says we have to set them free?"

"So we're gonna recruit them? Hey, they'll fit in great with us. I can see it now."

"We recruited Curtis."

"Look how well that turned out."

"We can hold them as hostages," Ben proposed. "Maybe our leadership can find some political use for them."

Martinetti blinked. "Maybe you don't realize what an asinine thing you just said. The enemy doesn't take hostages. And neither should we. It's against our protocol anyway."

Out of corner of his eye Ben saw Alan and Doug standing with full pack and listening. "Mart, if you do this, *no one* is going to support us. Do you have any idea what executing helpless black kids will do to our PR?"

"PR? We have no PR! This war is secret, remember?"

"You yourself said it may not be secret anymore, remember?"

Martinetti considered this and realized that Ben had a point. He then pointed east. "Then what about what *their* PR? Did you not see the daycare those bastards blew up? Goin' easy on the kiddies, were they? Or what about that home on Garrett? Did you see that kid trying to jump out of a window? Since when does the enemy give a shit about children?"

"They don't," Ben argued. "But the point I'm making is that embarrassing the enemy in terms of public opinion can be just as useful as a victory on the battlefield. If we can show the world that we have the ability to murder children and don't, while they do, it will be harder for them to gain domestic or international support. Meanwhile, in comparison we will be the good guys!"

Martinetti rolled his eyes and mugged for Alan and Doug. "You don't know any of this for sure. Do you?"

"You're right. I don't."

"Then we're done arguing," Martinetti said. "Break out your shovels, boys, and dig deep. I'll take care of the kids." Martinetti got down on one knee next to the oldest one, preparing to smother him with his bare hand.

"I love you, Mart, and I'm not gonna stop you if you think this is what we should do," Ben said, moving close to him. "But killing innocent, unarmed children, even in war time, is wrong. In and of itself, it is wrong. I'm not religious or anything, but if you do this—if *we* do this—for the rest of my life I'll be worried about our souls."

He noticed that Alan and Doug had their shovels out, but weren't anxious to start digging. Martinetti went from kneeling on one knee to two and sighed in exasperation. "You're not making this any easier, are ya?" he said.

Ben came a little closer. "We're better than this," he whispered. "Isn't that why we're fighting this war in the first place? Because we're better than they are?"

To this Martinetti had no ready response.

Chapter 47

Outrage over which event helped sway public opinion in America to support the Civil Rights Act of 1964?

A. the assassination of Malcolm X
B. the assassination of Robert Kennedy
C. the assassination of Martin Luther King, Jr.
D. the bombing of the 16th Street Baptist Church in Birmingham, Alabama in which four black children were killed. (correct)

The sounds of a large vehicle approaching from the road sharpened them once again to their surroundings. It was a quick and painful transition. Martinetti bounced to his feet without using his hands. "Guns out. Lights off," he ordered quietly. "Let's hope it's our new Horseman." He ran to his kit and unfolded his rifle. Alan and Doug did the same with theirs. They donned their night-specs. Martinetti motioned for Ben to come to him. He handed him a semi-automatic pistol. "Keep behind us," he ordered.

Ben took the gun. The four then crouched in the tall grass nearly two hundred yards from the RV and waited. It was Roland's RV. Ben and Martinetti exchanged a nervous glance.

"We don't have time to put on our apparition suits," Alan said. "They could kill us if they want. They got a machine gun on top of that thing."

"Not if they don't want to make noise," Martinetti said. "Machine gun fire would bring the cops. Or worse."

"They're gonna scan the area," Doug said. "Should we run?"

"Run where?" Martinetti asked. "What will that get us?"

"Guys, Roland wants me," Ben said. "I don't think he wants you."

"After what that little psycho got away with, I want him!" Martinetti said.

"Major, I would appreciate it if we didn't pick a fight with them right now." It was Alan. He didn't look scared. But he sounded it.

"Roger that," Doug said.

"I'm with ya, boys," Martinetti replied. "But Ben here is off limits. If Roland thinks he can arrest him, we're all gonna go round and round."

The RV parked next to theirs and shifted a few times before the door popped open. A man stepped down the stairs and into the open. Ben squinted, but couldn't recognize him. Whoever he was, he was too tall to be Roland. "It's Chuck," Martinetti said.

Chuck was alone, and seemingly unarmed. He waved to them with both arms. He knew exactly where they were hiding. "Come out! It's okay!" he called. He put his hands on his hips and kicked the dirt a few times. "We know where you are. Don't make me yell."

"Their conning tower isn't up," Alan said. "The door's shut behind him. If they're planning something, it'll be hard to pull off."

"I see that," Martinetti said. "But Roland and his boys could be sneaking up behind us in the woods. This could all be a trick to get us out in the open."

Chuck let his hands fall and turned back to the RV to speak with someone for a moment through the door. He then headed straight for the four confederates in the woods with his hands in the air.

"All right. I got this," Martinetti said, standing up. "Stay here. All of you."

"Major Martinetti!" Chuck called as soon as he could see him. He lowered his hands. "We understand your apprehension. We have the situation under control and would like to normalize relations with you and your men before our Horseman arrives."

Martinetti put him in his PVN and approached. His rifle was down, but Alan's and Doug's weren't from their hidden positions in the woods. "What do you mean 'under control'?" he asked.

"Colonel Turk has surrendered," Chuck said. "We threatened mutiny after he shot Ryder, and he capitulated. He surrendered his weapon and deactivated his DSAK. He's going to turn himself in as soon as our new Horseman arrives."

"So it took you till now to realize that he's a lunatic?"

Chuck bit his lip in embarrassment and looked at his feet.

Martinetti stepped up to him. Taller and only slightly less muscular, he seemed evenly matched with Chuck. He got close
enough to speak directly into Chuck's ear. "I don't trust you,
Captain. If you want to normalize things, fine. But all of you will
do it out here where we can see you."

"Right away, Major."

"Roland too."

Chuck nodded and jogged back to the RV. He knocked on the
door, and in moments all four were walking in single file. Roland was third to last and had his head bowed throughout the
little march. They stopped and stood shoulder to shoulder before Martinetti at the edge of the clearing. Alan and Doug still
had them in their sights.

"Like I said before, Major, we threatened —" Chuck began.

Martinetti held up his hand and cut him off. "Just a second,
Captain," he said, and then looked at Roland. "Colonel Turk, is
this true? Do you admit guilt in the murder of Sergeant Ryder
Adams?"

Roland nodded vigorously, splattering tears all around him.

"Did you also surrender your firearm and deactivate your
DSAK?" Martinetti asked.

Roland nodded again. "You can frisk me," he said.

Martinetti stepped back and motioned for Ben to come out of
the woods and frisk him. Ben had never frisked anyone in his
life but made all the motions on Roland's body that he thought
were appropriate. He stepped back when done. "He's clean," he
said, not knowing what else to say.

"Sir, I need to inform you that the lieutenants and I are currently carrying our handguns in our back holsters," Chuck said.

"That's fine, Captain," Martinetti said, now focusing even
closer on Roland. "Colonel, why did you kill Ryder?"

Roland looked up, his face a swollen mess of tears. He took in
breath to speak but hung his head again and began bawling.
Martinetti shoulder-slumped in annoyance. He looked first to
Ben and then to Chuck twirling his finger by his temple. Roland
wiped his face and looked up again with his wide, come-rescue-
me eyes. "First, I want to say to Lieutenant Cameron, Ben, that I
forgive you for stunning me. You did the right thing. I am not a

good soldier. Michael was right when he said I lack self-control."

"What about Ryder?" Martinetti asked.

"I was so mad at you, Ben," Roland explained. "After I woke up from being stunned I was *crazy*. Everyone knows you get hysterical when you wake up from a stun. I wanted so bad to leave you behind, Ben. To punish you. So I told Ryder to go, and he wouldn't go. And I kept telling him and telling him. Why didn't he listen? I was right in front of him. I know he could hear me. So why didn't he listen?"

"And what did Ryder say to you?" Chuck prompted.

"He said no," Roland answered, hiccupping like a child through a tantrum. "No one ever says no...to me. But Major, believe me, that wasn't me. I'm not...I'm not like that! I love white people, and I killed...I killed one of theh-eh-eh-em! And I'm sorry. I'm sorry! I am so-o-o-o sorry!"

Martinetti sighed. "We'll take that into consideration, Colonel."

Chuck cleared his throat. "Sir, please also take into consideration that we submitted the Colonel to a psychiatric evaluation with our med kit. After a battery of questions and an eMRI it concluded that the Colonel suffers from an antisocial personality disorder. I don't remember the specific condition, but we have the data in the RV. The kit said that it discovered poorly developed areas of the Colonel's limbic system. That's most likely why—"

"I got it, Captain. Thank you."

"It also prescribed medication that we could easily acquire by—"

"I said I got it! Thank you."

"Yes, sir."

Roland was now in full wail, face contorted in tempestuous grief. "I just want to win! I want us to get our country ba-hah-hah-hack! I would do anything! Anyth-hih-hih-hing!"

Again, Martinetti looked to Ben and Chuck. "What am I gonna do with this guy?" he asked.

Both men shrugged just as Roland came to the abrupt finale of his wails. He gasped twice and asked, "Who are they?"

Ben, Martinetti, and Chuck looked at Roland. He was point-

ing towards the three black children who were still lying on the
ground. One of them was beginning to stir.

"Oh, them," Martinetti said, scratching his head.

"Our girls secretly brought along three black kids from the
daycare," Ben said.

"What?" Chuck said, utterly aghast. He and his men, followed by Ben, Roland, and Martinetti, approached the children
as if they were active landmines. Alan and Doug came out of the
woods, no longer pointing their rifles. The eight men surrounded the children, giving them a wide radius. Roland remained
curiously silent as he stood between Chuck and Ben.

"The hell we gonna do with them?" Colton asked.

"Kill 'em," Chuck said. He looked to Martinetti. "That's why
you brought 'em out here, right?"

Martinetti stood to his full height and regarded Chuck. He
took a moment to compose his answer. "We're not gonna do
that, Captain."

Chuck was appalled. "What? Why not?"

"Because killing unarmed children is a big deal. And if we do
it, it's gonna be done by a Horseman or a general or by someone
very high up who knows a lot more about the bigger picture
than we do."

Chuck looked to the children and back to Martinetti. "We
can't let these kids live. We don't have the resources to take care
of them!"

"My mind is made up, Captain."

"Then I will have to remind you that taking prisoners or hostages violates protocol."

"I am aware of that."

"Then why are we violating protocol?"

"Because our protocols don't tell us to murder children."

"Sir, our war is not *bellum inter milites*, or war among soldiers!" Chuck insisted, pounding his fist into his palm. "It's *bellum inter cives*. War among citizens!"

"You learn that from Michael?" Martinetti asked.

"No. The military. Remember, to blacks and Muslims, no
whites are innocent. They kill us wholesale. If we want to win
this war, we can't consider them innocent either!"

Stunned for a moment by the power and bluntness of Chuck's argument, Martinetti bit his lip and shook his head. "I sympathize, Captain. I really do. But I've made my decision."

After a moment's silence, Roland pointed a finger in the air and announced, "I have the solution!" He looked at all of them, smiling like a true-believer in mid-epiphany. "I have the solution!" he repeated and then jumped in the air.

"What is it?" Martinetti asked.

"It's so simple!" Roland said, still jumping like a five-year-old anticipating his birthday cake.

"What's so simple?"

"This! The answer!"

Martinetti grunted his exasperation. "Colonel, get to the point!"

"The point is sacrifice! The biggest sacrifice ever!"

Martinetti grimaced and nodded. "Fuck it. I've had enough of this fruitcake. Captain, tie him up. We'll wait for the Horseman in the RVs."

Roland touched Martinetti entreatingly on the arm. "No. Hear me out!" Martinetti shrunk back and lifted his rifle. He relaxed when he saw Roland touch Chuck the same way, like a prophet seeking apostles. "This makes sense! My life is over anyway, so I'll take care of it! I'll make this right!"

"How?" Martinetti asked, suddenly suspicious. He took his finger off his rifle's trigger guard and placed it on the trigger. "How will you make it right?"

"Sacrifice," Roland said through a bright, halcyon smile. "My soul will burn in Hell for eternity…so yours won't have to!"

Without taking his eyes off of Martinetti, Roland snatched the handgun from Chuck's back holster. He stepped through the fuzzy darkness towards the sleeping children. He aimed the pistol at them. But an unexpected gunshot shattered the placid night and thwarted his transcendental sacrifice.

The bullet caught him just below the heart, wobbling him like a shockwave. His bowed legs provided a stable base and kept him upright in direct defiance of the firearm's incalculable power. It took all he had to remain standing as his usable blood supply drained from his brain. His desperate breaths sounded like raspy, drawn-out sneaker squeaks on a gymnasium floor. He bit at the air like a zombie as if that would reverse the asphyxiation which was almost done killing him. He dropped his gun. He tried reaching for something, anything, to keep from falling. He knew he had to stand. Beyond all things, and up until the very end, he knew he had to stand.

A man must stand.

Roland looked at the man who had just ended his life in an instantaneous blast of deadly force. It was Ben. He was still aiming his gun at him. Roland looked hard at him as if through a thickening fog. He blinked and licked his lips and dredged up the last three or four cubic centimeters of air he had left in his lungs to whisper two words. *"Fuck you..."*

Only Ben was close enough to hear. And by the time he did, Roland's body collapsed, pulling his head down, chin in the air, in a graceless swoon. After lurching lifelessly twice, he landed on his back with his arms spread wide as if to embrace the universe. His big, innocent eyes were now staring up at the darkening heavens and witnessing their terrible judgment.

***

Despite being trained soldiers, the men had been taken completely unawares. They, quite naturally, shouted and jumped back during the five-and-a-half seconds it took for the events to transpire. In the brief lull that followed, they reassembled these events in their minds and convinced themselves they were indeed irreversible. Then Chuck, Colton, and Jackson tried to rush Ben *en masse*. Fortunately, Alan and Doug had their rifles ready and deterred them.

Martinetti pointed his finger at Chuck. "No one touches him!" he said.

"That's fucking treason, Martinetti!" Chuck shouted, voice cracking in grief and shock. He was fully enraged and waiting for an excuse, any excuse at all, to lunge at Ben.

"It was a justifiable homicide," Martinetti countered.

"It was murder!"

"No, what Colonel Turk was about to commit was murder. In any case, he was a prisoner and a murderer himself who had just stolen a firearm."

"He didn't use it, did he?"

"And we were supposed to sit around and wait until he did?"

"He was attempting to follow protocol!"

"Yes, against my orders."

"And your orders violated protocol!"

"Stand down, Captain," Martinetti warned, still keeping his preternatural cool but raising his rifle anyway.

"I'll stand down," Chuck responded. "But as soon as the Horseman arrives, he's going to know every detail of what happened!" He pointed his finger at Ben. "Roland Turk was a personal friend of mine! I'll make sure you get court-martialed!"

"You don't have the authority to talk like that, Captain," Martinetti said.

Chucked glared back at him, still pointing at Ben. "Your boy just killed a man who spent *nearly a year* at the Marion Supermax!"

Martinetti smirked. "I heard it was four weeks."

"Ten months and change. I know because I was in the courtroom when the judge handed him his sentence! That sonofabitch never broke. And I *know* what he went through would have broken anyone!"

"That's not relevant, Captain."

"Oh, no? If not for him, the Sterling compound would have gone down like the one in Wahoo!"

Martinetti straightened his posture as if stretching out kinks. His smirk disappeared. "What Sterling compound?"

"Sterling, Colorado! The secret headquarters and last stronghold of the American White Nationalist Movement! Like most of our Horsemen, Turk and I were White Nationals. After Wahoo we were able to escape with our data and our tech and weapons and take the war underground because Roland Turk kept his mouth shut when it mattered! So, yeah! I think I have the authority! As soon as our new Horseman finds out what happened…" Chuck shifted a vindictive look at Ben and hissed, "…you'll fry!"

Ben felt his insides churn, but he stood firm. He knew that

despite Roland Turk's past heroics, the man had at some point lost his mind and become an outright liability to the movement. In the space of a day, he had murdered one innocent soldier and another, a high-ranking officer, who may or may not have been innocent. Ben mourned that very possibility—and his role in bringing it to be—while giving up on a brute force algorithm which could calculate the grievous loss an innocent Michael Archer would have meant for the revolution. Still, he had faith in the righteousness of his position. He knew he could defend his actions. And with Martinetti still standing before Chuck and not willing to concede the point, he knew Martinetti would too. But would that be enough? With radio silence between bases, Eli would not able to vouch for him unless a Horseman interceded, which very well might not happen. And aside from Martinetti and Eli he had no one. Fear began to creep through his body like a cancer.

Rumblings of two large vehicles silenced the men. Suddenly they were on the same side again. They retreated from the clearing and knelt down in the grass. They saw two muscle trucks park by the RVs. "They could be cops," Martinetti said.

"Or this could be our Horseman," Chuck said. "Do you know how they'll initiate contact?"

"No. Do you?"

"No."

"Well, Captain," Martinetti said. "I order you to walk up there and introduce yourself. And take your boys along with you."

Chuck shrank away. "But you said they could be cops."

"They probably aren't. Since when do cops drive around in muscle trucks? Just walk out there slow, Captain. You'll be fine."

"You sure about that?"

"No," Martinetti said with his trademark smirk.

Chuck obeyed the order with sullen hostility, and motioned for Colton and Jackson to follow him into the clearing. After they had gone, Martinetti said to Alan and Doug, "You guys, too."

Alan looked to Doug and then to Martinetti. "But you said—"

Martinetti stood and interrupted him. "It's all right. They're not cops."

"How do you know?" Doug asked.

"The brand of tire. We use a special Chinese brand. It's identical to an American product. But you can tell the difference if you really know what to look for."

Alan and Doug looked at each other. "Why didn't you tell the Captain that, sir?" Doug asked.

Martinetti winked. "I wanted to him sweat a little. Now go. We'll come out in a minute."

"Yes, sir," the men said and stepped out into the clearing. By this point, Chuck was nearly a third of the way to the muscle trucks. Someone was lowering one of their windows.

Martinetti turned swiftly, picked up his gear, and shoved it into Ben's chest. It was a Desert Storm-era, military-issue backpack. It contained everything a soldier could need on an agitation raid. Apparition suit, anaerobe, suicide vest, med kit, bombs, weapons, money, food. It weighed over forty pounds and made the wearer a very dangerous person. "Get out of here," Martinetti said. "Run."

Ben took the bag. "Really?"

"Yeah. There's a road about half a mile northeast of here. Take it north to Danville Parkway. After that, go wherever." Martinetti hung his night-specs on Ben's collar and started leading him briskly away from the clearing and deeper into the woods. The thickening night made the wood seem like a jungle. Only their breathing and footsteps disturbed the air.

"Won't they come after me?" Ben asked.

"Not if I have a say. And I will have a say. Chuck's not the only one who knew Roland Turk."

"You sure this is the only way?"

"Until Chuck cools down, yes. If you walk out there now they'll arrest you and probably execute you within twenty-four hours. I'm gonna need time to get a hold of Eli to corroborate your end. And after blowing up those choppers and this whole war going out into the fucking open who the hell knows how long that'll take?"

Ben hung his head and sighed. "I'm sorry. I messed up, didn't I?"

"No. You saved us all. This is the least I can do for ya." Martinetti pressed Ben forward even faster with his hand on his back. Ben had to start jogging to keep from falling forward.

"What about you?" Ben objected. "They could execute you, Mart."

"So what? I'm already dead, remember?"

Ben stopped and turned. "What?"

"Look, I'll get in trouble, but I'm a Major. It's much harder to do to me what they're gonna do to you if you stick around."

"You'll take care of those kids, right?"

"Yeah."

"I mean it, Mart," he said. It was an uneasy warning. With all that was happening, Ben knew he couldn't spare any more worry for those children. He had to rely entirely on Martinetti. "Keep 'em safe, and find a way to send them back to their families. I'm sure Sharon knows how to find them." Ben felt a warm tingle in his head as he realized that he at last remembered Sharon's name. The sensation vanished as he pondered the aching gulf he knew now existed between them. He would probably never see her again.

"Don't worry. I got it," Martinetti reassured him. That was all Ben needed to hear. Standing in a tiny oasis of air and grass, they were ambushed by insects, serenaded by the breeze. Ben turned towards Martinetti to acknowledge their parting somehow. Martinetti's face was little more than a silhouette over a purple, starless sky. A faceless friend, a moving bruise, a lurid, fleeting vision unexposed by the light of day.

The day. Ben considered the exhilaration of being a creature of the day once again. His insides suddenly twisted over what he was leaving behind, his eyelids soaking in tears. "All right," he said, offering Martinetti his hand. "Thank you, Mart."

Martinetti didn't take it. Instead, he moved close and whispered, "We're gonna call on you one day real soon. And when we do, you will come. I'm trusting you on this."

"Yes, sir."

Martinetti jammed his finger into Ben's chest. "And don't fucking grow a vagina on me and start blabbing about us. Understand?"

Ben smiled and watched as a thin, defiant smirk grew on

Martinetti's face. It was a comforting sight, and Ben was unspeakably grateful for it. "Never," he said, and then turned and disappeared into the woods.

***

Minutes later, he flagged down an old pickup truck on Sulphur Springs Road and offered the driver $200 to take him fifty-five miles to Louisville on the Indiana State line. The driver's wife said they could take him ten miles north to Springfield for $100, if he didn't mind climbing into the truck's bed and sharing it with half a dozen washing machines, that is. The driver said that he and the Missus ran a side business repairing and selling used washers and would lop fifty dollars off the price of the ride if he could help them deliver two to a motel up near Springfield. They were supposed to be there before sundown, but got tied up with a customer near Bradfordsville. Ben took them up on their offer and eagerly shook the man's hand. With barely any room to move between the washers in the truck's bed and with nothing to hold on to, Ben rocked violently with every bump and turn of their northward journey. He smiled. It was the smoothest ride he ever had.

Part 6: Muncie

Chapter 48

In volume five of *The Arabian Nights*, a Persian Prince named Kamar al-Akmar rescues a beautiful princess on the back of flying horse. What enabled the horse to fly?

A. the merciful will of Allah
B. the sinister magic of wizards
C. the graceful wings of the horse
D. the creative genius of Man (correct)

The Sun had risen well above the tree line by the time Ben witnessed Son Mensah arrive for work. It was nine seventeen in the morning. Still late, but early enough for Ben to suspect that something had drastically changed at BTC since his departure.

Son turned into the lot in his late model BMW and was forced to park in the back since the spaces close to the street had already been taken. He opened his door and hung an enormous foot out of his car as he rummaged through his car for something. His sandal dangled from his toes and then fell, revealing the stark contrast between his ivory-white sole and the dark brown of his ankle and leg.

He exited the car rear-end first and re-shod his foot. Holding a large black binder stuffed with papers, he closed the car door with his elbow. Ben noticed Son's dress—pressed tan slacks and a white collared button-down, which he attempted to tuck in *while walking to the office.* It was as if he were in a hurry. Ben could not imagine Son Mensah being in a hurry for anything. Now he knew that something must have changed at BTC. Ben also noticed that Son had lost weight. The slimmer body suited him.

Ben had stood in front of the building adjacent to the BTC offices since eight-thirty that morning, panhandling with other homeless types, nearly all of whom were black. Yellow lines painted on either side of a twenty-yard stretch of sidewalk demarcated the city's PCZ for this area. PCZ stood for Public Charity Zone, and duly licensed homeless individuals were entitled to panhandle there from eight until twelve in the morning and then from one until five in the afternoon after being allotted their hour-long, state-provided lunch and political action empowerment seminar. Ben had received his license that morning at the downtown homeless shelter shortly after he arrived in Muncie. The competition in the PCZ had been cutthroat. He had witnessed a fight among three men and two among women. And the people would not stop babbling and bickering in their predictable way. Ben was relieved beyond words to escape and join Son in the BTC parking lot. In his forty-seven minutes on the street he had collected eighty cents.

"Hi, Son!" he called.

Son had just crossed the street and stopped to size up this strange black man rushing to meet him. He had a lean, athletic build, a squashed nose, sunglasses, a dark green T-shirt, black pants, baseball cap, and heavy boots. He carried a full military pack over his shoulders. Son was not intimidated by such a presence but he did take a step back. "Do I know you?" he asked.

Ben stopped in front of him, removed his sunglasses, and smiled. "Yes, you do," he said. "I'm Ben Cameron."

Son looked sharply at the office and back at Ben, clearly refusing to believe what he had just heard. "Who are you?" he asked, doing a passable job of appearing nonplussed.

Ben smiled. "I'm Ben. We used to work together at BTC. Remember? We went to Little Rock last year. I helped you with your science items."

Son's hands rushed to his mouth as he finally recognized Ben through his African body mask. "Ben!" he exclaimed.

Ben held out a hand as a conciliatory gesture. "I know what you're thinking. I had a medical procedure done to change my appearance."

Son's head seemed to vibrate as if he were being shaken by a gentle tremor. "I must say, Ben, I am shocked to see you!" he said. He remembered to shake Ben's hand and did so firmly.

"How are things with you?" Ben asked.

"Oh, it is not good, Ben!" Son lamented. "We miss you here. We don't have the manpower for our work. We hired a woman to be in charge of item writing, but she's quitting. It's the second person we have hired for the job. New Jersey third and eighth grade are in trouble. New Mexico high school, we still have no one assigned. The GED people are mad at us. Even Arkansas science—"

"Arkansas?" Ben exclaimed. "Arkansas's easy! When I—"

"Ben," Son interrupted. "You have been gone a long time. Arkansas signed a new contract with new specs. They want twice the items now. They are very picky as well."

Ben nodded as a show of solidarity with his former colleague and then said, "Well, that's why I'm here. I'm hoping to write items again. Is there any way you can let me in as a guest and take me up to see Nigel?"

Son raised his chin about an inch. "Did Nigel fire you for visiting unauthorized websites?"

"Yes, he did."

"Am I to understand that these were racist websites?"

"Some were," Ben explained. "But my brother was visiting me that weekend. *He* visited those sites, and I didn't want to rat him out."

It took him a moment, but Son nodded. "Come," he said, leading Ben to the BTC steps. "We really could use you again."

"Thanks, Son."

"Did you know that Nigel was promoted to Vice President last month?"

"No way."

"He now leads all the testing projects."

"Huh. That's the job I wanted."

"Yes, well, it is giving him a heart attack," Son said as he opened the door for Ben. "Maybe the heart attack you give him will make him forget his first heart attack."

Ben laughed and looked around the tiny BTC lobby as Son reviewed the holographic instructions to request access for a guest. Ben linked his brand new personal device to the BTC sapserv for recognition. He was now Myles Percival Morphy, former resident of Jamaica who had just recently achieved U.S. citizenship and state residency through the Muncie downtown homeless shelter. He had a social security number, digital passport, and official state identification card right in his forearm. His occupation was listed as 'Scholar and minister of the Rastafari religion, Mendicant.'

Ben was still marveling at how Roland had actually come through for him with this new identity. Roland had never told anyone; he just did it. Ben hadn't caught on until he was almost out of Kentucky. This new identity enabled him to purchase a personal device and acquire a zero-income minority-borrower credit card from the federal government. At a restaurant in Louisville he ordered a submarine sandwich, an ice cream sundae, and a beer. He withdrew $10,000 cash, hailed a taxi, and made it to Muncie by morning. *Black Like Me Too*, huh? Ben smiled. Not a bad idea at all.

They were buzzed in, and Son led Ben through the familiar BTC hallway. Ben felt a twinge of discomfort given that that the last time he graced these halls he had been running for his life on a sprained ankle. As they passed the doors to the R&D department, he knew that Ariya was behind them, most likely barking commands in Farsi to her relatives or listening to one of her bodice-ripper e-books while writing items. He sighed like a schoolboy thinking about her and couldn't wait to surprise her once his interview with Nigel was over. Would she accept him with his new look? He had done some research on Eclumenicib while in transit across Indiana and learned that it could possibly restore him to his former pigmentation. His lips and nose would require plastic surgery in either case.

Nigel's office was now on the second floor where most of the BTC brass worked. Ben's breathing began to escalate as they approached his door, but the butterflies scattered when he reminded himself that he had been in situations far worse than this. With his new credentials as a numinous Negro, Ben figured the worst Nigel could do was tell him to go away.

Nigel's new office was even smaller than his last one. A motel-quality love seat stood to the left along with a cheap, wooden coffee table and a bookshelf filled with stuffed animals and internationalist tchotchkes. A little palace guardsman teddy bear waved the flag of England. Two reclinable chairs sat before his desk.

Nigel had his back to the door and remained that way after he bid them enter. Leaning heavily on his desk with his elbows, he was massaging his temples and applying the utmost focus on his work which glowed blue from the devices projecting all around him. He seemed thinner than before. Still, his garishly striped polo shirt clung to his body in all the wrong ways. Ben considered Nigel Polite to have the worst fashion sense of all gay men on the planet.

"Nigel, excuse me," Son began. He didn't know what else to say, so he placed his palms together and waited for his boss to face him. Nigel rubbed his eyes as if kneading dough and then spun around in his chair. It took him a few seconds to focus on whom Son had brought with him. Bags under his eyes looked almost like bruises, and his cheeks were insect-bite red. Nigel looked from one man to the other as if following a tennis match.

"Hello, Son," he said. "And whom do we have here?" He

posed this question directly to Ben. He appeared tired and sounded like it. He leaned back in his squeaky seat, folded his hands, and awaited a response.

Son looked at Ben as if for instructions, but Ben was not about to provide him any. Was he Myles Morphy or Zhenglong Hu? Or was he Ben Cameron for that matter? Was he an item writer or quantum gamer? A civilian, soldier, or spy? Ben smiled as he watched Son stammer through an introduction and then attempt to laugh off his embarrassment. Ben came to his relief by putting his hand on his shoulder. "Why don't you leave us, Son. Thanks."

"Of course," Son said, grateful for the interruption. "Good to see you both." With a wide wave, Son left the office and shut the door behind him.

Nigel sprang forward in his seat as if in an automobile coming to a hard stop. He practically slapped his desk with his forearms. "Who the hell are you?" he demanded.

Ben sat down, crossed his legs, and smiled wide. "You don't recognize me, Nigel?" he said. He discreetly established a PVN in case their conversation could be heard through the walls.

Nigel clamped his mouth shut as he studied Ben's imitation face. He came to the correct realization after four or five seconds but still couldn't believe it. In a genuine fight-or-flight response, he tucked in his chin and revealed hints of ligaments deeply submerged in neck fat. "Ben!" he whispered. It was more like a hiss, and it came through his teeth.

"Actually, my name is Myles P. Morphy now," Ben said, still with the smart-aleck grin. "From Jamaica, mon."

"What are you doing here?" Nigel growled.

"I'm here to give you the opportunity to hire me as an independent item writer," Ben said like a salesman.

"Get out," Nigel ordered. "I fired you once. I won't do it again."

Ben pointed his finger in the air. "No. You fired Ben Cameron, a white guy from San Diego. I'm a black guy from Jamaica. Myles P. Morphy, at your service."

Nigel stood and stepped around his desk with the obvious purpose of grabbing Ben by the collar and hauling him out of his

office. "I don't care what your name is or what medical procedure you've had. You will not—"

"Stop!" Ben commanded, pointing at Nigel. He uncrossed his
legs and stood, knowing that his experience and training would
give him a deep well of confidence before his fleshy former boss.
This confidence must have translated into intimidation since Nigel curtailed his trip to Ben's collar and reflexively stood there,
waiting for Ben to say something. "I'm here for a job," Ben said.
"And you will hire me."

"How dare you!"

"Is it daring? Yes, I would say it is. But forget that. The more
important question is whether you need me."

"I will determine what is important, Ben, or whoever you
are."

"Do you have items that need writing?" Ben asked. "Is there
a jam I can help you out of? Can Benchmark Testing use a man
of my talents and experience? I don't know how many different
ways I can ask this question."

"No," Nigel answered stiffly. "You are a white supremacist
who used a company device to visit white supremacy brood
sites. You are lucky I didn't report you to the FBI."

"But I was innocent. I didn't do any of that."

"I gave you a chance to keep your job. You should have taken
it."

"You gave me a chance to apologize for something I didn't
do. There was no presumption of innocence. I was just guilty of
being white, male, and Right-wing."

"I thought you were a libertarian."

"I've changed."

"Well, regardless, your device didn't go to those brood sites
by itself."

"It was my brother."

"What?"

"He was visiting for the weekend. He asked if he could surf
on my device. I said yes. That was it."

"Then why didn't you say so?" Nigel challenged.

"Because I'm not a rat!" Ben shot back. "I didn't know what
sites my brother went to. But I did know that if I gave him up to

you, you'd be obligated to report him to the FBI no matter where he'd been. Whereas I didn't think you would do anything to me...except fire me."

Nigel folded his arms. "Well, if you're not a rat, why are you ratting?"

"Because my brother died in a car crash," Ben said hotly. "Is that a good enough reason?"

Nigel sighed and hung his head. "Look, Ben. We are really busy here."

"Yes, you are! And why is that? It's because *you need me*. Just like you did in Little Rock. I *saved* this company, Nigel! And you know it!"

"We already have a lead content specialist."

"Yeah. She's quitting. Son told me."

Nigel cleared his throat. "That's not been finalized."

"Uh-huh. How's that working out for ya? Is she good? Don't answer because I already know. Son told me all the projects that are bombing. Arkansas? *Really*? When I was here I had them eating out of my hand!"

Nigel scrunched up his face and looked hard at Ben. "Why are you black?"

"You blackballed me, Nigel!" Ben said. "You said I was radioactive. The only way for me to get back into this industry and have a career again is to change my identity. And would you rather I *not* come back to BTC? I'm sure with my qualifications and skin color, ETS or Pearson would snatch me up in a heartbeat!" Ben knew that if Nigel acquiesced now, all was good. On the other hand, if Nigel kept up the third degree then Ben would be forced to stray closer to deception—if not lie outright—to keep his story plausible. Up till then he had stayed in the warm, fuzzy glow of the truth.

Nigel brushed aside the hair that was falling in his eyes but otherwise did not change his expression for what seemed like half a minute. Ben was heartened because he knew Nigel was at last taking his offer seriously. Nigel turned and shuffled through the spreadsheets and documents surrounding his desk, looking for something. "Is all your paperwork in order?" he asked.

"Yes."

"We'll do a background check."

"Of course."

"If anyone recognizes you here, I shan't be able to help you," Nigel warned.

"I'll work remotely. I will never set foot in this office again."

"Do you have a résumé?"

"I uploaded it to your sap-serv this morning. Filled out the application form too."

"Right. I'm looking for a few other documents you'll need. Is your net address on your résumé?"

"Yes."

"Okay. I'll send them to you."

"Thanks."

"I found your résumé," Nigel said, stopping his search. He pushed the document between them and paged through it. "Interesting. Do they really have a testing industry in Jamaica?"

Ben smiled. "I have no idea."

Nigel smiled back. It was his first one. "Of course. Why am I asking you?" He closed the document and turned back to Ben. "Ben, I cannot—"

"Don't call me Ben."

"Yes, ah, what is your name again?"

"Myles P. Morphy."

"Mr. Morphy, my one stipulation in rehiring you is that I cannot have you visiting unauthorized sites like that again. I will report you to the FBI and the Department of Homeland Security if you ever—"

"I got it, Nigel. I understand."

"Good."

"And here's *my* stipulation."

"What?"

"$50 an item."

Nigel blanched. "*What?*"

"Do you want me to fix your problems or not?"

"That's outrageous! The industry standard is only thirty!"

Ben folded his arms like an Indian chief. "I know what I'm worth."

Nigel pressed his lips together and seethed. "Thirty-five," he countered. Ben's shifted his glance and said nothing. "Okay. Forty," Nigel offered. Ben hardened his look and tortured Nigel with his silence. Nigel scowled at Ben and squirmed as if he had an unscratchable itch on his bottom. "Fine. You win. Fifty," he grumbled. "St. Clair's going to kill me."

They shook hands.

"And another thing," Ben said. "No more calling me the bottom of the barrel. *Nobody* calls me that."

"Did I say that to you? Oh, I did. Didn't I?"

"Yes, you did."

"But I didn't mean it literally. I was just trying to explain—"

"I don't care," Ben interrupted. "It was racist. It was offensive. And I'm not gonna tolerate it. This is the game you want to play? Fine. I'll play. But you have to play too. How would you like it if someone said you were the bottom of the barrel because you're gay?"

"Fair enough. I apologize."

"Good."

"I really did not mean to offend you, Ben."

"Myles."

"Myles."

"It's okay."

"Right." Nigel pointed his finger at Ben. "And no racist talk from you either. That's just as bad as visiting brood sites."

"Why are you concerned about that?" Ben asked. "I'll be working remotely."

"Because I am going to see if I can give you a management role as well." Nigel noticed Ben's look of surprise. "Don't worry. It won't impact your work load."

"Then why?"

"Because we need more minority managers," Nigel said through a forced, nervous laugh. "I believe you already know why."

Ben raised his chin and lowered it slowly. "Got some people you need fired, huh?"

"Yes."

"August Little?" Ben asked hopefully.

"Actually, August resigned several months ago, which is

good news for you. He now works for the Indiana chapter of the Equal Employment Opportunity Commission."

"That is more up his alley, isn't it?" Ben said. "How about that ugly shit Jamal?"

Nigel's face twisted in weary disgust. "Oh, he's a useless cunt."

"So you approve?"

"Sure. We started the process months ago, but with you we can speed things along. And save us some expense."

"I think we need to let Son go too, unfortunately," Ben added. "He's a nice guy, but—"

Nigel lifted one leg off the floor and sat on his desk. "I cannot fire him."

Ben jerked his head back an inch. "Why not? He's a fraud."

"No, he's not," Nigel said. "Well, not anymore. About four months ago we began a gentle approach of dismissing him. We couldn't fire him outright for obvious reasons, but as managers we could harass him until he decided to quit. It's a common technique. You put an employee on a tight re-training program and you micromanage him like a nagging wife until the poor tosser takes the hint."

Ben smiled. "Only Son didn't take the hint."

"He actually improved. The bloke put in the work and officially passed his re-training."

"That's great news," Ben said, genuinely pleased.

"Of course, he's still slow, and he doesn't know his onions like you. But at least now he's reliable. You ask him for forty reasonably challenging multiple-choice items and give him a week and that's what you'll get."

"A week? That's a long time for forty items."

"His acceptance rate in committee is better than yours." Ben fell back in his seat and made it squeak. Nigel shot him a wink and a goofy grin. "Well, almost better than yours."

Ben laughed and spun in his chair. "Did you miss me?" he asked.

"Absobloodylootely," Nigel said with a little shake of his head. "Although I didn't miss looking at your ugly chevy. And now it's come back even uglier."

"Yeah, well, it's an interesting story," Ben said, stroking his face.

Nigel covered his ears. "I don't wanna know! I don't wanna know! You probably broke the fucking law to arrange your face like that."

Ben smiled. "Nigel, you do not know the half of it."

"Gooooood!" Nigel exclaimed. "The less I know, the better. Now go home. Enjoy a three-day weekend. We'll start you on Monday. And don't forget the paperwork I sent you." Ben stood and they shook hands. "And welcome back!" Nigel said.

"Thanks. But before I go, I'm gonna say hi to Ariya. She's still in her old cube, right?" He felt the familiar tightening in his gut when he noticed Nigel's expression begin to sink. A defense mechanism against bad news, it was doubly crushing now that he had escaped the bunkers of a secret war. He was finally free, wasn't he? Nigel's plummeting discomfiture was telling him that no, he was not free at all.

"Oh, that's right," Nigel said. "You weren't here when it happened."

Ben's mind began to rattle considering all the bad things that could have 'happened' to Ariya during his absence. Like with a salad bar in Hell there were just too many ways to go wrong. Car crash. Breast cancer. Heart disease. Aneurysm. Mugging. Suicide? Pregnancy complications? Found out for her infidelities, beaten by her thuggish relatives, and then spirited back to Iran with full support of the U.S. government to face trial for adultery and the very real possibility of public execution? Ben knew that this last circumstance required the least amount of bad luck. It was also the only one that had had all the necessary parameters in place before he left Muncie. And he'd been gone a whole year. "What happened?" he asked, his fear beginning to curdle into anger.

Nigel's eyes opened wide with concern. "I don't know. She disappeared."

"*What?*"

"She just stopped coming into work."

"When!"

"A month ago. I can give you her last day. We called, we

wrote. There was no sign of her. It's one of the reasons we're in such a bind with New Mexico. When we lost her, we lost all of her item writers as well."

Ben began breathing rapidly and loudly though his nose. He remembered Son telling him that New Mexico was still without a lead. Why hadn't he inferred that that meant Ariya was gone?

"We notified the police," Nigel went on. "But they said there was nothing they could do. Their house was up for sale. Their real estate agent and their attorney said that she and her husband had simply left town. And you know how skittish authorities are about getting involved in marital issues...you know...among Muslims."

Ben remained silent. He was reverting into a soldier again, sharp, ready, lethal. Where some animals shed their skin, he was growing his back, skin that would defend against anything and never be shed again. He had been naïve to believe that his old life could ever be restored to him. This was war. Complete, total war. *Nothing* would ever be the same again. *He* would never be the same again. Embrace the race indeed. He resolved then and there to make it his life's purpose to grant Officer Charles Pendergast his ardent wish and then go to sleep with pleasant dreams one way or the other.

"Ben? Are you okay?" Nigel asked. "Answer me. Are you okay?"

Chapter 49

From 1450 to 1800 AD, approximately how many white Europeans were abducted by Barbary pirates or Crimean Tatars and sold into slavery throughout the Ottoman Empire and the Muslim world?

A. between 10,000 and 20,000
B. between 60,000 and 70,000
C. between 90,000 and 100,000
D. between 2.75 million and 3.75 million (correct)

Ben was grateful to Martinetti for many things, but most of all for giving him his agitation gear. It made possible the important things he was about to do. Immediately after parting with Nigel that morning, he searched the internet for any news item involving abducted Iranian women in Muncie and found nothing. He then ran the two-and-a-half miles to the Spice and Kabob restaurant to find the only person he knew who could possibly tell him Ariya's whereabouts: her old adversary Hassan Moammar Khan, the bulbous bullhorn bleater with the Abe Lincoln beard. Ben understood that such information would never be given up lightly to an infidel. He would have to strike when Mr. Khan would be most vulnerable, in his home in the middle of the night, and then mercilessly pry it out of him. Accosting him during work hours would be too risky given the witness potential of a city like Muncie. Ben considered and then rejected lying in wait inside the mosque where Mr. Khan held frequent rendezvous with his young protégées. That would take too long, and, in any event, he was sure the mosque had beefed up its security and photo-crystal systems thanks to Isaac's non-bomb from the previous summer.

Ben waited until the dinner rush to put tiny homing devices on all the cars in the S&K back lot where the employees parked. His plan was to wait until the restaurant closed and then keep a keen lookout with his night-specs as employees drove out of the lot. As soon as he could spot Hassan in his car, he would know which homing signal to follow. The flat, asphalt landscape surrounding the S&K however made holing up like a sniper too risky. It was as if the people in Muncie didn't believe in trees, he thought. Or at least not in peppering their city with little patches of swampland where men could hunt ducks all day and not be noticed. His ideal perch would have been within the thick yellow lines of a PCZ, like it had been that morning at Benchmark Testing. But the nearest PCZ was a half mile away, and panhandling was strictly forbidden after five in Muncie anyway.

To avoid suspicion, Ben made sure to float from one neighboring establishment to the next while maintaining a continuous bead on the S&K. He hopped from a café, to a bookstore, to a fast food restaurant, and ultimately to a laundromat, which he needed to visit anyway. He had even tried pretending to wait at a nearby bus stop which was catty-corner to the restaurant. This bought him forty-five minutes until a police officer drove up and politely informed him that the last bus for the day had come and gone over two hours ago.

Ben began tweaking his plan when, by ten-thirty that evening, only one car, a well-kept Mercedes, still remained in the lot. Ben deduced that it belonged to Hassan. Ben had not seen the restauranteur leave and, except for two in-and-out bathroom breaks, had maintained an admirably uninterrupted view of the S&K's parking lot the entire evening. Ben knew the restaurant closed at ten and suspected Hassan was working late, catching up on paperwork and whatnot as restaurant owners are wont to do. Ben figured that striking now would serve the dual purpose of catching Hassan while he was vulnerable and sparing himself the effort of breaking into the man's home and subduing his terrified wife and children. Who knew how difficult that would be?

Ben needed the apparition suit if he wished to confront Hassan in the restaurant and spent ten minutes sitting in the laundromat worrying about how he could put it on without anyone seeing. And how could he cross the street looking like a B-movie space robot without calling attention to himself? The area surrounding the S&K was well lit and exposed to considerable automobile and pedestrian traffic. Apparition suits were best used in unlit areas when trying to avoid surveillance from above. Ben also knew that the suit's spherical invisibility was unreliable, and he had no way of determining how quickly the battery would drain.

He needed a disguise to help him cross the street. Either that, or he would have to hope that neither witnesses nor photocrystal could identify him the day after the owner of the Spice and Kabob restaurant disappeared under mysterious circumstances. After wringing whatever information he needed from Hassan, Ben had every intention of killing him and cooking his pork-free corpse in an anaerobe. Not only was the man an obnoxious demagogue and pederast, he was also, in essence, the enemy, the very person who would benefit most if America were to bend its knee to Islam. If Ben *didn't* kill him, he had no doubt that Hassan would tip off Ariya's husband—or whatever Y-chromosomed reprobate that now owned her—that someone in a super villain suit was out to rescue her. So letting him live was not an option. Ben's utter lack of scruples in this matter lent him a certain martial clarity which, combined with adrenaline, made him feel like a perpetual motion machine.

As Ben sat back in his chair to allow an obese man and his hamper squeeze past, he knew he had his answer: snatch an extra-large shirt from one of the dryers, abscond with it to the bathroom, snap his pack in front, and then don the shirt. Instant fat man. Ben knew the plan was weak. He also knew it was better than no plan at all. He immediately took to checking the dyers, pretending to be looking for his own clothes. Fortunately for him the laundromat was nearly empty. He found what he needed in under two minutes.

Ben held up traffic as he shambled across the street in his recently purloined, golden yellow, extra-extra-large, Moroccan muumuu. It was elaborately embroidered at the chest and reeked of marijuana and body odor despite its recent washing. He had also filched a brightly-colored wool Rasta cap. Why be a minister of Jah if you can't look like a minister of Jah? Of course, Ben didn't want to overdo it with the theatrics and risk getting questioned by a police officer again. On the other hand, he understood the risk of being too quick. Should his little murder go swimmingly, he wanted to give the citizens of Muncie plenty to remember about suspicious overweight Rasta dudes hanging around the Spice and Kabob on the night the Bulbous Bullhorn Bleater got what was coming to him. Ben was banking on Eclumenicib, plastic surgery, and an extended stay in a sunlight-deprived arctic environment to eventually clear him of all wrongdoing should the authorities ever decide to look his way. Of course, he would indulge in such a luxury only after finding Ariya.

Ben nearly stopped on his heels when he reached the parking lot behind the restaurant. Three cars, not one, now occupied spaces there. The new ones were older model Japanese cars and not as well kept as Hassan's. Ben noticed that all lights in the building were off except for one shining dimly though a long, shuttered window on the second floor, the very room in which he'd met Ariya a year ago. He began to suspect there was more going on at the S&K than mere paperwork. Using his muumuu as a glove, he turned the knob of the back door. It was unlocked. Ben couldn't believe the arrogance of these people. They think they can come here and commit their heinous crimes practically out in the open as if we're already a conquered people. They make themselves quite at home in our part of the world, don't they?

He donned his apparition suit in the men's room and took a brief look in the mirror; in his black, bulky armor and flat, eyeless helmet he was a fearsome sight indeed. In seconds, he found himself at the foot of the stairs. He remembered that the pass code Ariya had given him for the portcullis lock contained a Persian name beginning with Q. It was the name of the man who had taken her bike riding through the butterfly forest on that horrible night years ago. But he couldn't remember the full name. A search on his personal device for Persian boy names beginning with Q refreshed his memory however. Qubad. In proper- not upper-case. Ben was willing to bet that Hassan Moammar Khan hadn't bothered to deactivate Ariya's pass code. His first try didn't work. But his second, Qubad1 followed by pound, did. Ben sneered in victory as the heavy door slid open for him.

Seeing the narrow stairwell, he remembered how the steps squeaked the last time he climbed them, so he activated his PVN to ensure a silent ascent. Just as he reached the hall he could hear a bed squeaking up ahead and the grunts and moans of men. The last door on the right was ajar. Ben shuddered as he imagined what was going on in there and anticipated the satisfaction he was going to feel when erasing such abominable people from the lists of the living. He drew his pistol just outside the door.

He kicked it open for maximum shock.

He noticed immediately that the full-sized bed and box frame was still there. He saw three naked bodies on it, two hairy and large and one hairless and not large. Ben's expanded peripheral vision told him someone was rushing him from his left. Someone big, bigger than Hassan. Ben raised his gun and pumped two bullets into the man's chest before even registering what he looked like. He didn't care. He stepped towards the bed and stunned all three members of the ménage à trois. He turned back to his left. Hassan, as naked as the rest of them except for a couple ostentatious gold chains around his neck, was seated in an upholstered rocking chair, apparently too dumbfounded to move. He still had his Abe Lincoln beard, but his soft, pudgy body was hairless as a boy's. A slender, long-haired Arab boy with peach fuzz under his nose had just climbed off of him and, with a high-pitched wail, bolted from the room. Ben followed him into the hall and stunned him before he could run three paces. In accordance with his training, Ben had kept his head turned in such a way that he never lost sight of the doorway behind him. Hassan stepped through it with a gun, but Ben had a bead on him with his before Hassan could raise it. Ben yanked the unconscious boy back by the hair until his gun was practically in Hassan's mouth. Hassan dropped his weapon and immediately began pleading for his life. Ben chuckled quietly, wondering if this stupid degenerate really entertained hope that he wouldn't kill him.

Ben shoved him back the in the room where the man seemed to lose all the starch in his legs. He fell onto the floor within kissing range of his freshly killed colleague. That got him back to his feet. Ben dragged the boy inside, shut the door, and locked it. Hassan began babbling in Urdu as he beseeched Ben to spare his life. Ben shut him up by punching him in the nose. It wasn't a hard shot because he wanted to keep the man conscious for the time being. Hassan sank to his knees anyway and commenced abject supplication at Ben's feet.

"Up. Up!" Ben commanded. The man obeyed, sniffing and wiping his now-runny nose. "Sit," Ben said, pointing to the rocking chair. The man fell into it, now realizing that his tormentor spoke English.

"Sir, I implore you to let me live," he said, eyes moistening. He used the King's English with impeccable clarity, and, even in duress, his voice had the pleasing, full-bodied tone of a natural orator. Even more extraordinary was the shamelessness with which he ignored the fact that he just been caught *in flagrante delicto* gang-debauching two pre-pubescent boys, the bodies of whom were now lying mere feet away on the floor.

"I am a law-abiding business man and restauranteur," he elaborated. "I have a wholesome, all-American family of six who are building the American dream as hard-working immigrants. I give routinely to numerous charities in the greater Muncie community. Furthermore, I am quite certain I can direct my accountant to deliver to you, my friend, a sizable donation—"

With his right hand, Ben tweaked the man's injured nose as if turning on a gas range. Hassan squeaked and shouted in pain. "Where is Ariya?" Ben asked.

"I-I beg your pardon, sir," he said. "Please do not hit me. Perhaps you have me mistaken for—"

Ben tweaked his nose again, this time to the breaking point. Hassan stamped his feet and smacked Ben's forearms a few times to make him stop. "Where is Ariya?" Ben asked him again. "Ariya Mohammadi."

"I swear to you, sir," Hassan attested with vigorous head shakes. "I do not know who that person is."

Ben holstered his gun and pinned the man's neck down with his left hand until the back of the chair struck the wall. With his right, he twisted his nose again, this time using leverage from his hips and shoulders to generate fearsome pressure. Feeling the cartilage fracturing beneath his fingers sent a euphoric rush through his brain. Hassan screamed throughout the tortuous ordeal and cradled his mangled proboscis in his hands the moment Ben let it go. Blood and snot leaked through his fingers, encrusting his beard.

"Do you know who Ariya Mohammadi is?" Ben asked.

The man was about to answer in the same fashion as before, but Ben silenced him by squeezing his neck and cocking his fist behind his ear. Ben loosened his hold just enough to let him answer.

"I do," he affirmed, voiced thinned by his injuries. "I do know of her."

"Where is she?"

"I swear to you, sir. I do not—"

Ben interrupted him with five consecutive punches to his nose. They were straight, hard shots, and the back of the rocking chair slammed into the wall with each one. It left a foot-long divot in the drywall.

"Where is she!" Ben demanded. He almost wanted Hassan to continue stonewalling because it would allow him to intensify the torture: breaking bones, chopping off fingers, flaying skin, castrating, mutilating. He briefly regretted wearing a helmet since it kept him from biting his face off like a bird of prey. In the presence of such evil, Ben saw himself becoming evil as well. It thrilled him but frightened him more. Only the thought of Ariya, innocent victim that she was, kept wrenching him away from the temptation.

But why? Why did the thought of this woman inspire him? Ben felt this question flash by as he waited for Hassan Moammar Khan to utter his last words. It wasn't as if Ben had had a lengthy, intimate relationship with Ariya. What was it about that one afternoon tryst which could drive him to fight like a beast to get her back into his life? Ben smiled because he knew he could never answer that question. Ariya Kayani was a bright, attractive, strong-willed woman who agreed to make love to him. But so had a lot of girls. She had given him her heart and made it his to break. Ben had had more than his share of that as well. Ben just liked her. He was drawn to her. He didn't know why.

But could he love her? He had sworn not to, of course. No sexual relations with non-whites, no exceptions. But Ariya *was* white, wasn't she? With her fair complexion, she certainly looked white. Shouldn't that be enough? She also identified as white. Ben remembered it well. She had looked him square in the face and said those three words: "White like you." In one thumping beat of his heart, he contemplated the courage it took to say such a thing, at a time when it was more dangerous to be white than not, especially for a woman. Chastened by the barbarous punishment placed upon her years ago in her home country, Ariya could have settled behind the bossed, gleaming shield of Islam and accepted her fate. She could have been a good Muslim and lived a long, healthy life with her husband and family. Instead, she chose to be with men like him. More importantly, she chose to be with *him*. Ben knew at that moment he would have to rely upon his heart to determine if he could indeed be with her. There was no other arbiter. Isn't that always the way?

He could only hope his brothers in the tunnels would understand.

Ben slammed Hassan against the wall once more and repeated the question. "Where is she?"

Hassan had difficulty speaking through the gore now spilling down his face. After three or four attempts Ben understood him. "Will you spare my life if I tell you?" Hassan asked.

"Yes."

"They are taking her to Tehran."

"Who's taking her?"

"Her husband. Her husband's brother."

"Why?"

"They discovered her adultery. She will have trial over there."

"Have they left yet?" Ben asked.

"I don't know."

"HAVE THEY LEFT YET?"

"I don't KNOW! You bastard!" Hassan spat at him. "Husband's brother came. He took her a month ago. But they had to go to Indy for religious deportation. Show her with attorney before state capital authorities. You know. These things take time."

"And how do I know you are telling the truth?"

"I am. It is my word."

"Where's proof? Do you have correspondence saved?"

Hassan nodded and reached for his shirt, which was on the floor nearby. Ben unholstered his weapon. "Never mind," Hassan said. "I get a handkerchief."

Ben pulled the gun back but he did not re-holster it as Hassan retrieved the handkerchief from his shirt pocket and tended to his brutalized nose. The deep, demarcating cut along its bridge made it seem as if the squashed, purple appendage were no longer part of his body. The handkerchief became unusable after ten seconds. Hassan activated his personal device and allowed Ben to scroll through his correspondence with Emad Mohammadi, Ariya's brother in-law. Hassan had been telling the truth. Ben then noticed one unopened correspondence from that morning. It revealed that five days ago Emad and Pooya, Ariya's husband, had returned to Tehran where Ariya was placed under immediate arrest. The trial would take place in three weeks.

Ben learned one other crucial piece of information. The infidelity in question had not been recent. Emad had mentioned 'last summer's adultery' as the reason for his grievance. Ben swallowed despite his dry mouth. Could *he* have been the reason for all this? "How did her husband know about her infidelities?" Ben asked.

Hassan shook his head, still clutching the bloody handkerchief. "Oh, I don't know, sir!"

"Did you tell him?"

"Oh, no. Of course not. I would never tell—"

"So you knew of her adultery?"

"How could I? I hardly knew the woman!"

"Well, if that's the case, then why did her husband's brother correspond with you about it?" Hassan tried to blow his nose. A blunder. He hooted in pain. Ben shook him. "Answer me!"

Hassan groaned. "He corresponded with me, sir, because that woman was inviting men into this room to perform her vile, criminal acts against Allah and her husband!"

Astounded, Ben waited a few moments before letting him go and stepping back. The man was being serious—indignant, even—as if the saddle on his little high horse were secure enough for such a brazen rebuke. He didn't see his own obvious hypocrisy. He could not hear the dissonance of his words. Something like this only appears in comedy, Ben realized. The child with chocolate smeared all over his mouth castigating his sister for reaching into the cookie jar. The barfly lecturing someone on honesty while saying he's not there when his wife calls. The bigot explaining in atrocious English why we should deport immigrants who can't speak English well. Such a gross double standard is impossible to ignore. To see someone ignore it *in front of others* takes us into a realm where day is night, and black is white, and right is wrong. That's why it's funny. It takes the hypocrisy that most people keep hidden and places it on the outside while the hypocrite himself acts as if it's still on the inside. This last part is key. The person has to act *as if.* If he doesn't, then the gag falls flat since the person will be forced to become embarrassed or self-conscious in order to preserve the dramatic ruse. A pratfall is never funny when one braces for the impact.

This stock comic trope was playing itself out before Ben's eyes and making him realize that comedy as truth is a terrifying thing. A person who creates a comic situation in front of others, especially the cruel kind, yet fails to see it as such, is lost in the eyes of God. Such a person does not care about how others might view the situation, which, by default, means that he does not care about others. He lives in a universe of one. Reason is no more than a MacGuffin to such a person, and redemption can no longer apply.

Ben gave the man an additional five seconds to reverse himself. Not that it would have mattered. He did not reverse himself, by the way. Any residual guilt Ben would have felt for what he was about to do dissipated like diaphanous dreams on a leisurely Sunday morning. Shooting an unarmed man is an act of cowardice, he knew. But this was a coward's war initiated by cowards who had invaded the West in the most cowardly fashion. And in order for Westerners to win this war they would have to behave like cowards too. He discharged a bullet into the man's forehead and watched with acute satisfaction as Hassan Moammar Hypocrite Pederast Khan slammed against the wall behind him and then pitched forward on the rebound in perfect adherence to the laws of physics. Hassan's expired body then slid to the floor face first with his rear end sticking ignominiously in the air. It was an apt emulation of Muslim prayer.

Ben had to act fast. Ben did not want to act fast. He felt his energy flagging and was torn between conceptualizing how he would engineer Ariya's unlikely rescue and cleaning up the crime scene all around him. It was still leaking blood at his feet. Present concerns first, he thought. He stepped back to make sure no blood got on him, and then set to the tedious, stomach-turning task at hand. Thirty minutes later, four grown men were being incinerated in an anaerobe in the middle of the room. Watching their ghostlike faces, Ben imagined they were fetuses of an extraterrestrial animal species or the mummified prey of a race of giant spiders. He didn't imagine that they were human beings. Two of them were still alive when he had put them in there, and one he saw twitch a few times before being engulfed in the bag's computer-blue nova.

Less than ten feet away, both boys snored languidly on the bed under the weight of heavy sedation. Ben had tucked them in nicely under the covers, and they resembled a pair of brothers from a broken home who have only each other for companionship. Ben felt good for not killing them, despite his worry. He suspected that he probably should have found room for them in the anaerobe. The logic was python tight: boy Muslims grow into man Muslims, and anywhere from twenty to twenty-five percent of man Muslims will do whatever it takes—lie, steal, cheat, sue, legislate, intimidate, protest, stab, shoot, burn, rape, bomb—to turn the world into one big uni-denominational caliphate. Ben also knew that the odds were pretty good that these two little slumbering cherubs actually hated his white Christian guts and would kill him if given the chance. Ariya had told him so back when they could both pretend that things were normal. If anything, she would know.

Ben had endured such a trial not too long before and was not about to do it again. He was not going to murder children. He looked at the inchoate faces of the two boys and hoped that one day they would meet a girl or read a book or hear a song or view a painting that would make them love life as much as he did. What's life without hope? What's humanity if we snuff out lives before they are fully formed?

Ben had to remove his helmet because it wasn't designed to collect tears. At first he wasn't sure why he was crying. As soon as he began thinking about Ariya again, however, he knew. He knew. He knew everything now about the dire and deadly test he was about to face except what he was going to do next.

Part 7: Tehran

Chapter 50

Before the Sun reached three meters above the horizon, at which point everyone knew the prayers would begin, it had been a beautiful, cloudless day with hummingbird breezes that tickle the skin and soothe the eyes and raise faces to Heaven.

Such an invigorating atmosphere makes breathing a sublime pleasure and thinking of death impossible. With days like these it's a wonder we die at all.

Everywhere in the city people were out of doors, enjoying each other's company in the orderly streets, in the fresh, verdant parks, and in the clean, modern facilities. Children ran and played and ate sweets. Teenagers flew kites and tossed Frisbees. Men smoked and played chess and backgammon on picnic tables and in outdoor cafes. Young mothers spread colorful rugs and blankets and chatted while tending to their little ones. Older ladies sipped tea and snacked on fruit and nuts while gossiping beneath beach umbrellas or from their window sills. Merchants set up temporary bazaars wherever they could, tirelessly hawking food, toys, trinkets, jewelry, and other items. Young and old alike wandered through the city, taking in and marveling at the prosperity teeming all around them. They moved slowly, almost reluctantly, as if they didn't want the day to end, the leisurely window-shopping, the spirited music from shaggy street musicians, the smell of grilled shish kebabs and incense and tobacco, the haze of a shade tree, the comfort of a street bench, the playful rush of wind between buildings, the hum of the city, the chatter of families, the laughter of friends, the giddy rhythm of life. Allah must be as great and as merciful as the prayer-song says he is to bless us with such wonder.

A cleric's voice, high-pitched and soulful, intoned a rhythmic Middle Eastern prayer through the vast stadium. The PA system broadcast it for miles and lent it a thin, news media ring that made it seem from another age, as if it were the soundtrack to televised history rather than a prayer said during Eid al-Fitr, the Feast of the Breaking of the Fast, which marks the end of the Islamic holy month of Ramadan. "Mohammed ... Mohammed ... Mohammed..." the man chanted between verses. This was the centerpiece of his song. The beginning. The end. The very point.

Thousands of men stood shoulder-to-shoulder with their palms outstretched towards Heaven and incanted along with their cleric. Sunlight fuzzed agreeably through the long, gossamer walls of the tent surrounding them. It was a serious, joyful time. Generations stood alongside each other according to the dictates of their prophet, awash in the eternal glory that is Allah. When the supplication had ended, the men standing in observance began to kneel on their prayer rugs. Some took longer than others. Some paused to straighten their slacks. Others paused to shake out their knees. But within ten seconds everyone in attendance had knelt to listen to their imam begin his sermon. One man however remained standing in the middle of the congregation. Was he refusing to kneel? He was taller than most and had a strange, gray-brown complexion with blue eyes and a curly brown beard. He had no mustache. A large saraband headdress and loose-fitting shalwar trousers indicated he could be a religious scholar. But he wore a light scarf around his neck as if he had just ridden in from the desert. His expression was blank, cold, dead. His body was there, in the tent, in the stadium. But he was clearly not of his body.

Others around him had suspected he was a drug addict or a schizophrenic. A lost soul searching for meaning on a holy day. It is written that all Muslims must show charity and kindness during Eid al-Fitr. Perhaps this was why the men surrounding him chose not to notice his odd behavior, his rapid breathing, his excessive sweating, his constant mumbling and fidgeting. Had they witnessed the public stoning six weeks prior on the city's outskirts they might have seen him there attempting to disrupt the executions. He had been mobbed by a crowd of young men and eventually had to be carried on his back to a nearby hospital by other protestors and activists. Had the men worshipping in the stadium that morning seen the fight he put up and desperation with which he wanted to spare the condemned women, they might have questioned his odd behavior. They might even have raised concerns with police and had him escorted from the stadium rather than have him disturb such a peaceful and beautiful holiday. But they hadn't seen the executions nor had they heard about anyone trying to disrupt them. The man seemed harmless enough, so they left him to worship in peace.

***

Six weeks prior, several women were being punished for their prodigious sins against Allah. In all cases, the women were accused of having adulterous relations with men on more than four occasions, which by law negates the possibility of forgiveness or repentance. Further, they had committed their sins in foreign countries and had to be transported back to their homeland to face trial. That they had been slandering the good name of Islam among the infidels further enraged the populace and convinced the judge to forego the more merciful sentence of 100 lashes. Last minute pleas for clemency by family members were ignored.

In their black chadors and headscarves, the adulteresses had been buried up to their shoulders to secure their helplessness as a gang of faceless men in black masks and checkered scarves pelted them with hand-sized stones. Most of the women accepted their fate with masochistic contrition. Some however struggled. One in particular taunted her tormentors, in English, and even managed to free an arm before a heavy, sharp-edged stone sliced open her forehead and smashed her resolve. The sickening crack of the impact intimidated even the stone-throwers, who paused in their righteous duty long enough to determine if the blow had fatally wounded their last surviving captive. A cheer went up when they realized that it had. In seconds, as the woman's face disintegrated into a font of blood and her one free arm flopped and twitched in the air, a rain of stones rendered an eternal quietus of the human spirit and convinced all in attendance of the wisdom of submitting to merciful Allah.

Six weeks later, the man who refused to kneel shouted something. It was in English, a forceful proclamation of some kind. It began with the word "Islam" and ended with a well-known American profanity. It put a halt to the sermon and caused everyone around him to rise. They did not understand exactly what he had said but in seconds they knew exactly what he intended to do. Seconds however were all that he needed. There were buttons on the vest beneath his tunic. He smiled grimly through his tears and pressed them twice.

A brilliant flash lit up the tent. Crippling shockwaves were followed by a murderous volley of shrapnel. Men were mowed down or were thrown up and out like confetti. Body parts sprayed blood and flew in grotesque directions and with such force that they became shrapnel as well, compounding the carnage. The attack ripped a bloody hole sixty feet in diameter in the human fabric of this holiest of holy days, killing over three hundred and injuring close to a thousand. It was a hellish perimeter, a warzone, an apocalyptic playground for the maimed and the dying. Insides, to put it not in the least bit comically, became outsides, and the color red permanently smeared the memories of all who had witnessed it.

Of the instigator himself absolutely nothing remained. He had placed explosives in his headdress and behind his scarf and under his trousers and in his shoes. He had even placed some in his nose and beard and in his mouth between lip and gum. His obvious purpose was to atomize. To start us all over again from scratch, at ground zero. Seconds after the detonation, particles of him and his devices were mingling with particles of his victims and their devices such that no extrication could ever be performed. *They would never know who he was.*

The history books would remain forever humbled by this miscellaneous killer, withholding glory yet stymied in their ability to condemn. Into the purgatory of memory he was flung, where, almost mockingly, he began to thrive.

Months and years later, when they retold the story of how a single Westerner, an American perhaps, had issued a proclamation inspired by forgotten nineteenth-century Spanish anarchists and then marred the beauty of the world which Allah, in all his love and mercy, had bequeathed to his children, they would have no one to blame. There would be no villain other than a vague foreign bogeyman who was, in essence, only guilty of doing to Muslims what Muslims had been doing to Westerners for nearly a century. Was this man a Christian? Was he a Jew? Was he black? Was he white? In some of their more honest moments, they knew this lack of certainty terrified them. A move had been played, indicating not just a change in tactics, but a change in strategy and in will. But it was *their* strategy and *their* will now being used against them. The Infidel was beginning to catch on, to fight cowardice with cowardice, and to leave scruples behind for the weak. He had finally gone on the attack, they knew. And they knew there would be more coming. For the first time in centuries, the infidel was fighting to win and was willing to die to deliver human retribution for the wrath of God.

ABOUT THE AUTHOR

Spencer J. Quinn is an essayist and novelist living in the United States. He is a frequent contributor to Counter-Currents/ *North American New Right*. This is his first book.

www.ingramcontent.com/pod-product-compliance
Lightning Source LLC
Chambersburg PA
CBHW031027030726
47497CB00004B/1038

* 9 7 8 1 9 4 0 9 3 3 7 4 0 *